John Bloundelle-Burton

Denounced

John Bloundelle-Burton

Denounced

ISBN/EAN: 9783744675499

Printed in Europe, USA, Canada, Australia, Japan

Cover: Foto ©Andreas Hilbeck / pixelio.de

More available books at **www.hansebooks.com**

A ROMANCE

BY

JOHN BLOUNDELLE-BURTON

AUTHOR OF
IN THE DAY OF ADVERSITY, THE HISPANIOLA PLATE, ETC.

" The adder lies i' the corbie's nest."
JACOBITE BALLAD

NEW YORK
D. APPLETON AND COMPANY
1896

CONTENTS.

CONTENTS.

DENOUNCED.

CHAPTER I.

A HOME COMING.

It was a wild and stormy sea through which the bluff-bowed Galliot laboured, as, tossed first from one wave to another, she, with the best part of her gear stowed away and no sail on her but a close-reefed main-topsail and a spanker, endeavoured to make her way towards the Suffolk coast. On the poop, the captain—a young man of not more than thirty—hurled orders and oaths indiscriminately at his crew, every man of which was a good deal older than himself, while the crew themselves worked hard at hauling up the brails, going out on the gaff to pass the gaskets, and stowing the mainsail-yard. But still she laboured and rolled and yawed, her forefoot pointing at one moment almost to the Dutch coast and at another to the English—she had left Calais thirty hours before, intending to fetch Dover, and had been blown thus far out of her course—and it seemed as though she would never get any nearer to the land she wished to reach. And, to make matters worse, lying some distance off on her starboard beam—though too far to be distinguished through the haze in the air and the spume of the waves—was a large vessel about which those on board could not decide as to whether she was one of King George's sloops or—a privateer. The young captain trusted it was the first, since he had no quarrel with either his Majesty or his navy, and had no men who could be pressed, while the passengers in the cabin—but this you shall read.

In that cabin there sat four persons, three men and a woman—the last of whom shall be first described. A woman young—of not more than twenty-four years of age—fair and well-favoured, her wheat-coloured hair brought back in a knot behind her head, above which, as was still the custom of the time for ladies when travelling, she wore a three-cornered hat. Wrapped in a long, collarless coat, square cut and possessing no pockets—also the custom of the time—it was still easy to perceive that, underneath, was a supple, graceful figure, and, when—as was occasionally the case—this long coat was thrown open so that the wearer might get a little relief from the stuffiness of the cabin, the beauty of that figure might plainly be perceived beneath the full scarlet waistcoat embroidered with gold lace, which, by its plenitude of pockets, atoned for the absence of any in the coat. Her face was, as has been said, a well-favoured one, oval, and possessing large blue eyes and delicate, thin lips, and with upon it even here, on this tossing sea, a fair rose and milk complexion, while in those large eyes the observer might have well imagined he saw a look of unhappiness. Also, too, a look of contempt whenever they rested on the man who, as she leant an elbow on one side of the table between them, leant one of his on the other.

They rested on him now with much that look as,

pushing over to her a glass of burnt wine which the cabin-boy has just brought in at his orders, as well as some ratafia biscuits, he said:

"I would counsel you, my lady, to partake of a little more refreshment. I have spoken with the master outside who says that by no chance can we make Harwich ere nightfall. Your ladyship, excellent sailor as you are, must have a care to your health."

"My health," she replied, "needs no care, either from myself or you. And when I am athirst I will drink, as when I am hungry I will eat. You had best offer your refreshments to our fellow-passengers."

The man to whom she spake was but two or three years older than herself—and was her husband, Simeon Larpent, Viscount Fordingbridge. He, too, was well dressed in the travelling costume of the day, wearing a black frock with a gold button, a black waistcoat trimmed with gold, black velvet breeches, and a gold-laced three-cornered hat, while on the table lay a silver-hilted hanger that slid about with every motion of the vessel. In looks he was her equal, being, however, as dark as she was fair, but of well-cut, even features and of a clear complexion. He wore, too, his natural hair, cropped somewhat short as though a wig might in other circumstances be easily assumed, but the absence of this article of dress in no way detracted from his appearance.

As her ladyship spoke he darted one swift glance at her from under his eyelids—a glance that seemed to embody in it a full return of all the coldness and contempt with which she had addressed him; and then, acting on her suggestion, he turned to the two other inhabitants of the cabin and said:

"Come, Father Sholto, and you, Fane, come and

take a sup of the liquor. 'Twill do you both good. Come and drink."

"Ah, the drink, the drink," exclaimed the latter, "well, give me a sup. Maybe 'twill appease a qualm. Kitty, me child," turning to Lady Fordingbridge, "why do ye not do as your husband asks? 'Tis a good stomachic—by the powers! how the barky rolls."

"I want nothing," her ladyship replied, lifting her eyes to him with almost as contemptuous a glance as when she had previously raised them to her husband, and then relapsing again into silence.

"I, too," said the other man, who had been addressed as "Father Sholto," "will take a sup, she does roll badly. Yet, my lord," he said, as he poured some out into a mug that stood by the liquor, "let me persuade you to be more guarded in your expressions. To forget, indeed," he went on, while his cold grey eyes were fixed on the other, "that there is such a person as 'Father Sholto' in existence for the present; that such a well-known ecclesiastic is travelling in your Lordship's esteemed company. For," he continued, after swallowing the liquor at a gulp, "I do assure you—Fane, see that the door of the cabin is fast! and that none of the crew are about!—you could not make your entry into your own country, could not return to make your peace with King George, the Elector of Hanover—with a worse companion in your train than the man who is known as 'Father Sholto.' Therefore——"

"Therefore," interrupted Lord Fordingbridge impatiently, "I will not forget again, Mr. Archibald. Enough!"

"Therefore," continued the other, as though no interruption had occurred, still in the cold, low voice

and still with the cold grey eyes fixed on his lordship,
"it is best you do not forget, at least, at present.
Later, if your memory fails you—I have known it
treacherous ere now—it will be of little importance.
Charles Edward, the Prince of Wales, is at Edinburgh,
soon he will be at St. James'; but until he is, remember what we are. You are the Viscount Fordingbridge, but lately succeeded to your father's title, and
a convert from his Jacobitism to Hanoverian principles; her ladyship here, who is ever to be depended
upon, follows your estimable political principles; her
respected father, Mr. Doyle Fane, has, he avers, no
politics at all; and I am Mr. Archibald, a Scotch merchant. You will remember?"

"*Peste!* Yes. I will remember. Tutor me no
more. Now, Fane, the sea abates somewhat—go and
discover if we are near the English coast. And, Mr.
Archibald, I have a word to say to my lady here, with
your permission. As I am at the expense of this passage, may I ask for a moment's privacy with her?
Doubtless the air on the deck will refresh you both."

"Precisely," replied the other. "We will not in-
trude unless it grows again so rough that we cannot
remain on deck. Come, Fane."

When both had left the cabin Lord Fordingbridge
turned to his wife who still sat, as she had done from
the beginning of Mr. Archibald's remarks, indifferent
and motionless as though in no way interested in what
had passed, and exclaimed:

"You hear, madam, the circumstances in which I
return to my own. 'Tis not too agreeable, I protest.
We are Roman Catholics, yet we come as Protestants,
Jacobites, yet under the garb and mask of Hanoveri-
ans. And in our train a Jesuit priest, arch-plotter,

and schemer, who passes as a respectable Scotch merchant. A sorry home coming, indeed!"

"If such duplicity is painful to your lordship's mind," his wife remarked, "'twould almost have been best to have remained in exile. Then you would have been safe, at least, and have done no outrage to your —conscience. And, later, when those who are fighting for Prince Charles have re-established him upon his grandfather's throne—if they ever do!—you could have declared yourself without fear of consequences."

No word, nor tone of her sneer was lost upon Lord Fordingbridge, and he turned savagely upon her.

"Have a care, my lady," he exclaimed, "have a care. There are ways in my power you little dream of by which if your defiance——"

"Defiance!" exclaimed her ladyship. "Defiance! You dare to use that term to me. You!"

"Ay! Defiance. What! Shall the daughter of Doyle Fane, the broken-down Irish adventurer, the master of the fence school in the Rue Trousse Vache, flout and gibe me—the man who took her from a garret and made her a lady—a peeress. I—I—"

"Yes!" she replied. "You! You—who have earned for ever her undying hatred by doing so; by making her a lady by lies, by intriguing, by duplicity. A lady! Yet your wife! Had you left me in the Rue Trousse Vache—in the garret over the fence school— whose wife should I have been now? Answer that, Simeon Larpent, answer that."

"The wife of a man," he said, quietly and calm again in a moment, for he had the power to allay the tempestuous gusts that overtook him occasionally almost as quickly as they arose, "who, if the fates are not more propitious than I deem they will be, rides at the present moment to his doom, to a halter that awaits him. A man who rides on a fruitless journey to England as volunteer with his cousin Balmerino in the train of Charles Edward; a man——"

"Whom," she interrupted again, "I loved with my whole heart and soul; whom I loved from the first hour my eyes ever gazed on him. A man whom you separated me from with your Jesuitical lies—they did well to educate you at Lisbon and St. Omer—a man who, if God is just, as I do believe, shall yet live to take a desperate vengeance on you. And for the reason that he may do so, I pray night and day that Charles Edward will fight his way to London. Then you must meet—unless you flee back to France again —then, Lord Fordingbridge, you must stand face to face with him at last. Then——"

"Then you trust to be a widow. Is it not so, my lady? You will be free then, and Bertie Elphinston may have the bride I stole from him. Is that your devout aspiration?"

"Alas, no!" she replied. "Or, if it is, it can never come to pass. If Bertie Elphinston saw me now he would shrink from me. He would not touch my hand. He would pass across the street to avoid me."

As she uttered the last words there came from over the swirling, troubled sea the boom of a cannon, accompanied a moment afterwards by harsh cries and orders from the deck of the Galliot, and by the rattling of cordage and a sudden cessation of the slight way that was still on the vessel.

"What does that gun mean?" asked Lord Fordingbridge as he started to his feet, while Fane and Mr. Archibald re-entered the cabin hastily.

"It means," said the disguised Jesuit, who spoke as coolly and calmly as ever, "that the vessel which has been following us since dawn is King George's—he forgot on this occasion to term the English king 'the Elector of Hanover'—Bomb-ketch the 'Furnace.' She has fired the gun to bring us to. Doubtless they wish to inspect our papers and to see there are no malignant priests or Jacobites on board. We are now in English waters and within two miles of Harwich, therefore they are quite within their rights."

"Bah!" exclaimed his lordship. "Let them come. What have we to fear?"

"Nothing whatever," replied Mr. Archibald. "The Viscount Fordingbridge is an accession to the usurper's Whig peers; a harmless Irish gentleman, such as Mr. Doyle Fane, and a simple Scotch merchant, such as I, can do no harm. While for her ladyship here——"

"Come, come on deck," said his lordship, "and let us see what is doing. Will it please you to remain here, my lady?" he asked, turning to his wife with an evil glance in his eye.

"Yes," she replied, "if they wish to see me I shall be found here."

The sea had abated considerably by now, so that already a boat had been lowered from the ketch, which was not more than five cables length from the Galliot by the time they reached the deck. It was manned by a dozen sailors while an officer sat in the stern sheets, and the brawny arms of the men soon brought it alongside. Then, while the seamen kept the boat off the Galliot with their hands and oars, the officer seized the man-ropes thrown over to him, and easily sprang up the accommodation ladder on to the deck.

"What vessel is this?" he asked fiercely of the captain, "and what passengers do you carry?"

"It is the Bravermann, of Rotterdam, sir," the young captain replied, "chartered at Calais to bring his lordship and wife with two other passengers to Dover. We are blown off our course, however, and——"

"Where are these passengers?" asked the officer.

"Here is one," said Lord Fordingbridge, coming forward, "and here two others whom I have accommodated with a passage. Her ladyship is in the cabin."

"Your papers, if you please."

His lordship produced from his pocket two large documents, duly signed by the English ambassador and countersigned by the first secretary of the Legation, while to them was also affixed a stamp of the Mairie; and the lieutenant, for such he was, glanced over them, compared the description of the viscount with that of the person before him, and then said he must see her ladyship.

"Come this way then," the other replied, and led him into the cabin. "My lady," he said to his wife, "this gentleman wishes to compare you with your description on our passports."

Very calmly Lady Fordingbridge turned her eyes on the lieutenant as he, touching his hat to her, glanced at the paper and retired saying he was satisfied. Then, turning to the others, he said, "Now your passports, quick."

Fane and Mr. Archibald also passed his scrutiny, though once he looked under his eyelids at the latter as if to make sure he was the man whose description he held in his hand, and then their passports were also returned to them.

"Let me see over the ship and also her papers," he said to the captain, and when this was done he seemed satisfied that his duty had been performed.

"You may proceed," he said. "Call the boat away," and with such scant ceremony he went to the ship's side and prepared to re-embark in his own cutter.

"Pardon me," exclaimed the viscount, stopping him, "but we have heard strange rumours in Paris of a landing effected in Scotland by the Prince of—the person known as the Young Pretender. Also we have heard he has reached Edinburgh and been joined by many persons of position in Scotland, and that an English army has set forth to oppose his further march. Can you tell me, sir, if this is true ?"

"I know nothing whatever on the subject," replied the lieutenant, curtly as usual. "His Majesty's land forces concern us not; our account is on the sea. And our duty is to search all unknown vessels proceeding to England to see that they bear neither Jacobites, pestilential priests, arms, nor money with them. Is the boat there ?"

Hearing that she had again come alongside, having kept off the Galliot to prevent her being stowed in, he descended swiftly to her without deigning to award the slightest salute to anyone on board. But as his men pulled off he saw the face of Lady Fordingbridge gazing out from the cabin porthole, and raised his hat to her.

"Yet," said Mr. Archibald to the viscount, as they sat once more in the cabin while the vessel now entered smooth water and drew close in to Harwich, "whatever his duty may be he has not been wondrous happy in carrying it out. For there are Jacobites, a pestilential priest, and money for the cause all in this ship together, arms alone being wanting. Faugh! he was a rough sea-dog, yet none too good a setter. Well, well. Perhaps in this town we may glean some news."

CHAPTER II.

A SUBJECT OF KING GEORGE.

THE month of May, 1746, was drawing to a close, and June was already giving signs of its approach, as my Lord Viscount Fordingbridge sat in the library of his house in Kensington-square and warmed his feet at the fire which, in spite of the genial spring weather, burned pleasantly on the hearth. By his side, on a table, lay the morning papers of the day to which he constantly referred, and which, after each occasion of doing so, he threw down with a very palpable expression of satisfaction.

"In truth," he muttered to himself, "nought could have gone much better. I am safe and—and the necks of all the rest are jeopardised. Jeopardised! Nay! 'tis much worse than that. Those who are caught must surely die, those who are not caught must be so ere long. As for Charles Edward himself he hath escaped. Well, let him go; I have no quarrel with him."

Again he took up one of the journals and read:

"This morning his Majesty's ship of war, Exeter, arrived from Scotland, having on board the Earls of Cromartie and Kilmarnock, and the Lord Balmerino. They have been committed prisoners to the Tower on a charge of high treason." "Ah," he mused, "that's well, so far as it goes, though for myself I care not whether their lordships finish on Tower Hill or are set free. Fools all! Yet they were near winning, the devil seize them! had they but pushed on from Derby they must have won, and the German who now sits secure would never have had my allegiance. Charles Edward would have transformed my title into that of a marquis, I doubt me if George will do as much in reward for my change of politics. But what I would fain know is, where is the wolf Elphinston, Balmerino's cousin? He fought at Culloden, I know well—recklessly, like a man sick of life. Perhaps 'twas for his lost love, Kitty! At least in Hawley's despatch he is mentioned as having killed four men of Barrell's regiment with his own blade. May Fate confound him! if taken his life is forfeit, but where is he?"

A knock came at the library door as he mused, and in reply to his answer Mr. Archibald entered. As usual, certainly since he left France, he was clothed as became the part he had now assumed, of a well-to-do Scotch merchant, there being only one new addition to any portion of his dress. His hat, which he threw carelessly upon the table, on the top of his lordship's journals, bore in it the *black* cockade!

"Ha, ha! my worthy merchant," exclaimed Lord Fordingbridge, as his quick eye perceived this, "my worthy dealer in brocades, broadcloth, and Colchester baize, so already thou trimmest the sails to catch the favouring German breezes. 'Tis well." •

"Stop this fooling," said the Jesuit, looking angrily at him; "is this the time for you to be joking and jeering when everything is lost? You have the journals there, you know well what has happened. The principals of the noblest cause, of the most sublime restoration that would have ever taken place, are prisoners with their lives in forfeit, some in London, some in Carlisle gaol, and some at Inverness, and you sit gibing there. *Pardieu!* sometimes I think you are a fool instead of the knave I once deemed you."

"If," said the viscount, scowling at the other as he spoke, "you deem yourself called upon to address me in such a manner, I shall be forced, Mr. Archibald, to also alter my style of address to you, and to speak both to and of you as the Reverend Archibald Sholto, priest of the Society of Jesus, and an avowed Jacobite. And you will remember that here, in England, at such a moment as this, to be so proclaimed could not be otherwise than fraught with unpleasant consequences to you. Moreover, you will have the goodness to remember that now—since the disastrous events, to your side, of Culloden, the Viscount Fordingbridge is a fervent Hanoverian."

"I will remember," said the priest, "that however desirous the Viscount Fordingbridge may be to espouse the cause of the House of Hanover, it is not in his power to do so, so long as there remains one Stuart to assert a claim to the throne of his ancestors. When that race ceases to exist, when no living Stuart is left to call for aid, then perhaps, you may be permitted to become Hanoverian, not before. Now, my Lord Fordingbridge, listen to me, while I go over the cards I hold in my hand against Simeon Larpent, my whilom scholar at St. Omer, who——"

"Nay!" exclaimed the other, "do nothing of the sort. I retract, I had forgotten. Recall nothing. Yet, for my safety, I must appear an adherent of King George. Indeed, to-morrow I attend his levée."

"For the good of the Stuart cause," the other said, "you will continue as you have begun since your return to this country, to appear an adherent of this King George; for the good of the cause that is not yet lost. There will be another rising ere long, be sure of that; if it comes not before, it will do so at the death of the present usurper. Now, listen to the news I bring you."

"What is it?" the other asked, while he paled as he did so. "What?"

"The worst that you can hear. Elphinston is in London."

"Elphinston here! Is he mad? His life is not worth an hour's purchase."

"He knows that," replied the Jesuit coolly, "as well as you or I do. Yet he heeds it not. Why should he? Are not other men's lives doomed who are now in London? Men who," he went on, speaking coldly and with great distinctness, "brought money into England to aid the cause; men," still his voice fell more and more crisp upon the other's ear, "who did endeavour to compass the death of George as he returned from his last visit to Herrenhausen; men who——"

"Silence, you Jesuit devil," interrupted the other. "Sometimes I wonder that you do not fear to speak as you do; that you do not dread that your own death may be compassed."

"I have no fear," replied the priest, taking snuff as he spoke, "so long as the walls of St. Omer contain my papers. Rather should I fear for those whose secrets would be divulged if I were to die. To die even suddenly, without being assassinated."

"Well! to your news," exclaimed the other.

"What of Elphinston! Where does he hide himself away?"

"At the moment," answered the priest, "he—and my brother Douglas——"

"So he is here, too!"

"He is here, too. They dwell together in lodgings at the village of Wandsworth. Perhaps later, if it goes ill with Balmerino, they may remove into the City."

"To make some mad attempt to save him!"

"Possibly. Meanwhile, do you not dread to meet the man yourself! You stole his bride from him, you will remember, and now he suspects how you brought it about. How will you answer to him for the falsehoods by which you persuaded her that he was already the husband of another woman?"

"By my sword," Lord Fordingbridge replied— though at the moment he was thinking of a far different manner in which Bertie Elphinstone should be answered.

"It will be your only plan," Sholto said. "For by treachery you can accomplish nothing. If Elphinston is blown upon he will know well who is his informer and will, in his turn, inform. Inform upon the man who plotted to have George's person seized by French pirates as he returned to England from France, the man who spread broadcast through England the reward offered by Prince Charles of £30,000 to whomsoever should seize and secure George——"*

"Why," exclaimed Fordingbridge, maddened by the other's taunts, "why do you persecute me like

---

* See appendix, note A. The reward offered by Charles Edward.

this? What have I ever done to you that you threaten me thus?"

"Recall," replied the Jesuit, "your vows at St. Omer, your sins since, your broken pledges, your cancelled oaths. Then answer to yourself why I do these things. Moreover, remember I love my brother —he has been my charge since his boyhood—and if Elphinston is betrayed Douglas must fall too. Also remember, Elphinston has been ever beloved by me. You have inflicted one deadly wound on him, you have wrecked his life by striking him through his love—think you that I will ever permit you to injure him again? Man!" the Jesuit said, advancing nearer to Fordingbridge as he spoke, and standing before him in so threatening a manner that the other shrank back from him, "if evil comes to Elphinston through you, such evil shall in turn come to you through me that I will rend your life for ever and always. Remember, I say again, remember."

He took his hat from off the table as he finished, and left the room addressing no further remark to the other. And, quietly as he ever moved, he was about to descend the stairs when Lady Fordingbridge coming from out an open door, stopped him.

"I wish to speak to you," she said, in a soft, low voice, "come within a moment," and, followed by Sholto, she led him back into the room she had just quitted. Here, too, a warm pleasant fire burned in the grate, while an agreeable aroma of violets stole through the apartment; and motioning her visitor to a seat her ladyship said:

"Is the news true? Are they—is Mr. Elphinston in London?"

"It is true, Kitty," he said. "Yet I know not how you heard it."

"From my father who dreads as much to meet him as the craven in his library must do." She paused a moment, then she continued, "Have you seen him?"

"Yes," he said, "I have seen him."

"And," she asked, wistfully, "did he send no word of pardon—to me?"

The Jesuit shook his head, though in a gentle kindly manner, ere he replied. "No, child. He spoke not of you."

She sat gazing into the embers for a few moments more; then she went on.

"Yet he must know, he cannot but know how basely I was deceived. You told me months ago that he had learnt some of the story from your brother's lips, who learnt it from you. Is there no room for pity in his heart? Will he never forgive?"

"If he thinks aught," said the Jesuit, still very gently, to her, "it is that you should never have believed so base a tale. So at least he tells Douglas. To me he has never spoken of the matter."

"Alas!" she said. "How could I doubt? Lord Fordingbridge I might have disbelieved, but my father!" and here she shuddered. "How could I think that he would stoop to practise such lies, such duplicity, on his own child?"

Father Sholto made no answer to this remark, contenting himself with lifting his hands from his knees and warming the palms at the fire. And so they sat, neither speaking for two or three moments. Then she said:

"Father, will you take a letter to him from me?"

This time he lifted his bushy eyebrows instead of

his hands, and looked at her from underneath them. Next he shrugged his shoulders, and then he said:

"Kitty, for you I will do anything, for you who have ever been a dutiful daughter of the Church, ay! and a loyal adherent to a now sadly broken cause. Yet, child, what use to write? Nothing can undo what is done; you must make the best of matters. Solace your wounded heart with the rank you have gained, with your husband's now comfortable means, your reception at the Court of the Hanoverian king, for king he is, and, I fear, must be. However great the evil that was done, it must be borne. You and Bertie Elphinston are sundered for ever in this world, unless——"

"Unless?" she repeated, with a swift glance from her eyes.

"You both survive him. Yet, how shall such a thing be! He is no older than Elphinston himself, and, much as he has wronged that other, no reparation, not even his life, would set things right. If Bertie slew him he could not marry his victim's widow."

"Alas! alas!" said Lady Fordingbridge, "the last thing he would wish to do now, even were I free, would be to have me for his wife. Me whom once he loved so tenderly."

Once more the Jesuit twitched up his great eyebrows and muttered something to himself, and then seemed bent in thought. And as Kitty sat watching him she caught disconnected whispers from his lips. "Douglas might do it," she heard him say; "that way the gate would be open. Yet he cannot be spared, not yet," until at last he ceased, after which, looking up from his reverie, he said to her:

"What do you wish to write to him, child? You, the Viscountess Fordingbridge, must have a care as to your epistles to unmarried men."

"Be under no apprehension," she replied. "Yet, if —if—he would pardon me, would send me one little line to say—God!—that he does not hate me—oh! that he who once loved me so should come to hate me —then, then I might again be happy, a little happy. Father, I must write to him."

"So be it," he answered. "Write if you must. I will convey the letter."

CHAPTER III.

THE next night Father Sholto, who was lodged in Lord Fordingbridge's house, took a hackney coach through the fields to Chelsea Church, and so was ferried across to Battersea. Then, because the evening was soft and mild and there was a young moon, he decided to walk on by the road to the next village, namely Wandsworth, which lay half an hour further on.

" Poor Kitty," he thought to himself, as he felt the packet she had confided to him press against his breast, "poor Kitty! Why could she not have believed in Bertie's truth? Surely anything might have been set against the word of such a creature as Simeon Larpent, pupil of mine though he be. *Peste!* why was not I in Paris when all was happening? By now they would have been happy. They could have lived in France or Italy. We, the Society," and he crossed himself as he went on, " would have found the wherewithal; or even in America they might have, perhaps, been safe. Yet now! Now! Elphinston is a heart-broken man; Kitty, a heart-broken woman. Alas! alas!

With meditations such as these, for political Scotch Jesuit as Archibald Sholto was, and fierce partisan of his countrymen, Charles Stuart and his father

James, there beat a kindly heart within him, he reached the long, straggling village street of Wandsworth. Then, turning off somewhat sharply to the right, he emerged after another five minutes upon a road above the strand of the river, on which, set back in shady gardens, in which grew firs, cedars, and chestnut trees, were some antique and picturesque houses built a hundred years before.

At one of these, the first he came to, he knocked three times on the garden gate and rang a bell, the handle of which was set high in the door frame; and then in a moment a strong, heavy tread was heard coming from the house to the gate.

"Who is it?" a man's voice asked from within.

"*Nunquam triumphans*,"* was the priest's answer, softly given, and as he spoke the postern door was opened, and a tall man stood before Sholto. In a moment their hands were clasped in each other's and their greetings exchanged.

"'Tis good of you, Archie, to come again to-night," his younger brother said to him; "have you brought more news? How fares it with those in the Tower?"

"Ill," replied the other. "As ill as may be. The trials are fixed, 'tis said, for July at latest. One will, however, escape. Tullibardine——"

"The Marquis of Tullibardine escape! Why, then, there is hope for the others!"

"Ay!" replied the elder brother, "there is, by the same way. Tullibardine is dying in the Tower. His life draws to a close."

"Pish! What use such an escape? But come in,

---

* "*Tandem triumphans*" was the motto emblazoned on Charles Edward's banner during the march into England. "*Nunquam triumphans*" was afterwards a password between Jacobites.

Archie. Bertie looks ever for you." Then he stopped on the gravel path and, gazing into the other's face as it shone in the moonlight, he said, "What of Kitty? Have you told her he is in London?"

"Ay," replied the Jesuit, "and have on me now a letter to him from her, suing, I believe, for forgiveness. Douglas!" he exclaimed, seizing the other by the arm, "Bertie must pardon her. You must make him. Otherwise——"

"What?"

"I fear I know not what. Her love for him is what it ever was, stronger, fiercer, may be, because of the treachery that tore them asunder; she thinks of him alone. And if she grows desperate Heaven knows what may be the outcome of it. Murder of Simeon! betrayal of him! Self-slaughter! She is capable of all or any, if goaded too far. He must forgive her."

"Forgive her!" exclaimed his younger brother. "Forgive her! Why, who shall doubt it; what possesses your mind? There is no fear of that. No, that is not what there is to fear."

"What then?" asked Archibald, bewildered.

"That if they should once again meet no power on earth could ever part them more. Even now he broods all day, and night too, on finding her, on carrying her off by force. There are scores of our countrymen in London in disguise who would do it for him at his bidding or help him to do it as well as to slay Fordingbridge. I tell you, Archie, he would stand at nothing. Nothing! Why, man, as we fought side by side at Prestonpans he muttered a score of times, 'Kate, Kate, Kate.' And once, as he cut down an officer of Fowke's dragoons, he exclaimed, 'Each Hanoverian dog who falls brings us so much the nearer to London and me to Kate.' Faith! though the battle lasted but four minutes, he muttered her name ten times as often."

"Come," said the other, "let us go in to him. I would I knew what is best to do. Ah, well! most affairs settle themselves. Pray Heaven this one may."

Over a fire, burning in an ancient grate constructed for the consumption of wood alone, they found Bertie Elphinston brooding, as his friend had described. And as all the Scotch had done who had sought a hiding-place in London after the defeat of the Stuart army in Scotland, any marks that might proclaim their nationality had been carefully exchanged—where the purse allowed—for more English traits and characteristics. Therefore Elphinston was now clad as any other gentleman of the time might be, plainly but well—a branched velvet coat with a satin lining, a black silk embroidered waistcoat, and breeches of velvet in keeping with the coat constituting his dress, while he wore his own hair, of a dark-brown colour and slightly curly. Against the side of the large open-mouthed grate and near to his hand there reclined an ordinary plate-handled sword, with the belt hanging to it as when unbuckled from the body; deeper in a recess might be seen two claymores, with which weapons the Scotch had recently inflicted such deadly slaughter on the Duke of Cumberland's troops.

"Ha, Archie!" exclaimed the young man, springing up from his chair and grasping the Jesuit's hand, "welcome, old friend. So you have found your way here once more. *A la bonne chance!* Yet," he went on, while his handsome face clouded again with the gloomy look that it had borne before lighting up at the entrance of their friend, "why say so! You can bring us no good news now—you can," he said in a lower voice, "bring me none. Yet speak, Archie, how is it with our poor friends?"

"As before. There is no news, except that their trials are fixed. Yet all bear up well, the head of your house especially so. He jests ever—p'raps 'tis to cheer his wife more than for aught else. She is admitted to see him, and brings and takes our news, and he sends always, through her, his love to you. Also he bids you begone from out of England, you and Douglas both, since there can be no safety for you in it. The king is implacable, he will spare none."

"And the Prince, our Prince," asked Elphinston, "what of him; is he safe?"

"He is not taken," replied the other. "We know nought else. But in truth, it is partly to endorse Lord Balmerino's injunction that I am here to-night. Both of you must begone. London is no place for Jacobites of any degree; for those who have recently fought the peril is deadly. Already the whole town is searched from end to end. The Tower is full of prisoners. From noble lords down to the meanest, it is crammed with them. Gallows are already being put up on Kennington Common; soon the slaughter will begin. My boys, you must back to France."

"Douglas may go if he will," replied Elphinston, looking at his comrade. "I remain here. I have something to do." Then he said quietly, "Where is Lord Fordingbridge?"

"At present in London, but he leaves for his seat in Cheshire to-morrow. Bertie," the Jesuit exclaimed, "if what you have to do is with him it must be postponed. To seek out Fordingbridge now would be your undoing."

"And his wife—does—does she go too?"

"No," the other replied, "she stays in London. Bertie, I have brought you a letter from her."

"A letter from Kate—Lady Fordingbridge—to me! To me! What does it mean? What can have caused her to write to me?"

"Best read the letter," replied the other. "And as you read it think—try to think—kindly of her. Remember, too, that whatever she was to you once, she is now another man's wife. However great a villain he may be, remember that."

"Give me the letter," Elphinston said briefly.

Sholto took from his pocket the little packet; then, as he gave it to the other, he said, "Douglas and I will leave you to its perusal. The night is fine, he can walk with me to Battersea. Farewell."

"Farewell," returned Elphinston. "And—and—tell her ladyship if there is aught to answer such answer will be sent."

"Be careful of your messengers. Remember. Danger surrounds you."

"I shall remember."

When they were gone, his friend saying he would be back in an hour's time, the young man turned the letter over more than once ere he broke the seal—it bore no address upon it, perhaps for safety's sake—and then, at last, he opened it and commenced its perusal. And as he did so and saw the once familiar handwriting, he sighed profoundly more than once. Yet soon he was engrossed in the contents. They ran as follows:

"I hear you are in London and that at last is it possible for me to do what I have long desired—though hitherto no opportunity has arisen—namely, to explain that which in your eyes may seem to be my treachery to you.

"Mr. Elphinston, when you and I last parted, I was your affianced wife; I write to you now as the wife of another man to ask you for your pardon. If I set down all as it came to pass it may be that, at least, you will cease to hate my memory—the memory of my name. Nightly I pray that such may some day be the case. Thereby at last I may know ease, though never again happiness in this world.

"When you quitted Paris a year ago you went, as you said you were going, to Rome on a message to the Pope connected with the Cause. Alas! you and Father Sholto had not been sped a week ere very different tidings reached me. My father—God forgive him!—first poisoned my ears with rumours—which he said were spread not only over all Paris but also at St. Germains, Vincennes, and Marly—that it was on no political matter that you had departed. It was known —even I knew so much, I had jested with you about it, had even been sore on the subject—that Madeleine Baufremont, of the Queen's Chamber, admired you. Now, so said my unhappy father, with well-acted misery, it was whispered that she and you had gone away together. Moreover, he said there was no doubt that you and she were married. He even named the church at which the marriage had taken place at Moret, beyond Fontainebleau."

"So, so," muttered Bertie Elphinston, as he read. "I see. I begin to see. 'Tis as I thought, though I did not know this. Well, a better lie than one might have hoped."

. "Next," the letter continued, "there came to me the man who is now my husband—then, as you know,

the Honourable Simeon Larpent, his father being still
alive. Needless to tell you, Mr. Elphinston, of how
this man had ever sought my love; first, because of
our poverty, in a manner alike disgraceful to both,
and next, when that design failed, in a more honourable fashion. Yet, of no avail when you—— But
enough. You also know well how every plea of his was
rejected by me.

"He, too, told the same tale. He protested to me
that on the morning you left St. Germains Madeleine
Baufremont set out on the same southern road, that
your carriages met and joined at Étampes, and that
thence you travelled together to Moret."

" The devil can indeed speak the truth," muttered
Bertie, as he read thus far.

"Still, I would not—I could not—believe. Our
last parting was fresh in my mind, ay! in my heart;
our last vows and last farewells, our projects for the
future, our hopes of days of happiness to come—forgive me if I remind you of them—they are wrecked
now! I say I could not believe. Yet, wherever I
looked, wherever I made inquiries, there was but one
answer. The English, Scotch, and Irish gentlemen
who frequented my father's house all gave the same
answer, though none spake the words I feared. Some,
I observed, regarded me with glances that were full of
pity—for which I hated them—others preserved a silence that was worse tenfold than speech, some smiled
in their sleeves. And Larpent was ever there—always,
always, always. And one day he came to where I was
sitting and said to me, 'Kitty, if you will indeed know
the truth, there is a witness below who can give it to
you. The *curé* of Moret has come to Paris with a pe-
tition to the king against the exactions of the Seigneur.

Kitty, he it was who made Bertie Elphinston and Madeleine Baufremont man and wife."

"'So be it,' I replied. 'Yet, remember their marriage makes ours no nearer.' 'It will come,' he replied. 'I can not believe that my reward will never come.' Whereon he left the room and came back with the *curé*. Alas! he told so plain a tale, describing you with such precision and Madeleine Baufremont also, that there was, indeed, no room left for doubt. Yet still I could scarce believe; for even though you had not loved me, even though your burning words, your whispers of love had all been false, why, why, I asked again and again, should you have stooped to such duplicity? If you had tired of me, if that other had turned your heart from me to her, one word would have been enough; I must have let you go when you no longer desired to stay by my side. Mr. Elphinston, I wrote to you at Rome, to the address you had given me and to the English College there; I wrote to Father Sholto—alas! I so much forgot my pride, that I wrote to Douglas, who had then joined the squadron commanded by Monsieur de Roquefeuille for the invasion of England. I could not part from you yet"—these words were scored out by the writer, and, in their place, the sentence began—"I could not yet believe in your deceit, in your cold, cruel betrayal of a woman who had trusted in you as in a god; it seemed all too base and heartless. Yet neither from you nor the Sholtos came one line in answer to my prayer."

Elphinston groaned bitterly as he read the words. He knew now how easily the trap had been laid.

"Then, at last, I did believe. Then, at last, I renounced you and your love. I denied to my own

heart that I had ever known a man named Bertie Elphinston, that I had ever been that man's promised
wife. I tore you from my heart for ever. It was
hard, yet I did it. Time passed, no intelligence came
of you or Madeleine Baufremont. I even heard that
the Duc de Baufremont had petitioned the king that,
if you again entered French territory, you should be
punished for abducting his daughter. Yet, as the days
went on, I allowed Simeon Larpent to approach me no
nearer on the subject. So he and my father concocted
a fresh scheme by which I was at last led to consent
to become his wife. We were, as you know, poor,
horribly poor; the *Cours d'Escrime* hardly provided
for our needs. Often, indeed, I had wondered how we
managed to subsist so well on what seemed to me to
be nothing. My father talked vaguely of an allowance to him, in common with other refugees from
England, from the French king or from the Chevalier
St. George, or the Scotch Fund. Now—for at this
period the old Lord Fordingbridge died—he said we
had been subsisting for some time on money lent, or
we could, if we chose, consider it given to us, by the
present lord. He would never, my father said, demand repayment; indeed, such was his lordship's respect for him and his admiration for me, that he would
cheerfully continue his allowance, or, since he was now
very well-to-do, increase it. So I learnt that I had
been dependent for the bread I ate, the dress I wore,
to this man. Need I say more! You know that I became the wife of Lord Fordingbridge.

"A month had not passed ere I knew the truth as
to how I had been duped and deceived—as to how I
had been false to you. De Roquefeuille's squadron
was driven back by Sir John Norris, and Douglas

Sholto returned to Paris.   He told me all ; that it was your kinsman and namesake of Glenbervie who had left Paris with you to espouse Madeleine Baufremont, and that you—tied under a solemn promise to in no way let his approaching marriage with her be known —had kept the secret even from me.   Alas! had you given me one hint, spoken one word, how different all would have been!   Yet, I do not reproach you for fidelity to your friend ; I only ask that when you think of me—if you ever think at all—as not trusting you, you will recollect that your own silence made it possible for me to doubt.

"One word more, and I shall not trouble you further.   It is to beseech you to quit London at once, to put yourself in safety, with the seas between you and the English Government.   For, even though you might lie hid from the vengeance that will fall on all followers of the prince who may be caught, I fear that private malice, aided by personal fear of you, may lead to your betrayal.   Be warned, I beseech you.   Farewell and forgive.

"CATHERINE FORDINGBRIDGE."

CHAPTER IV.

THE letter written by Lady Fordingbridge, read in conjunction with some other remarks made by other persons who have been introduced to the reader's notice, may serve to inform him of the state of affairs that led to the position in which things were at the period when this narrative commences, namely, the month of May, 1746. A few other words of additional explanation alone are necessary.

At the time when Cardinal Tencin (who looked forward to becoming the successor of Fleury as Prime Minister of France, and who owed his elevation to the purple as well as to the Primacy of France to the influence of the old Pretender) persuaded Louis XV. to support the claims of the Stuarts as his great-grandfather and predecessor had done, Paris was, as is well known to all readers of history, full of English, Scotch, and Irish Jacobites. These refugees from their own countries were to be found in all capacities in that city, some serving as the agents of the exiled Chevalier de St. George, who was now resident at Rome, and others as correspondents between the followers of the Stuarts in London, Rome, and Paris; also, some resided there either from the fact that their presence would not be tolerated in England or its dependencies, and some because, in their staunch loyalty to the fallen

House, they were not disposed to dwell in a country which they considered was ruled over by usurpers. To this class belonged the late Viscount Fording-bridge, a staunch Cheshire nobleman, who had been out in the '15, had afterwards escaped from the Isle of Skye, and had also had the good fortune to escape forfeiture of his estates, owing to the fact that, though he had been out himself, he had neither furnished men, arms, nor money, so far as was known.

But also in Paris were still others who, loyal Jaco-bites as they were, and followers of a ruined party, were yet obliged to earn their bread in the best way they were able. Thus Doyle Fane, Kitty's father, an Irish gentleman of good family who had himself seen serv-ice under France and Austria, eked out a slender allowance—paid irregularly by James Stuart—by les-sons in swordsmanship, of which art he was an expert master. Some, again, obtained commissions in French regiments, many, indeed, being glad to serve as sim-ple privates; while several who were more fortunate—and among whom were Douglas Sholto and Bertie Elphinston—obtained positions in the Garde du Roi or the Mousquetaires, or other corps, and so waited in the hopes of a descent on England in which they would be allowed to take part by resigning tempora-rily their French commissions.

Of priests affecting Stuart principles there were also several, some, as was the case with Archibald Sholto, being temporarily attached to St. Omer, at which there was a large English seminary for the edu-cation of young Catholics, but all of whom were fre-quently in London and Paris, plotting always restless-ly for the overthrow of the present reigning House in England, and for the restoration of the discarded one.

Fane's residence at this period, which was shortly before the expedition of Charles Edward to recover, if possible, the throne of England for his father, was a popular resort of many of the exiled English, Scotch, and Irish, principally because, in the better classes of men who were still young, the practice of the sword was unceasing, and also, perhaps, because in the next house to his was a well-known tavern, "Le Phœbus Anglais," kept by a Jacobite, and a great place of assembly for all the fraternity. But for the younger men there was an even greater attraction than either the advantages of continued practice in swordsmanship or a cheap but good tavern—the attraction of Kitty Fane's beauty.

Kitty kept her father's house for him, kept also his accounts, made his fees go as long a way as possible, and his bottle last out as well as could be the case when submitted so often to the constant demands on it, and was admired and respected by all who came to the little house in the Rue Trouse Vache. Besides her beauty, she was known to be a girl who respected herself, and was consequently respected; and as Doyle Fane was also known to be a gentleman by birth, and Kitty's mother to have been a daughter of one of the oldest families in Ireland, none ever dreamed of treating her in a manner other than became a lady.

Of declared lovers she had two, one whom she disliked for reasons she knew not why—at first; the other whom she adored. Simeon Larpent, heir to the then dying Lord Fordingbridge, was one; Bertie Elphinston, of the Regiment of Picardy, the other. With Larpent, however, the reasons why she disliked him soon made themselves apparent. He was crafty by nature, with a craft that had been much fostered at

St. Omer and Lisbon, where he was educated, and he was, she thought, lacking in bravery. When other men were planning and devising as to how they could find a place in that army which—under Count Saxe, to be convoyed to England by De Roquefeuille—was then forming, he made no attempt to become one of its number, giving as his reasons his father's ill-health and his opinion that he could better serve the Cause by remaining in France. Yet Bertie Elphinston had at the same time a delicate mother residing at Passy, and Douglas Sholto was in poor health at the moment; and still they were both going.

Moreover, Simeon Larpent's admiration was distasteful to her. He had then but recently come back to Paris from Lisbon, from which he brought no particular good character, while he appeared by his conversation and mode of life to have contracted many extremely bad habits. In the Paris of those days the practice and admiration of morality stood at a terribly low point, yet Simeon Larpent seemed more depraved than most young men were in that city even. In a morose and sullen fashion he revelled in all the iniquities that prevailed during the middle of Louis XV's reign, and his name became noted in English circles as that of a man unscrupulous and abandoned, as well as shifty and cunning. Moreover, even his Jacobitism was looked upon with doubtful eyes, and not a few were heard to say that the hour which witnessed his father's death would also see him an avowed Hanoverian. That such would have been the case was certain, had not, however, the old lord's death taken place at the very moment when Charles Edward made the last Stuart bid for restoration in England. But at such a time it was impossible that the new peer could approach the English king. Had he done so it would have been more than his life was worth. At the best, he would have been forced into a duel with some infuriated Jacobite; at the worst, his body would have been found in the Seine, stabbed to the heart.

Meanwhile those events which Lady Fordingbridge had spoken of in her letter to Bertie Elphinston had taken place; nothing was heard by her either of her lover or the Sholtos, and she became the wife of Fordingbridge. For a month he revelled in the possession of the beautiful woman he had coveted since first he set eyes on her; then she found out the truth and his lordship had no longer a wife except in name. She had one interview with him—alone—and after that had taken place she never willingly spoke to him again. Her pride forbade her to separate from him, but with the exception that the same roof sheltered and the same walls enclosed them, they might as well have dwelt in different streets. Against all his protestations, his vows, his declarations that love, and love alone, had forced him to play the part he had, she turned a deaf ear; she would not even open her lips if possible, to show that she had heard his words. She had come to hate and despise him—as she told him in that one interview —and her every action afterwards testified that she had spoken the truth.

And now, when the married life of Lord and Lady Fordingbridge had arrived at this pass, the time was also come when scores of Jacobites, militant, priestly, or passive as they might be, poured into England. For Charles Edward had landed at Moidart, Tullibardine had displayed at Glenfinnen the white, blue, and red silk standard of the prince, the march southward had begun. Following on this news—all of which reached Paris with extraordinary rapidity—came the intelligence of the Battle of Preston, the capture of Edinburgh, Charles's installation at Holyrood, the rout of Cope's army, the march into England, and the determination of George II. to take the field in person against the invader. And among those who received their orders to at once proceed to England was Lord Fordingbridge, such orders coming from out the mouth of the restless Father Sholto.

"But," exclaimed his lordship, "I have no desire to proceed to England. My unhappy married life—for such it has become—will be no better there than here. And in France, at least, matrimonial disputes are not regarded."

"Your desire," said the priest, "is of no concern. I tell you what is required of you—there is nothing left for you but to conform. We wish a goodly number of adherents to the Stuart cause—indeed, all whom it is possible to obtain—to be in London when the prince and his army arrive, as it is now an almost foregone conclusion they will do. You must, therefore, be there. Only, since you are of a calculating—not to say timorous—nature, and as no Jacobite nobleman will be permitted to enter England until the prince is in London, you will travel with papers describing you as a nobleman who has given in his adherence to the House of Hanover. I shall go with you—it is necessary that I keep you under my eyes as much as possible; also it is fitting that I should be in London. In either case my services will be required, whether we are successful or not."

In this way, therefore, his lordship returned to England in company with his wife and his wife's father as well as the Jesuit. Only, he made several reservations in his own mind as to how he would manage his own political affairs, as to how, indeed, he would trim his sails.

"For," said he to himself, "whether I become Hanoverian or remain Jacobite will depend vastly on which side wins. Once in England I shake off this accursed hold which Sholto and all the other priests of St. Omer have on me; nay, if Hanover comes up uppermost, Sholto himself shall be laid by the heels. There will be a pretty sweep made of the Jesuits if Charles gets beaten. If he drives out George, why, then—ah! well, time enough to ponder."

The events of three months soon showed to which side victory was ultimately to belong. Cumberland destroyed the Scotch army, Charles Edward was in hiding in the land he had entered attended by such bright hopes and prospects; all who had fought on his side were either dead, in prison, or fled. And Simeon Larpent, Viscount Fordingbridge, was—quite with the consent for the time being of Archibald Sholto—an avowed Hanoverian and received into favour by the Hanoverian king, though with a strong watch kept on all his actions by that king's Ministers.

CHAPTER V.

On the day after Bertie Elphinston received the letter from his lost love, Lady Fordingbridge, his lordship himself set out from London to journey into Cheshire, there to visit his estate in that county. He had previously intimated to his wife—who had told Father Sholto of the fact—that he intended being absent from London for some weeks; indeed, had asked her whether it was her desire to accompany him. To this question or invitation her ladyship had, however, returned the usual monosyllabic answer which she generally accorded him, and had briefly replied " No." Then being pressed by him to give some reason for her refusal to so accompany him, she had turned round with that bright· blaze in her blue eyes which he had learnt to dread, and had exclaimed :

" Why pester me—especially when we are alone—with these useless questions and formalities? We have arranged, decided the mode in which our existences are to be passed, if passed together—it is enough. We remain together ostensibly on the condition that I share this house with you—I will have no other part in your false life. And if you cannot conform to this arrangement, then even this appearance of union can—had best be—severed."

The viscount bit his lips after her cold contemptuous tones, yet, with that strange power which he possessed, he overmastered the burning rage that rose up in his heart against her. Only he asked himself now, as often before he had asked himself, would he always be able to exercise such control—able to refrain from bursting forth against her, and by so doing put an end to the artificial existence they were living?

But now the morning had come for him to depart for the country; outside in the square he could hear the horses shaking their harness while his carriage waited for him; it was time for him to go. Therefore he went to his wife's morning-room and found her ladyship taking her chocolate.

"I come, madam," he said, with that usual assumption of courtliness which he always treated her to since they had become estranged, "to bid you farewell for some few weeks. I will notify you by the post of my proposed return. Meanwhile your ladyship need not be dull. You have the entry now to the Court circles, you have also your respected father with you in this house. And there are many friends of your younger days in London"—he shot an evil, oblique glance at her out of the corner of his eye as he said this, which was not lost on her—"to wit, Mr. Archibald and—and—others. Doubtless ere I return you may have renewed some of your earlier acquaintanceships. They should be agreeable."

For answer she gave him never a word, but, stirring her cup of chocolate leisurely, looked him straight in the face; then she let her eyes fall on the journal she had been perusing and again commenced to do so as though he were not in the room.

"Curse her," muttered her husband to himself as her indifference stung him to the quick, "curse her, ere long the bolt shall be sped." After which he exclaimed:

"My lady, as is ever the case, I perceive my presence is unwelcome. Once more I bid you adieu," and took himself out of the room and also out of the house. And so he set forth upon his journey.

For a young man on the road to his old family seat, Lord Fordingbridge was that morning strangely preoccupied and indifferent to the events around him, and sat in his carriage huddled up in one corner of it more like an elderly sick man than aught else. The cheerful bustle of the village of Islington, the pretty country villas at Highgate, the larks singing over Finchley Common and Hadley Green, had no power to rouse him from his stupor—if stupor it was— nor either had the bright sun and the warm balmy spring air that came in at the open windows. A strange way for an English nobleman to set out upon his journey to the place where his forefathers had dwelt for ages! A strange way, indeed, considering that he might be regarded as an extremely fortunate man. The head of a family with strong Stuart tendencies, and suspected of himself participating in those tendencies, he had yet been at once received into favour by the King on returning to London. This alone should have made his heart light within him, for he had but now to conform to that King's demands to pass the rest of his existence in peace and full enjoyment of his comfortable means—to feel that his father's and his family's Jacobitism was forgotten, that all was well with him. George was now welcoming to his fold every exiled Jacobite who had not openly fought or plotted and schemed against him in the recent invasion, and many peers and gentlemen who had long lived abroad in exile were hastening to tender their adherence to the German king, feeling perfectly sure that, after the events of the past three months, the day of the Stuarts was past and gone for ever.

Why, therefore, could not Simeon Larpent look forward as hopefully to the future as all his brother exiles who had returned were doing? Why! Was it because of the enmity of his wife to him, an enmity which he knew could never slacken ; or was it because of his fear of that other man whom he had so deeply wronged ; or because of what his scheming mind was now fashioning? This we shall see.

The roads were heavy with the recent spring showers so that the four horses of his coach could drag it but tediously along them, and it was nightfall ere South Mimms was reached, and night itself ere they arrived at St. Albans, and Lord Fordingbridge descended at the Angel. To the bowing landlord he gave his name, and stated that he wished a bed-room and a parlour for himself, and a room for his men ; and then, as he was about to follow his obsequious host up the broad staircase, he said, pulling out his watch :

"It is now after seven. At nine I expect to be visited by a gentleman whom I have appointed to meet me here. His name is Captain Morris. You will please entertain him at my cost to-night, and do so at your best. On his arrival, if he hath not supped, ask him to do so ; if he hath, show him in at once to me. Now I will prepare for my own meal."

Again Boniface bowed low—lower even than before, after he had become acquainted with his visitor's rank and position—and escorted him to a large, comfortable bed-room on the first floor, in which a cheerful fire burnt in the grate. And throwing open two heavy folding-doors, he showed next a bright sitting-room, also with a fire, and well lit.

"This will do very well," said his lordship. "Now send my servant to me with my valise. And let him wait on me at table."

All through the repast he partook of the viscount meditated gloomily and gravely, eating but little of the substantial meal provided by the landlord, drinking sparingly, and addressing no remark to his servant. Then when he had finished, he had his chair drawn up before the fire, a bottle of wine and another of brandy placed on the table, and, bidding the servant withdraw and bring Captain Morris to him when he should arrive, he again fell to meditating and musing, speaking sometimes aloud to himself.

"It is the only way," he muttered, in disconnected sentences, "the only way. And it must be done at one swoop; otherwise it is useless. So long as one of them is free I am fettered. The only way! And—then—when that is accomplished—to deal with you, my lady. Let me see." He began counting on his fingers and tapping the tips as still he pondered, touching first his forefinger, then the second and third, and once or twice nodding his head as though well satisfied with himself.

"As for Fane," he muttered next, "he scarce counts. Yet he, too, must be taken care of. But of that later. Doubtless when I begin with my lady—Vengeance confound her!—he will become revengeful,

4

but before he can do so—well, he will be harmless. So, so. It should work."

The clock struck nine as he spoke, and he compared it with his great tortoiseshell watch, and then sat listening. The inn was very quiet, he doubted if any other travellers were staying in it, especially as the coach from London passed through early in the day, but outside in the street there were signs of life. The rustics bade each other good-night as they passed; a woman's laugh broke the air now and again; sometimes a dog barked. And at last, above these sounds, he heard a horse's hoofs clattering along the street as though ridden fast.

"That," said his lordship, "may be he. 'Tis very possible. For one of his Majesty's servants, he is none too punctual."

As he spoke the horse drew up with still more clatter at the porch below his window, and he heard a clear, firm voice ask if Lord Fordingbridge had that day arrived from London. And two or three moments later his servant knocked at the door, and, entering, said that Captain Morris was come.

"Has he supped?"

"He says he requires nothing, my lord, but desires to see you at once. He rides to Hertford to-night, he bid the landlord say, and has but little time at his disposal."

"So be it. Show him in," and a moment later Captain Morris entered the room.

A man of something more than middle age, this gentleman's features, aquiline and clear cut, presented the appearance of belonging to one in whom great ability as well as shrewdness and common sense were combined. Tall and extremely thin, his undress riding-habit of dark blue embroidered with gold lace set off his figure to extreme advantage, while the light sword he carried by his side, his gold-trimmed three-cornered hat with its black cockade, and his long riding boots all served to give him the appearance of an extremely gentlemanly and elegant man.

"Welcome, sir," said Lord Fordingbridge, advancing to meet him with extended hand, while at the same time he noticed—and took account of—the clear grey eyes, the thin lips, and aquiline nose of his visitor. "Welcome, sir. I am glad you have been able to reach here to-night. To-morrow I must resume my journey. Be seated, I beg."

"The orders which I received from London," replied Captain Morris, in a clear, refined voice that corresponded perfectly with his appearance, "made it imperative that I should call on you to-night. As your lordship may be aware, in this locality I have certain duties to perform which can be entrusted to no one else."

"I am aware of it," Fordingbridge replied. Then he said, "Before we commence our conversation, let me offer you a glass of wine or brandy. The night is raw, and you have doubtless ridden long."

Captain Morris bowed, said he would drink a glass of wine, and, when he had poured it out of the decanter, let it stand by his side untouched for the moment. After which he remarked:

"I understand, my lord, that I am to receive from your lips to-night some information of considerable importance to his Majesty, touching those who have been engaged in plotting against his security. May I ask you to proceed at once with what you have to tell me? I have still some distance to ride to-night, and also other work to do."

"Yes," answered Fordingbridge, "you have been exactly informed. Yet—how to tell—how to begin, I scarcely know. My object is to put in the King's hands—without, of course, letting it be known that the information comes from me—some facts relating to several notorious Jacobites now sheltering in London. Men who are," he continued, speaking rapidly, "inimical to his Majesty's peace and security, hostile to his rule, and, if I mistake not, bent at the present moment in endeavouring in some way to effect a rescue of the Scotch lords now in confinement at the Tower."

A slight smile rose upon his visitor's face as he uttered these last words; then Captain Morris said quietly:

"That is hardly likely to come to pass, I should imagine. The Tower does not disgorge its victims freely, certainly not by force. As for the Scotch lords, I am afraid they will only quit the place for their trials and afterwards for Tower Hill."

"Yet," remarked Lord Fordingbridge, "the attempt may be made. Of the men I speak of, two are desperate, and both fought at Culloden and the battles that took place during the Pretender's march into England. They will stop at nothing if," with a quick glance at the other, "they are not themselves first stopped."

"Give me their names, if you please," said Morris, with military precision, as he produced from his pocket a notebook, "and where they are to be found."

"Their names are Bertie Elphinston and Douglas Sholto—the former a kinsman of the Lord Balmarino.

Both have lived in exile in France, serving in the French King's army, one in the *Garde du Roi* at first, and then in the Regiment of Picardy. The other, Sholto, has served in the Mousquetaires."

"Their names," said Captain Morris, "are not in the list," and he turned over the leaves of his note-book carefully as he spoke. "But for you, my lord, these men might have escaped justice. 'Tis strange nothing was known of them."

"They crossed from France with Charles Edward. Many names of those who accompanied him are probably not known. You may rely on my information. I myself returned but from France some weeks ago. I know them well."

"Indeed!" exclaimed Captain Morris. "Indeed! Your lordship doubtless came to support his Majesty shortly after so many of his enemies crossed over."

"Precisely. But I will be frank. I should tell you I am myself a converted—perverted, some would say —Jacobite. My father, the late lord, died one. I do not espouse his political faith."

Captain Morris bowed gravely; then he said:

"And you know, therefore, these gentlemen—these Scotch rebels."

"I know them very well. Shall I furnish you with a description of their persons?"

"If you please;" and as the captain replied to the question, he—perhaps unwittingly—pushed the un-tasted glass of wine farther away from him into the middle of the large table, where it remained un-drunk.

After the appearance of Elphinston and Sholto had been fully given and noted in the captain's book, he asked:

"And where are these men to be found, Lord Fordingbridge?"

"They shelter themselves in the village of Wandsworth, near London, in an old house on the Waterside, as the strand there is called. It is the first reached from the village."

Again this was written down, after which Captain Morris rose to take his departure, but my lord's tale was not yet told. Pointing to the chair the other had risen from, he said:

"I beg you to be seated a moment longer. There is still another—the worst rebel of all—of whom I wish to apprise you. A priest."

"A priest! You speak truly; they are, indeed, his Majesty's worst enemies. A Jesuit, of course?"

"Of course. With him it will be necessary to use the most astute means in the Government's power to first entrap him, and then to deal with him afterwards. He should, indeed, be confined in total solitude, forbidden, above all things else, to hold any communication with other rebels."

"You may depend, Lord Fordingbridge, on all being done that is necessary, short of execution."

"Short of execution!" interrupted the other. "Short of execution! Why do not the scheming Jesuits—the mainspring of all, the cause of the very rebellion but now crushed out—merit execution as well as those who routed Cope's forces and hewed down Cumberland's men? *Grand Dieu!* I should have thought they would have been the first to taste the halter."

"Possibly," replied the captain in passionless tones, and with an almost imperceptible shrug of his shoulders, "but at present no Jesuit priests have been executed. I doubt if any will be. The Government have other punishments for them—exile to the American colonies, and so forth. Now, my lord, this priest's name and abode."

"He is brother to Douglas Sholto, an elder brother by another mother, yet they have ever gone hand in hand together. Named Archibald, of from thirty-eight to forty years of age. Crafty, dissimulating, and——"

"That is of course," said Captain Morris. "Now, tell me, if you please, where this man is to be found. Is he also in hiding at Wandsworth?"

"Nay," replied the other—and for the first time the informer seemed to hesitate in his answer. Yet for a moment only, since again he proceeded with his story. "He is disguised, of course; passes as a Scotch merchant having business between London and Paris, and is known as Mr. Archibald." He paused again, and Captain Morris's clear eyes rested on him as, interrogatively, he said:

"Yes? And his abode?"

"Is my own house. In Kensington-square."

This time the officer started perceptibly, and fixed an even more penetrating glance upon the other than before. Indeed, so apparent were both the start and look of surprise on his face that the traitor before him deemed it necessary to offer some excuse for his strange revelation.

"Yes," he said, "in my own house. It has been necessary for me to let him hide there awhile the better to—to entrap—to deliver him to justice."

"Your lordship is indeed an ardent partisan," coldly replied Captain Morris; "the King is much to be congratulated on so good a convert."

"The King will, I trust, reward my devotion. The

Stuarts have never shown any gratitude for all that has been done for them—by my family as much as any. Now, Captain Morris," he went on, "I have told you all that I have to tell. I have simply to ask that in no way shall it be divulged—as, indeed, I have the promise of his Majesty's Ministers that nothing shall be divulged—as to the source whence this information is derived. It is absolutely necessary that I appear not at all in the matter."

"That is understood. The Secretary of State for Scotch affairs, from whom I receive my instructions, knows your lordship's desire, without a doubt."

"Precisely. It is with him I have been in communication. Yet, still, I would make one other request. It is that Father Sholto may not be arrested in my house. That would be painful to—to—Lady Fordingbridge, a young and delicate woman. He can easily be taken outside, since he quits the house fearlessly each day."

"That too," replied Morris, "I will make a note of for the Secretary's consideration. I wish you now, my lord, good evening," saying which he bowed and went toward the door.

"If I could possibly prevail on you to refresh yourself," said Fordingbridge, as he followed him to it, "I should be happy," and he held out his hand as he spoke.

But the captain, who seemed busy with his sash, or sword belt, did not perhaps see the extended hand, and muttering that he required no refreshment, withdrew from the room.

Nevertheless, when he reached the bar in the passage below he asked the smiling landlady if she could give him a glass of cordial to keep out the rawness of the night air, and to fortify him for his ride. Also he asked, in so polite a manner as to gratify the good woman's heart, if he might scrawl a line at her table whereat she sat sewing and surrounded by her bottles and glasses. Buxom landladies rarely refuse politenesses to persons of Captain Morris's position, especially when so captivatingly arrayed as he was in his undress bravery, and as he wrote his message and sealed it she thought how gallant a gentleman he was.

Then he looked up and enquired if there was any ostler or idle postboy about the place who could ride for him with a letter to-morrow morning to Dunstable, and receiving a reply in the affirmative, paid for his cordial, the hire of the next morning messenger and his horse's feed, and so bade her a cheerful goodnight.

In the yard, while his animal was being brought out, he looked with some little interest at his lordship's travelling carriage, inspected the crest upon its panels and the motto, and, tossing the fellow who brought the nag a shilling, and seeing carefully to his holsters, rode away into the night.

Upstairs, my lord, standing before the fire, noticed the unemptied glass of wine, and, remembering that the captain had not chosen to see his outstretched hand, cursed him for an ill-conditioned Hanoverian cur. Downstairs, the hostess, being a daughter of Eve, turned over the captain's letter addressed to "Josias Brandon, Esq., Justice of the Peace," and would have given her ears, or at least a set of earrings, to know what its contents were. Had she been able to see them they probably would have given her food for gossip for a twelvemonth, brief as they were. They ran :

" The Viscount Fordingbridge passes through Dunstable to-morrow in his coach on his road to Cheshire. From the time he does so until he returns through your town to London, he is to be followed and watched and never lost sight of. Let me be kept acquainted with all his movements—by special courier, if needful.—NOEL MORRIS, CAPTAIN."

CHAPTER VI.

BETWEEN Lady Fordingbridge and her father a better state of things existed than that which prevailed between her and her husband. Indeed, Kitty, who could not forgive the treachery of the man who was now her husband, could not, at the same time, bring herself to regard her father's share in that treachery in as equally black a light. She knew that it was the actual truth that he had been much in debt to Simeon Larpent (as he was then), and she had persuaded herself also to believe that which he constantly assured her was the truth—and, perhaps, might have been—that Larpent would have proceeded against him for his debt, in spite of the story Fane had been instructed to tell to the effect that the other was very willing to continue their creditor. Moreover, old and feeble as her father was now—broken down and unable any longer to earn bread to put in their mouths, she did not forget that, until the events of the last few unhappy months, he had been an excellent parent to her. For, hardly and roughly, by long days of weary work, the bread had been earned somehow, the roof kept over their heads, the clothes found for their backs. Hour after hour, as she remembered, the worn-out old Irish gentleman—once the brilliant young military adventurer—had stood in the room set apart for the

fencing school, giving his lessons to men young enough
to be his sons; and also she recalled how every night,
it seemed to her, he was more fatigued than before,
his back a little more bowed, his weariness greater.
And as—even after the marriage had taken place into
which she had been hoodwinked—she thought of all
this, and of how he had grown older and more feeble
in his fight to keep the wolf from the door, she almost
brought herself to forgive him entirely for the great
wrong he had done her.

She sat thinking over all this on the morning after
her lord's departure for the country, while opposite to
her, toasting his feet in front of the fire, her father
sat. The old man was well dressed now; he was comfortable and without care—an astute Irish attorney
settled in Paris had tied the viscount up as tightly as
possible in the matter of jointure, settlements and
dowry for Kitty, not without remonstrance from Fordingbridge, which was, however, unavailing; and out of
her own money she had provided for her father. And
as her eyes rested on him she felt that, badly as he had
behaved to her, she was still glad to know that his
laborious days were past. At this time Kitty was very
near to forgiving him altogether; her strong, loving
heart remembering so much of all he had done for her
in the past, and forgetting almost all of his wrong-
doing.

"What do your letters say to ye, Kitty, this morning?" asked Doyle Fane, who, after more than forty
years' absence from his native land, still retained some
of its rich raciness of tone and.accent. "Ye've a big
post there before ye, me child."

"Very little of any importance," she replied. "The
night coach through St. Albans brings me a letter from

his lordship trusting I shall be happy during his enforced absence. Faugh! Also there is one by the
French packet from Kathleen Muskerry. Her uncle,
the priest at Marly, is removed to St. Roch. Lady
Belrose, whose acquaintance I made a month ago at
Leicester House, writes desiring me to accompany her
to the masquerade at Vauxhall."

"Good, me child, good. And what for not? 'Twill
do ye good to see some life, to——"

"To see some life!" she repeated, "see some life!
In the midst of death all around us!"

"Death!" the old man repeated. "Death! Faith,
I did not know it. What death is there around
us?"

"Father!" she exclaimed, looking at him, "is
there not death all around—threatening those whom
we love—whom we loved once? Do you not know
that London is at the present moment full of followers
of the unhappy prince, who, if they are caught, must
be doomed? Do you not know that the Tower, Newgate, the New Gaol over the water in Southwark, is
crowded with such men, all of whom have soon to
stand their trial for high treason—men of whom we
have known many, some of whom were your pupils?
Father, this is no time for masquerades."

For a moment the old man gazed at her with solemn eyes, as though endeavouring to penetrate her
mind, to discover if behind her words there lay any
hidden meaning; then he asked:

"Are there any—any whom—we know particularly
well among these threatened men? You may tell me,
Kitty. You may trust me—now."

"Is not Father Sholto in jeopardy?" she asked,
while her eyes also rested on him much as his had

dwelt on her.　Perhaps she, too, was wondering if he guessed to whom, more than all others, her remarks applied.　"If he were discovered would he not share the gaol, if not the scaffold?　He told us yesterday that there was a newly-made law against any Jesuit priests from France who should be found in England." *

"Are there any—any others?" he almost whispered.　But still her clear blue eyes regarded him, and she spoke no word.

"Well, well," he said a moment after.　"Perhaps it may be, even after so many years, that I do not deserve your confidence.　Yet, Kitty, I was nigh as much deceived in some things as you were.　Child," he said, leaning across the table as he spoke, "I swear to you I thought that man who came to us was, in truth, the priest, the *curé* of Moret.　How could I know he was a paid creature of Larpent's, a vile cheat, instead of the man who, as I supposed, had tied the hands of Bertie El—— ?"

"Stop," said his daughter, "stop!　Don't mention that again.　Let it be done with, forgotten; dead and buried.　It is past!　Over!　I—I—am Lord Fordingbridge's wife."

"Yet I must ask.　I must know.　Nay, I do know. Fordingbridge hinted as much to me ere he set out. Kitty," and now his voice sank to a whisper that none but she could have heard, even though in the room, "is he in London?"

"Yes," she whispered also, softly as a woman's whisper ever is.　"Yes.　He is here.　Oh, father! for the love of God, betray us—him—no more.　For if

---

* See Appendix, note B—"Jesuit Priests in England."

you do, it will not end this time with broken hearts, but with death."

"Betray you," he said, "betray you again! Why will you not believe me once more? See, Kitty, see here," and as he spoke he rose from his chair and stood before her. "I swear to you that I am true in spite—in spite of what I once did, partly in ignorance —unwittingly. I myself loved Elphinston and always despised Larpent. And I did—honestly, I did—believe that he had married Mademoiselle Baufremont."

"Well, she said, "well, he had not. Enough of that. And, since you ask me to trust you once again as I trusted you before, I answer you—remember his life, as well as Douglas Sholto's, are in your hands— he is in London. Both are here."

"'Tis madness," he murmured, "madness. For, Kitty, as sure as he is here he will be betrayed. Fordingbridge will denounce him."

"Alas!" she replied, almost wringing her hands, "alas! I fear as much myself. Yet Father Sholto says not—that it is impossible. For, he declares, should harm come to either of them through him, he will cause him also to be denounced. He knows some secret as to Fordingbridge's doings that, he says, would bring him to the block for a surety, which secret, if he turns traitor, he will use most remorselessly. And, do what he may, at least he is harmless now. He will be in Cheshire for a month. By that time I pray that both the others may be beyond the seas."

"Have you seen him?" he asked, still in a low voice.

He knew that in London at this time walls almost had ears, and that every footman or waiting-maid might be a spy of the Government—especially in a house but recently re-opened after many years of dis-use, and, consequently, possessing a staff of servants new to their employers and taking neither interest nor sympathy in their affairs. Also he knew that, in the garb of servants, many a Government agent was care-fully watching every action of his or her temporary employers. London especially had but recently re-covered from too great a fright to cease as yet to fear for its safety, and saw a bugbear in many harm-less strangers now in its midst; the house of a noble-man returned recently from France—the birthplace of the late invasion—and known to be a Catholic, would, therefore, be a particularly likely object to be subjected to supervision, quiet yet effectual.

"No," she replied; "no, I have not seen him. God forbid I should. And if I did, the only words I could, I think, find heart to utter would be to beseech him to fly at once. Oh! father, father, I dread some awful calamity, though I know not in what form or shape it may come."

As she spoke, a tap was heard at the door, and, a second afterwards, Father Sholto entered the room, while so much had her ladyship's fears and tremors overcome her and her father that both exclaimed at once, in the same words, "Is all well?"

"In so far as I know," he replied, after having ex-changed morning greetings with them. "As well as all will ever be. Why do you ask? Have you reason to dread aught?"

"No, no," Kitty replied. "Still, I know not why, I am strangely uneasy, strangely nervous to-day. Some feeling of impending ills seems to hang over me."

"Yet," said Sholto, "if omens are to be supposed

to have any power, no such feeling should trouble you to-day. Kitty, I bear good news——"

"Good news!" she exclaimed. From——"

"From an acquaintance of mine—one who is in the office of the Scotch Secretary of State. Nay," he went on, seeing the look of disappointment on her face, and knowing she had expected matter of a different kind, "'tis worth hearing. Among the names of those now in London for whom diligent search is being made —the names of those who, if found, are doomed— three do not appear—three in whom we are concerned."

"Thank God!" exclaimed Lady Fordingbridge and her father together. "They are——"

"Our two friends across the river and—and— myself."

"Therefore you may escape at once?" she asked. "All of you? There is nothing to keep you here in England—the Cause is broken, it can never be regained now—you can all depart in peace?"

"Yes," he said, "we can." But letting his eye fall on Fane, he took her a little apart and said:

"Kitty, we have the chance of getting across the water; at least, we are safe at present. I, you know, can go at any moment; there is nothing to detain me. The glorious work, the accomplishment of which I crossed over to see, will never be done now—I may as well go. But—shall the others go too? It rests with you to say."

"With me," she said, looking up at him; "with me? Why, how should I prevent them going? Oh Archibald, if I could see them I would beg them on my knees to go while there is yet time."

"One will not leave England without the other;

Douglas would never go without Bertie.   And, Kitty, Elphinston will not go yet."

"Not yet! Why not? What does he tarry for? Is it to take vengeance on my husband, to—to——"

" To see you."

"To see me," she said, clasping her hands convulsively together, while from her soft blue eyes there shone so bright a light that Father Sholto knew how deeply the love still dwelt in her heart for the poor wanderer and outcast; "to see me. Oh! say, does he forgive—has he sent me one word of pardon, of pity?"

"Ay, child, he forgives, if he has aught to forgive. Those are his words. Yet, he bids me say, he must see you, speak with you; then—then he will go away for ever. Now," Sholto went on, "'tis for you to decide. If you see him, there is naught to prevent his going; only—I must tell you, it is my duty as a priest, though you need but little caution from me—remember this man loves you now as much as he ever loved you, and—you are another man's wife."

Fane had left the room when the others drew apart —perhaps he guessed that Sholto had some message for his daughter—so that now they could speak at ease. For a moment Lady Fordingbridge seemed lost in thought—as though struggling between conflicting desires, the one to see again the man she loved, the other to know that he was safe, a third to remember that, however hateful to her Lord Fordingbridge was, she was still his wife. Then suddenly she said:

"You are right. 'Tis best we should not meet. Yet—yet—you say he will not quit England without our doing so."

"I fear not. And time is precious. Remember,

though the names are not in the list, they may be at any moment. Or he, or both of them, 'may be denounced. Many of Cumberland's and Cope's regiments are back in London ; they may be recognised by some against whom they fought, and, if that were the case, their chance of existence would be small. Kitty, if you are strong enough, as you should be, 'tis almost best that you should see him. Then he can go in peace."

" I am strong enough," she replied. " Have no fear of me ; I have none of myself. Yet, how can it be ? He cannot come here—I cannot go to him. But oh ! to hear from his own lips that he forgave me, that he would think of me sometimes without bitterness."

" What answer shall I give him, then ? "

" Does he await one ? "

" Eagerly. If you bade him meet you in George's Throne-room he would contrive to be there."

" When do you see him again ? " she asked.

" To-night, after dark."

" So be it. To-night you shall bear him a message from me. Now, leave me a little while. At dinner we will meet again. Then, then, I will ask you to carry a note to him."

When she was alone she went to the standish and, taking pens and paper, wrote two notes. The first was easily despatched ; it simply told Lady Belrose she would accompany her and her party to Vauxhall on the following night. The next took longer, caused her much deliberation.

She pined to see the man whom in her own heart she accused herself of having deceived ; yet she dreaded the hour when she should stand face to face with him. Alas ! how could she look into his eyes—

eyes that she feared would look back but sternly upon her—and plead for forgiveness, remembering that, had she but trusted and believed in him, they who now met as strangers would by this time have been man and wife a twelvemonth. Yet, it was not only to gratify her own desire to once more touch his hand and hear his voice, even though that voice should reproach her, that she desired to see him. It was also to save him, since he would leave the country, he had said, after they had once met.

So, at last, she decided it should be so. She would see him once, would take his pardon from his own lips—Sholto had said that he forgave her—and then she would bid him go and consult nothing but his own safety and that of his true and tried friend.

She took the pen in her hand again and drew the paper towards her, but, at first, she knew not what to say. In the previous letter she had sent him the words and ideas had come easily enough, for then she was writing a straightforward narrative with, in it, a sad plea for forgiveness. But now it was different. She was making an assignation with a man she had once loved—once!—she was deceiving her husband.

"Bah!" she said, as this thought rose to her mind. "If 'tis deception let it be so. Out of his deceit to me is borne mine to him."

Whereon once more she pondered a moment on what she should say, and then wrote:

"Lady Fordingbridge will be at the masquerade at Vauxhall to-morrow night. May she hope she will hear none but gentle words there?"

That was all.

CHAPTER VII.

THE rejoicings into which London broke out when,
at last, the Scottish rebellion was decisively crushed
caused Ranelagh and Vauxhall Gardens to be, perhaps,
more frequented in the warm spring and summer of
1746 than they had ever been previously. Indeed,
after the fright which had fallen upon the capital
when the news came that the Highland troops were
at Derby and within four days' march of London, it
was not very astonishing that the inhabitants should,
on the removal of that terror, give themselves up to
wholesale amusement. Six months before, imminent
ruin stared them in the face; the Bank of England, by
that time regarded as being almost as stable an insti-
tution as it is now considered, had only escaped closing
its doors by the oft-quoted artifice of paying the demands made on it in sixpences. Regiments engaged
in foreign campaigns—Ligonier's Horse and Hawley's
and Rich's Dragoons—had been hurried home from
Williamstadt; Admiral Vernon and Commodores Bos-
cawen and Smith were each at sea with a squadron
looking for ships carrying the invaders; while fifty
merchantmen, styled "armed cruisers," were patrol-
ling the Channels round our shores. Also, as an outcome of the panic, the inhabitants of London had pur-
chased for the army about to take the field against the

Pretender, 12,000 pairs of breeches and the same number of pairs of woollen gloves, 12,000 shirts, 10,000 woollen caps and pairs of stockings, and 9,000 pairs of woollen spatterdashes; while, not to be outdone by the other citizens, the managers of the then existing London theatres offered to form the members of their various companies into volunteers attached to the City regiment.

But, ere the springtime had come, the invasion was over, the danger past. The young Duke of Cumberland, fresh from his triumphs in Flanders, had not only destroyed the rebel army, but had taken terrible and bloody vengeance upon all who had opposed him. Therefore London—indeed, all England—slept again in safety at night, and with the arrival of summer had plunged with greater fervour than ever into all its usual enjoyments. Amongst the enjoyments of the former none were more popular than those of Ranelagh and Vauxhall Gardens, the latter being more generally known and spoken of at that period as the Spring Gardens. Here, on the warm evenings which May brought with it, until the fashionable world departed for its country seats, or for Bath, Epsom, or Tunbridge, went on one continual round of pleasures and festivities—one night a masquerade, another a concert, vocal and instrumental, where, among others, the mysterious Tenducci—whose sex was always matter of discussion—sang and warbled, sometimes in a man's voice, sometimes in a woman's; illuminations took place every evening, and, as they died out and the company departed, the nightingales might be heard singing in the neighbouring fields and groves.

It was on one of these warm May nights that the wherry which brought Lady Belrose's party from Pimlico Fields to the Spring Gardens arrived at the latter place, while, as the boat touched the shore, from the gardens might already be heard the orchestra playing. In the wherry sat, of course, Lady Belrose herself, a still young and still good-looking woman, who, being a widow, thought herself entitled to always have in attendance upon her some beau or other, and who, to-night, had brought two, one a young lad from Oxford, the other almost as young a man, Sir Charles Ames. By her side sat Lady Fordingbridge, whose plain evening frock contrasted somewhat strongly with that of her friend, who was arrayed in a gorgeous brocade silk, while one of her cavaliers carried over his arm a green velvet mantle laced with gold, in case the evening turned cold and she should .have occasion for it.

"I protest," said her ladyship, as stepping ashore she put on her mask, in which she was copied by the others—"I protest the very sound of the fiddles squeaking makes me long for a dance. Mr. Fane," she said, turning to that gentleman, who formed the last member of the party, "am I to have you for a partner to-night?"

Fane bowed and responded politely that he only trusted his old age and stiff joints would not prevent him from making himself acceptable, on at least one occasion, to her ladyship; while Sir Charles Ames, turning to Kitty, desired to know if she would so far favour him as to give him a dance.

But Lady Belrose, who had already gathered from her friend that she only made one of the party because of a serious and grave interview which she anticipated having with a gentleman whom she might meet at the *fête*, here interposed and, in a few well-chosen words, gave the baronet to understand that to dance was not Lady Fordingbridge's desire that evening. "She is not well," she said, "and will simply be an onlooker. Meanwhile, doubtless I can find you a sufficiency of partners among other friends." To this the young man protested that there was no need for Lady Belrose to endeavour to find him partners among her friends, since, if she would but condescend to be his partner, he could not possibly desire any other, and so, with these interchanges of politeness, they entered the gardens.

On this particular night at Vauxhall—the opening masquerade of the season—the fashionable world, as well as those who, though not in that world themselves, loved to gaze on the happier beings who were of it, assembled in large numbers and in a variety of costumes. Scaramouches in their black dresses, toques and masks, with rush lances in their hands, mingled with dancing girls clad in the Turkish costumes still known in these days as "Roxanas," in memory of the infamous woman who had first worn this garb; shepherdesses walked arm-in-arm with men dressed as grave and reverend clergymen; assumed victims of the Inquisition, invested in the San Benito, pirouetted and twirled with brazen-faced and underclad Iphigenias and Phrynes—for the world was none too modest in those days!—mock soldiers, knights and satyrs, harlequins, and men in wizard's garments danced and drank, laughed and shouted with milkmaids, nuns, and Joans of Arc. And to testify, perhaps, the fact that they had not forgotten the dangers through which the country had recently passed, and also, perhaps, to hurl one last taunt at their crushed and broken foes, many of the maskers had arrayed themselves in the garbs of their late enemies —for some strutted round and round the orchestra pavilion and banqueting room dressed as Highlanders or French officers, others as miserable Scotch peasants having in their hands flails and reaping hooks. Others, again, had even attempted to portray the character of the unhappy Charles Edward, now in hiding in the Scotch wilds, and, as they danced and sang or drank their glasses of ale and ate their two-penny slices of hung-beef, and endeavoured even by their conversation to ape what they imagined to be the Scotch dialect. At the same time, outside all this seething, painted, and bedizened crowd were many others of the better classes, such as those who formed Lady Belrose's party, or visitors of a similar degree, who contented themselves by concealing their identity with masks, vizards, and dominos, or with hoods and laces.

In a somewhat retired spot beneath where stood a noble statue of Handel, now nearing his last days, executed by Roubiliac, and at the back of which were a small wooded green and bosquet in which were many arbours, Lady Belrose and her friends sat down to watch the kaleidoscopic crowd. Here, Sir Charles Ames, summoning a waiter, bade him bring refreshments for the party—viz., some iced fruits and a flask of champagne—and they being partaken of, he invited her ladyship to honour him by becoming his partner in a *quadrille de contredanse*, a new style of dancing introduced into the French ballets a year or so before, and but just come over to London. This the sprightly lady accepted at once, having already perfected herself in the new divertissement under Duharnel's tuition; but, on her other cavalier desiring also

the honour of Lady Fordingbridge's hand, Kitty refused, on the ground that she knew not the dance, and
neither was she very well.

"I' faith, Kate," said Lady Belrose, as she shook
her sack over her great balloon-shaped hoop and fast-
ened her mask more tightly under her hood, "yet have
you lost but little to-night. The quadrille is well
enough in our own houses or on our country lawns;
here, I protest, the noise, the dust, and the stench of
the oil lamps, to say nothing of the unknown and,
doubtless, unclean creatures with whom we rub shoulders and touch hands, do not recommend it over-
much. However, lead me to it, Sir Charles, since you
will have it so," and in another moment she, with her
partner and the others who formed the sets, were bowing and curtseying to each other.

Meanwhile Mr. Wynn, Lady Belrose's second string,
having begged that he might be allowed to find a partner and himself join in a set, since Lady Fordingbridge
was so obdurate (he, too, had been learning the new
dance from Monsieur Duharnel), took himself off, so
that Kitty and her father were left alone together.
And now it was that she, after scanning each male
figure that was "more than common tall," began to
tremble a little in her limbs and to feel as though she
were about to faint. For in that portion of the crowd
which was not dancing and which still followed its
leaders round and round the orchestra pavilion, thereby illustrating the words of Bloomfield, a poet of the
period, who wrote:

> First we traced the gay circle all round,
> Ay—and then we went round it again—

she saw two forms that, she doubted not, were those

for whom she looked—partly in eagerness, partly with nervousness.

These maskers did not walk side by side, but one behind the other, and, possibly, to ordinary onlookers would not have appeared to have any connection with each other. Yet Kitty knew very well that, inseparable in almost all else, they were now equally so. The first, who was the tallest, was clad in a costume, perhaps unique that night in the Spring Gardens, perhaps almost unique among the many costumes that have ever been assumed since first masquerades were invented. It was that of the headsman. Arrayed in the garb of that dismal functionary, a rusty black velvet suit, with the breeches and black woollen stockings to match, the masker might yet have failed to inform those who saw him of the character he wished to portray, had it not been for at least one other accessory. On his back, strapped across it, he carried the long, narrow-bladed axe used for decapitation, its handle fringed and tasselled with leathern thongs. Yet there were other tokens also of the part he represented. In a girdle round his waistcoat he bore a formidable knife having a blade a foot long and an inch and a half deep— the knife with which the doomsman finished his ghastly task if the axe failed to do its duty, as had too often happened. His mask, too, was not that of the ordinary reveller at such places as this, not a mask made ostensibly to conceal the features, yet, as often as not, revealing them almost as clearly as though it had not been assumed; instead, it was long and full, covering not only the eyes and the bridge of the nose, but also the whole of the upper part of the face, and leaving only visible the lower jaw and the two ends of a thick brown moustache that hung below it. Alone by that

moustache would Kitty have known the wearer, if by
no other sign.   It had been pressed too often against
her own lips for her to forget it !   Yet, also, would she
have known him without it.   His companion, the man
who followed after him, was not so conspicuous by his
appearance.   He, indeed, wrapped in a long brown
woollen cloak which descended to his shoes and must
have been more than warm on such an evening as this,
with at his side a Scotch claymore, or broadsword, and
on his head a Scotch bonnet—the mask, of course,
being worn—passed among the crowd as an excellent
representative of their now despised and fallen enemies.   Yet, had that crowd known that amongst them
stalked in reality one whose prowess had been terribly
conspicuous when exhibited against their own soldiers,
they might not have gazed as approvingly as they now
did on Douglas Sholto.

As Kitty regarded these two figures—still trembling
and feeling as though she were about to faint—she
saw the eyes of the former one fix themselves upon
her, and observed him hesitate for a moment ere continuing his course, then, in an instant, he went on
again in the stream that continued to revolve round
the orchestra pavilion.   And she knew that a few moments would bring him again before her.

"Father," she said, nerving herself to that interview which she so ardently desired, yet which, womanlike. she almost feared now, "the green behind looks
cool and inviting, especially now that the sun is gone
and the lamps are lit.   I will stroll down there awhile
and take the air.   Meanwhile, rest you here—there is
some more champagne in the flask—and keep these
seats until the others come back.   The *contredanse*
will be finished just now."

"Mind no gallant treats ye rudely, child. The crowd is none too orderly as regards some of its members. Ladies alone, and without a cavalier, may be roughly accosted."

"Have no fear," she said, "I can protect myself. I shall be back ere Lady Belrose takes part in the next dance," saying which she turned and went down the walk that led between the grassy lawn and the arbours, in each of which now twinkled the many-coloured oil lamps. And, as she so turned, that portion of the maskers in which was the man dressed as the headsman passed by the chair she had just vacated, and she knew that he must have seen her rise and move away.

A few moments later she was aware that such was the case. A heavy tread sounded behind her—she had now advanced considerably down the path and had almost reached a rustic copse, in which were two or three small arbours—another instant, and the voice she longed yet feared to hear, the voice that she thought trembled a little as it spoke, addressed her:

"Is Lady Fordingbridge not afraid to separate herself from her party thus?" she heard Bertie Elphinston say—surely his voice quivered as he spoke. "Or does pity prompt her to do so; pity for another?"

"Lady Fordingbridge," she replied, knowing that her own voice was not well under control, "has no fear of anyone, unless it be of those whom, all unwittingly, she has injured." Then, scarcely knowing what she said, or whether her words were intelligible, and feeling at a loss what else to say, she gazed up at him and exclaimed, "You come to these festivities in a strange garb, sir. Surely the executioner's is scarcely a suitable one for a night of rejoicing."

"Yet suitable to him who wears it. Perhaps 'tis best that I who may apprehend——"

"Oh, Mr. Elphinston!" she exclaimed suddenly, interrupting him, "it was not to hear such words as these that I came here to-night. You know why I have sought this meeting; have you nought to say to me but this?"

"Yes," he replied, "yes. But let us not stand here upon the path exposed to the gaze of all the crowd. Come, let us enter this arbour. We shall be unobserved there."

She followed him into the one by which they were standing, and—for she felt her limbs were trembling beneath her—sank on to a rustic bench. And he, standing above her, went on:

"The letter that you sent to me asked that I should pity and forgive you. Kate, we meet again, perhaps for the last time on earth; let me say at once, there is nothing for me to forgive. If fault there was, then it was mine. Let mine, too, be the blame. I should have told you that Elphinston of Glenbervy was about to marry Mademoiselle Baufremont. Yet, he had sworn me to silence, had bidden me, upon our distant kinsmanship, to hold my peace, had sought my assistance to enable him to wed the woman whom he loved. How could I disclose his secret even to you? How could I foresee that a scheming devil would turn so small a thing to so great an account?"

"But," she said, gazing up at him and noticing— for both had instinctively unmasked at the same time —how worn his face was, how, alas! in his brown hair there ran grey threads though he was still so young; "but why, to all those letters I sent, was no answer vouchsafed? I thought from one or from the other some reply must surely come. Have you forgotten how, for many years now, we four—Douglas and Archibald, you and I—had all been as brothers and sister—until—until," she broke off, and then continued: "how we had vowed that between us all there should be a link and bond of friendship that should be incessable?"

"I have forgotten nothing," he replied, "nothing. No word that was ever spoken between us, no vow, nor promise ever made."

Again the soft blue eyes were turned to him, imploringly it seemed; begging by their glance that he should spare her. And, ceasing to speak of his remembrance of the past, he continued: "Circumstances, strange though they were, prevented any one of us from receiving your letters—or from answering them in time. I was lying ill of Roman fever at the English College; Archibald Sholto was in Tuscany in the train of Charles Edward, Cardinal Aquaviva having provided their passports; Douglas was with De Roquefeuille, and received your letter only on his return to Paris, where it had been sent back to him. Kate, in that stirring time, when the prince was passing from Rome to Picardy, was it strange no answer should come?"

"No, no," she replied. "No," and as she spoke she clasped both of her hands in her lap, and bent her head to hide her tears. Then she muttered, yet not so low but that he could hear her: "Had I but waited! but trusted!"

"It would have been best," he said very gently. And as he spoke, as though in mockery of their sad hearts, many of the maskers went by laughing and jesting, and the quadrille being finished the band was playing the merry old tune of " The Bird that danced the Rigadoon."

"You hear the air ?" she said, looking up suddenly again. "You hear? Oh! my heart will break."

"Yes," he answered, " I hear."

CHAPTER VIII.

"FORTUNE! AN UNRELENTING FOE TO LOVE."

THAT song in the old days in the Rue Trousse-Vache had been the air which Bertie Elphinston had whistled many a time to Kate to let her know that he was about to enter the "*salle d'escrime*," or to make her look out of the window and see the flowers he had brought her from his mother's garden in the suburbs. Also, on a Sunday morning early, he had often stood beneath the window of her room and had piped the "Rigadoon" to remind her that it was time for them to be away for their day's outing. For in those happy times—alas! but a year ago—these two fond, happy lovers had spent every Sabbath together and alone. Arm in arm the whole day; or, when the soft summer nights fell over the Bois de Boulogne, or the woods of St. Germain or the Forest of Fontainebleau, his arm round her waist and her soft fair head upon his shoulder, they had wandered together, taking a light meal here and there at any roadside *auberge* they happened on, and then both going back to supper, at her father's little house, where, as they had done all day, they talked of the future that was before them.

And now the future had come and they were parted for ever! No wonder that the old French song which had found its way to England grated harshly on their ears.

6

"Thank God, 'tis finished," he said, as the orchestra struck up a dance tune next. "For us, to our hearts, it awakens memories best left to slumber for ever." Then sitting down by her side on the rustic bench, he continued: "Kate, you wrote in your letter to me," and he touched his breast involuntarily as he spoke, so that she knew he bore it about him, "that there was private treachery to be feared. Is it to be feared from him?"

"Alas!" she whispered, "I almost dread 'tis so. He is not satisfied yet; he——"

"He should be! He has all I wanted."

"To injure you," she continued, "would be, as he knows, the best way to strike at me."

"To strike at you?"

"Yes, to repay me for my scorn and contempt—my hate of him."

"You hate him!" he exclaimed.

"From the depths of my heart. How can it be otherwise? His treachery—when I learnt it—made me despise him; his conduct since has turned my contempt to hatred. Oh," she exclaimed, "it is awful, terrible for a woman to hate her husband! Yet what cause have I to do aught else? When he speaks—though I have long since ceased to reply to anything he says—his words are nothing but sneers and scorn; sometimes of you, sometimes of me. And he gloats over having separated us, of having taken your place, while at the same time he is so bitter against me that, if he dared, I believe he would kill me. Moreover, he fears your vengeance. That is another reason why, if he could betray you to the Government, he would."

"'Tis by betrayal alone that we can be injured,"

Bertie said, thoughtfully. " None of our names are known, nor in the proscribed list. Yet how can he do it ? He it was who planned the attack upon the Fubbs * to be made when the Elector crossed from Holland ; he who disseminated the tracts, nay, had them printed, counselling his taking off. He was worse than any—no honest Jacobite ever stooped to assassination !—and many of us know it."

" Be sure," she replied, " that what he could do would be done in secret ; Bert—Mr. Elphinston, who is that man who has passed the arbour twice or more, and looks always so fixedly at you ? "

" I know not," he replied, " yet he has been ever near Douglas and me—he and another man—since we entered the gardens. Perhaps a Government spy. Well, he can know nought of me."

The man she had mentioned was a tall, stoutly-built individual, plainly enough clad in an old rusty black suit of broadcloth, patched black stockings and thick-soled shoes with rusty iron buckles upon them, and bore at his side a stout hanger. He might be a spy, it was true, but he might also have been anything else, a low follower of the worst creatures who infested the gardens, a gambling-hell tout, or a bagnio pimp. Yet his glance from under his vizard was keen and penetrating as it was fixed on them, but especially on Elphinston, each time he passed the summer house wherein they sat.

But now their conversation, which to both seemed all too short and to have left so much unsaid, was interrupted by the advent of Douglas Sholto, who came

---

* The remarkable name of one of the royal yachts of George II.

swiftly down the shell-strewn path, and, seeing them in the arbour, paused and entered at once.

"Kitty," he said, grasping her hand, "this is not the greeting I had intended to give you, though it's good to look upon your bonnie face again. But, Bertie, listen. We are watched, followed, perhaps known; indeed, I am sure of it. One of those fellows who have kept near to us, and whom we saw at Wandsworth as we set forth—I see the other down the path —spoke but now to three soldiers of the Coldstreams. Perhaps 'twas to identify us; you remember the First Battalion at Culloden," he added grimly; "perhaps to call on them for help. Bertie, we must be away at once."

"'Tis as I suspected," said Lady Fordingbridge, now pale as ashes and trembling from head to foot. "My words have too soon come true. How, how has he done it?"

"Farewell, Kate," said Bertie Elphinston, "we must, indeed, hasten if this is true. Yet first let me take you to your father and friends. Then," with a firm set look on his face, he said, "Douglas and I must see our way through this, if 'tis as he suspects. Come, Kate."

"No, no," she said, imploringly. "Wait not to think of me. Begone while there is yet time. Lose no moment. Farewell, farewell. We may meet again yet."

But ere another word could be said a fresh interruption occurred. From either end of the path that ran between the arbour and the lawn, both spies—for such they soon proclaimed themselves—advanced to where the others were; the first, the one of whom Kate had spoken, coming back from the end by the bosquet, the other from the platform where the orchestra and dancing were. And in the deepening twilight, for it was now almost dark, the three soldiers of the Coldstreams came too, followed by two others belonging to the "Old Buffs," a regiment also just brought back to London after Falkirk and Culloden. And behind these followed a small knot of visitors to the gardens who had gleaned that there was something unusual taking place, or about to do so.

"Your names," said the first man, who had kept watch over the movements of Elphinston, as he came close to the two comrades, while his own companion and the soldiers also drew very near, "are, if I mistake not, Bertie Elphinston and Douglas Sholto. Is that the case?"

"My friend," said the former, "I would bid you have a care how you ask persons unknown to you, and to whom you are unknown, what their names are. It is a somewhat perilous proceeding to take liberties with strangers thus."

"You are not persons unknown to me. I can give a full description of your actions during the last year, which would cause you to be torn limb from limb by the people in this garden. As it is, I require you to go with us to the nearest magistrate, where I shall swear an information against you, and——"

"By what process," asked Douglas Sholto, "do you propose to carry out your requirements? By your own efforts, perhaps?"

"By our own efforts, aided by those of five soldiers here, of several others now in the Spring Gardens, and by the general company herein assembled, if necessary. But come, sirs, we trifle time away. Will you come, or won't you?"

For answer Douglas Sholto dealt the man such a blow with his fist that he fell back shrieking that his jaw was broken; while his comrade, calling on the soldiers for aid in the name of the King against rebels who had fought at Culloden, hurled himself on Elphinston, with his sword drawn and in his hand. But the latter, drawing from his back the long lean-bladed axe, presented so formidable an appearance, that the other shrank back appalled, though he called on the soldiers still for assistance.

"Beware," said Elphinston, as he ranged himself by the side of his friend, "beware! We are not men to be played with, and, as sure as there's a heaven above, if any of you come within swing of my arm, I'll lop your heads off!"

"The hound fought at Culloden; I saw him there," said one of the Coldstreams. "By heavens, I'll attempt it on him if he had fifty axes," and so saying he sprang full at the young Scotchman. As he came, the latter might have cleft his head open from scalp to chin, but he was a soldier himself; and the other had not drawn the short sword he wore at his side ere he flew at him. Therefore, he only seized him by the throat as he would have seized a mad bull-dog that attacked him, and in a minute had hurled the fellow back among the others. But now all the soldiers as well as the two police agents had had time to draw their weapons, and seven gleaming blades were presented at the breasts of the two young men when a timely assistance arrived.

Sir Charles Ames burst through the crowd on the outskirts of the antagonists, his own bright court rapier flashing in the air, and following him came Mr. Wynn and Doyle Fane, also with their weapons drawn.

"For shame! For shame!" said Sir Charles. "Five great hulking soldiers and two others against two men. Put up your weapons, or we'll make you."

"Put up your own," said one of the Old Buffs; "they are rebels. Curse them! We have met before," and as he spoke he lunged full at the breast of Elphinston.

"Hoot!" said Fane, the spirit of the old swordsman, the old Irishman, aroused at this, "if it's for tilting, my boys, come along. It's a pretty dance I'll teach ye. There, now, look to that." And with the easiest twist of his wrist he parried the soldier's thrust at Elphinston, with another he had slit the sleeve of the man's uniform to the elbow, while a thin line of blood ran quickly out from his arm.

"My word," he continued, "I've always said the worst hands in the world with a sword were soldiers—of these present days. Your mother's broom handles would suit ye better," whereon he turned his point towards another.

Meanwhile Sir Charles Ames had placed himself by Bertie and Douglas, and had already exchanged several passes with the others, when, stepping back a moment into the arbour, he saw to his intense astonishment the figure of Kitty, she being in a swoon, and consequently unconscious.

"Lady Fordingbridge," he murmured, "Lady Fordingbridge. So, so! A little assignation with our rebel friends. Humph! I'd scarce have thought it of her. However, 'tis no affair of mine, and as she's Molly Belrose's friend, why, I must be the same to her friends." Whereon he again took his place alongside the two Jacobites and assisted at keeping the others at bay.

But the crowd still augmented in their neighbourhood, and while the soldiers—all of whom had of late fought in Flanders as well as Scotland, and were as fierce as their chief, Cumberland—were pressing the others hardly, some of the livelier masqueraders began to feel disposed to assist one side or another. Therefore, 'twas almost a riot that now prevailed in the Spring Gardens; and as among the company there were numerous other Jacobites, who, although they had probably not been out with Charles Stuart, were very keen in their sympathies with his cause, they took the opportunity of joining the fracas on their own account and of breaking the heads of several Hanoverian supporters. And also, gathering that the scene arose from the attempted apprehension of two of their own leaning, they gradually directed their way towards the arbour where the affray had begun—summarily knocking down or tripping up all who opposed them, so that the next morning many shopboys, city clerks, and respectable city puts themselves appeared at their places of business with broken crowns, bruised faces, and black eyes.

At present nothing serious had occurred beyond a few surface wounds given on either side; the soldiers and police agents were no match for the five skilful swordsmen to whom they were opposed, and the latter refrained from shedding the blood of men beneath them.

"Yet," said Sir Charles Ames to Mr. Wynn, while he wiped his face with his lace-embroidered handkerchief, "if the canaille do not desist soon I must pink one for the sake of my gentility. Wynn, where is Lády Belrose during this pleasing interlude?"

"Safe in the supper room," replied the young beau. "She is very well. I saw to that. Ames, who are these stalwart Highlanders whose cause we espouse?"

" The devil himself only knows," replied the worldly exquisite. " Ha! would you?" to one of the Coldstreams as he tried a pass at him. " Go home, my man, go home. I know your colonel; you shall be whipped for this. Yet," he whispered to his friend, " I do think these knocks are *pour les beaux yeux de madame*. What's that shout?"

"The constables, I imagine."

"The more the merrier! Ha! Wynn, we are borne along the path. The deuce take it, we have lost the shelter of the arbour!"

"For Heaven's sake," whispered Elphinston to the baronet, "as I see you are a gentleman, go back and look to Lady Fordingbridge. I cannot see her after to-night—sir, on your honour, tell her 'All is well.' She will understand."

"On my honour, I will," the baronet replied. " London will be too hot for you—perhaps for me, too. I do fear I'm a little of a Stuart myself; but listen, my aunt, Lady Ames, lives at Kensington, by the Gravel Pits; direct a letter to—to the fair one, under cover to my respected relative, and she shall get it. Oh, no thanks, I beg; I have my own *affaires de cœur*. I know, I know——"

And now the *mêlée* became more general, and gradually the partisans of both sides were borne asunder, two only keeping together, Bertie and Douglas.

"Where is Fane?" whispered the former.

"With Kate. I saw him in the bower with her. Heaven grant——"

He was interrupted by a man who at this moment ranged himself alongside them both, and who muttered, "Follow me, through the copse here. There is an exit by which you can escape from the gardens.

Back yourselves to the copse as easily as you can, then watch my movements."

"To leave her thus is impossible!" exclaimed Elphinston. "I cannot."

"Tush, nonsense!" replied Sholto, "her father is with her and our dandy friends by now. Come, come, we can do better for her and all of us by escaping than by being taken."

"But Fane; they will arrest him."

"If they do he has his answer. He was protecting his daughter. And her position will assure his. Come, Bertie, come. Once outside, we can seek new lodgings in another part of the town; put on new disguises. Come."

All the time this colloquy had taken place they had still been struggling with others, though by now the affray had lost the sanguinary character it once threatened to possess. The soldiers and the agents were separated from them by a mass of people, among whom were many of their sympathisers; but none were using deadly weapons, rather preferring buffeting and hustling than aught else. So that, as the tall man entered another summer house and, dragging Sholto and Elphinston after him, shut a door which guarded its entrance, the thing was done so quickly that the two originals of the disturbance had disappeared in the darkness ere they were missed.

"This," said the man, "is a private entrance and exit, reserved for some very high and mighty personages whom I need not mention. They are good patrons of ours—I am the proprietor's, Mr. Jonathan Tyers, chief subordinate. Also a Scotchman like yourselves, or by now you would probably have been taken. Hark to them!"

The people were howling outside, "Down with the rebels!" "Find the Culloden dogs and cut them to pieces!" etc., the soldiers' voices being heard the loudest of all, while in response many shouted, "Charlie Stuart for aye!" and some bolder spirits shrieked a then well-known song, "The Restoration," which had been originally composed in honour of the return of Charles II.

"Come," said the tall man, "come, your safety is here." Wherewith he opened another door in the back of the arbour and showed them a quiet leafy lane which was entirely deserted. There," he continued, " is your way. Follow the grove in this direction, and 'twill bring you to Kennington," and he pointed south ; " the other leads to the river. Fare ye well, and if you are both wise, quit London as soon as you have changed your garments. For myself I must go round to the front entrance; if I go back through the gardens I may be called to account by the mob for your escape."

Upon which, and not waiting for his countrymen's thanks, he took himself off quickly.

."Which way now, Bertie?" asked Douglas. "Wandsworth is done with. Where to ?"

"To Kensington. I, at least, must watch the square to see if Kate gets safe back to her home."

"Then we go together. Only, what of these accursed clothes ? We must make shift to get rid of them."

CHAPTER IX.

DENOUNCED.

To put the river between them and their late antagonists and would-be captors naturally occurred to the young men as their wisest plan, although as, urged by Douglas, the other strode towards it, he more than once reproached himself for coming away and leaving Lady Fordingbridge behind. Nor could any words uttered by his friend persuade him to regard his departure as anything else than pusillanimous.

"She went there to meet me; to see me once again," he repeated, "and I have left her to Heaven knows what peril. These men know me—know us—. well enough for what we are. 'Tis not difficult to guess whence comes their knowledge! They may accuse her of being a rebel, too. Oh! Kate, Kate! what will be the end of it all; what the finish of our wrecked and ruined lives?"

"No harm can come to her, I tell you," replied his comrade. "Why, man, heart up! Has not the fox, Fordingbridge, made his peace with George; how shall they arrest his wife or her father as rebels? Tush! 'tis not to be thought on. Come, fling away as much of this disguise as possible. We near the end of the lane, and I can hear the shouts of the watermen to their fares; and still we must go a mile or two higher up and take boat ourselves."

As he spoke he discarded his own woollen cloak, and tossed it over a high fence into the grounds of a country house by which they were now passing, while, slowly enough, for his heart was sore within him, Bertie imitated his actions. The axe (which, like the principal part of his dress, had been hired from a costumer or fashioner—a class of tradesmen more common even in those days than these, since fancy dresses were greatly in demand for the masques, *ridottos al fresco*, and fancy dress balls which took place so frequently) had been lost in the latter part of the riot, and now he discarded also the peculiar mask he had worn, producing from his pocket the ordinary vizard used at such entertainments, and which the forethought of Douglas had induced him to bring. For the rest, his clothes would attract no attention. They were suitable either to a man whose circumstances did not permit of his wearing velvet, silk, or fine broadcloth, or to one who had assumed the simple disguise of a superior workingman. The headsman's knife, however, he did not discard, but slipped up his sleeve, and Douglas retained his sword.

And now they drew near to the end of the lane, when, to their satisfaction, they perceived an alley running out of it and parallel to the course of the river, as they supposed, by the aid of which they might be enabled to follow its course for some distance without coming out on to the bank where, at this moment, there would be many persons from the garden taking boat to the other side.

"Fortune favours us up to now," exclaimed Sholto to his moody companion, as they turned into this smaller lane; "Heaven grant it may continue to do so!" Then, changing the subject, he said, "Bertie, lad, who do you think set those bloodhounds on us? 'Twas some one who knew of our hiding-hole. As we remarked, we were followed from Wandsworth."

"Who!" said Elphinston, stopping to look in his friend's face and peering at him under the light of the stars, "who, but one? The man whom I have to kill; whom I am ordained to kill sooner or later."

"You will kill him?" the other asked, stopping also.

"As a dog, when next I see him—or, no, not as a dog, for that is a creature faithful and true, and cannot conceive treachery—but as some poisonous, devilish thing, adder or snake, that stings us to the death when least we expect the blow. Why," he asked, pausing, "do you shudder?"

"I know not," replied Douglas; "yet I have done so more than once when his name has been mentioned. I know not why," he repeated, "unless I am fey."

"Fey! fey!" echoed Elphinston. "Let him be fey! He should be! It is predestined; his fate at my hands is near. He cannot avoid it."

As they ceased speaking they continued on their way until, at last, the lane opened on to a dreary waste of fields and marshes which stretched towards the very places which they most desired to avoid, Battersea and Wandsworth; while opposite to them, on the other side of the river, were the equally dreary marshes known as Tothill and Pimlico Fields.

"I' faith," said Douglas, as his eye roamed over all this extent of barrenness, which was more apparent than it would otherwise have been owing to the late rising of the moon, now near its full, "I' faith, we're atwixt the devil and the deep sea—or, so to speak, the river. How are we to cross; or shall we go back and over the bridge at Westminster?"

"Nay," replied Bertie; "as we came down the lane I saw a house to the right of us; doubtless 'tis to that the lane belongs. Now, 'tis certain there must be boats somewhere. Let us down to the shore and see. Hark! there is the clock of Chelsea Church striking. The west wind brings the sound across the marshes. Ha! 'tis eleven of the clock. Come, let us waste no time."

They turned therefore down to the river's bank, walking as quietly as possible so that their feet should make no more noise than necessary on the stones and shingle, for it was now low tide; and then, to their great joy, they saw drawn up by the water's edge a small wherry in which sat a man, and by his side he had a lantern that glimmered brightly in the night.

"Friend," said Elphinston, "we have missed our way after leaving the Spring Gardens; can you put across the river? We will pay you for your trouble."

The fellow looked at them civilly enough, then he said, "Yes, so that you waste no time. I have business here which I may not leave for more than a quarter of an hour. Wilt give me a crown to ferry you across?"

"The price is somewhat high," said Douglas. "Yet, since we would not sleep in these marshes all night, nor retrace our steps to Westminster Bridge, we'll do it."

"In with you, then," replied the man, "yet, first give me the crown; I have been deceived by dissolute maskers ere now." Then, when he had received the money, he said he supposed Ranelagh or the New

Chelsea Waterworks * would do very well. "Aye," said Douglas, "they will do," whereupon, having taken their seats, the man briskly ferried them across.

Yet, as they traversed the river, the fear sprang into their hearts that they had been tracked from Vauxhall, that even yet they were not safe from pursuit. For scarcely were they half way across the stream when the man's lantern, which he had left on the bank—perhaps as a signal—was violently waved about in the air by some hand, while a couple of torches were also seen flickering near it and voices were heard calling to him.

"Ay! ay!" the man bellowed back; "ay! ay! What! may I not earn a crown while you do your dirty work? In good time. In good time," he roared still louder, in response to further calls from the bank, while he pulled more lustily than before towards the north shore.

"What is it?" asked Elphinston. "Who are they who seem so impatient for your services?"

"A pack of fools," the man replied. "Young sprigs of fashion who have been quarrelling there," nodding towards Ranelagh Gardens, to which they were now close, "quarrelling over their wine and their women, I do guess, and two of them have crossed over to measure the length of their swords. Well, well; if one's left on the grass I'll be there pretty soon to see what pickings there are in his pockets. 'Tis the fools that provide the wise men's feasts," whereon this philosopher pulled his boat to the bank, set the young men ashore, and, a moment

---

* Inaugurated 1724.

later, was quickly pulling away back to the duelling party.

Ranelagh itself was shut up as they stepped ashore, all its lights were out and the hackney coachmen and chairmen gone with their last fares; and of that night's entertainment—which was sure to have been a great one in rivalry to its neighbour and opponent at Vauxhall—nothing was left but the shouting figures of those on the other bank, and, perhaps, a dead man on the grass of the marshes, with a sword-thrust through his lungs and his wide-staring eyes gazing up at the moon. It seemed, therefore, that they must walk to Kensington, since no conveyance was to be found here.

"Not that the distance is much," said Bertie Elphinston, who had before now walked at nights from Wandsworth and Chelsea to the Square, simply to gaze on the house that enshrined the woman he had loved so much; perhaps also to see the place where the man dwelt whom he meant to kill when the opportunity should arise—"but 'tis the hour that grows so late. If they have gone home at once from the gardens without being disturbed by any of the police agents, she must be housed by now—and—and—I cannot see her again."

"At least you can wait. If not to-day, then to-morrow you can meet, surely. All trace of us is lost now, we shall never go back to Wandsworth—we must send the landlady our debt by some sure hand—a change of clothes and hiding place will put us in safety again. And as for messages, why, Archibald will convey them."

"Archibald!" exclaimed the other with a start. "Archibald! Heavens! we had forgotten!—what have we been thinking of? He may be taken too."

"Taken! Archibald taken! Oh, Bertie, why should that be?"

"Why should it be! Rather ask, why should it not be? Do you think that tiger's whelp who has set the law on us will spare him? No, Simeon Larpent means to make a clean sweep of all at once; his wife's old lover, that lover's friend, and the priest who knows so much of his early life and all his secrets, plots and intrigues against first one and then the other, Jacobite and Hanoverian alike. I tell you, Archibald is in as great a danger as we are!" and he strode on determinately as he spoke.

Their way lay now towards Knightsbridge by a fair, broad road through the fields, and between some isolated houses and villas that were dotted about; and as by this time the moon was well up, everything they passed could be seen distinctly. Of people, they met or passed scarcely any; the road that, an hour or so before, had been covered with revellers of all degrees wending their way back from Ranelagh to the suburbs of Chelsea, Kensington, and Knightsbridge, or to what had, even in those days, been already called "The Great City," was now, with midnight at hand, as deserted as a country lane. Yet one sign they did see of the debaucheries that took place in Ranelagh as well as in the Spring Gardens; a sign of the drunkenness and depravities that prevailed terribly in those days among almost all classes. Lying at the side of the road, where, doubtless, they had fallen together as they reeled away from the night's orgie, they perceived two young men and a young woman— masked, and presenting a weird appearance as they lay on their backs, their flushed faces turned up to the moon, yet with the upper part hidden by the black vizard. It was easy to perceive that all had fallen together and been afterwards unable to rise—as they lay side by side they were still arm in arm, and, doubtless, the first who had fallen had dragged the others after him. The two young men seemed from their apparel to be of a respectable class, perhaps clerks or scriveners, their clothes being of good cloth, though not at all belaced; as for their companion, the bacchante by their sides, she might have been anything from shopgirl or boothdancer down to demirep.

"Now," said Douglas, "here is our chance for disguise. These fellows have good enough coats and hats—see, too, they sport the black cockade. Well, 'twill not hurt them to sell us some apparel." Wherewith he proceeded to lift the nearest sot up and relieve him of his coat, waistcoat, and hat. Apparently the fellow thought he was being put to bed by some one, as he muttered indistinctly, "Hang coat over chair—shan't wear it 'gain till Sunday"—but as Douglas slipped a couple of guineas into his breeches pocket he went to sleep peacefully enough once more. As for the other young man, he never stirred at all while Bertie removed his garments, nor when he put into his pocket a similar sum of two guineas, and also his copper-cased watch, which had slipped from out his fob.

"They are somewhat tight and pinching," remarked Douglas as he and his friend donned their new disguise, "even though we are now as lean as rats after our Scotch campaign."

Yet, tight as their new clothes were, they answered, at least, a good purpose. It would have taken a shrewd eye to recognise in these two respectably clad men—in spite of their coats being somewhat dusty from having lain in the road while on the backs of their late masters, the headsman and the Highlander who, a few hours before, had walked round and round the orchestra pavilion at Vauxhall.

After this they went forward briskly towards Kensington-square, attracting no attention from anyone indeed meeting few people, for at this distance from the heart of the town there was scarcely anyone ever stirring after midnight, and it was somewhat past that time now. As they neared Kensington, it is true, they were passed by a troop of the Queen's Guards (as the 2nd Life Guards were then called) returning, probably, from some duty at St. James's Palace, but otherwise they encountered none whom they need consider hostile to them.

In the square there was, when they reached it at last, no sign of life. The watchman in his box slumbered peacefully, his dog at his feet, and in the windows of the houses scarcely a light was to be seen. Nor was there any appearance of activity in the house belonging to Fordingbridge, though Bertie thought he should have at least seen some light in the room which he knew, from enquiry of Sholto, to be Kate's.

"'Tis strange," he said, "strange. Surely they must have returned from the masquerade by now. After crossing the water a coach would have brought them here in less than an hour. 'Tis passing strange!"

"They may have got back so early," hazarded Douglas, "that already all are a-bed. Or they may have gone on to Lady Belrose's, in Hanover-square. A hundred things may have happened. And where, I wonder, is Archie? He surely will be in bed."

"Can he be arrested? It may be so."

"God forbid! Yet this darkness and silence seem to me ominous. What shall we do?"

"Heaven knows. Hist! Who comes here?" and as he spoke, from out of one of the doorways over which was, as may still be seen, a huge scallop-shell, there stepped forth a man. Enveloped in one of the long cloaks, or roquelaures, still worn at the period, and with the tip of a sword's scabbard sticking out beneath it, the man sauntered leisurely away from where they were standing, yet as he went they could hear him humming to himself an air they both knew well. It was that old tune "The Restoration"—which they had heard once before this evening!—to which the Highland army marched after it had crossed the border.

Presently the man turned and came towards them slowly, then as he passed by he looked straight in their faces, and, seeming satisfied by what he saw, he muttered, "A fine spring night, gentlemen. Ay, and so it is. A fine night for the young lambs outside the town and for the hawks within—though the hawks get not always their beaks into the lambs too easily; in fact, I may give myself classical license and say they are *non semper triumphans.*"

"In very truth," replied Bertie, "some—though 'tis not always the hawks—are *nunquam triumphans.* That is, if I apprehend your meaning."

"Ay, sir," said the man, dropping his classics and changing his manner instantly. "You apprehend me very well. Sir, I am here with a message for you from a certain Scotch trader, one Mr. Archibald; also from a certain fair lady——"

"Ah!"

"Or rather, let me say, without beating about the bush, I brought to a certain fair lady, to-night, a message from Mr. Archibald, while she, considering it possible that a certain, or two certain brave gentlemen might appear in this square to-night, did beg me to remain in this sad square to deliver the message."

"Sir," said Elphinston, teased by the man's quaint phraseology, yet anxious to know what the message really was that had been sent from Father Sholto to Kate, and on from her to him, "sir, we thank you very much. Will you now please to deliver to us that message?"

"Sir, I will. It is for that I am here." Then without more ado he said hastily, "The worthy trader has been warned from a friend, a countryman of ours, who is connected, or attached, so to speak, to the Scotch Secretary of State's Office, that he may very possibly be cast into durance should he remain there," and he jerked his thumb at Lord Fordingbridge's house as he spoke; "whereon, seeing that precaution is the better part of valour, the worthy trader has removed himself from the hospitable roof there," upon which he this time jerked his head instead of his thumb towards the house, "and has sought another shelter which, so to speak as it were, is not in this part of the town, but more removed. But, being a man of foresight and precaution, also hath he gone to warn two gallant gentlemen residing at a sweet and secluded village on the river to be careful to themselves remove——"

"That," said Douglas, "we have already done. Yet his warning must have got there too late."

"And," continued their garrulous and perspicacious friend, "also did he request and desire me to attend here in the square until a certain fair lady should return from the gallimanteries and *ridottos al fresco* to which she had that evening been."

"And did the certain fair lady return?" asked Elphinston, unable to repress a smile at his stilted verbiage.

"Return she did. In gay company! Two sparks with her, dressed in the best, though somewhat dishevelled as though with profane dancings and junkettings—one had his coat ripped from lapel to skirt—and an elderly man—I fear me also a wassailer!—with a fierce eye. Then I up and delivered the worthy—hem!—trader's message, when, lo! as flame to torchwood, there burst forth from all a tremendous clamjamfry such as might have been heard up there," and this time he jerked his head towards where Kensington Palace lay.

"As how?" asked the young men together. "Why should they make a clamjamfry?"

"Hech!" answered their eccentric countryman, "'tis very plain ye ken not women—nor, for that matter, the young sparks of London! This is how it went. One certain fair lady—from whom I bring you a wee bit message—wrung her hands and wept, saying, 'Betrayed, betrayed again! The veellain! the veellain!' whereby I think she meant not you; the other fair lady, who is maybe an hour or so older, stormed and scolded and screeched about unutterable scoundrels, yet bade the other cease weeping and seek her house, to which she was very welcome; while the two young men uttered words more befitting their braw though unholy dishevelled apparel, and spake of him," and here the nodding head was wagged over to Fordingbridge's house again, "as though he were Lucifer incarnate—though that was not the name, so to speak as it were. And for the old man with the fierce eye, hech! mon, his language was unbefitting a Christian."

"And the message the lady scrawled. What is it?"

"'Tis here," the other replied. "You must just excuse the hasty writing——" but ere he could finish his remark Bertie had taken a piece of paper from his hand which he brought out from under his cloak, and, striding to where an oil lamp glimmered over a doorway, read what it contained. The few lines ran as follows:

"We are once more betrayed. He has, I know, done this. I leave his house and him for ever from to-night. I pray God you may yet escape. If you ever loved me, fly—fly at once. Lose no moment.—KATHERINE."

CHAPTER X.

IT was on a bright afternoon, a week after the events which have been described, that Lord Fordingbridge's travelling carriage drew up in front of his house, and my lord descended in an extremely bad humour. There was, perhaps, more than one reason why he was not in the most amiable of tempers, the principal one being that the news which he had hoped to receive ere he again made his entrance into London had not come to hand.

All the time that he had been on his Cheshire property—which he had found to be considerably neglected since his father's departure for France—he had been expecting to receive, from one source or another, the information of the arrest of those three enemies of his, about whom he had given information sufficient to bring them to justice. Yet none had come. Daily he had sent to the coach office at Chester for the journals from London, but, when he had perused them, he still failed to find that any of the three had been haled to justice. Nor was there even a description in any of them of the scene at Vauxhall—which, had he found such description, might have been exceedingly pleasant reading. But, in truth, nothing was more unlikely than that he should find it. A fracas at either Ranelagh or the Spring Gardens was by no means likely to be chronicled in either the " London Journal" or the "Craftsman," or any other news-sheet of the period, since in those days the ubiquitous reporter was unknown, or, when he existed, did not consider anything beneath a murder, a state trial, or an execution worthy of his pen. Also the proprietors of Ranelagh and Vauxhall, and similar places of entertainment, took very good care to keep anything unpleasant that happened out of the papers. Nothing short, therefore, of Mr. Jonathan Tyers sending an account of what had occurred in his grounds to the papers of the day with the request that it might be inserted—accompanied, perhaps, by a payment for such insertion—would have led to the publication of the matter, and that the worthy proprietor of the Spring Gardens would do such a thing as this was not to be supposed.

Also, my lord had received no news from his wife, nor her father, which astonished him considerably. For he had supposed that, in about a week's time, the post would bring him a letter full of accusations, reproaches, and injurious epithets from her ladyship, who, he felt sure, would at once connect him with the arrest of the three men—yet, no more from her than from the public prints did he gather one word. So that at last he began to have the worst fears that, after all, the Government had bungled in some way and that the victims had escaped. It was, therefore, in a very ill humour that he again returned to London, cursing inwardly and vehemently at any delay necessitated by the changing of horses, by nights spent at inns on the road, and by the heavy roads themselves; and at St. Albans, where he once more slept, by receiving no visit at all from Captain Morris, to whom he had written saying that he would be there on a certain evening and would be pleased to see him.

Instead, however, he received a visit from another person who had troubled his mind a great deal during the past week or so ; a somewhat rough, uncouth-looking fellow, who seemed to have dogged his footsteps perpetually—who had passed him soon after he left Dunstable on his journey down, whom he saw again at Coventry and at Stafford, and who, to his amazement, now strode into the apartment he occupied as hitherto, and stated that he brought a message from the Captain.

"Hand it to me, then," said his lordship, regarding the man as he stood before him in his rough riding cloak and great boots, and recognising him as the fellow who had appeared so often on his journey.

"There is nothing to hand," the other replied. "Only a word-of-mouth message."

"A word-of-mouth message! Indeed! Captain Morris spares me but scant courtesy. Well, what is the message?"

"Only this. The work has failed, and the birds have escaped from the net. That's all."

"Escaped from the net!" his lordship said, sinking back into the deep chair he sat in, and staring at the uncouth messenger. "Escaped from the net! But the particulars, man, the particulars! How has it come about? Are the Government and their underlings a pack of fools and idiots that they let malignant traitors escape thus?"

"Very like, for all I know, or, for the matter of that, care. The captain's one of their underlings, as you call them, and I'm another. Perhaps we're fools and idiots."

"You are another, are you?" said his lordship,

looking at him, " another, eh? Pray, sir, is that why you have dogged me into Cheshire and back again as you have done, for I have seen you often? Am I a suspected person that I am followed about thus? Am I, sir?"

"Very like," again replied this stolid individual. " Very like, though I know not. I received my orders at Dunstable to keep you in sight, and I kept you, that's——"

" Leave the room. Go out of my sight at once!" exclaimed Lord Fordingbridge, springing from his seat and advancing toward the man. " Go at once, or the ostler shall be sent for to throw you out. Go!"

When the man had departed, muttering that "fool, or idiot, or both, he'd done his duty, and he didn't care for any nobleman in England, Jacobite or Hanoverian, so long as he done that," the viscount gave himself up to the indulgence of one of those fits, or rather tempests, of passion, which, as a rule, he rarely allowed himself to indulge in, and cursed and swore heartily as he stamped up and down the room for half an hour.

" Everything goes wrong with me," he muttered, as he shook his fist in impotent rage at his own reflection in the great mirrors over the fireplace, " everything, everything! If that infernal captain had only gone to work as he should have done on the information I gave him, they would all have been lodged in gaol by now—two of them doomed to a certain death and the other to a long imprisonment or banishment to the colonies. And now they are fled—are free—safe, while I am far from safe since Elphinston is at large; and am suspected, too, it seems, since, forsooth, that chuckle-headed boor is set to follow me."

This latter thought was, perhaps, as unpleasant a one as any which rose to his mind, since if he were also suspected it might be the case that, while he had denounced the others, they—or probably Archibald Sholto alone—might have denounced him. And at this terrible thought he quaked with fear, for he knew what an array of charges might be brought. Nay, it was the very fear of those charges being brought, combined with his other fear of Elphinston wreaking vengeance on him for having deceived and stolen his promised wife, that had led to his betraying the three men who alone could denounce him. And now they were all free, instead of being in Newgate or the Tower, and he, it seemed, was as much suspected as they!

He tossed about his bed all night, made a wretched breakfast, and then set out for London, determined at all hazards to discover exactly what had happened, or perhaps to find out that nothing had happened. Yet as he went he mused on what his future course should be, and came to at least one determination.

"I will send her ladyship packing," he said, with a sardonic grin. "I have had enough of her and her airs and graces, and she may go to Elphinston or to the devil for aught I care. I have a surprise to spring upon her, a trump card, or, as the late Louis was said to call that card, '*La dernière piece d'or*,' because it always won. And, by Heaven, I'll spring it without mercy!"

. In which frame of mind his lordship arrived in front of his town house. But now a new matter of astonishment arose, also a new fuel for his humours; for the house appeared deserted, the blinds were drawn down in all the windows. He could perceive no smoke arising from any chimney, there was no sign of life at all about the place. He bade his manservant get down from beside the coachman and tug lustily at the bell, while all the time that the man was doing so he was fretting and fuming inwardly, and at last was meditating sending for the watch and having the door forced, when it was opened from the inside, and the oldest servant in his establishment, a decrepit, deaf old man, who had acted as caretaker for many years during his and his father's absence abroad, appeared.

"Come here, Luke, come here," his lordship called loudly to him; "come here, I say," and he motioned that he should descend the steps and approach the travelling carriage, from the door of which he was now glaring at him. But, whether from fright or senility, or both combined, the other did not obey him, and only stood shivering and shaking and feebly bowing upon the threshold.

"What devil's game is this?" Fordingbridge muttered to himself as he now sprang out and ran up the steps, after which he grasped the old man by the collar and, dragging him toward him, bawled in his ear question after question as to what cause the present state of the house was owing. But the old fellow only shivered and shook the more, and seemed too paralyzed by his master's violence to do anything but wag his jaws helplessly. Hurling him away, therefore, with no consideration at all for either his age or feebleness, Fordingbridge rushed through the hall ringing a bell that communicated with the kitchens and another with the garrets, calling out the names of male and female servants, and receiving no answer to any of his summons. Then, tired of this at last, he bade his manservant bring in his valises and ordered the travelling carriage off to the stables.   But by now the old servitor seemed to have recovered either his breath or his senses somewhat, and coming up to his lordship in a sidling fashion, such as a dog assumes when fearful of a blow if it approaches its master too near, he mumbled that there was no one else in the house but himself.

"So I should suppose," Lord Fordingbridge replied, endeavouring to calm himself and to overcome the gust of passion with which he had once more been seized, "so I should suppose; I have called enough to have waked the dead had there been any here."   Then once more regarding the old man with one of his fierce glances, he shouted at him in a voice that penetrated even to his ears, "Where are they all ?   Where is her ladyship ? " in a lower voice.   "Where are the servants ? "

"Gone, all gone," Luke replied, "all gone.   None left but me."

"Where are they gone to ? "

The old man flapped his hands up and down once or twice—perhaps he performed the action with a desire to deprecate his master's anger—and looked up beseechingly into his face as though asking pardon for what was no fault of his, then replied :

"Her ladyship has gone away—for good and all, I hear, my lord."

"Ha !   Where is she gone to ? ".

"To Lady Belrose's, I am told.   She—she—they— the servants say she will never come back."

The viscount paused a moment—this news had startled even him !—then he muttered, "No, I'll warrant she never shall.   This justifies me."   And again he continued, still shouting at the old man, so that his valet upstairs must have heard every word he uttered :

"And the servants, where are they ?"

"All gone too. They were frightened by the police and the soldiers—"

"The soldiers! What soldiers ?"

"They ransacked the house to find Mr. Archibald. But he, too, was gone. That terrified all but me—me it did not frighten. No, no," he went on, assuming a ludicrous appearance of bravery that was almost weird to behold, "me it did not frighten. I remember when, also, the soldiers searched the house for your father, his late lordship with—he! he!—the same re——"

"Silence!" roared Fordingbridge. "How dare you couple my father's name with that fellow? So Mr. Archibald is also gone! But what about the soldiers? The soldiers, I say," raising his voice again to a shriek.

"Ah, the soldiers," Luke repeated. "Yes, yes. The soldiers. Brave soldiers. I had a son once in their regiment, long ago, when Dunmore commanded them; he was wounded at—um—um——" and he stopped, terrified by the scowl on Lord Fordingbridge's face.

"What," bawled the latter, "did they do here—in this house? Curse your son and your recollections, too. What did they do here—in my house?"

"They sought for Mr. Archibald—her ladyship being gone forth. But he, too, was out—ho! ho—and— and he never came back. Then the captain—a brave, young lord, they say—said you were known to be fostering a rebel—they called him a rebel Jesuit priest!— that you were denounced from Dunstable, and that you must make your own account with the Government. Then the maids fled, and next the men—they said they owed you no service. Ah! there are no old faithful servants now—or few—very few."

"Go!" said Fordingbridge, briefly—and again his

look terrified the poor old creature so, that he slunk
off shivering and shaking as before.

Slowly the viscount mounted the stairs to his saloon, or withdrawing room, and when there he cast
himself into a chair and brooded on what he had
heard.

"Harbouring a rebel—a rebel Jesuit priest," he
muttered. "So! so! am I caught in the toils that I
myself set? Pardieu, 'twould seem so. I denounce a
rebel, and, unfortunately, that rebel lives on me—is
housed with me. I never thought of that! It may
tell badly for me; worse, too, because I brought him
to England in my train. How shall I escape it?"
And he sat long in his chair meditating.

"The captain said," he went on, "that I must make
my own account with the Government. Ah, yes, yes;
why! so indeed I must. And 'tis not hard. Make
my account! Why, yes, to be sure. Easy enough.
I, having embraced the principles of Hanover, and
being now firm in my loyalty to George, do, the better
to confound his enemies, shelter in my house one whom
I intend to yield up to him. Well! there's no harm in
that, but rather loyalty. Otherwise," and he laughed
to himself as he spoke, "I might lay myself open to
the reproach of being a bad host; of not respecting
the sacredness of the guest."

Eased in his mind by this reflection and by the excuse which he had found, as he considered, for appeas-
ing the Government and satisfying it as to his reasons
for sheltering a Jesuit plotter, he rose from his seat
and wandered into the other rooms of his house, view-
ing with particular interest and complaisance the one
which had been her ladyship's boudoir, or morning-
room.

8

"A pretty nest for so fair a bird," he muttered, as he regarded the Mortlake hangings and lace curtains, the deep roomy lounge, the bright silver tea service, and—as blots upon the other things—bunches of now withered flowers in the vases. "A pretty nest. Yet, forsooth, the silly thing must fall out of it; wander forth to freedom and misery. For they say, who study such frivolities, that caged birds, once released, pine and die even in their freedom. *Soit!* 'tis better that the bird should escape and die of its own accord than be thrust into the cold open by its master's hand. And that would have happened to your ladyship," and he laughed as he spoke of her, "had you not taken the initiative. My Lady Fordingbridge," uttering the words with emphasis, nay, with unction, "I had done with you. It was time for you to go."

A little clock on the mantelpiece, a masterpiece of Tompion's, chimed forth the hour musically as he spoke; he remembered his father buying it as a present for his mother the year before they fled to France; and turning round to look at it he saw, standing against its face, where it could not fail to be observed, a letter addressed to him. Opening it, he found written the words, "I have left the house and you. I know everything now." That was all; there was no form of address, no superscription. Nothing could be more disdainful, nor, by its brevity, more convincing. And, whatever the schemes the man might have been maturing in his evil mind against the writer, yet that brief, contemptuous note stung him more than a longer, more explanatory one could have done.

"So be it," he said again, "so be it." Then he bade his man come and dress him anew, and afterwards call a hackney coach. And on entering the

latter when ready, he ordered the driver to convey
him first to the Duke of Newcastle's (the Secretary of
State), and later to Lady Belrose's in Hanover-square.

"For, to commence," he muttered, as he drove off,
"I must square his grace, and then have one final
interview with my dearly beloved Katherine. Newcastle has the reputation of being the biggest fool in
England—he should not be difficult to deal with;
while as to her—well, she is no fool but yet she shall
find her master."

CHAPTER XI.

ARCHIBALD'S ESCAPE.

FORTUNE had, indeed, stood the friend of those three denounced men, otherwise they must by now have been lying—as Fordingbridge had said—in one of the many prisons of London awaiting their trial; trials which—in the case of two at least—would have preceded by a short time only their executions and deaths; deaths made doubly horrible by that which accompanied them, by the cutting out and casting into the fire of the still beating hearts of the victims, the disembowelling and quartering and mangling.

Yet, if such was ever to be their fate—and they tempted such fate terribly by their continued presence in London, or, indeed, in England—it had not yet overtaken them; until now they were free. How Douglas Sholto and Bertie Elphinston had escaped the snare you have seen; how Archibald Sholto eluded those who sought him has now to be told.

Kate had no sooner departed in a chariot, sent for her by Lady Belrose, to take a dish of tea in company with the other members of the proposed party before going on to Vauxhall, than Mr. Archibald, who had a large room at the top of the house, was apprised by the servant that a Scotch gentleman awaited him in the garden.* On desiring to be informed what the gentleman's name and errand were—for those engaged as the Jesuit now was omitted no precautions for their safety—a message was brought back that the visitor was an old friend of Mr. Archibald's, whom he would recognise on descending to the garden, and that his business was very pressing. Now Archibald was a man of great forethought—necessity had made him such—and therefore, ere he descended to the garden, he thought it well to take an observation of this mysterious caller, who might be, as he said, a friend or, on the other hand, a representative of the law endeavouring to take advantage of him.

The opportunity for this observation presented itself, however, without any difficulty. On the back-stairs of each flight in the houses of Kensington-square there existed precisely what exists in the present day in most houses, namely, windows half-way up each flight, and, gazing out into the garden—up and down the gravel walks of which the visitor was walking, sometimes stopping to inspect or to smell some of the roses already in bloom, and sometimes casting glances of impatience at the house—Archibald saw the man who, later on, was to deliver Kate's message to Bertie.

"Why!" he exclaimed to himself, "as I live 'tis James McGlowrie. Honest Jemmy! Indeed, he can come on no evil intent to me or to those dear to me. Yet—yet—I fear. Even though he means no harm he may be the bearer of bad news," and so saying he passed down the stairs and to the man awaiting him.

---

* At this period most of the houses in Kensington-square had large gardens at the back. Those on the west side, where Lord Fordingbridge's is supposed to be situated, covered what is now known as Scarsdale-place.

"James," he said, addressing the other in their native brogue, "this is a sight for sair een. Yet," he went on, "what brings you here? First, how did you know I dwelt here, and next, what brings you?—though right glad I am to see you once again."

"I have a wee bit message for ye, Archibald," said the other, shaking him warmly by the hand, "that it behoves you vary weel to hear. And," dropping at once into the verbosity that was to so tease, while at the same time it amused, Elphinston some hours later, "not only to hear, but, so to speak, as it were, to ponder on, yet also to decide quickly over and thereby to arrive at a good determination. D'ye take, Archibald Sh——, I mean, so to speak, Mr. Archibald?"

"Why, no," said the other, with a faint smile, "I cannot in truth say that I do. James McGlowrie, you can speak to the point when you choose. Choose to do so now, I beg you."

"To the point is very well. And so I will speak. Now, Archie, old friend, listen. Ye ken and weel remember, I doubt not, Geordie McNab, erstwhile of Edinburgh."

"Indeed I do."

"So—so. Vary weel. Now Geordie McNab is come south and has gotten himself into the Scotch Secretary of State's office, for Geordie is no Jacobite! —and there he draws £200 a year sterling — not Scotch. Oh, no. Geordie is now vary weel to do, and what with the little estate his poor auld mother left him, which, so to speak, yields him thirty bolls and firlots of barley, some peats at twopence per load, and many pecks of mustard seed at a shilling, and——"

"Jemmy, Jemmy," said the other, reproachfully,

"was this the important errand you came here upon?"

"Nay, nay. My tongue runs away with me as ever. Yet, listen still. Geordie is no Jacobite, yet, i'faith, there's a many he's overweel disposed to, among others an old schoolfellow o' his, one Archibald."

"One Archibald! Ha! I take you. And, Jemmy, is he threatened; has he aught to fear from the Scotch Secretary's office?"

"The warst that can befall. Ay, man, the very warst. So are also two friends of his, late of—hem—a certain army that has of late made excursions and alarums, as the bard hath it."

"So! I understand! We have been informed against, blown upon. Alas! alas! We were free but for this—our names not even upon the list."

"Yet now," said McGlowrie, "are they there. Likewise also your addresses and habitments—all are vary weel known. My laddie, ye must flee out o' the land and awa' back to France, and go ye must at once. There's no time to be lost."

"I cannot go without warning the others—without knowing they are safe." Then, while a terribly stern look came into his face, he said, "Who has done this thing, McGlowrie, who has done it?"

"Can ye not vary weel guess? 'Tis not far to seek."

"Ay," the Jesuit answered, "it needs no question. Oh! Simeon Larpent, Simeon Larpent, if ever I have you to my hand again, beware. Oh! to have you but for one hour in Paris and with the Holy Church to avenge me, a priest, against you!" Then changing this tone to another more suitable, perhaps, to the occasion and the danger in which he stood, he asked:

"What do they mean to do? When will they proceed to the work, think you?"

"At once; to-night, perhaps; to-morrow for certain. Go, Archie, go, pack up your duds and flee, I say. Even now the Government may have put the officers upon your hiding-place; have told the soldiers at Kensington to surround the house. Lose no time."

"But the boys—the boys at Wandsworth. What of them?"

"They shall be warned, even though I do it myself. But now, Archie, up to your room, bring with you—in a small compass, so to speak—your necessaries, and come with me."

"But where to? Where to?"

"Hech! with me. I have a bit lodgment, as you will know vary weel soon, in the Minories; 'tis near there poor Lady Balmerino lodges—though they promise her that after her lord is condemned, as he must be—as he must be!—she shall be lodged with him in the Tower to the last; come with me, I say. For the love o' God, Archie, hesitate no longer."

Then indeed, Archibald Sholto knew that, if he would save himself and help the others, and—as he hoped—wreak his vengeance on the treacherous adder that had stung them, he must follow honest James McGlowrie's counsel. So, very swiftly he passed up to his room, collected every paper he possessed, and carried away with him a small valise, in which were a change of clothes, several bank bills and a bag of guineas, Louis d'ors, and gold crowns. Then he returned to the garden where McGlowrie was still walking up and down as before, and announced that he was ready to follow him.

"Only," he said, "we will go as quietly as may be, and without a word. I will not even tell the servants I am going, Heaven knows if they are not spies themselves. I will just vanish away, and, as I hope, leave no trace. Come, Jemmy, there is a door behind the herb-garden that gives into the lane, and the lane itself leads to the West-road. If we can cross that in safety we can pass by Lord Holland's—he is Secretary of War now, and of the Privy Council—yet that matters not to us; behind his leafy woods we shall come to the other road. Then for a hackney or a passing coach to the city. Only, the boys, Jemmy, the boys! What of them?"

"Have no fear. If they are not warned already by Geordie McNab 'twill surprise me very much, and once I have seen ye off to the Minories I'll be away to Wandsworth myself. Thereby I'll make sure. Come, Archie, come. The evening draws in. Come, mon."

"I will. Only, Jemmy, stick your honest nose outside the garden gate and see that neither soldiers, spies, nor men of the law are there. If it is as you say, the house may even now be surrounded."

McGlowrie did as the other requested, going out and sauntering up and down the lane, but seeing no signs of anyone about who might threaten danger. To a maid-servant, drawing water from a well which served for many of the gardens of the houses, he gave in his pleasant Scotch way the "good e'en," and remarked that "the flowers were thirsty these warm May nights, and required, so to speak as it were, a draught to refresh 'em"; and to a boy birdnesting up a tree he observed that it was a cruel sport which would wring a poor mither's heart, even as his own mither's would full surely be wrung should he be torn away from her grasp, even as he was tearing the young from the nest. But, all the time he was delivering these apothegms, his eye was glancing up and down the lane, and searching for any sign of danger. And, seeing none, he went back to Archibald Sholto and bade him follow since all was clear.

"And now," said he, as they passed to the left of Holland House and so reached Kensington Gravel Pits, "let us form our plans. First, there are the two young men, who must of a surety have been warned by Geordie, yet, supposing he should have failed, must yet be warned, so to speak. Now, shall I get me away——"

"Alas!" said Sholto, "I have just recalled to mind that, if they are not already on their guard, 'tis now too late. They were to go to the masquerade at Vauxhall; are there by now. 'Tis certain. One of them had an appointment with—with the wife of the double-dyed scoundrel who owns the house we have but just now quitted."

"Hoot! Ma conscience! With his enemy's wife. Vary good! Vary good! Perhaps 'tis not so strange the man is his enemy. Weel, weel, 'tis no affair of mine, yet I like not this trafficking wi' other men's goods. But since they are away on this quest they need no warning. Now for yourself, Archie. Get you away to the Minories—here is the precise address," and he slipped a piece of paper into his hand, "go there, lie perdu, and await my return."

"But Kate! Lady Fordingbridge! I must let her know of my absence; what will she think when she re-

turns home and finds me gone? And the others—
they may be taken when they also return to their
homes."

"Leave't to me. I will await my lady's return
from these worldly doings—ma word! a married
woman and meeting other men in such sinfu' places!
—even though she comes not till the break o' day—as
is very likely, I fear, under the circumstances! And,
meanwhile, for the others we must trust to Geordie."

"No," said Archibald Sholto, "we will not trust to
Geordie, true as I believe him to be. This is the best
plan. If you will wait—as I know you will—until her
ladyship returns, though it will not be for some hours
yet, I apprehend, I will make my way to Wandsworth,
find out if they are warned, and, if not, will myself
wait their return. Then I will accept your shelter in
the Minories for a time until we can all three get safe
back to France. For France is now our only refuge
again, as it has so often and so long been before."

"Humph!" said McGlowrie, "perhaps so 'tis best.
None know you at Wandsworth?"

"None. No living soul except the woman of the
house—a true one. Her father fell in the Cause in the
'15' at Sherriffmuir. She is safe."

"So be it. Then away with you to yon village, and
trust me to manage things in this one. Now, off
wi' you, Archie, but first make some change in your
clothing."

"But how? I have no other clothes but those I
wear."

"Hoot! a small changement is easy, and sometimes, so to speak as it were, effectual. Off with that
hat and wig." And as he spoke he took off each of
his.

"You will lose by the exchange, Jemmy," said Archibald. "Mine is but a rusty bob and a poor hat; both yours are very good."

"No matter. To-morrow at the lodgment we will change again."

Therefore, with his appearance considerably altered, Archibald Sholto prepared now to set out for Wandsworth. But ere he did so he said one word to honest James McGlowrie.

"Jemmy," he remarked, "make no mistake about Ka—Lady Fordingbridge and this meeting with Bertie Elphinston to which she has gone. She is as good and pure a woman as ever lived and suffered. I have known her from a child, gave her her first communion; there is no speck of ill in her."

"Lived and suffered, eh?" repeated the other.

"Ay, lived and suffered! The man she has gone to meet was to have been her husband; they loved each other with all their hearts and souls; and by foul treachery she was stolen from him by that most unparalleled scoundrel, Fordingbridge. Remember that, Jemmy, when you see her to-night; remember she is as pure a woman as your mother was, and respect her for all that she has endured."

"Have no fear," said Jemmy, manfully, "have no fear. Although ye are a Papist, Archie, and a priest at that, I'll e'en take your word for it."

So, with a light laugh from the Jesuit at the rigid and plain-spoken Presbyterianism of his old schoolfellow and whilom fag, they parted with a grasp of the hand, each to what he had to do. That James McGlowrie carried out his portion of the undertaking has been already told, as well as how, after the information he gave Lady Fordingbridge, she decided to accept Lady Belrose's offer of her house as a refuge, if only temporarily; and how he afterwards became a messenger from her to Bertie Elphinston.

As for Archibald Sholto, he, too, did that which he had said would be best. He made his way from Kensington to Chelsea and so to Wandsworth, only to find when he had arrived there that his brother and friend had long since—for it was by then nine o'clock—departed for Vauxhall. Therefore he said a few words to the landlady—herself an adherent of the Stuarts, as she, whose father had fallen at Sherriffmuir, was certain to be—telling her that it was doubtful if they would ever return to their lodgings, but that, if they did, she must manage to send them off at once. He told her, too, the address of the Minories where he could be communicated with, under cover to McGlowrie, and, since he it was who had sent them as lodgers to her house, he gave her some money on their account. Then he left her and, thorough and indomitable in all he did, made his way to the Spring Gardens.

"If they are there," he thought, as he waited outside the inn in Wandsworth—an old one, known then, as now, as the Spread Eagle, while the horse was being put into the shafts of the hackney coach he had hired, "I may see them in time to warn them. Dressed as the executioner, the woman said of Bertie and Douglas, without any disguise, though in a garb that will be supposed to be one in that place; there should be no difficulty in finding them if they are still there. Thank God, they were not caught in their lodgings."

He did not know, nor could the landlady have told him—not knowing herself—of how they had been watched and followed from the village to Vauxhall;

so he passed his time on the lonely drive through the Battersea marshes in meditating how this last act of treachery of Lord Fordingbridge was to be repaid. For that it should be so repaid, and with interest, Archibald Sholto had already determined. "Though not for his baseness to me so much," he muttered, "as to those whom I love. For since to me, a priest, there can be no home, no wife, no children, I have centred all my heart upon those three—my brother, our friend Bertie, and poor, bonnie Kate. And those it is against whom he has struck. May God forget me if I strike not equally, ay! and with more certainty than he has done, when my hour comes."

A good friend was Archibald Sholto, Jesuit though he was, but a terrible foe. As you shall see.

On his way to the garden he passed half a dozen young men of fashion who, from their talk and actions, he knew to be about to assist at a duel, and, forgetting that he was in secular garb, he could not forbear from addressing them in his priestly character and begging them to desist from the sin they contemplated. But they bade him pass on and not interfere in what concerned him not, while one, striking at the horse with his clouded cane, caused the animal to dash off upon the uneven road or track. These, doubtless, were the men for whom the boatmen who ferried Bertie and Douglas across later on were waiting.

So he reached the gardens, but only to find that most of the company was already gone, and that, with the exception of a few revellers who would keep the night up so long as it were possible, none of the masqueraders remained. Yet, even from these he gathered enough to set his mind fairly at rest; for, happening to hear one of them speak of the "merry disturbance" which had taken place that night, and also boast somewhat loudly of how he had assisted the Jacobites in resisting the limbs of the law, he, by great suavity and apparent admiration of the speaker's prowess, managed to extract from him a more or less accurate account of what had taken place.

Thus he learned that, in some way, his brother and friend had made their escape—aided, of course, by the pot-valiant hero to whom he was listening—and also that the "ladies of fashion" and the gentlemen by whom they were accompanied had also departed without molestation. "Though," continued the narrator, as he swallowed the last drop of brandy in his glass and then looked ruefully at the empty vessel, "I know not if they would have been allowed to go so freely had not I and my friend assisted in protecting them."

After that Archibald withdrew, and, on foot, made his way to the City, while as he crossed London Bridge nearly two hours later—for he was weary with all that had happened that day—the sun came up and lighted with a rosy hue the Tower lying on his right hand.

"Ay," he muttered. "Ay, many's the poor aching heart within your walls this morning besides the doomed Balmerino, Cromartie, and Kilmarnock—for nought can save them; thank God that some at least are free at present. But how long will they be so? How long? How long?"

CHAPTER XII.

HEY! FOR FRANCE.

DURING the time which elapsed between the eventful proceedings of that day and the time when my Lord Fordingbridge—agitated by receiving no news in Cheshire from his wife—returned to London, all those whom this history has principally to deal with met together with considerable frequency.

For, whether the clue was lost to the whereabouts of Elphinston and the Sholtos, or whether the Government was growing sick of the wholesale butchery of Jacobites which was going on in Scotland and England—though it would scarce seem so, since two of the lords in the Tower and some score of other victims were yet to be executed and their remains to be brutally used—at least those three friends were still at large. Archibald Sholto was in hiding at James McGlowrie's lodgings in the Minories, in the neighbourhood of which that honest gentleman was much engaged in the grain and cattle trade between London and Scotland and also Holland and France. Farther east still was Bertie Elphinston, he being close to the spot where the unhappy Lady Balmerino, his kinswoman, was lodged; while in the West End, or rather the west of London, at the Kensington Gravel Pits, and under the roof of no less a person than Sir Charles Ames, Douglas had found a home and hiding place.

As for Kate and her father, they were in Hanover-square, the guests of Lady Belrose, and were to remain as such until the former had had an interview with Fordingbridge. "For," said Kate to her friend who, although a comparatively new one, was proving herself to be very staunch, "then I shall know, then I shall be able to decide; though even now my decision is taken, my mind made up. Who can doubt that it is he who has done this? He and no other. No other!"

"Indeed, dear," replied her hostess, as she bade her black boy—a present from her devoted admirer, Sir Charles—go get the urn filled, for they were drinking tea after dinner, "indeed, dear, no one, I think, from all that you have told me. Yet if you leave him, what is to become of you and Mr. Fane? You have, you say—pardon me for even referring to such a thing—no very good means of subsistence. I," went on her ladyship, speaking emphatically, "should at least take my settlement. I would not, positively I would not, allow the wretch to benefit by keeping that. No, indeed!"

"If," replied Kate, "'tis as I fear—nay, as I know it is, I will not touch one farthing of his. Not one farthing. I will go forth, and he shall be as though I had never seen or spoken to him."

"But," asked the more practical woman of the world, "what will you do, dear? You cannot live on air, and—which is almost worse—you cannot marry someone who will give you a good home. And you so pretty, too!" she added.

"Marry again!" exclaimed Kate, her eyes glistening as she spoke. "Heaven forbid! Have I not had enough of marriage? One experience should suffice, I think."

"It has indeed been a sad one," answered Lady Belrose, who had herself no intention of continuing her widowhood much longer, and was indeed at that moment privately affianced to Sir Charles Ames. "But, Kate, if your monster were dead you might be happy yet."

"No, no," the other replied, "never. And he is not dead, nor like to die. I am, indeed, far more likely to die than he—since the doctors all say I am far from strong, though I do not perceive it."

"But what will you do?" again asked the practical hostess. "How live? Mr. Fane has, you say, no longer sufficient youth or activity to earn a living for you at the fence school—can you, dear, earn enough for both?"

"I think so," Kate replied, "by returning to Paris. That we must do—there is nothing to be earned here. But, in Paris, Archibald Sholto has much influence in the court circles; he knows even the King and—and—the new favourite, La Pompadour, who has deposed Madame de Châteauroux. Also he is a friend of Cardinal Tencin, who owes much to the exiled Stuarts. It is, he thinks, certain that some place either at the court, or in the prince's household—if he has escaped from Scotland, which God grant!—or in the Chevalier St. George's, at Rome, might be found for me—a place which would enable me to keep my old father from want for the rest of his life."

"Kate, you are a brave woman, and a good one, too, for from what you have told me your father himself has behaved none too well to you, and——"

"I must forget that," the other replied, "and remember only how for years he struggled hard to keep a home for us, to bring me up as a lady. I must put away every thought of his one wrong to me and remember only all that he has done for my good."

Meanwhile Kate's determination to part from her husband—if, as no one doubted, he it was who had endeavoured to betray the others to the Government—was well known to her three friends; and therefore, with them as with her and her father, preparations were being hurried on by which they also might return to France. For them there was, as there had been before the invasion of Scotland and England, the means whereby to exist; Douglas and Bertie had not sacrificed their commissions in the French regiments to which they belonged, and Archibald was employed by the Stuart cause as an agent, was also a member of the College of St. Omer, and was a priest of St. Eustache. That Bertie Elphinston would ever have left London while his kinsman and the head of his house, Arthur, Lord Balmerino, lay in the Tower awaiting his trial and certain death was not to be supposed, had not a message come from that unhappy nobleman ordering him to go. Also, he bade him waste no time in remaining where he was hourly in danger and could, at the same time, be of no earthly good.

"He bids me tell you, Bertie," said Lady Balmerino, in a meeting which she contrived to have with the young man on one of those evenings when both were lodged in the Eastend, and while she wept piteously as she spoke, "he bids me tell you that it is his last commandment to you, as still the head of your house and the name you bear, to flee from England. The rank and title of Balmerino must die with him, but he lays upon you the task of bearing and, he hopes, perpetuating the name of Elphinston honourably. Also he sends you his blessing as from a dying old man to a young one, bids you trust in God and also serve the House of Stuart while there is any member of it left. And if more be needed to make you fly, he orders you to do it for your mother's sake."

After that Elphinston knew where his duty lay—knew that he must return to France. It was hard, he swore, to leave England and also, thereby, to leave the scoundrel Fordingbridge behind and alive, still he felt that it must be so. Fordingbridge merited death—yet he must escape it!

But he had one consolation, too. Ere long Kate would be back in Paris—it was not possible that her husband could be innocent—therefore he would sometimes see her. A poor consolation, indeed, he told himself, to simply be able to see the woman who was to have been his wife yet was now another man's—no power on earth, no determination on her part to sever her existence from Fordingbridge could alter that!—yet it was something. Consequently, he with the others set about the plans for their departure.

Now, to so arrange and manage for this departure, they looked to James McGlowrie, who had both the will and the power to help them.

An old acquaintance of his in Scotland, when both were boys who had not then gone forth into the world, McGlowrie had kept up an occasional correspondence with Archibald Sholto until the present time, and thereby had been able to afford him assistance and had proved himself invaluable when Fordingbridge informed against them. Indeed, had McGlowrie not known where Archibald Sholto was living when in London, Geordie McNab's information derived from the Scotch Secretary's Office could never have been utilized, and Archibald Sholto must at least have been taken. And now he was to be even more practically useful than before—it was in his cattle-trading boats that all were, one by one, to be conveyed to the continent. "Though," said Jemmy, as he arranged plans with them one night in a little inn at Limehouse where they were in the habit of meeting, and where there was little danger of their being discovered, "I can give none of ye any certain guarantee, so to speak as it were, of ye getting over in safety. Infernal sloops o' war and bomb-ketches, and the devil knows what else, are prowling about the waters looking for rebels, and as like as not may light upon the one or other of you."

"We must risk that," said Bertie. "Great heavens! what have we not risked far worse?"

"Vary weel," replied McGlowrie; "then let one of you begin the risk to-morrow night. And you it had best be, Mr. Elphinston. My little barky drops down the river then, and once you're round the North Foreland you will be safe, or nearly so, to reach Calais. Be ready by seven to-morrow night."

"Why do you select me to go first, Mr. McGlowrie? I have quite as many, if not more, interests in England than either Douglas or Archie."

"Um!" muttered honest Jemmy, who did not care to say that he thought a man who was philandering about after a married woman was best got out of the way as soon as possible, though such was, indeed, his opinion, he being a strict moralist. "Um! I thought the noble lord had laid his commands on ye to be off and awa' at anst. The head of the family must be obeyed."

"Also," said Archibald Sholto, "you have your mother to think of. We have no mother. Bertie, you had best go to-morrow night."

"And you have seen Kate," whispered gentle Douglas Sholto, who took, perhaps, a more romantic view of things—for he had known of their love from the first and, from almost envying them at its commencement, had now come to pity them, "have made your farewells. If you get safe to France you must of a surety meet again—for Fordingbridge is a villain, and she will keep her word and part from him—is it not best you go at once?"

"You and I have always gone together, Douglas, hand in hand in all things," his friend replied; "I like not parting from you now."

"Still let it be so, I beg you. Remember, once we are back in Paris all will be as happy as it has been before, or nearly so, and there will be no Fordingbridge there. He, at least, will not be by us to set the blood tingling in our veins with the desire to slay him."

"So be it," said Bertie, "I will go."

This being therefore decided, McGlowrie gave his counsel as to what was to be done. The "little barky" of which he had spoken was in the habit of taking over to Calais good black cattle in exchange for French wines (what did it matter if sometimes the bottles were stuffed full of lace instead of Bordeaux?), silks, and ribbons, and it was as a drover he proposed Elphinston should go. The duties would be nothing, and the assumption of them would be a sufficient explanation of his being on board.

"And then," said he, "when once you set your foot on Calais sands you can again become Captain Elphinston of the regiment of Picardy, and defy King Geo—hoot! what treason am I talking?"

It was the truth that he had seen Kate again since

the night of the conflict at Vauxhall, and then, stung to madness by the renewed villainy and treachery of her husband, he had pleaded to her to let him seek out Fordingbridge and slay him with his own hands. But, bitterly as she despised and hated the man who had brought them such grief and sorrow, she refused to even listen to so much as a suggestion of his doing this.

"No, no, no!" she exclaimed, shuddering at the very idea of such a tragedy. "No, no. What benefit would it be to you or to me to have the stain of his blood on our hands?"

"It would remove for ever the obstacle between us," he said; "would set you free; would place us where we were before."

"Never, never," she replied. "I have been his wife—though such by fraud and trickery—and if he were dead, God knows I could not mourn him; yet I will not be his murderess, his executioner, as I shall be if I let you slay him. If he fell by your hand, I could never look upon your face again. Moreover, even were I hardened enough to do so—which I am not—do you not know that the French law permits no man to become the husband of a woman whose first husband he has slain? We should be as far apart then as ever—nay, farther, with his death between us always."

"I know, I know," he said, recognising, however, as he did so that there was no possibility of his taking vengeance on Fordingbridge, since by doing so he would thus place such a barrier between them. "Yet there are other lands where one may live besides France and England. There is Sweden, where every soldier is welcome; there is——"

"Cease, I beseech you, cease! It can never be. If in God's good time He sees fit to punish him, he will do so. If not, I must bear the lot that has fallen to me. Meanwhile be assured that once I find he has done this act of treachery, I shall never return to him."

"And we shall meet in Paris—that is, if ever I can get back there?"

"Yes," she answered. "We shall meet in Paris; for it is there I must go. There, at least, I must find a means of existence; though, since now we understand, since we have forgiven each other—is it not so? —'twould perhaps be best that we should not meet again."

"No, no," he protested. "No, no. For even though this snake has crept in between us—so that never more can we be to each other what—what—my God!—what we once were; so that there must be no love, no passing of our days, our lives, together side by side—yet, Kate, we can at least know that the other is well if not happy; we can meet sometimes. Can we not? answer me."

"Oh, go!" she exclaimed, breaking down at his words and weeping piteously, as she sank into a chair and buried her head in her hands. "Go! In mercy, go! I cannot bear your words; they break my heart. Leave me, I beseech you!"

So—because he, too, could bear the interview no longer, and could not endure to see her misery—he left her, taking her hand and kissing it ere he departed, and whispering in her ear that soon they would meet again.

CHAPTER XIII.

THE hackney coach drew up at Lady Belrose's house in Hanover-square a couple of hours after it had left Kensington-square, and Lord Fordingbridge, descending from it, rang a loud peal upon the bell.

For some reason—the whereof was perhaps not known to him, or could not have been explained by even his peculiarly constituted mind—he had attired himself for the two interviews with great care. His black velvet suit, trimmed with silver lace—for he wore mourning for the late viscount—was of the richest; his thick hair was now confined beneath a handsome tye-wig, and his ruffles and breast lace were the finest in his possession. Yet he, knowing himself to be the unutterable scoundrel he was, could scarcely suppose that this sumptuousness of attire was likely to have much effect upon the woman who had deserted him for a cause which he had not the slightest difficulty in imagining. Perhaps, however, it was assumed for the benefit of the Duke of Newcastle, with whom he had had a satisfactory interview.

"Lady Fordingbridge is living here," he said quietly, but with a sternness he considered fitting to the occasion, to the grave elderly man who opened the door to him—a man whose appearance, Lady Belrose frequently observed, would have added respectability to the household of a bishop—"show me to her."

The footman looked inquiringly at him for a moment; he was not accustomed to such imperious orders from any of her ladyship's visitors, however handsome an appearance they might present. Then he said:

"Lady Belrose lives here. Lady Fordingbridge is her guest. And if you wish to see her, sir, I must know whose name to announce."

"I am her husband, Lord Fordingbridge. Be good enough to announce that, and at once."

The staid man-servant gave him a swift glance—it was not to be doubted that many a gossip had been held below stairs as to the reason why Lady Fordingbridge had quitted and caused to be shut up her own house, only to come and dwell at his mistress's—then he invited his lordship to follow him into the morning room on the right of the door.

"I will tell her ladyship," he said, and so left him.

When he was alone, Lord Fordingbridge, after a hasty glance round the room, and a sneer at the portraits of a vast number of simpering young men which hung on the walls—her admirers, he considered, no doubt—took a seat upon the couch and pondered over the coming interview with his wife.

"It is time," he thought, "that things should draw to a conclusion. For," he said, as though addressing Kate herself, "I have had enough of you, my lady. You have long ceased to be a wife to me—never were one, indeed, but for a month, and then but a very indifferent spouse, a cold-hearted, cold-blooded jade; now it is time you should cease to be so much in even name. So, so. You shall be stripped of your borrowed plumage; we will see then how you like the position of affairs. I myself am heartily sick of them."

He had no premonition of what Kate might be about to say to him when she should enter the room in which he now sat; yet he had a very strong suspicion that her remarks would consist of accusations against him of having betrayed the Sholtos and Elphinston.

"Well, well," he said, "let her accuse. I have the last card. It is a strong one. It should win the trick."

Yet at the same time, strong as any card might be which he held in his hand, he would have given a good deal to have known where at the present moment those three men might be harbouring whom he had endeavoured so strongly to give to the hangman's hands. And once, as a sudden thought came to his mind—a thought that almost made the perspiration burst out upon him—a thought that they might all be in this very house and appear suddenly to take vengeance on him for his treachery!—he nearly rose from his seat as though to fly while there was yet time. But, coward though he was, both physically and morally, he had strength to master his impulse, and, in spite of his fears that at any moment Elphinston, whom he had wronged the worst of all, might enter the room, to remain seated where he was.

Still his eyes sought ever the hands of the clock as moment after moment went by and his wife failed to come, until at last he was wrought to so high a pitch of nervousness that he started at any sound inside and outside of the house. A man bawling the news in the street or blowing the horn, which at that time the newsboys carried to proclaim their approach, set his nerves and fibres tingling; the laughter of some of the domestics in the kitchens below him had an equally jarring effect, and when a loud knock came at the street door he quivered as though the avenging Elphinston was indeed there. Then, at last, the door opened suddenly, and his wife stood before him.

He saw in one swift glance that she was very pale—she, whose complexion had once been as the rose-blush—and this he could understand. It was not strange she should be so. What he could not understand was the habit in which she appeared, the manner in which she was attired. Ever since she had become his wife he had caused her to be arrayed in the richest, most costly dresses he could afford; had desired, nay, had commanded, that in all outward things she should carry out the character of Lady Fordingbridge; that her gowns, her laces, her wigs, should all be suitable to his position.

Yet now she appeared shorn of all those adornments which his common, pitiful mind regarded as part and parcel of his dignity. The dress she wore was a simple black one, made of a material which the humblest lady in the land might have had on, without lace or trimmings or any adornment whatsoever. Also on her head there was no towering wig, nor powder, nor false curls; instead, her own sweet golden hair was neatly brushed back into a great knot behind. Nor on her hands, nor on her neck, was any jewellery, save only the one ring which, from the day he had put it on her finger, she had ever regarded as a badge of slavery.

"Madam," he said, rising and advancing towards her, while as he did so she retreated back towards the door, "Madam, I have come here to desire an explanation from you as to why I find you gone from my house and living under the shelter of another person's roof. And also, I have to ask," he continued, letting his eye fall upon the plainness of her attire, "why you present yourself before me in such a garb as you now wear? I must crave an immediate answer, madam."

"I am here to give it," she replied. "And since I do not doubt that it is the last time you and I will ever exchange words again in the world, that answer shall be full and complete. But, first, do you answer me this, Lord Fordingbridge. Was it by your craft that Mr. Elphinston and Douglas and Archibald Sholto were denounced?"

She spoke very calmly; in her voice there was no tremor; also he could see that her hands, in one of which she held a small packet, did not quiver.

"Madam," he replied, endeavouring to also assume a similar calmness, but not succeeding particularly well, while at the same time one of those strong waves of passion rose in his breast which he had hitherto always mastered when engaged in discussion with her, "madam, by what right do you ask me such a question as this? What does it concern you if I choose to denounce Jacobite plotters to the Government? Nothing! And again I ask why you have left my roof for that of the worldling with whom you have taken refuge, and why you appear before me in a garb more befitting a mercer's apprentice than my wife?"

"Your equivocation condemns you. Simeon Larpent, it was you who played the spy, you who were the denouncer of those three men. I knew that there could be no doubt on that score."

"And again I say, what if I did? What then? What does it concern you? What have you to do with it?"

"I have this to do," she replied; "but that which is to be done shall be done before witnesses," and stepping to the bell rope, she pulled it strongly, so that the peal rang through the house.

"Witnesses!" he exclaimed. "Witnesses! None are required. Yet, be careful; I warn you ere it is too late. If you summon witnesses to this interview, they may chance to hear that which, to prevent their hearing, you would rather have died. Be careful what you do, madam."

As he finished, the footman opened the door, and, without hesitating one moment, she said to the man:

"Ask the two gentlemen to step this way."

"Two gentlemen!" he repeated; "two gentlemen! So, this is a trap! Who are the two gentlemen, pray?" and as he spoke he drew his sword. "If, as I suspect, they are the two bullies—your lover, whom you meet at masquerades, whom you give assignations to, and his friend—they shall at least find that I can defend myself."

In truth, bold as he seemed, he was now in great fear. He expected nothing else but that, when the door again opened, Sholto and Elphinston would appear before him, and he began to quake and to think his last hour was come. His treachery was, he feared, soon to be repaid.

She made no answer to his vile taunt about her lover, nor did she take any heed of the drawn sword that shook in his hand; had she been a statue she could not have stood more still as she regarded him with contempt and scorn.

Then the door did open, and Sir Charles Ames and Douglas Sholto entered the room. The first he did not know; had, indeed, never seen him before; but at the sight of the other he grasped his weapon more firmly, expecting that ere another moment had passed the hands of the young Highlander would be at his throat, and that he would have to defend his life against him. To his intense surprise Sholto treated him with as much indifference as if he too had been a statue; after one glance—which, if disdain could have the power to slay, would have withered him as he stood—he took no further heed of him. As for Sir Charles Ames, he, observing the drawn weapon in the other's hand, smiled contemptuously, shrugged his shoulders, and then took his place behind Lady Fordingbridge and by the side of Douglas.

"Sir Charles and you, Douglas," she said, "forgive me for asking you to be present at this interview, yet I do so because I desire that in after days there shall be one or two men, at least, to testify to that which I now do." Then, turning towards her husband, who still stood where he had risen on her entrance, she said:

"Simeon Larpent, since first I met you—to my eternal unhappiness—your life has been one long lie, one base deceit. The first proposals ever made to me by you were degrading to an honest woman, were infamy to listen to. Next, you obtained me for your wife by more lies, by more duplicity, by more deceit. Also, from the time I have been your wife, you, yourself a follower of the unhappy house of Stuart by birth and bringing up, have endeavoured in every way to encompass the death of three followers of the same cause, because one of those men was to have been my husband had not you foully wronged him to me; because the other two were his and my friends."

She paused a moment as though to gather fresh energy for her denunciation of him; and he, craven as he was, stood there before her, white to the very lips, and with his eyes wandering from one to the other of the two listeners. Then she continued:

"For all this, Simeon Larpent, but especially for that which you have last done, for this your last piece of cruel, wicked treachery, for this your last bitter, tigerish endeavour to destroy three men who had otherwise been safe, I renounce and deny you for ever."

All started as she uttered these words, but without heeding them she continued:

"For ever. I disavow you, I forswear you as my husband. I have long ceased to be aught to you but a wife in name; henceforth I will not be so much as that. I have quitted your house. I quit now and part with for so long as I shall live your name, the share in the rank that you smirch and befoul. From to-day I will never willingly set eyes on you again, never speak one word to you, though you lay dying at my feet, never answer to the name of Fording-bridge. I return to what I was; I become once more Katherine Fane."

He, standing before her, moistened his lips as though about to speak, but again she went on, taking now from off her finger the one ring that alone she wore. Placing it on the table, she continued:

"Thus I discard you, thus I sever to all eternity the bond that binds me to you; a bond that no priest, no Church, shall ever persuade or force me into again recognising." And with these words she placed also on the table the package she had brought into the room with her.

"There," she said, "is every trinket you have given me, except the jewellery of your family, which you have possession of. At your own house is every dress and robe, every garment I own that has been bought with your money. So the severance is made. Again I say that I renounce you and deny you. From to-day, Lord Fordingbridge, your existence ceases for me."

It seemed that she had spoken her last word. With an inclination of her head towards those two witnesses whom she had summoned to hear her denunciation, she moved towards the door, while they, after casting one glance at him, the Denounced, standing there—Sir Charles Ames, conveying in his looks all the ineffable disdain which a polished gentleman of the world might be supposed to feel towards another who had fallen so low, and Douglas ·regarding him as a man regards some savage, ignoble beast—prepared to follow her.

Then, at last, he found his voice—a harsh and raucous one, as though emotion, or hate, or rage were stifling its natural tones—and exclaimed ere they could quit the room:

"Stay. The last word is not yet said. You, Katherine Fane, as you elect, wisely, to call yourself henceforth, and you, her witnesses, listen to what I have now to say. This parley, this conference, call it what you will, may justly be completed."

She paused and looked at him—disdainfully, and careless as to what he might have to say in this her final interview with him—and they, doing as she did, paused also.

Then he continued, still speaking hoarsely but clearly enough:

"You have said, madam, that you renounce and deny me for ever; that you are resolved never more to share my rank or title, nor again to bear my name. Are you so certain that 'tis yours to so refuse or so renounce at your good will and pleasure?"

"What, sir, do you mean by such questions?" asked Sir Charles Ames, speaking now for the first time. But Lord Fordingbridge, heeding him not, continued to address her, and now, as he spoke, he raised his hand and pointed his finger at her.

"You have been very scornful, very cold and disdainful since first we came together, madam, treating me ever to your most bitter dislike, while all the time every thought and idea of yours was given to another man—all the time, I say, while you continued to bear the title of the Viscountess Fordingbridge. Once more, I ask, are you so sure that this title was yours to fling away, the husband yours to renounce and deny in your own good pleasure?"

And his eyes glared at her now as he spoke, and she knew that the devil which dwelt in him had got possession.

"Be more explicit," she said, "or cease to speak at all. If I could think, if I could awake as from an evil dream and learn that I had never been your wife, never plighted troth with you, I would upon my knees thank God for such a mercy."

"Those thanks may be more due than you dream of. How if I were to tell you——?"

"What?" fell from the lips of all, while Douglas took a step nearer to him, and Sir Charles felt sure that in another moment they would be told of some earlier marriage. "What?"

For answer he went on, one finger raised and

pointing at her as though to emphasize his remarks:

"You have taunted me often with the Jesuit education I received at St. Omer—at Lisbon. Well, it was true: such an education I did receive at both places. Only, madam—my Lady Fordingbridge!—Miss Fane!—have you never heard that one so educated may, at such places, receive other things? may become acolytes, priests? What if *I* became such? what would you then be—a priest——?"

"It is a lie!" she exclaimed, "and you know it."

"Are you so sure? Can you prove—or, rather, *disprove* it? Answer me that—answer, if you are sure that you share my name and rank—have power to renounce them."

As he finished, Douglas sprang at him and, in spite of his drawn sword, would have choked the life out of him on the spot had not Sir Charles interceded, while at the same moment Kitty's voice was heard bidding him desist.

"Even so," she said, "true or untrue, it is best. The infamy, if infamy there is, must be borne. At least, I am free. Free! Am justified after these hints!"

"Ay," Lord Fordingbridge said, "you *may* be free. To do what, however? To fling yourself into your lover's arms to-night—only, where will you find him? Newgate, the Tower, the New Gaol in Southwark are full of such as he; 'tis there, Mistress Fane, that doubtless you must seek him."

"And 'tis there," said Douglas Sholto, an inspiration occurring suddenly to his mind, "that you shall join him. The King has issued orders for every Jesuit priest to be arrested who shall be found, or denounced, in these dominions, and, Jacobite though I am, with my life at stake, I will drag you there with my own hands ere you shall be suffered to escape. You have proclaimed yourself, shown us the way ; by your own lips shall you be judged."

CHAPTER XIV.

FLIGHT.

THAT Douglas had spoken out of the fury of his heart and, consequently, without thought, was, however, very apparent at once; for when Kate had quitted the room, leaving Fordingbridge free from the grasp of the former—since Douglas, a second after he had seized him, flung him trembling and shivering on the couch—Sir Charles Ames spoke and said, as he drew Sholto aside to where the other would not hear them:

"It would indeed serve the scoundrel right if he were treated as you suggest. Only, unfortunately, it is not possible. First of all, I believe this insinuation is a lie."

"I am sure of it. If he had ever been admitted a priest my brother must have known of it, and, in any circumstances, the truth can soon be proved by him. A letter to the head of the Jesuit College at Lisbon from another Jesuit such as Archibald is will prove his statement to be false."

"Yet even," said Sir Charles, "were he a Jesuit priest and so subject to arrest and imprisonment in this country, you would stand in far too much danger to bring it about. Also, he can tell too much, as he would undoubtedly do if he was himself given up. Let us consider what is best."

143

"I," replied Douglas, speaking in an even lower whisper, so that the villain could not possibly hear him, "go to-night, as you know. Archie probably to-morrow, or the next night, and Bertie is already gone. Surely it might somehow be done."

"Impossible," replied Sir Charles, "impossible. Remember, we are in Lady Belrose's house; we must bring no scandal upon her. No, that way will not do."

"What then?" asked Douglas. "What then? For I am determined that his power of doing any harm shall be forever quenched now. We have him in our hands, and we will hold him fast."

As he spoke he glanced where the traitor sat glowering at them from the sofa. He seemed now to be thoroughly cowed, thoroughly alarmed also for his own safety, and his piercing black eyes scintillated and twinkled more like the eyes of a hunted, timorous creature than those of a man. Indeed, as Douglas looked at him, it seemed as though Fording-bridge were really mad with terror. Yet, abject as he now was, the other shuddered again, as he had more than once shuddered before when speaking of or looking at the man.

"We must get him away from this house," said Sir Charles. "I will have no disturbance here. Come, let us take him to the park. There we can talk at freedom, and, I think, so persuade his lordship of our intentions that henceforth he will be harmless. Do you agree?"

Douglas nodded, whereon Sir Charles, advancing into the room again, addressed Lord Fordingbridge.

"My lord," he said, in his coldest, most freezing manner, "it were best you sheathed that sword," and he pointed to it as it lay beside him on the sofa. "Such weapons are unfitted to a lady's house, and you may be at ease—no injury is intended you."

Fordingbridge gazed at him—still with the terror-stricken look in his eyes, the glance almost of madness or, at best, of imbecility; yet he did as the baronet bade him, and replaced his weapon. But he uttered no word.

"We shall be obliged," continued Sir Charles, "if you will accompany us to St. James's Park. We have something to say to you."

"If," said Fordingbridge, finding his voice at last, "you intend to make me fight a duel with that man, I will not do it. He——"

"There is," interrupted Douglas, "no thought of such a thing. My sword is not made to cross one borne by you."

"Very well," replied the other meekly, "I will come." But, a moment later, he burst out into one of his more natural methods of speaking, and cried, "You have the whip hand of me for the moment, but we shall see. We shall see."

"We shall," replied Sir Charles, calmly; "but if your lordship is now ready we may as well depart. We have already encroached somewhat on Lady Belrose's hospitality."

The grave manservant seemed somewhat astonished, when he opened the street door at a summons from the bell, to observe the three gentlemen go down the steps together and enter the hackney coach which was still waiting for the viscount. Also he was surprised—since he and all the other servants in the house had gathered a very accurate knowledge of what had transpired in the small saloon—to witness the courteous manner in which Sir Charles motioned to his lordship to enter the vehicle before him, and then entered it himself, followed by Douglas. Next, he heard the direction given to the man to drive to St. James's Park, and retired, wondering what it all meant. After the words he had—by chance, of course —overheard in the room, he, too, naturally supposed that a duel was about to be fought; but being a discreet man, he only mentioned this surmise to his fellow-servants, and took care not to alarm his mistress.

Arrived in the park and the coach discharged by Sir Charles, who even took so much of the ordering of these proceedings upon himself as to pay the man the hire demanded, the former, still with exquisite politeness, requested Fordingbridge to avail himself of a vacant bench close by, since he and his friend, Mr. Sholto, had a few words to say to each other before they laid their deliberations before him. And Fordingbridge, still with the terror-stricken look upon his face and the vacillating glance in his eyes, obeyed without a word.

And now the others paced up and down the path at a short distance from him, but always keeping him well in their view, and the deliberations mentioned by Sir Charles took some time in arriving at. But they came to an end at last, and the baronet, drawing near to the bench where Fordingbridge was seated, proceeded to unfold them to him.

"My lord," he said, speaking with great clearness and cold distinctness, "you may perhaps think that I should have no part in whatever has transpired between you and others. Yet I think I have. It fell to my lot—to my extreme good fortune—to be of assistance to the Viscountess Fordingbridge, for so I shall continue to call her in spite of your observations and disclosures this morning, which I do not believe. It fell to my lot, I repeat, to be of some service to her ladyship on a certain night a week or two ago. That service was rendered necessary by your betrayal of a cause which you had once espoused, of a man whom you had previously injured cruelly, and of another man, Mr. Douglas, who had never injured you. Therefore, I was of assistance to her ladyship, who was more or less under my charge and protection that evening, and I am glad to have been able to do so."

"I wish," muttered Fordingbridge hoarsely, glaring at him, "that you had been at the devil before you did so."

"Doubtless. But I was not. That service, however, and your visit to-day to the house of a lady who is shortly about to honour me by becoming my wife, justifies me, I think, in taking some part in these proceedings, though only as spokesman. In that character I now propose to tell you what Mr. Sholto intends to do."

"What?" gasped Fordingbridge, moistening his lips.

"First," said Sir Charles, unsparingly, "when he has left the country, which he will do almost immediately, to denounce you to His Majesty's Government. You are pledged by every oath that can be regarded as sacred in any cause to the House of Stuart——"

"No!" exclaimed Fordingbridge. "No. I am now an adherent of the House of Hanover."

"I am afraid even that will be of little avail to you. For, if you are, you are a double traitor. It was you who planned the attack on the 'Fubbs,' which brought the King from Herrenhausen at the outbreak of the

Scotch Invasion ; you who circulated the papers offer-
ing a large reward for his assassination ; you who, but
a month or so ago, brought over with you Father
Sholto, the most notorious plotter among the Jesuits."

"I denounced him," whined Fordingbridge. "I
denounced him. That alone will save me from the
King's anger."

"That," replied Sir Charles, "is possible. I am
willing to allow it. But you are by your own confession a Jesuit priest, therefore you will be subject to
all the punishments and penalties now in force against
such persons. Also, you will have let loose against you
the whole of the anger of the Jesuits—should His Majesty be inclined to spare you—when Mr. Sholto has
informed them of your treachery. You, as one yourself, can best imagine what form that anger is likely
to take."

Fordingbridge gasped as he stared at the baronet ;
and now, indeed, it seemed as if the light of idiocy
alone shone in his eyes.

"But," went on Sir Charles, "you have also something else to reckon with, namely, the punishment
which your brother religionists may see fit to accord
to you for having, as a priest—as you suggest yourself—gone through the form of matrimony. I have
not the honour to be of the Romanist religion myself,
therefore I do not know what shape that punishment
may take, but, from what Mr. Sholto tells me, it is for
your own sake to be hoped that you have hinted a lie
and are, indeed, no priest."

"Let me go," said Fordingbridge, "let me go."
Then he muttered, "Curses on you all. If I could kill
you both as you stand there, blast you both to death
before me, I would do it."

"Without doubt," replied Sir Charles; "but if you will pardon my saying it, your schemes for injuring others seem to fall most extraordinarily harmless. And I trust your aspirations for our ill will not take effect until, at least, we have had time to put some leading Jesuits in France—if not here—in possession of your true character."

"Curse you both, curse you all," again muttered Fordingbridge impotently.

"Now," continued Sir Charles, "I propose to accompany your lordship as far as the door of your own house. Once I have seen you safe there, care will be taken that you shall find no means of communicating in any way with those who have it in their power to injure our friends. When, however, they are beyond your reach you will be free from observation, and will be quite at liberty to devote yourself to making another peace with the Government and with the—Order of the Jesuits. My lord, shall we now proceed to Kensington-square?"

"Have a care," said Fordingbridge, with an evil droop of his eye at him, "have a care, however, for yourself. If they escape me, you may not. A harbourer of Jacobites, an abettor in their escape from England and from justice, I may yet do you an evil turn, Sir Charles Ames."

"I do not doubt it if you have the power. But, Lord Fordingbridge, you have so much to think of on your own behalf, you will be so very much occupied in you own affairs shortly—what with the State on one side and the Church (your Church) on the other—that I am afraid you will have but little time to devote to me. And I think, my lord, I can hold my own against you. Now, come."

Douglas shook hands with Sir Charles as they stood apart once more from the wretched man, and after one hearty grasp strode away through the park, leaving the other two alone. Yet he did not hesitate to acknowledge the truth of the baronet's last whispered words to him.

"Lose no time," that gentleman said as they parted, "in putting the sea between you and England. Also induce your brother to go at once. I have frightened the craven cur sufficiently to keep him quiet for a day or so—alas! mine are but idle threats. The Government must find out his villainies for themselves, while for his Church you must put them on the scent, but afterwards I cannot answer for what he may do. Once he finds that they are but idle threats he may go to work again. Begone, therefore, both of you, and let me hear when you are safe in France."

"Have no fear," Douglas replied; "by to-morrow, if all is well, we may be in Calais. McGlowrie sends another vessel to-night. If possible, Archie and I, Kate and her father, may be in it. But the day grows late, there is much to do. Again farewell, and thanks, thanks, thanks for all."

"He is safe from you," said the baronet, turning, after Douglas was gone, to Fordingbridge. "Now, my lord, I am ready."

"I will not go with you," replied the other, some spark of manliness, or perhaps shame, rising in his breast at the manner in which he was dominated by this man whom, until to-day, he had never seen nor heard of. "I will not go with you."

And he drew back from him and laid his hand upon the hilt of his sword.

"No?" inquired Sir Charles, with his most polished

air. Then he continued: "I am sorry my enforced society should be so unwelcome." As he spoke he glanced his eye round the grassy slopes of the park and across the low brick wall which at that time separated it from Piccadilly. "I regret it very much. But, my lord, I must not force myself where I am disliked. Therefore, since I see a watchman outside who appears to have little to occupy him, I will, with your lordship's permission, ask him to accompany you and see you safely home. Or, stay," and again his eye roved over the grass, "there is a sergeant's guard passing towards Buckingham House—your lordship can see their conical caps over the bushes—I will summon them and relieve you of my presence, since it is so distasteful."

"Oh!" exclaimed Fordingbridge, "if ever the time should come—if ever the chance is mine!"

"It is not at present," replied the baronet. Then, with an air of determination which until now he had not assumed, he stamped his foot angrily and exclaimed: "Come, sir, I will be trifled with no longer. Either with me, or the watch, or the soldiers. But at once. At once, I say!"

And Fordingbridge, knowing he was beaten, went with him.

A coach was found at the park wicket, into which they entered and proceeded to Kensington, no word being uttered by either during the drive. Then, when they had arrived outside Fordingbridge's house, Sir Charles, with a relaxation of the courteous manner that he had previously treated the other to, said, coldly and briefly:

"Remember, for two days you will have no opportunity of injuring anyone. That I shall take steps to prevent. Afterwards, you will have sufficient occupation in consulting your own welfare," and, raising his three-cornered hat an inch, he entered the coach again. Only, he thought it well to say to the driver in a clear, audible voice which the other could not fail to hear:

"Drive to Kensington Palace now; I have business with the officer of the guard."

With those terrifying words ringing in his ears—for Fordingbridge knew how, at that time, soldiers quartered in the neighbourhood of suspected persons acted as police act in these days, and were employed often to make arrests of persons implicated with the State—he entered his house, locking himself in with a key he carried. Then he proceeded at once to ring the bells and shout for the deaf old servitor, Luke, but without effect. There was no response to the noise he made, no sound of the old man's heavy, shuffling feet, and he began to wonder if he, too, had taken flight like the rest of the servants. Yet, even if he had, his master meditated, it would matter very little now. He was himself about to take flight. London was too hot to hold him.

A coward ever from his infancy, there could have been no better plan devised to frighten this man from doing more harm to those whom he wished to injure than the one adopted by Sir Charles Ames; while the latter's statement that he had business with the officer of the guard at Kensington Palace was the culminating point to the other's fears. Moreover—although his mind appeared to him to be strangely hazy and distraught now, and unable to retain the sequence of that day's events—he recognised the fearful weapon he had drawn against himself in suggesting that he was a Jesuit priest. Upon that statement, testified to by Sir Charles, a man of responsible position, he would certainly be arrested at once; while, if proof could be obtained that he was in truth a priest, or had ever been trained to be one, the most terrible future would lie before him.

As he thought of all this in a wandering, semi-vacant manner, he set about doing that which, since the interview in the park, be had made up his mind to do. He would fly from England, he would return to France. Yet, he reflected, if in France, Paris would still be closed to him. There the Jesuits were in possession of terrible authority, although an authority not recognised by the Government; if they knew what he had done, even in only betraying Archibald Sholto to the English authorities, their vengeance on him would be sharp, swift, terrible. And in Paris also—he could not doubt it—would soon be Bertie Elphinston and Douglas, even Archibald himself. No, it must not be Paris. Not yet at least!

But he must be somewhere out of London, out of England, and he set to work—still in a dazed, stupefied manner—to make his plans.

He went first to his own bed-room, to which was attached a small toilet or dressing-room, and, unlocking an iron-bound strong box, took from it some money—a small casket of Louis d'ors and English guineas, a leather case stuffed full of bills of exchange and several notes, among them a large one drawn by a Parisian money-lender on a London goldsmith. Then, next, he opened a false tray, or bottom, in the strong box, and from it took out several shagreen cases which he slipped into his pocket. These contained all his family jewels.

Yet the man's fear was so great that he might even by now have been denounced by Sir Charles Ames to the officer of the guard at Kensington Palace, that more than once he rose from the box and, on hearing any slight noise in the square, ran to the window and peered out of it and down into the road, and then came back to his task of packing up his valuables. And all the while as he did so he muttered to himself continually:

"The notary must see to all—I will write to him from France. He had best sell all and remit the money. England is done with! Neither Hanoverian nor Jacobite now. Curse them both and all." Then he laughed, a little sniggering, feeble laugh—it was wondrous that, in the state his mind was and with the ruin which was upon him, he could have been moved by such a trifle!—and chuckled to himself and said:

"If Luke comes back now he will find the door barred forever. A faithful servant! A faithful servant! Well, his home is gone. Let him go drown himself."

He fetched next all the silver which he could find about the house, and which had been brought forth on his return from the coffers where it had lain since his father's flight into France years ago—candelabras, old dishes and baskets and a coffee pot, with a tankard or so—and hurled them into the strong box and locked it securely.

Then, after once more peering into the square and seeing that all was clear, he descended to the hall, opened the door an inch or two and again glanced his eye round, and, a moment later, drew the door to and went forth into the night.

CHAPTER XV.

UNITED.

ALL through Picardy, from Artois to the Ile de France, from Normandy to Champagne, the wheat was a-ripening early that year, the trees in the orchards and gardens of the rich, fruitful province had their boughs bent to the earth with their loads, and, so great was the summer heat, the cattle stood in the rivers and pools for coolness, or sought shelter under the elms and poplars dotted about by the river's banks.

Yet, heat notwithstanding, the great bare road that runs from Calais through Boulogne, Abbeville, and Amiens, as well as through Clermont and Chantilly and St. Denis to Paris, had still its continuous traffic to which neither summer nor winter made much difference, except when the snows of the latter belated many diligences and waggons—for it was the high road between the coast and the capital. And thus it was now, in this hot, broiling June of 1746. Along that road, passing each other sometimes, sometimes breaking down, sometimes, by the carelessness of drunken drivers or postillions, getting their wheels into ditches and sticking there for hours, went almost every vehicle that was known in the France of those days. Monseigneur's carriage, drawn by four or six stout travelling roadsters—wrenched for the occasion from the service of Monseigneur's starving tenants—

and with Monseigneur within it looking ineffably bored at the heat and the dust and the inferior *canaille* who obtruded themselves on his vision—would lumber by the diligence, or Royal Post, farmed from Louis the well-beloved—so, loved, perhaps, because he despised his people and said France would last his time, which was long enough!—or be passed by a *desobligéant*, or chaise for one person, or by a fat priest on a post-horse, or by a travelling carriage full of provincials *en route* for Paris. Also, to add to the continuous traffic on this road in that period, were *berlins à quatre chevaux*, carriers' waggons loaded with merchandise either from or to England, countless horsemen civil and military, and innumerable pedestrians, since the accomplishment of long journeys on foot, with a wallet slung on the back, was then one of the most ordinary methods of travelling amongst the humbler classes.

Seated in the *banquette*, or hooded seat, attached to the back of the diligence from Calais to Amiens, on one of these broiling days in June of 1746, were Kate Fane—as now she alone would describe herself or allow herself to be styled—and her father. They had crossed from England in the ordinary packet-boat a day or two before, and were at this moment between Abbeville and Amiens, at which latter place they proposed to remain for the present at least. To look at her none would have supposed that, not more than a week or two before, this golden-haired girl, now dressed in a plain-checked chintz, with, to protect her head from the heat, a large flapping straw hat, had been discarded by the man whom she had imagined to be her husband; had been told that she was, possibly, no lawful wife. For she looked happier, brighter at this time than she had ever done since she went

through a form of marriage with the Viscount Fordingbridge, because—though not in the way that he
had falsely insinuated—she was free of him.

"What was it Archie said to ye?" asked her father
as the diligence toiled up a small hill, the road of
which was shaded by trees from the burning sun.
"What was it he said to ye in the letter you got at
Calais? Tell me again; I like not to think that my
daughter has been flouted and smirched by such a
scoundrel as that. Lawfully married, humph! Lawfully married, he said, eh?"

"Lawfully married enough, father," Kate replied.
"Lawfully enough to tie me to him for ever as his
wife. But," she went on, "lawful or not lawful, nothing shall ever induce me to see him, to speak with him
again."

"Read me the letter," said Fane; "let me hear all
about it."

"Nay, nay," answered his daughter, "time enough
when we get to Amiens, when we shall all meet again.
Oh, the joyful day! The blessed chance! To think
that to-night we shall all of us be together once more!
All! all! Just as we used to be in the happy old times
in the Trousse Vache," and she busied herself with taking a little wine and water from a basket she had with
her, and a bunch of grapes and some chipped bread,
and ministering to the old man.

So, as you may gather from her words, those who
had been in such peril in England were back safe in
France. Bertie Elphinston had crossed, disguised, of
course, as a drover, unmolested by "infernal sloops o'
war and bomb-ketches"—to use honest McGlowrie's
words—or anything else. And, also, the Sholtos had
come in the same way, finding, indeed, so little let or

hindrance in either the river or on the sea, that they began to think the English King's rage and hate against all who had taken part in the late rebellion were slacked at last. They were, in truth, not nearly glutted yet, and the safe, undisturbed passage which they had been fortunate enough to make was due to that strange chance which so often preserves those who are in greatest danger.

Still, they were over, no matter how or by what good fortune, and that night—that afternoon, in another hour's time—all would meet at the Inn, *La Croix Blanche*, in Amiens.

At Calais Kate had learned the welcome tidings; a letter had been given into her hands by no less a person than the great Dessein himself—hotel-keeper, *marchand-de-vin*, job-master, and letter of coaches, chaises, and post-horses, and plunderer of travellers generally!—and in it was news from Father Sholto, as he might safely be called here in France, and from Bertie and Douglas.

Sholto's letter told her all she desired to know, viz., that Fordingbridge's suggestion of his being a priest was a lie, "the particulars of which," the Jesuit wrote, "I will give you at Amiens when we meet." Bertie's, on the other hand, told her—manfully and, of course, as a woman would think, selfishly—that he regretted that it was an implied lie. "Because," wrote he, "had it been the truth, we might have become man and wife within twenty-four hours of meeting, and now we are as far apart as ever." Some other details were also given, such as that Father Sholto was in residence for the time being at the Jesuit College, and that Bertie had rejoined his regiment and was now on duty at the Citadel. Douglas was at the

Croix Blanche, and would take care that suitable rooms were kept for them, though, since it happened to be the great summer fair-time, the city was full of all kinds of people, and rooms in fierce demand at every hostelry.

These letters, received by Kate as they landed from the packet-boat in the canal at Calais, were sufficient to prompt her to lose no time in hastening onward—north. The diligence, she found, left the hospitable doors of Monsieur Dessein at five o'clock on summer mornings, and did the distance of sixty miles to Amiens in eleven hours, which Dessein spoke of approvingly —and falsely—as being the fastest possible. Still they could not afford anything that was faster—for they had little money in their purse these days. Therefore, at dawn, they clambered into the *banquette*, which happened to be vacant, and set out upon their road.

And now, as the diligence skirted the river Somme, and drew near to Picquigny, the towers of the cathedral *Nôtre Dame d'Amiens* came into sight, and the ramparts of the city. And, because it was fair-time, the roads were full of people of all kinds streaming towards it; of market people, with their wares, and waggons of fruit and vegetables, and poultry, of saltimbanques and strolling actors, strong men, fat women, dwarfs, and giants—since in those days fairs were not much different from what they are now, only the play was a little rougher and the speech a little coarser even among the lowest.

Nevertheless, amidst the ringing of the cathedral bells, as well as those of the Collegiate Church and Amiens' fourteen parish churches, the diligence arrived at last, and only one hour late, at the office of the *Poste du Roi*, and there, walking up and down in front of it, were Bertie and Douglas, both in their uniforms, and waiting for them.

"How did you know, Mr. Elphinston," Kate asked, glad of the bustle and confusion in the streets caused by the fair and by the arrival of the diligence, "that we should come to-day? We might not have crossed from England for another week—nay, another month, for the matter of that."

"We should have been here all the same," Bertie replied. "I am not on duty at this time in the day, and Douglas would have come every afternoon. We have watched the arrival of the diligence, Kate, for the last week—since—ever since you wrote to say you were about to set out."

"I did not know I told Archie that."

"No, but you told me. Have you forgotten all you wrote to me, Kate?"

"No," she said, in a low voice, and with her soft blush. "Yet, remember, Ber——Mr. Elphinston—we are as far apart as ever. Archie says I am, in truth, that man's wife."

"I remember," he replied; "I must remember," and he led the way into the inn, which was close by the *Poste du Roi*.

The young men had been fortunate enough to secure a room for themselves and the new arrivals, where they could sit as well as take their meals apart, in spite of the inn being crowded. Nay, those who crowded it now were scarcely of the class who require sitting-rooms, nor, in some cases, bed-rooms even; many of them being very well satisfied to lie down and take their rest in the straw of the stables. For among the customers of *La Croix Blanche* were horse-dealers from Normandy and from Flanders; the performers

at the booths, the strolling actors, mendicant friars—
if friars they were!—vendors of quack medicines, and
all the *olla-podrida* that went to make up a French
fair. These cared not where they slept, while of those
who sought bed-rooms there were *commis voyageurs*,
ruffling gentlemen of the road, bedizened with tawdry
lace, and with red, inflamed faces beneath their bag-
wigs *à la pigeon*—on whom the local watch kept wary
eyes—large purchasers of woollen ribbons and ferrets,
serges, stuffs, and black and green soap for the Paris
market, in the production of all of which things Amiens
has ever been famous, as well as for its *pâté de canard.*
Nor did any of these people require private rooms for
the consumption of their food, but, instead, ate together at the ordinary, or fed in the kitchen among
the scullions and their pots and pans.

Therefore, undisturbed, or disturbed only by the
cries that arose from below, as evening came on and
the guests' table became crowded, Douglas and Bertie
ministered to the wants of Kate and her father, and
compared notes of the passages they had made across
from England. Also they spoke of their future, Kate's
being that which needed the most discussion.

" Prince Edward is safe," said Bertie, " of this there
is no doubt. He is known by those of this country,
though by none in England, to be secure with Cluny
in the mountain of Letternilichk, near Moidart. Off
Moidart is the " Bellona," a Nantes privateer, with
three hundred and forty men on board, and well armed.
She will get him away, in spite of Lestock's squadron,
which is hovering about between Scotland and Brit-
tany. Now, Kate, when he arrives in Paris, as he will
do shortly, his household will be a pleasant one. Your
place must be there."

"In the household of the prince!" exclaimed Kate.

"Ay! in the household of the prince. Nay, never fear. You will not be the only woman. The Ladies Elcho and Ogilvie will be with you; also old Lady Lochiel. Oh, you will be a bonnie party! While, as for Mr. Fane, some place must also be found."

"But who is to find these places?" she asked.

"Archie," replied Douglas. "He has interest enough with Tencin to do anything. Indeed, from finding a post at court to obtaining a *lettre de cachet*, he can do it."

"Why," said Bertie to him aside, noticing that he turned pale as he spoke, "did you shiver then, Douglas, as I have seen you do before now? You do not fear a *lettre de cachet* for Vincennes or the Bastille— and—and—we are not talking of the man at whose name I have seen you shiver before."

"I—I do not know," his companion replied. "It must be that I am fey, or a fool, or both. Yet, last night I dreamt that Archie was asking the minister for a *lettre de cachet* to consign someone—I know not whom—to the Bastille, and—and—I woke up shivering as I did just now."

"It could not be for you, at least," answered the other.

"Perhaps," replied Douglas, moodily, "for someone who had injured me. Who knows?"

Whatever reply his stronger-minded friend might have made to this gloomy supposition, which was by no means the first he had known Douglas to be subjected to, was not uttered since at that moment Archibald Sholto himself entered the room.

His greetings to Kate were warm and, at the same time, brotherly. He, too, remembered how for years the little party assembled now in *La Croix Blanche* had all been as though one family; he remembered the black spot that had come amongst them; that to Fordingbridge, whom he himself had introduced into Fane's house, was owing most, if not all, of the evil that had befallen them. Also he recalled that, but for Fordingbridge's treachery, neither he, nor Bertie, nor Douglas would have been forced to flee out of England for their lives; that Kate would never have forfeited her position nor have had the foul yet guarded suggestion hurled against her that she was no wife, but only a priest's mistress. Then, when their first welcomes and salutations were over, he spoke aloud to her on the subject that, above all, engrossed their minds.

"Kitty," he said, "is Fordingbridge gone mad? For to madness alone can such conduct as 'his be attributed."

"I do not know," she replied. "I cannot say. All I know is that he is a villain and a traitor—that I have done with him for ever. Yet he must be mad when he throws out so extraordinary a hint as that he is a priest. He could not have been a priest, and you not know it—could he?"

Up from the guests' room below there came the hubbub of those at supper, the shouts of the copper captains for more petits pigolets of wine, mixed with the clattering of plates and dishes, the calls of other travellers for food, and the general disturbance that accompanies a French inn full of visitors, as Father Sholto answered gravely:

"My child, he might have been a priest and I not know it; God might even have allowed so wicked a scheme to enter his heart as that, being one, he

should go through a form of marriage with an innocent woman. But, my dèar, one thing is still certain,
he was not, is not, a priest—I know it now beyond
all doubt; you are as lawfully his wife as it is possible for you to be."

"What—what, then, was the use of such a statement, such a lie, added to all the others which—God
forgive him!—he has already told since first he darkened our door?"

"'The gratification of his hate, his revenge against
you and all of us. He hated you because you had never
loved him, and had at last come to despise him; he hated
Bertie because you had always loved him" (as he spoke,
the eyes of those two met in one swift glance, and then
were quickly lowered to the table at which they sat);
"he hated me because I knew him. And, remember,
until he had put himself in the power of Douglas and
Sir Charles Ames by insinuating himself to be what he
was not—a priest—he thought that I should soon be
removed from his path for ever. Once in the power of
the English Government, my tongue would have been
silenced; it would have been hard to prove, perhaps,
that he was not a priest; that you were a lawful married woman."

"Yet, surely, it could have been proved in some
way. And—and—of what avail such a lie to him?
Knowing he is not a priest, he would not have dared
to take another wife."

"Perhaps," replied Sholto, "he had no desire to
take another. If he is not mad, he had but one wish,
to outrage and insult you, and thereby avenge himself
upon you. Moreover, he must have some feelings
still left in him—your very renunciation of him may
have led to his denial of you."

"How have you found for certain that he is no priest?"

"In the easiest manner. A letter to the 'General' at Rome, another to the 'Provincial' at Lisbon, and, lo! a reply from each to the effect that neither under the name of Simeon Larpent nor the title of Viscount Fordingbridge had anyone been ever admitted to the Society of Jesus. At St. Omer, I knew, of course, such a thing could not have happened; nay, I knew more: I knew that neither as novice nor acolyte, even, had Fordingbridge ever been admitted, nor had he submitted to any of those severe examinations which all must pass through ere they can become these alone. As for priest—well, it was impossible, impossible that he could be one and I not know it, never have heard of it."

"So, Kate," whispered Bertie to her, "you are still Lady Fordingbridge. As far apart as ever—as far apart as ever."

"Surely," said she to him, as now they talked alone and outside the general conversation that was going on, "surely it is better so. I have renounced him, it is true; willingly I will never see nor speak to him again; he and I are sundered for ever. Yet—yet—Bertie," and for the first time now, after so long, she called him frankly by the old, familiar name, "I could never have come to you had I been that other thing. You could not have taken such as I should have been for your wife."

He looked at her, but answered no word. Then he sighed and turned away.

They sat far into the evening talking and making plans, while still, through the warm summer night, the noise of the crowded city came in at their windows and nearly deafened them. And this is what they decided upon for the future.

The troop to which Bertie Elphinston belonged in the Regiment of Picardy would be removed, later on, to quarters at St. Denis, and at about the same time Douglas would rejoin his regiment in Paris, while his brother Archibald was about to depart for St. Omer, where he should remain for some time. He had, he said, nothing more to do now in the world, since the restoration he had hoped so much from had failed altogether. Therefore, because at present there was no need for Kate to go to Paris, and because, also, her father became more and more ailing every day, they decided to remain at Amiens, to live quietly there in lodgings, and to have at least the friendship of the two young men to cheer them. There was still a little money left from the sale of Doyle Fane's fencing school in Paris—indeed, it had never been touched since Kate's marriage—which would suffice for their wants, especially since Amiens was cheaper than Paris to reside in. Then, when the time came, they would all move on to the capital, and there, as they told each other, try to forget the black, bitter year which had come and separated them all from the happy life they had once led together.

"Only," said Bertie once again that night to her, ere he went back to the Citadel, "only, still we are parted; the gulf is ever between us. O Kate, Kate! if it were not for that."

And once more for reply she whispered:

"'Tis better so, better than if it had been as he, that other, said. At least I am honest; if—if freedom ever comes, no need for you to blush for me."

"Nay," he said, "none could do that, knowing

all. For myself, Kate, I would it had been as the wretch said. Then the bar would not be there."

"But the blot would."

With which words she left him and the others, going with her father to the rooms prepared for them.

Meanwhile, as now the full night was upon them, the hubbub and the uproar grew greater in the inn. Back from the booths and open-air theatres came the mummers and the mountebanks, the mendicant friars with their pills and potions, balsams, styptics, and ointments, the Norman and Flemish horse dealers— the latter drunk and shouting for more drink—and all the rest. And they distributed themselves about the *Croix Blanche*, as, indeed, they were doing in every other hostelry in Amiens, and laughed and shrieked and howled and cursed as they sought their beds in the straw or the garrets, and turned the ancient city into a veritable pandemonium.

"I will walk with you a part of the way," said Douglas to his brother and Bertie as they rose to depart. "This narrow street is hot and stuffy, especially with the fumes that arise from the revellers below. The night air will be cool and refreshing before sleep."

And buckling on his sword he went down with them, and out through the still crowded inn yard.

At the Jesuit College he parted with Archibald, and went on a little farther with Bertie, and then, saying that he was refreshed with the coolness, bade him also good-night.

"It is good for us all to be together again, Bertie, boy, is it not?" he exclaimed as they shook each other by the hand; "good to think that, with but a few intervals of separation when on service, we shall scarcely ever be parted more. Nothing is wanting now but that you and Kate could come together lawfully."

"That," replied the other, "seems never likely to be permitted to us. Well, we must bear it, hard as it is. Yet, Douglas, I am as honestly glad as you can be that we are safe back in France with all our troubles over."

"Yes," replied Douglas, "with our troubles over. Yet I wonder where that rogue ingrain, Fording-bridge, is?"

He was soon to know.

CHAPTER XVI.

"TREASON HAS DONE HIS WORST."

SOME of those who came to Amiens as attendants upon the fair had not yet sought their beds, whether in the straw of the stables, on the brick floors of the kitchens, or in the sweltering garrets under the red-tiled roofs. Night birds, however, were most of these, creatures who found their account in roaming the streets, seeking whom they might devour. Night birds, such as the bellowing, red-faced bullies who had been shouting all day for drink and food in the *Croix Blanche*, and who, managing to keep sober in spite of all their potations, sallied forth at midnight. For it was then their work began. Then horse dealers, merchants, buyers, dissolute members of the local *bourgeoisie* and the *petite noblesse*, making their way to their lodgings or houses, found themselves suddenly seized by the throat or from behind, and their watches, trinkets and rings taken from them and their purses cut—nay, might deem themselves fortunate if their throats were not cut too.

Once or twice men of this stamp passed Douglas after he had quitted his friend—fellows in soiled finery with great swords by their sides, and with their huge hats drawn down over their faces—who looked at him askance, seeing his sword also by his side and noting his well-knit form and military bearing. But, as they observed his glance fixed keenly on them and his hand ready enough to his weapon, they passed on with a surly "Good-night."

Making his way back to the inn, Douglas came to a sudden halt as he arrived under the *Beau Dieu* on the pillar of the great west doorway of *Nôtre Dame d'Amiens*, for, in the open space in front of that entrance he saw two of these very night birds standing, evidently, as he supposed at first, planning and concocting some villainy. Regarding them from behind a buttress of that old cathedral of Robert de Luzarches, he could observe them and all their movements plainly enough, since the full moon was high in the heavens by now; and, although the towers obscured somewhat the light, a great stream of it poured down into the place before the west doorway and with its rays illuminated the space.

Great brawny fellows they were, he could see; good types of the half swashbuckler, half highwayman of the period—the class of men who would be found one day fighting as mercenaries at Placentia or Raucoux, another robbing a church or some lonely grange, another hung or broken on the wheel, or swinging in chains on a gibbet on some heath or by the seashore.

"By St. Firmin!" he heard one say to the other, while he balanced something in his hand which sparkled in the moonlight as he gazed down at it, "who would have thought the scarecrow had such valuables upon him? *Regardez moi ça!*" and again he moved what he had in his hand, so that it glittered as though on fire.

"'Tis enough," replied the other, "we have done well this fairing. Now for Paris and *vogue la galère!* We have the wherewithal to amuse ourselves for a year. Come, let us ride to-night; to-morrow he may raise a hue and cry. Come, the horses are outside; the gates do not shut till midnight. Hark! it wants but a quarter," he broke off as the big clock above them boomed out that hour. "Come," and clasping his companion's arm they disappeared round the other side of the cathedral.

The first impulse of Douglas was to seize these men, if possible; the next, since they were two to one, to follow them to the gate and there to call on the watchman to prevent their exit. And knowing that some robbery had been committed, perhaps some murder— as was very likely—he was about to put this idea in practice when his action was arrested by what startled him far more than the sight of the two scoundrels regarding their stolen wealth had done.

That which so startled him was a man's form creeping up behind him in the shadow of the cathedral, a man who had come so near to him without his knowing it that, as Douglas turned and faced him, he sprang out at him and endeavoured to seize him by the throat. And as he did so he shrieked out, "Villain, thief, give me back my property! Give it back, I say, or," and he hissed the words out, "I will kill you! See, I am armed: you have left me this," and he brandished a long knife that shone in the moonlight—into which Douglas had now dragged him—as the jewels had heretofore shone.

Of the man himself, nor of his dagger, Douglas had no fear; he was stronger than his antagonist, and his hand held the other's, which grasped the weapon, as in a vice. But what appalled, almost unnerved him, was that he knew the voice—and he knew the man. It was Fordingbridge.

"You fool!" he cried, "do you not know me? I am Douglas Sholto," and as he said the words he felt the other's hold relax, felt him disengage himself and stagger back against the wall of the cathedral, where, the moon lighting up his pale, cadaverous face, he stood gasping and glaring at him.

"Douglas Sholto!" he muttered, whispering to himself, "Douglas Sholto here? So, you herd with thieves and robbers, do you? Where are they gone, those others? Where, where, I say?"

"To the gates, I imagine. Beyond them by now," for as he spoke the hour boomed forth from the clock in the tower above, and was repeated by all the other clocks in the city. "Your property, Lord Fordingbridge, is gone. I cannot say that I am sorry for it, though, had you not come when you did, I was about to follow the men who robbed you and have them stopped at the gate. Now, knowing whom they have despoiled, I can only say I rejoice that for once you have met with scoundrels as great as yourself."

Glowering, staring at him intently, the other leaned back against the cathedral, while from his eyes there shone a light which looked like the light of madness. Nay, in that moment Douglas decided in his own mind that he was mad. Still, so great a villain did he know Fordingbridge to be, that, gentle as he was to all others, he could feel no pity towards him. Instead, he said:

"So, my lord, not content with having nearly sacrificed our lives in England, you have tracked us all to this place, doubtless in furtherance of some scheme of your own, though what it is I cannot even guess. You can harm no one here. Your spite——"

"It is false," said Fordingbridge; "I have done no

such thing. I am myself on the road to Paris"
—he did not say that he was a fugitive from England—"and I have been robbed of all—jewels, money,
bills."

"To Paris!" echoed Douglas. "I am afraid you
will scarcely be welcome there. The base hint you
gave about being a priest will surely lead you into
trouble—for it is a lie, as my brother has discovered,"
and he saw the other start at his words. But he went
on: "Moreover, there are many ardent adherents of
the Stuart cause in Paris. How do you imagine they
will receive the intelligence that you, a supposed adherent yourself, endeavoured to betray three others to
their doom in London? Lord Fordingbridge, take my
advice, do not go to Paris."

In truth, he had no intention of going to Paris, as
has been already told. After much deliberation, when
he stole away from his house at Kensington, and during the time occupied in escaping to France, he had
been meditating much upon where he should live,
where go to until the trouble he had brought upon
himself by his own evil actions should have blown over.
Money he did not want, having a large sum in France
that had been invested by his father, as well as that
which he could procure from his property in England,
and so, at last, he decided that he would for some time
at least take up his abode at Amiens. There he was
comparatively near Paris if he wished at any time to
visit the capital, and at the same time he was but a
day's journey to the seaports of Calais and Boulogne,
should he find it necessary at any time to quit France
suddenly. Full of these ideas, and certain that it
would not be long before he could either return to England or take up his position in Paris, he had come on

to Amiens and was now staying at a larger inn than the *Croix Blanche* under the name of Mr. Chester—which had been his mother's.

He had come out that night, partly driven forth by the shouts and carousings that were going on in his own hostelry in the same manner that they were in all the others in the city, and which, with his brain in the state it had been for some time now, were maddening to him. And partly, also, he had been driven forth by discovering that a large group of English visitors had arrived during the afternoon, the very sight of whom was terrifying to him, since amongst them were· one or two young men of fashion whom he had more than once met at King George's levees. Therefore, he had determined to wander about the city until it was time to go to bed, and then to return and keep his room until the English party had gone on to Paris the next morning and the hubbub of the fair was over. But near the cathedral he had been attacked and robbed of his money and trinkets—which, for precaution, as he imagined, he had kept on his person—and in endeavouring to follow the thieves he had stumbled on Douglas Sholto.

"No one would know that I was in Paris," he said, with a cunning leer in his eyes, as he answered the other's remark. "No one, no one."

"On the contrary," replied Douglas, "everyone would know—Bertie, my brother, your wife, all."

Again the other leered at him with so sidelong a glance, with such a snake-like look, that Douglas, remembering how Archibald had said that night that he must be mad, began to feel sure that he was, indeed, in the presence of a demoniac—a creature whose pursuit of evil had turned his brain. And again, for some reason, the young man shuddered violently as he looked at him, as he had shuddered more than once before.

"No," hissed Fordingbridge, glinting his eyes round the open space in front of the great cathedral, which, with the exception of the spot where they stood, close up by the door, was now bathed in moonlight. "No; they do not know, they will never know. They think I am still in England; that I shall not leave it."

"Indeed! Will they think so to-morrow when I tell them I have met you to-night?"

"Tell them to-morrow! To-morrow?" he whispered. "How can you do that, Douglas Sholto?"

"Very easily. They are all here."

"Here!" He almost screamed the word "here," and his eyes roved round the place as though he thought they might be hiding behind some buttress, or pillar, ready to spring out on him.

"Ay, here. One, who seeks for you ever, at the Citadel, another at the Jesuits' College, and your wife at an inn in the town."

Fordingbridge reeled back against the cathedral walls once more as he heard this unexpected disclosure—he had until now imagined that Douglas was alone in Amiens; and there he stood absolutely paralysed with apprehension. In Amiens! The very place he had selected for a refuge. In Amiens. They would know all to-morrow, all. And he would be brought face to face with Elphinston, who would slay him, he never doubted; with Archibald Sholto, who would denounce him to the Jacobites, of whom there were many in this city as well as Paris; to the Church, which he had slandered by falsely stating himself to be one of

its priests. A Church which, he knew—had reason
enough to know—was sufficiently powerful to resent
any affront to it; a Church which—though the Inquisition had no foothold in France—could make its
vengeance felt. And he remembered he had bound
himself to that Church by many oaths to further the
Stuart cause in England, and had ended by denouncing three of its most active partisans! No need for·
Elphinston to force him to fight; no need for the
Jacobites to take vengeance on him for his treachery;
Archibald Sholto would see that the punishment was
accorded.

As he stood there, while Douglas remained regarding him, he thought it all out as well as his disordered
mind would permit; remembered that but for the
hated form of the man before him they would never
know he was in France. And if they never knew,
then he might remain in peace until things could be
smoothed over in England. But could they be so
smoothed? He must know that first.

"You drove me out of England," he said, or rather
whined; "now you would drive me out of France";
and he folded his hands across his breast as he spoke,
and stood shaking before the other.

"Your own cowardice, your own wickedness, drove
you out," replied Douglas. "Nought else. And, Lord
Fordingbridge, because I would not have you regard
us upon the same bad level as yourself, let me tell you
this: None of us are spies, denouncers, informers.
None. We do not shift from white to black cockade
to save our necks nor to gratify a base hatred. You
were not denounced by us to the English Government
even after your execrable lies at Lady Belrose's; we
but frightened you into silence till we had time to

quit England ourselves. You have been terrified by a bugbear—by your own evil nature."

Alas! poor Douglas. He was no match for this crafty, frenzied villain. He told more than he should. He showed Fordingbridge that England was still open to him; he presented him with the knowledge that, besides himself, there was no one knew of his presence in France.

In a moment the wretch had grasped this fact; in another he had resolved on what he would do. His glittering eye still upon Douglas, who stood there calmly contemptuous, his left hand idly resting on his sword hilt, and his right in the lace of his ruffles, he asked:

"Is this true?"

For answer Douglas shrugged his shoulders and replied, "All men are not born liars."

Alas! poor Douglas. Unready as he was, he had no time to save himself.

With a harsh, raucous cry the other sprang at him; the knife, which he had held hidden in his sleeve so long, gleamed in the moonlight; a moment later and it was buried in Douglas's bosom.

"So," said the assassin, "in this way I am free of France too."

As he struck the unhappy man the latter reeled back three paces and then fell prone in the full blaze of the moonlight, while the murderer, with a hurried glance round, prepared to skulk away in the deep shadow thrown by the cathedral walls on a side street. Yet, as though the horror of the deed he had done were not enough for him to carry away, he knew that it had been observed.

As he turned to fly, he saw looking at him from a

window in a darkened room the white face of a
woman distorted with terror; a face from which the
eyes seemed starting. And, as he crept by the buttress in the shadow, he also saw her raise her finger
and point as though denouncing him.

CHAPTER XVII.

GASCONISM.

THE summer waned, the autumn came, and poor, gentle Douglas lay in his grave, but still his murderer had never been discovered.

Yet in connection with that murderer, or rather in connection with the murder itself, some extraordinary facts had been forthcoming which, after all, but served to surround it more and more with mystery. These you shall hear.

When that white-faced woman, whose threatening finger had pointed at the assassin as he fled, recovered from her horror—she was but a poor concierge who had happened to be seeking her bed—she rushed forth into the open place where Douglas's body lay, and there, with wild and piercing shrieks, awakened all who dwelt round the cathedral. At first she conveyed to those who hurried to the spot the idea that it was she who was the shedder of blood, for, as she threw herself down by the victim's side to see if any spark of life remained, her own white night garments became stained with the dreadful fluid, so that those hurrying to the scene imagined that they saw a guilty woman screaming over her own evil deed.

But as she grew more composed she was able to tell her tale coherently; to relate how, in curiosity, she had stood watching those two conversing there;

how she had seen the blow struck, and the murderer flee into the darkness. She was very poor, she said, every sou was worth taking account of; therefore, on moonlight nights, she sought her bed without candle-light. Yet now she bemoaned her thrift, for had she but burnt a light it might have alarmed the assassin— have saved the unhappy victim.

"But *mort de ma vie!*" exclaimed the chief of the watch, who by this time had arrived with two or three of his subordinates, " why not rush out and follow the man; why not at least open the window and scream? *Peste!* you women can do that if a mouse scampers across the floor or your husband reproves you, yet, behold! when a man is done to death you hold your tongue."

The poor affrighted creature, still whimpering and shivering, explained that she had no thought of mur-der being about to be done; she had supposed they were two friends parting for the night; there was no sign of argument or quarrel, and, when the deed was done, she thought she had swooned for a moment or so. She could say no more.

"*Peste!* " again exclaimed the chief of the watch— a tetchy man given to examining all kinds of charac-ters from midnight revellers and wassailers to house-breakers and worse, " why not do something better than swoon? And I'll be sworn, too, that you would not know the fellow again even though he came back this instant itself."

But to this the woman protested her dissent. She would know him again anywhere, at once or at a long interval, adding with a shudder that "for ever and as long as she should live, his features were stamped into her memory."

"What was he like, then?" asked the chief, "how clad?"

"Fairly tall," she replied, "though not so tall, I think, as *that*," and she glanced at poor Douglas's body lying in the centre of the crowd that surrounded it. The chief of the watch, and a doctor who had come from out a house near, had examined it at once on their arrival, and, alas! there was no life left in it. The gentle spirit had flown.

"Also," she went on, "the assassin was very dark, his eyes of a piercing nature, his face white as a corpse—as *that*," and again she glanced at the dead man; "but the whiteness might be from horror, *mon Dieu!* it was a terrible face, the face of a devil, terror-stricken; the face of a fiend. But no remorse, oh, no! only fear—it might be of himself."

"And his clothes?" asked the chief. "What of them?"

"Sombre, dark. All dark. Scarce any lace at sleeves or breast, neither aigrette nor cockade, nor galloon to his hat; no sword."

"Not a bully, then, nor *filou?* No appearance of a knight of the road? Hein?"

"No," the woman replied, "no." Then, reflectively, she said, "It was, I think, no murder for gain nor greed. Nay, could not have been. He stooped not, went not near the—the body after it fell. More like, I think, a deed of hate, of bitter, hot rage. Who knows? Perhaps a wife stolen, a daughter wronged. All is possible. For see, *it*," and again she glanced down, "was young, and—and, *mon Dieu, il était beau!*"

So they all said who gazed upon the handsome features now setting rigidly in the blaze of the moon. "*Il était beau.*"

"Well," said the chief, "we must not stay here. He must be removed. Meanwhile, I must to the officers of the guard; none must pass the gates at daybreak except under strict scrutiny. And the body must be searched to see if we can gather who and what he is. Alas! alas! The woman speaks well. He was handsome."

But now an exclamation arose from the crowd, while one or two stooped hurriedly to the earth, and the first picked up something that, as he held it out, glistened in his hand. It was an unset stone, a ruby.

" *Tiens*," said the chief, turning it over in his hand, "what's this ? A ruby, and unset," he repeated. Then meditatively, " It may have fallen from a setting worn by one or other, victim or murderer—from, say, a ring, a collar, a brooch for cravat, or ruffle. Has he upon his body," he said to his attendant, "any setting to which it might by chance belong ?"

The man bent down and inspected poor Douglas's form, then he rose and shook his head.

" Neither ring nor chain that I can see. Nought that is likely to have held such as that stone."

" Humph !" mused the chief, "humph !" Then he whispered to himself, " If anyone pass the gate to-morrow with an unfilled setting—bah! *Non! non! non!* He that has the setting belonging to the ruby will scarcely show it. Yet, that the murderer owns it is most likely. If it had been lost by anyone who has lately worshipped here," and he glanced up at the cathedral over which the daffodil dawn was coming now from the east, " there would have been hue and cry enough. *Allons*," he said aloud. "To the watch house. And, *bonne femme*, come you with us to testify."

Then, turning to his underlings, he said, "Bring him with you—find a plank or door. And—and—be gentle with him. *Pauvre garçon!* Has he a mother, I wonder?"

For three or four days the search went on, those whom he had loved so aiding it in every way. Archibald, stern, silent, inwardly crushed; Bertie mad with grief and despair; Kate broken-hearted. The lower parts of the city were ransacked and received visits from the watch and the exempts, but nothing came of it except great discomfort to the denizens thereof. Nothing! And—which perhaps was not strange—never to one of those who had so loved him came the veriest shadow of a thought as to who the murderer was. It was not possible, indeed, that such a thought should come. He, they imagined—if ever in their sorrow they let his foul memory enter their mind—was in England. No, they never dreamt of him. They began, therefore, at last to think, as all the world which went to make up Amiens thought, that some of the outcasts, the thieves and scoundrels who had visited the city at fair-time, had taken his bright young life. Yet, strange to say, if such were the case, he had not been robbed. His pocketbook was on him, his purse untouched. There was little enough in either, it was true, yet, the night-birds would have had them had they been his slayers!

Then, at last, it seemed that the murderers were caught.

There rode up to the south gate, on the fifth day, a sergeant and three troopers of the Regiment of Picardy, and with them they had—bound with ropes—two villainous-looking scoundrels, fellows in stained and tawdry riding coats, with brandy-inflamed faces, one having a broken leg, so that as he sat on his horse he groaned with every movement it made.

The sergeant's story was brief and soon told to the captain of the guard, while Bertie Elphinston, summoned to hear it, stood by hollow-eyed and sad, wondering if he was to learn that in these swashbucklers he saw the assassins of his poor friend.

"*Monsieur le capitaine*," said the sergeant, "by orders received from you we have scoured the roads for the last few days. Then, last night, we put up at the *Dragon Volant*, outside of Poix, and here we found these two *larrons*. This one—this creature here—who calls himself Jacques Potin, was abed with his broken leg, his horse having thrown him; the other one, who names himself Adolphe d'Aunay, was nursing him. *Ma foi!* a strange patient and a strange nursing. From the room they occupied came forth howlings and singings and songs of the vilest, mixed with oaths and laughter sufficient to have awakened their grandfathers in their prison graves. 'Twas this drew my attention to them, *Monsieur le capitaine*. Passing their door, attracted by their roars and singings, I was also led to stop and listen, because, the uproar over, I next heard this conversation: 'Curse you and your leg too!' said he who calls himself D'Aunay; 'if 'twere not for your accident we should have been in Paris now, safe and free with our prize disposed of. Your drunkenness, whereby you got your fall, has ruined all.' '*Mon petit choux*,' said the other, 'bemoan not; here we are snug and comfortable. Our *logement* is good, the food of the best, the wine of the most superior. What would you more? And we have the jewels, which are a small fortune, and the money— *bonnes pieces fortes et trebuchantes*—for our immediate wherewithal. As for the bills and bonds—well, we have destroyed them, so they can tell no tales. *Mon enfant*, be gay.'

"Upon this," went on the sergeant, "I arrested them and found these."

Whereupon the man produced from his pockets numerous gold coins, French and English, Louis d'ors and double Louis d'ors, some gold quadruple pistoles, and a handful of English guineas. And also he brought forth, wrapped in a filthy handkerchief, a considerable quantity of pieces of jewellery containing superb precious stones. There were two necklaces, innumerable rings and bracelets, and a woman's tiara of rubies and diamonds. And from this latter—the rubies and diamonds being set alternately—one of the former was missing.

"Alas!" said Bertie aside to his brother captain, "that proves nothing as regards my poor friend. He possessed no jewels, nor, in the world, one-half of that money. He had nought but his pay and a little allowed him by the Scot's Fund. These men may be his murderers, but all this is the result of another robbery—perhaps another murder."

"Nevertheless," said the captain of the guard, "we will hear their story. Observe, a stone is missing from the tiara, and such a stone was found where your friend was slain." Then turning to the two fellows before them, he said curtly, "Now, your account of yourselves. And explain your possession of all this," and he swept his hand over the plain guard-room table, whereupon the money and the jewellery had been temporarily placed.

"Explain!" exclaimed the man who was called D'Aunay and who appeared to be the boldest of the two—while he regarded the captain with an assumed air of fierceness and disdain. "Explain! What shall I explain? That we are two gentlemen of Gascony."

"*Sans doute*," the captain muttered under his teeth.

"*Oui, monsieur, sans doute*," repeated the fellow, who had overheard his whisper. "Of Gascony, I repeat. From Tarbes, and resident at Paris."

"Amiens scarcely lies on the route between those places," the captain remarked quietly.

"Permit that I make myself clear. We had been to your great fair in this fine city, and, by St. Firmin, had much enjoyed ourselves and were riding back to Paris when, by great misfortune, my friend, who suffers much from a painful and distracting vertigo, fell from his horse. Naturally, I remained to solace and console him, and 'twas there that your sergeant—who, you will pardon me for saying, possesses not manners of the highest refinement and appears to combine the calling of a *mouchard* with that of a soldier—burst in upon our privacy, and has added to his insults by dragging us back here."

"You have your papers, doubtless?" the captain asked.

"Doubtless—at Paris. They are there."

"Is it usual for gentlemen of—of Gascony to travel with such jewellery and gems as these?"

"*Monsieur le capitaine*," said the man named D'Aunay, "you will pardon me if I say that it is usual for gentlemen of Gascony to do precisely whatever it seems best to them. At the same time they are respecters most profound of the law. Therefore, monsieur, if you have had any complaint of jewellery stolen, I am willing to give a more full account of that which is in our possession."

He was a bold villain—yet, perhaps, more of a crafty one. On the road from Paris to Amiens his sharpness had gathered something from the troopers, chatting among themselves, of what they were being brought back for, and he knew that it was for murder, and not robbery, that they were wanted. Therefore, being innocent of the former, he brazened it out as regards the latter, though all the while thinking that there was, probably, as great a hue and cry after those who had robbed the man near the cathedral as those who had murdered the other one.

That the captain of the guard was nonplussed his equally sharp eyes saw at once; and he drew himself up a little more to his full height and regarded the other with a still more assured air of haughty disdain. However, the captain went on:

"There was a murder committed five nights ago in the Place de la Cathédrale——"

"*Nom d'un chien!*" interrupted D'Aunay, "is it murder we are accused of next? Excellent! Go on, monsieur. There are still other crimes in the decalogue."

"No, you are not accused of it. But circumstances require explanation. First to me, afterwards, perhaps, to the law. One circumstance is that in your jewellery," and he emphasised the "your" very strongly, "there is a stone, a ruby, missing from the tiara. Now——"

"It is found?" exclaimed the cunning vagabond, with an admirable assumption of gladness. "Ha! that is well, monsieur; these are joyous tidings. That tiara was my mother's, La Marquise d'Aunay. I am indeed thankful."

"It was found on the spot where the murder took

13

place—the spot where the victim's body was also found."

"*Vraiment!* And that spot was——?" he asked, with still greater coolness.

"I shall not tell you. Indeed, it would be best for you to say what spots you were in on that night."

"On that night; monsieur speaks of which night?"

"The 28th. The last night of the fair."

"The 28th! Jacques, *mon ami*," to his friend, "correct me if I forget to mention any place we visited. *Vonons.* We supped at nine—*tiens*, the *paté de canard* was excellent; we must instruct our cook in Paris to attempt one. Then we visited the theatre, a vile representation of '*Les Précieuses*,' I assure you, monsieur. Next, because in Gascony we never forget, amidst all our troubles of after years, our early religious instruction, we decided to attend the evening service at La Cathédrale; there was a large and reverent crowd, monsieur——"

"*Dame!*" exclaimed the captain, turning to Bertie; "I can do nothing with the fellow." Then, re-addressing D'Aunay, he said:

"I have finished with you, sir. Your next examination will be before the Procureur du Roi," and he ordered the two "gentlemen of Gascony" to be confined in the guard-house until that official should interrogate them.

Yet they were too much even for this astute old lawyer, who had learned his craft in Paris in the Law Courts of the Grand Monarch, as they had learned theirs in half the gaols of France.

D'Aunay insisted first on knowing who charged them with having stolen the jewellery; where the person was who had lost it or had it stolen; and if the unhappy young man who had been so monstrously and cruelly done to death was known, or even supposed, to have been possessed of any similar jewellery? Having achieved victory over the Procureur in this respect, in the doing of which he exhibited such virtuous indignation, accompanied by strange exclamations and shrugs and bangings of the bench in front of him, as to nearly terrify the representative of the law into releasing him, he began on a new tack.

"Summon the good woman," he exclaimed, "who saw the murder done. By St. Firmin, if she says one of us is the man, then to the wheel with us! Also call the watch at the southern gate; if he in turn says that we did not pass through ere midnight—I hear the excellent female places the assassination after the first quarter past the hour had struck—then, I say, to the wheel with us! *Sacré nom d'un chien!* were ever gentlemen treated thus before? *Sacré mille tonnerres,* is this France in which we are?"

The woman was summoned, and instantly replied, "No, neither of the messieurs before her was the man. No resemblance whatever. She was certain. That face she could never forget. It was a devil's. On her most sacred oath, neither were concerned in the awful scene."

The watchmen at the gate affirmed that both men passed out before midnight struck—the hour for the gate to close on *fête*-days. There was no possibility of his being mistaken—one, the big man, swore at him for having half closed the gate, thinking the last person had gone through for that night; the other insulted him and jeered at him, and flung a sou at his feet.

"So," said the old Procureur du Roi, "you seem free of this crime. Yet, I misdoubt me but you are the lawful prey of the gibbet. The sergeant heard you speaking of your plunder. That you have stolen the jewellery no one can doubt——"

"Produce the owner," interrupted D'Aunay, on whom a clear light had now dawned. "We ask nothing but that."

"Also you swear by St. Firmin. He is a saint of Picardy, not of the south of France."

"It would be strange if I did not swear by him. In the few hours we were here we heard everyone we met swear terribly by him. He must, indeed, be a saint of Picardy—*surtôut* of Amiens."

"Also," went on the judge, "you spoke truth when you said you had been to the theatre and to the Cathedral——"

"Naturally, monsieur. It is ever my habit. To shun the truth is impossible to me."

"But your actions were suspicious. Both at the theatre and the cathedral you were observed to place yourselves, to force yourselves, nearest to those who presented the appearance of greatest wealth——"

"*Finissons!*" roared D'Aunay now in virtuous indignation. "Enough. Produce more tangible reasons for this detention, these insults, or release us. Your charges have all fallen to the ground; you now begin a fresh one equally baseless. Yet, because I love justice and respect the law—its administrators I cannot always respect—if anyone has been robbed at either theatre or church, bring them forward, and we will meet that charge too."

"You will be released," said the Procureur; "you are now free. But the jewellery will be retained for the present. Later on it may be returned to you."

So, not without many protestations, the fellows

went away from Amiens, D'Aunay breathing maledictions against the barbarous laws which permitted honest gentlemen to be arrested and their property confiscated. Yet, he swore, the end was not yet arrived at; when they reached Paris they would soon set the highest legal authorities at work. Also he edified the good people of Amiens by the tenderness and care with which he assisted his suffering friend to mount his horse.

Later in that day they halted for an evening meal on the cool grass at the wayside, and, as D'Aunay helped his comrade from his wallet, he said:

"Jacques, *mon ami*, observe always the advantage of truth. Had I not mentioned our visit to the cathedral in the earlier part of the evening that cursed ruby would almost have sunk us." Then he wagged his head and took a drink of wine.

"Yet," he continued, "I understand it not. Let us consider. We took the plunder close by the cathedral. In front of the cathedral that other one was slain. None claim the jewels—*peste!* 'tis hard to lose them. What do you make of it?"

"A fool can see," replied Jacques, as he shifted his wounded leg into an easier position. "Any fool can see that. It was our friend who——"

"Precisely," said D'Aunay. "Precisely. *Allons!* To Paris."

"And the ruby fell out when we were examining the spoil!"

"Again, precisely. And remember, Jacques, that if we ever meet our friend who once owned the jewels it would be worth while attacking him. Also, above all, Jacques, remember the truth is best. *Allons!* To Paris!"

CHAPTER XVIII.

"WHAT FACE THAT HAUNTS ME?"

AFTER that all hope was given up of discovering who had murdered Douglas. From the first, from the moment Bertie saw the jewels taken from the two vagabonds by the sergeant, he felt that neither of them were the culprits. Yet, all asked each other whenever they met, "If not these scoundrels, who then?"

"He had no enemy in France, in the world," said Bertie, as they sat one night in the lodgings which Kate had hired for her father and herself. "Why, why should any creature have taken his life? In his regiment he was most popular—nay, beloved. Oh! oh! I cannot understand it."

And now, since, as has been said, the summer was waning—for Douglas had been dead three months when they talked thus—their little circle was about to be broken up once more. One was gone for ever, they said in whispered tones, he could never come back; could those who still remained be once more united after they separated at Amiens?

Bertie, with his troop and one other of the Regiment of Picardy, was to proceed to St. Denis; Kate and her father were to go to Paris; Archibald was to remain behind at Amiens.

Over the latter a great change had come since his

brother's death.   He had always been a quiet and reserved man—perhaps from the very nature of his calling—one who never said more than was absolutely
necessary to any person on any subject; now he
seemed to have retired entirely within himself and to
have but two things in this world to which his life was
devoted : his Faith, and his determination to find the
murderer of Douglas.

"And," he said to Bertie, "I shall do it.   Have no
fear of that.   I shall do it.   I have now an idea—
though an idea of so strange, so extraordinary a
nature, that I hardly dare to let myself believe that it
can ever take a tangible shape."

"And may I, may Kate, know nothing of that idea ?
Remember how we both loved him."

"No," Sholto replied.   "No.   It may come to
nothing—must, it almost seems certain, come to
nothing.   Yet, if the secret can be unravelled, I will
find the way to do it.   Then, when I am sure, if ever
I am, you shall know all.   Nay, you will most as-
suredly know all."

"Will you tell us—tell me—no more than this ? "
asked Bertie.

"I will tell you nothing.   It is possible I may be
mistaken ; more than possible.   If I am not, then you
will know."

And with this the other had to be content, and
to prepare to proceed to his new quarters outside
Paris.

The Jesuit's idea was, indeed, one about which he
might well say that he could not believe it should ever
assume a tangible shape.   It was nothing else than
that he believed he had seen those jewels—especially
that tiara—before.

He had examined them many times since they had been taken away from D'Aunay and his companion and kept in the custody of the Mayor of Amiens—had turned them over and over in his hands; scrutinised the settings to see if he could observe any mark or inscription upon them. But there was nothing—no coronet engraved inside the tiara with a name, or initials, such as might well have been looked for in such costly gewgaws—nothing! Yet the tiara forced itself upon his memory, seemed to be a thing he had seen before—worn upon a woman's head at some great ceremony. Especially he seemed to remember one diamond to the extreme left of the diadem, a yellow, light brown stone that had flashed out a different light from its fellows beneath the gleams of many-lustred candelabras. But where? Where? Where?

"Almost," he whispered to himself, "I seem to see, as through a mist, the head, the face that was beneath it. Dark hair, grizzled grey; pale olive complexion; lines of care. Who was it? Who? If I could remember that."

At night as he lay upon his truckle bed, or as he walked by the banks of the Somme, or held the jewels in his hands—for more than once he went to see them —he mused on all this. Nay, when the memory of his beloved brother and his cruel death was more than usually strong upon him, he would ponder upon the idea that was ever in his mind as he stood at night, solitary and alone, in the Place de la Cathédrale before the great west door, and on the very spot where his loved one had fallen. But still memory failed him, or, as he came near believing now, he was the sport of a delusion.

Practised by long training in every mental art, he

took next to recalling each scene of splendour—for in some such scene it was, he felt sure, that he had seen that gleaming hoop worn, if he had ever seen it at all —in which he had ever taken part from the time he had been ordained a priest, from the time when, an ardent enthusiast of the Stuart cause, he had mixed in the great court circles. Scenes at Versailles, at Marly and Vincennes, St. Germain and Fontainebleau—for he had been amidst them all—were recalled carefully, yet still the phantom of the dark-haired woman with the threads of grey running through that hair evaded him. He had known so many such, he told himself, wearily; had seen so many women to whom jewels and adornments were the natural accompaniments, that, perhaps, it was not strange he should forget. Also, he reflected, how easy for him, who had seen countless jewelled head-dresses worn, to imagine that he remembered this particular one !

Yet he could swear he remembered that yellow, brown diamond !

Tortured thus by his struggles with the dim shadows of his memory, he bade farewell to the others as they departed, and left him alone in the city so bitterly dear to him.

"Farewell, Kate," he said, "farewell. God bless you ! You are separated, as I think, for ever from a man utterly unworthy of you; yet you have still the consolation of being without dishonour—ay, without speck or blemish. He will never trouble you again, I do believe. Let him, therefore, go his evil way, and go you yours in peace and happiness. I would that I could see a way to your obtaining the one happiness that should belong to you; wish it for your sake and Bertie's. But it cannot be. Not yet, at least. There-

fore bear up. Heaven in its mercy will, I know, protect and prosper you."

"Good-bye, good-bye, Archie," Kate replied, as she
sobbed unrestrainedly. "Oh, how unhappy we are!
We looked forward to so much in this meeting here,
and see—see how it has ended! Shall we ever be
happy again?"

"In Heaven's mercy," he said, "in Heaven's mercy."
Then he kissed her on the brow, shook hands with her
father, and went his way back to his gloomy life, and
now still more gloomy thoughts. Yet never in those
thoughts—no, not even though they had sometimes
spoken of the man himself—did it dawn upon him
that here was the one who might be the murderer of
Douglas.

Bertie was already gone, the two troops of the Regiment of Picardy having marched out a day or so before, the blare of their trumpets and the clatter of the
horses' hoofs having awakened the city early. And he
had seen Kate—dawn though it was—glancing from
her window to look at him, to wave him her farewell.

"Yet," he had said to her overnight, "it must not
be for long, Kitty. It seems to me that we grow
nearer to one another as trouble falls—at least, there
can be no assassin's knife to come between us. Kate,
I shall come and see you as often as I can get leave to
visit Paris; even though you are in a King's—a future
King's—house, as I still hope—I may come. Is it
not so?"

"Yes," she said, "you may come always. Oh,
Bertie, we are parted for ever—our lives, our hopes,
all—yet if I could not sometimes see you, know that
you are well, happy—you will be happy, will you not,

when this great sorrow is eased by time?—I think I should die. Surely it cannot be wrong, remembering what we once were to each other, what we once were to have been, to wish to know and hear of you."

"What we once were to have been!" he repeated, in almost a whisper. "To have been. O Kate! O Kate! Those plans, those projects for the future!" His voice broke and failed him as he continued: "You have not forgotten them! Kate, do you remember how once we pictured ourselves growing old together, how we meditated on the time that should come when, our lives done with, we should rest together in some calm and peaceful grave?"

"No," she said, "no," and sprang to her feet excitedly. "No! no! no! I will not remember—will recall nothing, for if I do I shall go mad. Remember nothing—'tis best so. Go, Bertie Elphinston, go to your duties, as I will go to mine. Let us forget everything—except—except——" she faltered, changing in a moment womanlike—"that it was I who ruined and cursed both our lives."

He soothed her as best he could, reproaching himself for having revived such memories; reproaching himself, too, for the silence that had led to her believing him false. And once he said, as he had said in England when first they met again:

"Mine was the fault, let mine be the blame. Yet, unhappily, both have had to suffer. Surely something must arise to end that suffering ere long."

He did not know it, could not, indeed, know it; yet the end was far off still. There were more vigils of sorrow to be kept by both, more grief and pain to be endured.

Nor when she said between her tears, "If we were

to be parted again now, if I should never see your face more, my heart would break," could she know what lay in front of them—black, dark, and lowering.

Her future was in a way provided for. The Cardinal Tencin, in spite of being somewhat out of favour now and retired to his archbishopric of Lyons—for when a French prelate was in disgrace his punishment was that he should attend to his diocese instead of being in Paris!—had still entire influence over the exiled Stuarts. Therefore it was to him that Archibald Sholto applied on behalf of Kate, and through him that she was to be appointed to the small court now being formed round Charles Edward in Paris.

That unhappy prince—though fortunate in some things, especially in his escape from Scotland after the rebellion—had now landed at Roscort, three leagues west of Morlaix, from the " Bellona," of St. Malo, and was safe once more in Paris. His adventures since the defeat of Culloden had been truly marvellous, and his escapes not less so ; twice he was in danger of being shot, five times in danger of being drowned, nine times he was pursued by men of war and armed vessels of King George, and six times he escaped being captured by what seemed to be miracles. Also he had been almost famished for want of food and drink, and had had to lie out on the bare heaths or wild mountains and to shelter in caves.

Yet now he had entered Paris again, had been graciously welcomed by the French King and Queen, and was in treaty for a fine house in the Quartier St. Germain. It was to that house that Kate, with her father, was to go, there to form two of his small court.

At first when she took up her residence in it she was happy. She was among friends she had known in Paris, many of them also comrades of Bertie who had fought in the last invasion and themselves escaped. The Lords Ogilvie and Elcho were there with the ladies of their family; there, too, were old Lochiel and young Lord Lewis Gordon; the young Lochiel also, and Captain Stafford, who had lain long in Newgate in irons, yet was now escaped and free.

Also she was happy because Bertie was able to come and see her, and on one occasion, with all the othres, including herself, accompanied the prince when he went to pay his respects to Louis at Versailles.

" Faith, Kate," he whispered to her on that evening, when, Charles Edward being at supper with the royal family, they strolled together up and down the mirrored galleries of the palace, " 'tis even better than the old days, were it not that dear Douglas has left us," and he sighed. " But," he went on, " you are provided for—that, at least, is well, or as well as things are ever likely to be."

She said, " Yes, it is well, so far." Then she continued :

" Still, Bertie, I am unhappy."

" Unhappy ?"

" Yes. Unhappy because I never know when that man—my husband—may cross my path again. Oh, if I could be sure I should never see him more!"

" At least he can never harm or annoy you. Have no fear of that. Remember, he knows that Archibald and I are in Paris, and, of course, believes that Douglas is here also. His dread of us will keep him away. He will trouble you no more. And if he should come

—which is of all things most unlikely—why, I shall be near at hand to shield and protect you."

"You will always be near me?" she asked. "Always now? Oh, promise, Bertie; promise me that you will never disappear again."

"Of course, I promise. Why, where should I go to?" and he laughed as he asked. "My life is now bound up with the regiment. Short of campaigns nothing can take me far from you."

"Yet," she replied, "I fear—fear always. It is only when you are near that I feel safe—feel that I have one who is a brother to stand between me and harm."

"Yes," he said, "as a brother. It can never be anything else than that now—yet, as a brother, I will not fail you."

So they went back to Paris as they had come, the royal visit being over.

And then it seemed at last as if, with some few changes, things were to be almost as they had once been, though it is true that, instead of the old house in the Rue Trousse Vache, she and her father were lodged in a mansion which was in fact a palace, that Douglas was gone out of their life forever, and that she was a wife in name, though nothing else.

Bertie came at least once a week to Paris from St. Denis, both to pay his respects to his prince—as he regarded always Charles Edward—and also to see her, and brought her flowers from the gardens round that old town. But he brought no news from Archibald as to his having been successful in discovering who the murderer of Douglas was. The priest had, indeed, written to them once or twice from Amiens, but he either refrained from mentioning the subject at all, or, if he did so, said that he could discover nothing, and that any idea he might have had on the matter was, he now feared, a futile one.

"I began to also fear," Bertie said, as he talked it over with Kate, "that it was indeed a futile one—that never now will he be avenged. Poor Douglas! Who could have desired his life—who have struck so foul a blow?"

"It must have been," she answered, "as we at first thought, a murder in the hope of robbery afterwards."

"Or," said Bertie, "as sometimes I think now, the offshoot of another—an undiscovered murder. What if those vagabonds who called themselves Gascon gentlemen had previously slain someone else who was possessed of all that jewellery, and Douglas had come across them at the time, and, in endeavouring to save that other, was slain himself?"

"No," she said, "no. That is impossible. No other victim's body was found, and there was no place where they could have hidden it away, or, having hidden it, could not also have disposed of his. Besides, remember: The woman—the concierge—saw only one other slay him, and that other was neither of the Gascons. Nor was his sword drawn. No, we must seek elsewhere for the solution of that crime."

Thus they talked it over and over whenever they met. Surely it was natural that they should do so, seeing how much he had been to them, and how awful a blow his assassination was, but never did they arrive at any thought or idea of who was the actual murderer.

And, as they so discussed it day by day, the autumn departed as the summer had done, and the winter was almost upon them. Already the leaves lay in heaps at the roots of the trees, the swallows were all gone, the nights were long and dark, and Douglas slept un-avenged in his grave. And still the troubles, the griefs and sorrows of this luckless man and woman were not yet at an end.

Another blow was still to fall upon them—it was close at hand now, though they knew it not.

CHAPTER XIX.

"WHICH WAY I FLY IS HELL—MYSELF AM HELL!"

IT was the feast of St. Denys, the patron saint of France.

Over all the land, from north to south and east to west, the churches and cathedrals were crowded on that day with worshippers bringing offerings and gifts to the altars, praying for the saint's aid to be still continued to them, asking for pardon for past sins, for prosperity in the future. On that day the King himself went in state to Notre Dame, accompanied by his brilliant court. In the provinces, governors of fortresses and of departments did the same thing at the local cathedrals; prisoners were released because of the anniversary of St. Denys, while some of the worst among them were executed—both as an example, and because it was the great *fête*-day and a holiday when other people required to be amused.

In Amiens, as in all the other cities boasting a beautiful cathedral and possessed of a strong religious element, it was the same as elsewhere. From morning until night the bells clanged at intervals from the towers of Notre Dame and the fourteen parish churches; processions innumerable took place, masses of all kinds—Capitular, Conventual, Missa Cantata, Missa Fidelium, Mass High and Low—were said and sung, accompanied by Kyrie, Gloria, and Credo, by Sanctus, Benedictus, and Agnus Dei.

But at last all was over—of a religious nature. The crowds that had filled Notre Dame d'Amiens were streaming out to other forms of celebration of the *jour de Patron*. It was the turn of the theatres now and the family gatherings, of the dance and song and jest among the better classes; the turn of the supper party and the wine-shop and the *courtesan* for the remainder of the day—or rather night.

Yet, for those who still were willing to continue their religious devotions, still to regard the occasion more as a fast than a feast, the opportunity presented itself and was availed of by many. In every church in the city, in the cathedral above all, worshippers still knelt in prayer, though the hour grew late; at the confessionals hidden priests still listened to the sins —real or imaginary—of those who knelt before them.

In that cathedral with, still lingering about it, the odour of the incense that had been used that day, with the organ still pealing gently through the aisles, while at intervals the *voix céleste*, in flute-like tones, seemed almost to utter the soul's cry, "Oh, Agnus Dei, qui tollis peccata mundi, miserere mihi!"—those confessors sat there, and would sit until midnight struck, to listen to and absolve all those who sought for pardon.

"My son," came forth the muffled voice of one, his face being hidden in the impenetrable darkness in which he sat—a darkness still more profound since many of the lights in the great edifice had either been extinguished or had burnt themselves out, "the confession is not yet all made. Therefore, as yet there can be no absolution. Confess thy sins! Continue!"

Kneeling outside, the stricken creature thus addressed, its wild hair streaming down its back and meeting with the other unkempt hair on cheek and chin, its eyes gleaming, like a hunted animal's, around and up and down the dusky aisles, and glancing at pillars as though fearing listeners behind each, went on:

"My life, oh, holy father, was in his hands. He knew all; knew I was in France, and that he could give me up to justice to those whom I had wronged. Oh, father, *mea culpa, mea culpa!* Absolve me! absolve me!"

"Tell first thy sin," the muffled voice said again. "Thou hast not yet told all. Deceive not the Church. Confession first, then absolution."

The penitent groaned and wrung his hands, threw back the locks from his face, and then, with that face pressed close to the confessional, hissed in a whisper:

"Father, I was mad—am mad, I think. I was sore wrought; but half an hour before I had been assaulted and robbed by two villains of much wealth in jewels —and—and—I feared he would denounce me for my crimes, make my presence known. So, holy father— in my frenzy, in my fear—I struck him dead. I slew him. Have mercy on me, God!"

"Where slew you him?" the priest's stifled voice continued.

"There, father—without, by the west door. Oh, pardon, pardon, that here, on holy ground that should be sanctuary, I took his life!"

It seemed almost to the wretch outside the confessional that the priest had uttered a gasp, had started in his seat, as he heard these words; yet presently he spoke again:

"The victim being the young Scots officer found murdered more than three months past?"

"'Tis so, holy father. 'Tis so. Oh, pardon! Pardon me! *Mea culpa, mea culpa!*"

"What restitution have you made?" the voice was heard to ask. "What restitution propose to make?"

"I know not what to make, father. I cannot call him back to life. What can I, must I do?"

"Have you wronged others—man, woman, or child? Think! trifle not with the Church. There are, doubtless, others."

"Oh, father, I have been an evil liver—a bad husband; bad friend. Set my feet but in the right way! show me the path. And oh! father, absolve me of this sin of blood. Above all, that!"

"Confess all," the priest said, "confess all."

Then, still shivering there, while more and more the shadows grew within the great temple and it became more and more empty, the wretched assassin went on, though ever and again glancing behind the stately column and pillars as though fearing that unseen listener. He told how, determined to gain possession of a woman whose beauty maddened him—the more so because she despised him, or, at least, regarded him not—he had tricked her into the belief that the man she really loved had jilted her. Also how, when even that brought them no nearer, he had married her. How, later on, when wearied and exasperated by her hate and scorn, he had denied her as his wife, hinting that he was himself a priest; yet it was a lie, for he was no priest, having never been more that a lector.

"Almost," came forth the confessor's voice again, "art thou beyond absolution—beyond pardon."

"No! no! no!" wailed the wretch.

"Twice hast thou used our holy Church to aid in thy deceit. First, when thou suborned a villain and caused him to pretend he had performed the holy office of marriage; next, when thou falsely claimedst the office of priest to disavow thy lawful wife. Man, how shall I absolve thee? Yet, be more careful, or thy soul is lost for ever. Hast thou done more evil than this, committed more outrages against the Church?"

Because, perhaps, the wretched creature was half mad with terror now, with a new terror for his soul—whereas before he had but feared for his body—he told all that he had done; how, indeed, he had still further sinned against the Church in that he had set on foot a plot having for part of its intent the ruin of a priest of that Church, a Jesuit, one Sholto. It was all told at last.

For so long did the confessor sit silent in his unseen place that the miserable penitent, thinking no absolution would come forth to him, began to tremble, even to weep, and to call on him again for pardon and for pity. But at last the other spoke:

"Art thou well-to-do in the world?" he asked. "What are thy means?"

Yes, he said he was well-to-do; he had large means in both England and France. What portion should he set aside to appease both God and the Church?

"All," answered the priest. "All."

"All!" he gasped. "Go forth a beggar!"

"All. Ay, all. Better go forth a beggar, stand naked in the market-place, than strip thy soul of its last chance of salvation."

"All!"

"To the last sol, the last dénier—excepting a provision for thy unhappy wife. Thou art the shedder of blood, the blasphemer of the Church and its holy offices, thy soul is clogged with guilt. I know not, even then, and with all else that thou must do, if it can ever find expiation."

"Say not so, father; absolve me, pardon me! See! see! I will do it. Before God I swear, in this His house, that I will do it! I will become a beggar, part with all. Only, father, give me His pardon. Pardon, and set me free!"

"Yet, still more," said that voice, "must thou do. Listen!"

And from his lips there fell so deep a charge that the murderer, kneeling there, knew that to save his soul in heaven he must forego all hopes of future peace on earth. Nevermore was he to touch meat nor aught but the coarsest black bread, never drink but water, never sleep soft, nor lie warm again. And there was worse even than that. He was to go forth to wild, savage parts of the world, there to pass the rest of his existence in trying to preach God's goodness and mercy to the heathen who knew Him not. On the promise that he would do this the priest would give him absolution; otherwise he would refuse it, and his soul must go to everlasting perdition.

He promised, and he was absolved!

Still sitting there, the last in the cathedral that night—for all were gone now except those who were to guard it until midnight had struck—he became the prey of even worse horrors than he had been before; he was absolved as regards his soul, yet into his mind a new fear had arisen for his body—a fear that became a spectre. He had thought that once or twice he had recognised in the tones of the priest's voice some that were familiar to him; now he felt sure that they were. He had confessed to his bitterest enemy on earth—to Archibald Sholto! to the brother of the man whom he had murdered!

This was the meaning of the awful doom passed on him—the doom of ruin, beggary, and starvation, of expatriation to wild and savage lands. To him! He had confessed to him of all others! Yet, was it so, or was he, in truth, mad? He had heard of madmen who knew that they were mad and who could yet be so cunning as to contend with that madness, wrestle with it, subdue it—for a time. Let him do so now. Let him think it all out. Was it, in truth, Archibald Sholto?

It might well be.

For three months he had been in hiding in a small village near Amiens, watching over the course of events connected with his assassination of Douglas, avoiding, above all others, yet keeping them ever under his own view, two persons. One was Archibald, the other the woman who had seen his face on that night—the white-faced woman in the darkened room who had raised her finger and pointed as he did the deed.

"Avoided them," he muttered now, as he sat there in the dark, watching the sacred lamp that burned unceasingly above the high altar, but still engaged always in peering into the deep shadows and blackness in which the huge pile was now enveloped—"avoided them. O God, how have I avoided them! Yet, drawn irresistibly to where they were. Little does he know how I have seen him officiating at his own church, or she how I have passed her close, though unseen; even peered into her room at night from the street, when, dragged here by—by—the fierce desire

to stand again upon the spot where—where he fell.
Once, too, she felt, unwittingly, my presence. As I
brushed against her in the street she shuddered and
drew back from me. Something revealed that one
accursed had touched her."

He moaned aloud as he sat there, his head buried
in his hands; then, because his mind was now disordered and he was half mad, half sane, a smile came on
the evil face that he turned up as the moon's rays
came through the great rose window and lighted all
the nave. "Yet," he murmured, "it was in the confessional under the seal of confession. If it was
Douglas's brother, he can do naught. Naught! Confession is sacred. That seal cannot be broken. But
was it he? Was it? Was it?

"His face I could not see, but the tones were like
unto his," he continued. "And once he started—I
am certain of it. O God, have I told his brother
all? His brother! His brother!"

Above, from the great tower, there boomed the
striking of the hour—midnight. And again he shuddered and moaned and whispered with white lips:

"The very hour, the hour that I cannot hear, can
never hear again, without agony and horror unspeakable. The hour told by the same clock that told it on
that night of blood. I must go," he wailed in low,
broken tones, "must go there. He draws me to the
spot; I see his finger beckoning me nightly. His eyes
met mine once, a month ago, as I reached Paris. I
thought I was free and had escaped, yet they dragged
me back to this accursed spot. I must go. I must go.
He waits for me. Ever—ever when the moon is near
her full. I am absolved by him, his brother, yet he is
always beckoning me and makes me go."

A hand fell on his shoulder as he sat there, and he started up with almost a shriek, and with his own hand thrust in his breast—perhaps to draw some hidden knife, perhaps to still the leap his heart gave.

"Monsieur," a voice said, the voice of the old sacristan, "permit that I disturb your pious meditations. But all are gone now, including the priests. The cathedral is about to close."

"Yes, yes," he muttered low, "I will go. I will go. I have stayed too long."

"By the west door, if it pleases monsieur. It is the only one open."

"The west door," the terrified creature muttered as he left the old man putting out the last remaining lights, and so made his way towards the exit indicated. "By the west door. It must needs be that. It is the nearest to the spot, and he will be there waiting for me, the moonlight shining in his glittering eyes as he beckons me to him, the glare of reproach in them. I must go. I must go."

Down the long aisle he crept, shaking as with a palsy as he went, starting and almost crying out again as a bat flew by and brushed his hair with its wings, going onward to what he dreaded to see, the phantom of the murdered man which his distracted brain conjured up nightly.

"He will be there," he muttered again. "He will be there."

He reached the great west door—striking against the bell ropes hanging in the tower, and gasping at the contact—and then paused at the wicket let into the door, dreading to go out through it to meet the ghostly figure that he knew awaited him.

Still, it must be done, and with another gasp, a

smothered groan, he stepped out through the wicket into the shadow thrown by the cathedral wall, and gazed upon the moon-illuminated spot where Douglas had fallen dead.

And once more he smothered a shriek that rose to his lips.

Standing above that spot, its back to him, but as he could tell by the bent head, gazing down upon it, there was the figure of a man—a man still as death itself ; a man bare-headed.

"You have come again," he hissed in terror. "Again ! Again ! Mercy ! Mercy !

Swiftly the figure turned and faced him—its eyes glistening in the moonlight as he had said—and advanced towards him.

"Douglas !" he screamed. "Douglas ! Mercy !"

"No," the figure said. "No. Not Douglas. Archibald."

CHAPTER XX.

AVENGED.

HE had fallen grovelling to the earth as that figure turned its face towards him, and now he remained in the same position.

As he did so Archibald Sholto knew for certain that he had found his brother's murderer. In the moment of witnessing that frenzied terror there had flashed into his mind the knowledge of who had been the wearer of the tiara with the one yellow-brown diamond in it; the recognition of the dark head streaked with grey with which his thoughts had been filled for weeks, yet without certainty—the head of the murderer's late mother! He knew all now. She it was who had worn the diadem in the great ceremonies he had taken part in; the rejoicings at the peace of '38, the almost equally great rejoicings at the death of the Emperor Charles, and many others. She, Lady Fordingbridge, his mother, had worn it often; often had he observed the strange light emitted by that blemished jewel; and now, from the tiara in which it still remained, a ruby was missing, and had been found on the spot where his brother had been done to death. Therefore he knew that that brother's assassin was before him. God had given him into his hands.

He bent forward over the crouching creature at his feet; in a low voice he said:

"So, I have found you, Simeon Larpent. Even though you are armed to-night as you were on that other night; even though you bear about you the weapon with which you slew him, you cannot escape me."

"You can do nothing," the other said, turning up an evil eye at him and then rising to his feet—"nothing! Your tongue is sealed. What I confessed was under the sanctity of the confessional; you dare tell naught."

At once the Jesuit's clear mind grasped the facts —at once he perceived that the murderer had been cleansing his soul before a confessor—and thought that he was that confessor.

"I told you all," Fordingbridge went on, "all, all. And you absolved me, pardoned me, though the punishment you meted out to me was hard. Have you not vengeance enough? To go forth a beggar and an outcast—to wander in savage lands until I die— surely, surely, that is enough. Let me go in peace."

"Not yet," Archibald Sholto answered; "not yet."

"Not yet!" the other repeated. "Not yet! What more would you have? All is told—you know all now. Shall I repeat what I said in there? I slew him here upon this spot because he would have warned you and Elphinston that I was in France, and—you absolved me. It is enough."

"You slew him here upon this spot," the Jesuit said, and he pointed with his finger to the place, " upon this spot. You acknowledge it?"

"Have I not said? You have absolved me." It was strange how, from the repetition of this phrase, he seemed to take comfort. "You have absolved me."

"You are mistaken," the other said, while as he spoke he drew nearer to the murderer, though keeping ever a wary eye upon him. "Mistaken! I have heard no confession for a week."

"What!" exclaimed Fordingbridge, springing back a step or so, while now his eyes glared round the deserted cathedral place—again like the eyes of some hunted or trapped wild beast. "What! It was not you in there? Not you!"

"No. Not I. Simeon Larpent, you are doomed. You divulged your crime under the seal of the confessional in the cathedral; you have divulged it openly here with no such seal to protect you. Murderer! You are in my power!"

As he spoke he saw the other do that which he had been anticipating. He saw his hand steal to his breast; he knew that he was searching for some weapon concealed there. But he feared him not; he, too, was armed. Ever since he had sought for the assassin he had carried about with him a small pistol, knowing that if, by any strange chance, fortune should throw him across the villain's path, such weapon might be needed. To-night he had come out to gaze again on the place where the deed had been done, never thinking, never dreaming, that there of all places on the earth that murderer should be found, yet not neglecting the precaution of being armed. Now that precaution stood him in good stead.

"Draw no hidden weapon from your breast," he said, as he saw the hand go to it; "remember, I am not as Douglas was, but am forewarned; and if you bring forth one, I will slay you here on the spot as you slew him, and save the hangman his office," and as he spoke he showed the other the little inlaid pistol, its barrel glistening in the moon's rays.

"You know nothing," the other hissed at him now, "nothing. I have told you nothing—you have no witnesses. My word is as good as yours, even if I let you take me—which I will not," he continued, "which I will not."

"No witnesses?" said Archibald; "no witnesses? Nay, look behind you. Look! I say. No other witness is required."

Affrighted at his words—thinking, perhaps, that the terrible spectre that haunted him always now might be standing menacingly behind him—he glanced round, and what he saw struck nearly as much horror to his crime-laden brain as could have done the ghost of his victim.

Advancing from an open door by the side of the cathedral there came a woman, her face white as any ghost's or leper's, her eyes distended, her hand uplifted and pointing at him. Indeed, so appalling was her ghastliness, the whiteness of her face being made doubly so by the rays of the moon falling upon it, that the dazed, stricken creature hid his own face in his hands and recoiled as she advanced.

"It is he," she said. "It is he. Nightly almost he comes when the moon is up. Seize on him, seize him! Let him never escape again," and still she pointed at the man shivering between them.

"Fear not," Archibald said. "Fear not." Then turning to Fordingbridge, while he held the pistol pointed at him, he continued: "Come! Resistance is useless. I have sworn here, upon this spot, to avenge Douglas; I will keep my oath. Till you stand upon the scaffold you are mine."

"He has a weapon to his hand," the woman said, still with her own pointing at him as if it were the hand of Fate. "See!" Then, as though she were one inspired, she said, as she turned to him, "Give me the knife."

Whether his mind was gone at last, or whether fear had so overcome Fordingbridge that he was no longer master of his actions, Sholto was never able to decide. Yet, from whichever cause it was, he obeyed his ghastly denouncer in so far that, as she spoke to him, the dagger dropped to the earth. And she, picking it up, placed it in the priest's hands, saying:

"It is borne in on me that with this he slew that other one. I feel it—know it."

"You will testify that he is the murderer?" Sholto said. "You do not doubt?"

"Doubt!" she exclaimed, turning her wan, white face on him. "Doubt! How should I doubt? He has haunted me since that awful night—haunted me, almost driven me to my death. Oh, you know not! I have risen at night from my bed to see him standing there, muttering, grimacing over that very spot, so that, as I gazed on him from out the darkness of my room, I have swooned again as on that night I swooned. Had I been a man, nay, had I had a man to call on, I would have gone forth and seized him. Yet, when I have told others that nightly, almost, the murderer came and gloated over the space where he slew the other, they derided me, said I was mad, would not even watch themselves. Oh, the horror of it! the horror of it!"

"The horror is ended for you now, poor woman," the priest said. "Never more will he affright your sight when you rise from your bed. Yet do me one service, I beg you.   Put on some clothes, for the night air gets cold "—she had, indeed, come forth from her room—where she had again been watching in terror, fearing to see another murder—in little else than her night raiment—" and go fetch the watch.   I will see that he escapes not."

The woman went away at his request, and coming out from the house, at which she was the concierge, with a cloak thrown over her shoulders, sped down the darkened streets, while once more the avenger and his prey were left alone.   But they spoke no more to one another now; only stood there silent, facing each other.   Yet once, after a few moments' pause, Fordingbridge chuckled audibly and whispered to himself.   God only knows what was in the wretched man's mind as he did so; Archibald, at least, made no attempt to discover.

For himself he was contented.   Fate had thrown into his hands the assassin of his beloved brother—that was enough.

Presently the woman came back, and with her three of the watch, armed and with a lantern borne in the hands of one, and into their custody the Jesuit gave Fordingbridge.   Yet, since he could not feel at ease until he had seen the other safe under lock and key, he accompanied them to the prison—to which the guard-house was attached—and handed him over to the officials there.

"To-morrow," he said, "I will formally lay my charge against him before the Procureur du Roi; till then, I pray you, keep him safe.   He is the murderer of the young Scotch officer who was slain outside the cathedral, and was my brother, as all Amiens knows."

"Never fear, monsieur," said the chief of the watch; "we will keep him safe enough. Our cage is strong."

.   .   .   .

A few nights later than the one on which the murderer, Fordingbridge, had been taken to the prison, Bertie Elphinston, riding up to the northern gate of Paris, demanded admission. It was a cold, raw night this—one of those October evenings common enough to the north of France, when the moisture hangs like rain-drops on every bush and bramble, and when the rawness penetrates to the inside of man, making him think of drams of brandy and Nantz as the best preventive of chill and cold.

He would not have ridden in to-night, would not have left the comfortable fire in the officers' quarters of the St. Denis Caserne to splash through six miles of wet roads, only it was Thursday, the day on which he invariably went to Paris, partly to pay his respects to Charles Edward, partly to see his mother and Kate. Also, if he did not come on Thursday there was no other opportunity for him to do so for a week; there were only the officers of two troops quartered in the old town, and but one night a week granted to each for leave. Therefore he was loath to lose his turn, and to go a whole fortnight without seeing the two creatures dearest to him in the world.

"A rough, raw night," he said to the man at the gate as he passed in, "a night better for indoor pleasures than the streets. You have the best of it," glancing in at the bright fire in the man's room, "much the best of it."

"*Mais oui, Monsieur le Capitaine*," said the custodian—who knew him very well—following his glance as it rested on the blazing hearth and his little girl playing with a pup before it. "*Mais oui.*" Then he said, as Bertie stooped down to tighten the buckle of his stirrup leather, "Was monsieur expecting, *par hasard*, to meet anyone hereabouts to-night? Any friend or person with a message?"

"No," replied Elphinston, partly in answer to his question, partly in surprise. "No one. Why do you ask?"

The man shrugged his shoulders in the true French manner, then he said:

"Oh, for no serious reason—but," and he paused and then went on again: "There came yesterday an unknown one to me who asked how often Monsieur le Capitaine Elphinston rode into Paris. I knew not your name then, monsieur, but his description was graphic, very graphic, so that at once I knew he meant you. Moreover, the other officers of monsieur's regiment come not so regularly on any day, some come not at all."

"'Tis strange," Bertie said; "I know no one who need ask for me in this mysterious manner, especially as there is no mystery about me. My life is simple and open enough, I should suppose. Six days a week in garrison at St. Denis, one night a week in Paris; there is not much to hide."

"So I told the man, Monsieur le Capitaine; not much to hide. *Voyez-vous*, I said, here is the captain's life so far as I know it. He rides in every Thursday evening about six of the clock, leaves his horse, as I have heard him say, at an inn in the Rue St. Louis, sees his friends, sleeps at the inn, and rides out of Paris again at six in the morning to his duties. Not much mystery in that, *mon ami?* I said to him. Not much mystery in that."

"And what did he say to you in return?" asked Bertie.

"Little enough. Remarked that he had made no suggestion of mystery; indeed, was not aware of any reason for such; only he desired to see you. Asked if you wore your military dress, to which I answered *ma foi!* no. The uniform of the Regiment of Picardy was too handsome, the cuirass too heavy for ordinary wear, the gold lace too costly; and that monsieur was always well but soberly attired. Also that his horse, a bright bay, was a pretty creature, as she is, as she is," whereon he stroked the mare's muzzle affectionately, for he himself was an old cavalryman and knew a good horse when he saw one.

"Well," said Bertie with a laugh, "you have described me accurately, so that my friend should know me when he sees me. However, I must not linger here. Good-night. Good-night, *Bébé*," to the child playing with the dog, both of whom he, who loved children and animals, had long since made acquaintance with.

As he rode through the narrow streets towards the inn where he always put up for the night. he reflected that it might have been wise to ask the gate-keeper for a description of the man who had been anxious to obtain that of him; but since he had not done so there was no help for it. Yet he could not dismiss from his mind the fact of the unknown having inquired for him —and by name, too—nor help wondering who on earth he could be. He pondered over every friend he could call to mind, old comrades in the French King's service by whose side he had fought, or comrades in the late English invasion; yet his meditations naturally amounted to nothing. The man might have been one of them or none of them, and, whoever he was, no amount of cogitation would reveal him. He must wait and see what the mysterious inquirer might turn out to be.

He rode into the inn he used in the Rue St. Louis, put up his horse, and after personally seeing it attended to—for it had done duty before starting for Paris—went into the guests' room and made a slight meal, after which he ordered a coach to be called to take him to Passy, where his mother lived.

Later, when Bertie Elphinston had disappeared from all human knowledge from that night, the search that was made for him elucidated what had been his movements and actions up to a certain point, after which all clue was lost. What those movements were have now to be told.

Quitting his mother after an hour's visit, he found the same coach standing outside the *auberge* in the street of the little suburb, and, again hiring it, proceeded to the mansion of Charles Edward, on the Quai de Théatin—to which he had removed from the Château de St. Antoine, where he had resided for a short time as the guest of Louis XV—and here he spent two more hours with his countrymen in attendance on the prince, and with Kate. At this place he had finally dismissed the coach, and as he left the house an episode arose which recalled to his mind the unknown person who had inquired for him at the north gate.

As he descended the steps of the mansion he saw, to his surprise, that, lurking opposite by the parapet which separated the Quai from the river, was a man who had been standing near him when he hired the coach outside his inn on the other side of the Seine, and who, still more strangely, had been standing outside the inn at Passy when he quitted his mother's house.

That this man was following him was therefore scarcely to be doubted, and, determined to see whether such was the case, he crossed the road, stared under his hat, which was drawn well down over his features, and then walked slowly on towards the Pont Neuf. Also, he took the precaution of loosening his sword in its sheath.

If he had had any doubts—which was not the case —they would soon have been resolved, since, as he proceeded along the narrow footway by the parapet, the man followed him at the same pace. Then, instantly, Bertie stopped, faced around, and, walking back half-a-dozen paces, said to him:

"Monsieur has business with me without doubt. Be good enough to explain it," and now he lifted his sword in its scabbard so that, while he held the sheath in the left hand, his right grasped the handle.

"I—I——" the man stammered. "Yes, Monsieur Elphinston——"

"Monsieur Elphinston! so you know me?" and a light flashed on his mind. "Monsieur Elphinston. Ha! Perhaps it was you who inquired for me at the north gate yesterday?"

"Yes, monsieur," the man replied respectfully; "it was I who did so."

"Who are you, then? What is your affair with me that you track me thus?"

"I am servant to Carvel, the exempt. I have orders to keep you in view."

"Servant to an exempt!* What, pray, has an

* A tipstaff, or executor of warrants for the Government.

exempt to do with me ?" Bertie asked in astonishment.

"That, monsieur," the man said, still very respectfully, "I cannot say. I but obey my orders, do my duty. I received instructions that you were to be kept under watch from the time you entered Paris, and I am carrying them out—must carry them out."

"Where is this exempt to be found, this man Carvel ? We will have the matter regulated at once. Where is he, I say ?"

"If monsieur would be so complaisant as to follow me—it is but across the Pont Neuf—doubtless monsieur will make everything clear."

"Lead on," Bertie said, "I will follow you, or, since you may doubt me, will go first."

"If monsieur pleases."

At this period, and indeed for long afterwards, Paris was too often the scene of terrible outrages committed on unprotected persons. Men—sometimes even women—were inveigled into houses under one pretence or another and robbed, oftentimes murdered for whatever they might chance to have about them, and, frequently, were never heard of again. That this was the case Bertie knew perfectly well, yet—even after the mysterious murder of his friend at Amiens— he had not the slightest belief that anything of a similar nature was intended towards him. First, he was a soldier and known by the man behind him to be one; he was armed, although now dressed as a civilian, and therefore a dangerous man to attack. And, next, none who knew aught of him could suppose that it would be worth while to endeavour to rob him. The Scots officers serving in France were no fit game for such as got their living by preying on their fellow-creatures.

Still he could not but muse deeply on what could possibly be the object of any exempt in subjecting him to such espionage, while at the same time he hastened his footsteps over the bridge so as at once to arrive at a solution of the matter.

"Here is the bureau of Monsieur Carvel," said the spy, as on reaching the northern side of the river he directed his companion to a house almost facing the approach to the bridge; "doubtless he will explain all."

"Doubtless," replied Elphinston. "Summon him."

The door was opened an instant after the man had rapped on it, and another man, plainly dressed and evidently of the inferior orders, though of a respectable type, admitted them to a room on the left-hand side of the passage; a room on the walls of which hung several weapons—a blunderbuss, a musquetoon or so, some swords—which Bertie noticed were mostly of fashionable make with parchment labels attached to them—and one or two pairs of gyves, or fetters. Also, on the walls were some roughly-printed descriptions of persons, in some cases illustrated with equally rough wood-cuts.

"So!" said the man, looking first at the spy and then at Elphinston. "So! Whom have we here?"

"Monsieur le Capitaine Elphinston," the other replied. "Learning, Monsieur Carvel, your desire to meet with him from me, he elected to visit you at once."

"*Tiens!* It will save much trouble. Monsieur le Capitaine is extremely obliging."

"Sir," said Bertie sternly, "I am not here with the intention of conferring any obligation upon you. I wish to know why I, an officer of the King, serving in the Regiment of Picardy, am tracked and spied upon by your follower, or servant. I wish a full explanation of why I am subjected to this indignity."

"Monsieur, the explanation is very simple. An order signed by the Vicomte d'Argenson has been forwarded to me for your arrest, and with it a lettre de cachet."

"A lettre de cachet!"

"Yes, monsieur. A lettre de cachet, ordering me to convey you to the Bastille."

"My God!"

CHAPTER XXI.

THE BASTILLE.

"La Bastille! où toute personne, quels que soient son rang, son âge, son sexe, peut entrer sans savoir pourquoi, rester sans savoir combien, en attendant d'en sortir sans savoir comment."—SERVAN.

"ON what charge is that letter issued?" asked Elphinston a moment later, when he had recovered somewhat from the stupefaction into which the exempt's last words had thrown him. "On what charge?"

"Monsieur," the man replied, "how can I answer you? Nay! who could do so? Not even De Launey, the Governor, could tell you that. These *billets-doux* are none too explicit. They order us, the exempts, in one letter to arrest; the Governor, in another, to receive. But that is all. It is from the examiners, the judges, from D'Argenson himself, wise child of a wise father! that you must seek an explanation."

"But there is no possible reason for it, no earthly charge that can be brought against me. It must be a mistake!"

"So all say," the exempt exclaimed, repressing a faint smile that rose to his features. "Yet, here is the name, very clearly written," and he took from his pocket the lettre de cachet, impressed with a great stamp, and read from it:—'Elphinston. Scotch. Capitaine du Regiment de Picardy. Troop Fifth, at St. Denis.' That is you, monsieur?"

"Yes," Bertie said with a gasp. "It is I. No doubt about that."

There rose before his mind, as he spoke, every story, every legend he had ever heard in connection with the Bastille. And although it is true that, in the days when that fortress existed, it was not regarded in so terrible a light as time and fiction have since cast upon its memory, it still presented itself in a sufficiently appalling aspect. Men undoubtedly went in and came out after very short intervals of incarceration—some doing so two or three times a year—yet, if all reports were true, there were some sent there who never came out again. Moreover, few who were committed could ever learn the reason whereof until they were ultimately released, and no communication whatever, except by stealth and great good fortune could be made with the outer world. From the time the gates closed on them they were lost to that outer world for the period—long or short—which they passed there. This knowledge alone, without the aid of time and fiction, was, indeed, sufficient to make Elphinston gasp.

"When," he asked, after another pause for reflection on the state in which he now found himself, "does that lettre de cachet come into operation—when do you propose to put it into force?"

"Monsieur," replied Carvel, with a swift glance at him and another at the man standing behind, "it *has* come into operation ; it is already in force."

"You mean——?"

"I mean that you have surrendered yourself without having to be sought for—without having to be arrested. Please to consider it in that light, monsieur."

"To consider it in the light that I am to be conveyed to the Bastille from here—at once?"

"If monsieur pleases. Though not at once—not
this immediate instant. Monsieur de Launey prefers
to receive those who are sent to him at eight o'clock
in the morning. That is his hour of reception."

Again Bertie paused an instant, then said:

"In such case I may advise my friends of this detention. It will ease their minds—and it can be done
before eight o'clock. It is now scarcely midnight."

"I regret to have to say No, monsieur," and Bertie
started at his reply. "Such would be against all order,
all rule. From the moment the persons named in the
lettres de cachet are in our hands they can have no
further communication with their friends."

"What if I refuse to comply with your demands—
with the demands of that lettre de cachet? What then,
I say?"

"Monsieur is here," the exempt replied, "that is
sufficient. It is too late for him now to retreat. We
are furnished with attendants for escorting to the Bastille those who are arrested; monsieur will perceive it
would be vain for him to contend against us. There
are at the present moment half-a-dozen such attendants
in this house."

"So be it," said Bertie, "I will not contend. Some
absurd mistake has been made that will be rectified as
soon as I have seen the Governor."

"*Sans doute*," replied the exempt; "meanwhile let
me suggest to monsieur that he should rest until it is
necessary to set out. He may yet have some hours of
refreshing sleep."

"I do not desire to sleep," Bertie said, "only to be
left alone. Is that impossible, too?"

"By no means. We have a room here in which monsieur may remain at his ease. But," and he pointed to the labelled swords hanging on the walls, "it is our habit to disembarrass all who are brought here of their weapons. Those who are arrested at their own houses or lodgings leave them in custody there. But monsieur may rest assured of his weapon being quite safe. If he comes out to-morrow or—or—or—a month later, say, it will be at his service."

"If," replied Bertie, taking off his diamond-cut civilian sword, "it had been the weapon of my profession, you should never have had it. As it is—take it."

"Keep it carefully," said Carvel to his men, "until Monsieur le Capitaine returns. I guarantee you 'twill not be long ere he does so. I myself believe, monsieur, a mistake has been made. 'Tis not with such metal as you that Madame la Bastille is ordinarily stuffed."

After this, and on receiving Bertie's word of honour that he had no other weapon of any kind, knife nor pistol, about him, he was shown into a room at the back of the house, where the exempt told him he would be quite undisturbed—a room the window of which, he noticed, was cross-barred, and with, outside the window, a high blank wall. Here he passed the night in reflections of the most melancholy nature, wondering and wondering again and again on what unknown possibility could have led to this new phase in his existence. At one moment—so far afield did he have to go to seek for some cause for his arrest—he mused, if by any chance Fordingbridge could have come to Paris and, exercising some to him unknown influence, have procured the lettre de cachet. Yet he was obliged to discard this idea from his mind as he had discarded others, when he reflected that nothing was more unlikely than that the minister of the King would have signed an order for the incarceration of one Englishman at the request of another. But, with this conjecture dismissed, he had to content himself and remain as much in the dark as before.

At seven o'clock the exempt came to him and told him that it was time to set out.

"A coach is ready, monsieur," he said, "all is now prepared. Would you desire to make any toilette before your departure?"

Bertie said he would, and when he had done this, laving his face and washing his hands in a basin brought him by two of Carvel's attendants, he announced that he was prepared to accompany him.

"Perhaps when I have seen the Governor of the Bastille," he said, "I shall better understand why I am confided to his keeping."

To which once more the other replied, "*Sans doute.*"

Everything being therefore ready, Carvel and Elphinston entered the coach, while, of four men who had appeared on the scene that morning, two went inside with them, and the others, mounting horses, rode on either side of the vehicle. In this way they progressed through the small portion of the city necessary to be traversed, arriving at the fortress exactly as the great clock over the doorway—decorated with a bas relief representing two slaves manacled together—struck eight. That their destination was apparent to those members of the populace by whom they passed it was easy to perceive. Women and men, hurrying to their shops and places of business, regarded the party with glances which plainly showed that they knew whither they were going, the former doing so with terrified and uneasy looks, the latter according to their disposition. Of these, some laughed and made jeering allusions to the morning ride which the gentleman was taking; some frowned with disapproval; and some there were who muttered to one another, "How long? How long shall we groan under the tyranny of our masters?" while others answered, "Not for ever! It cannot be for ever, though the good God alone knows when the end will come. Perhaps not even in our day!"

"Descend, monsieur," said the exempt, as the coach drew up; then, turning to some sentinels within the gate which opened to receive them, he remarked, '*Couvrez-vous, messieurs.*"

Surprised at this order, which Bertie did not understand, he glanced at the soldiers standing about and observed that, as he approached them, they removed their hats from their heads and placed them before their faces until he had passed by, so that they could by no means have seen what his appearance was like. And to the inquiring look which he directed to his captain, the exempt replied, with a slight laugh:

"Madame la Bastille endeavours ever to be a polite hostess. She thinks it not well that these fellows, who are not always in her service, should be able afterwards to recognise her guests when they have quitted her hospitable roof. *Vraiment!* her manners are of the most finished. Come, Monsieur Elphinston, Jourdan de Launey attends us.* He rises ever at seven, so as to welcome those who arrive early. Come, I beg."

---

* Governor of the Bastille from 1718 to 1749, and father of the last governor of that prison, Le Marquis Bernard Réné Jourdan de Launey, who was brutally murdered by the populace on the fall of the Bastille in 1789.

Following, therefore, his guide, and followed by the men who had escorted them, Bertie crossed a drawbridge and a courtyard, and then arrived at a flight of stone stairs let into the wall, at which was stationed an officer handsomely dressed, who, on seeing Elphinston, bowed politely to him and requested that he would do him the honour to accompany him to the Governor. Then, turning round on the exempt's followers who came behind them, he said in a very different tone:

"Stay where you are. Do you suppose we require your services to welcome the arrivals? And for you, Monsieur l'Exempt, we will rejoin you later." Whereon he opened a small door off the staircase and led Bertie into a room.

A room which astonished the young man as he stepped into it; for, although he had often talked with people in Paris who had been imprisoned in the Bastille, and had heard that some parts of it were sumptuously furnished, he had not imagined that even the Governor possessed such an apartment as this. It was, indeed, so large as to be almost a hall, though the gorgeous hangings of yellow damask fringed with silver and with lace made it look smaller, while at the same time they imparted a brilliancy to the vastness of the room; and some cabinets, bureaux, aud couches distributed about also served to give it a comfortable appearance. In front of a blazing fire—so great, indeed, that the wonder was that any mortal could approach near it—there stood, warming his hands, the Governor, De Launey himself, while seated close by at a table covered with papers was a miserable-looking person who was engaged in writing.

No man, possibly, ever presented a greater contrast between his own appearance and the dreaded position which he occupied than did Jourdan de Launey, then an old man approaching his end. He was very thin and very bald, with beady black eyes and a rosy face which gave him the appearance of extreme good humour, while that which rivetted the attention of everyone who saw him for the first time was the extraordinary shaking, or palsy, that possessed him always. Even now, as he stood before the huge, roaring fire, holding out the palms of his hands to it and lifting first one foot and then another to its warmth, he shook and shivered so that he seemed as though dying of cold.

To him the handsomely apparelled officer—whom Bertie soon learned bore the rank of the "King's Lieutenant of his Majesty's fortress of the Bastille"—addressed himself, saying that the Captain Elphinston had arrived; whereon De Launey turned his back to the fire, regarded Bertie for a moment, and then held out a long, white, shivering hand, which the other, as he took it, thought might well have belonged to a corpse.

"Sir," he said, in a voice of extreme sweetness, though somewhat shaken by his tremblings, "you are very welcome, though I fear this abode may scarcely be so to you. Yet I beg of you to believe that what can be done to put you at your ease and make you comfortable shall be done. Moreover, permit me to tell you that which I tell all my visitors who are not of the lower classes, nor murderers and ruffians, who need not to be considered, that your visit here by no means brings with it a loss of self-respect or of social position. The Bastille is not a prison, as the *canaille* think; is not Bicêtre nor even Vincennes; it is a place where gentlemen are simply detained at the pleasure

of his Majesty, and when they go forth they go un-
stained. If you will remember that, Monsieur le
Capitaine," he continued with increased sweetness of
voice, "you will, I think, repine less at our hospitality."

Bertie bowed, as, indeed, he could not but do to
such extreme politeness, no matter how much he re-
sented his incarceration, then he said:

"Sir, I am obliged to you for your civility. Yet,
monsieur, if you would add to it by telling me with
what I am charged and why I am brought here at all,
you would greatly increase my obligation."

"Monsieur le Capitaine," replied the Governor, "I
regret to refuse—but it is impossible. That you cannot know until you appear before the Lieutenant of
the Civil Government, or Examiner, who comes here
at periods to examine our visitors. Then, by the questions he will ask, you will undoubtedly be able to surmise with what you are charged."

"And when will he come, monsieur?"

"I know," he replied, with a shrug of his shoulders
which so blended into one of his shivers that it was
almost imperceptible, "no more than you do. He
comes when it pleases him, or, perhaps, I might more
truthfully say, when he has time, and then he interro-
gates those whom, also, it pleases him. Sometimes it
is our latest guest"—De Launey never by any chance
used the word "prisoner"—"sometimes those who
have been here for years. And some there are who
have been here for many—but no matter!" Then,
turning to the King's Lieutenant, he bade that officer
give him Captain Elphinston's *mittimus*, or the stamped
letter containing the order for his reception and security.

16

This letter he read carefully, during which time it shook so in his palsied hands that Bertie could not but wonder how he could distinguish the characters in it; after which he looked up with his good-humoured smile and said:

"Sir, I felicitate you. You are of the first class of guests; beyond restriction you will have little to complain of. The King"—and he raised his tottering white hand to his forehead as though saluting that monarch in person—"is, you know, your host; your pension will be of the best. Secretary," he said, turning round sharply to the man at the table, "read to the captain the bill of fare for the principal guests."

This man, who seemed, at least, to derive no great good from his position, seeing that he was miserably clad in an old suit of ragged Nismes serge, a pair of old blue breeches loose at the knees, and a wig which had scarcely any hair left on it, began to read from a paper, when, to Bertie's astonishment, a very different voice from the soft tones he had recently been listening to issued from the Governor's lips; and in a harsh, commanding way De Launey exclaimed:

"Fellow, stand up before gentlemen! *Mort de ma vie!* do you dare to sit and read before us?" Whereon the wretched creature sprang up as though under the lash, and began hastily to gabble out:

"*Déjeuner à la fourchette.* Potage. A quarter of a fowl or a slice of ox beef. A pie, a sheep's tongue or a ragout, biscuits, and rennets. A quarter septier of wine, to suffice also for dinner and supper. Dinner: A loaf, soup, petite pâtés, roast veal or mutton, pigeon or pullet, or beef and toasted bread. Supper: A fish of the season, or a bird and a chipped loaf. By order of the King, to the extent of 150 sols a day."

As he read from his paper—to which the visitor paid but little attention, since he cared nothing about the meals he might receive—De Launey nodded and wagged his head with approbation, and, when he finished, exclaimed:

"A noble King! Fellow," to the secretary, "begone! Go seek the turnkey, Bluet, and bid him prepare for Monsieur le Capitaine the second chamber of the chapel."

"The second chamber of the chapel! The best apartment!"

"*Mon Dieu!*" exclaimed De Launey, while he shook terribly, "do my infirmities render me unintelligible? Ay, the second chamber; and for you, if ever you misunderstand me again, the vault under the ditch where the malefactors lie!" Then, putting out his long, white, trembling hand—while all the time he smiled blandly—he nipped the man's arm between two fingers and repeated, "Where the malefactors lie! Where the man was eaten alive by rats! *Tu comprends, cher ami?* · Go. The second chamber in the chapel for Monsieur le Capitaine. *Va!*"

The man left the room quickly, casting a glance, half of terror and half of hate, on De Launey, who, after regarding him till he was gone, turned round to Elphinston with his pleasant smile, and said, "A vile wretch that. Yet a useful one, and bound to me by the deepest ties of gratitude. Sent here by the Jesuits some years ago. Ha! ha! The holy fathers know how to obtain the lettres de cachet! for an unspeakable crime—the corruption of a nun to Protestantism. I saved his life by telling them that he was the man who had been eaten by the rats, though 'twas another. Thus I bound him to me for ever. He writes a most beautiful hand, knows the history of every man in the Bastille, and—ha! ha!—draws no recompense. The Inquisition injured my family once—they burnt an aunt of mine in Seville—therefore I love to thwart them."

Bertie inclined his head to show that he heard the Governor's words; then the latter continued in his mellifluous strains:

"Now, Captain Elphinston, I must tell you that you should try and make yourself as comfortable as possible here. Above all, do not dream of an escape. Many have done so; few have succeeded—the Abbé du Bacquoy alone of late years.* For the walls are thick—oh, so thick!—between each room there is a space of many feet—the windows are barred; so, too, are the fireplaces; the ceilings cannot be reached by two men standing one on the other's shoulders. Moreover, a visitor seen outside his window, or on the roofs or walls, could not escape the eyes of the sentries, and would be shot—poof!—like a sparrow. Monsieur, let me beg you, therefore, to content yourself with our hospitality. Later on—if you are not recalled—we will perhaps give you some companions; we wish our guests to have the enjoyment of society. Monsieur le Capitaine, here is Bluet, who will conduct you to your apartment. *Au revoir.* I trust sincerely you will be at your ease."

Again the ice-cold, shivering hand clasped that of Elphinston, De Launey bowed to him with as much grace as though he were taking part in a minuet, and, following the turnkey, who had come in with the secretary, the prisoner went forth to his chamber.

Descending the stairs and out by the small door in

---

* Latude's successful escape was made some years after the date of this narrative—viz., in 1750.

the wall, he passed again through the Corps de Garde, all the members of which once more instantly took off their hats and held them before their faces. Then he was led across a great court and in at a square door painted green, and so up three small steps on to a great staircase, at the bottom of which were two huge iron doors that clanged with an ominous sound behind him. At the head of this staircase were three more gates, one after the other—wooden gates covered with iron plates—and when these were locked behind Elphinston also, another iron-bound door was opened, and he stood within a great vaulted room, some sixty feet long and about fifteen in breadth, and the same in height.

"*Voilà!*" exclaimed the secretary, "behold the second room of the chapel. *Mon Dieu!* a fine apartment for an untitled guest! But the old animal will have his way. Yet, why this room of princes? 'Twas here the man with the iron mask died, they say; here that the Duke of Luxembourg and the Marshals de Biron and Bassompière once reposed."

"At least," said Bertie, casting his eyes round the vault—for such it was—"I trust there was more accommodation for those illustrious personages than there appears for me. Am I to sleep on the floor, and lie on it also in the day? There is neither bed nor chair here."

"All in good time, brave captain," replied Bluet, the turnkey, who even at this early period of the morning appeared to be half drunk—"all in good time, noble captain. I shall make your room a fitting boudoir for a duchess ere night. Have no fear."

"Now," said the secretary, "give up all you have about you."

"What!"

"All, everything," replied the other. "Oh, be under no apprehension; we do not rob the King's guests; oh, no! Every visitor to this delectable castle has to do the same, even though he be a prince of the blood. I shall give you a note for what you hand me, and on your sortie you will see all is as you handed to me. Yet the old *cochon*, De Launey, loveth trinkets for his wife—young enough to be his daughter; if you have a ring or a jewel, you can part with it; it will be to your advantage."

"Friend," said Elphinston, "I am a soldier who has fought in hard wars, sometimes without even receiving a sol of any pay—as in the last campaign in Scotland—what should I have? See, I have no rings on my fingers, no watch to my pocket, no solitaire to my cravat. Yet, here is my purse with a few Louis d'ors and one gold quadruple pistole; count those, if you will," and he pitched it into the secretary's ragged hat as he spoke.

The man told over the coins, muttering that the large piece was *bien forte et trébuchante*, then made an accurate note of them and gave the list to Bertie. "All," he said again, "will be returned you on your exit, unless you choose to give them to Bluet and me. We get little enough, though God knows we have also little enough—at least, I have—of opportunities for spending. Yet even here one may have his little pleasures," and he winked at Bertie, who turned from him in disgust.

"No trinkets on the bosom," he went on questioningly, "no lockets, nor crosses, nor reliquaries of saints? Humph!"

"There is," replied Elphinston, "on my breast a

bag of satin, in which is a lock of hair—the hair of the woman whom I love. Fellow, do you think I will let you take that, or even fasten your foul eyes on it! Ask me no more; otherwise I will speak to the Governor."

"It is against the rules," said the other, "quite against the rules, yet——"

"Curse the rules!"

"Yet," he said, "so that when you leave us you will give me one, only one of those pieces, I will not insist."

"Leave me," said Bertie, and his voice was so stern that, followed by the turnkey, the man slunk out of the room, and a moment afterwards the heavy door was locked and barred on him.

CHAPTER XXII.

DESPAIR!

Left alone at last, he walked up and down the huge chamber, or vault, his mind full of melancholy, heart-broken reflections.

"My God, my God!" he muttered, "what have I done that thus Thou lettest Thy hand fall so heavily on me? What fresh sin committed, that this fresh punishment should be mine! I have lost the one thing I cared for in this life, lost her; now I am incarcerated here in this place of horror, this place where men's existences, even their very names, are forgotten as much as though they had lain for years in their graves; this place which may be my grave." Then, a few moments later, his heart and courage returned to him, and he murmured to himself again:

"Yet, I will not repine. That abject creature spoke of others who had been here and yet escaped, obtained their liberty, all but him, the hapless Masque de Fer, who drew his last breath in this gloomy dungeon. Bassompière, Luxembourg, De Biron, all went forth to the world again. How many men have I not known myself who have been here? There was one, the old Comte de Tilly, who told me he had been incarcerated thirteen times, and that, whenever he saw the exempts in the street, he took off his hat to them, and asked if by any chance they happened to be seek-ing for him.   And these walls," he exclaimed, looking up at the blackened sides of the room, "seem to bear testimony to many who have inhabited the place."

They did, indeed; for, written all over the grimy and smoky sides of the vault, were records left by those who had been incarcerated.   In one part of the room near the barred fireplace, through which a child could not have crept, were the words: " The widow Lailly and her daughter were brought into this hell on the 27th September, 1701 "; in another place was the name of a Neapolitan prince, one De Riccia, with his remarkable motto beneath it, " Empoisona ove Strangola."   And there were scores of other names, of all countries: one, that of the Chevalier Lynch, gentleman, of Sligo in Ireland; another, Jean Cronier, *rédacteur*, " Du Burlesk Gazette," Holland; a third, Magdalen de St. Michel, while in a different hand underneath was written, " who slew her husband, a King's sailor; " yet another, " the *Curé* de Méry, falsely accused of rioting and drunkenness "; and many more.   And, still continuing his sad patrol of the room, he saw that at each corner of it were statues of the four Evangelists, so that he understood now why it should be called the " Room of the Chapel," though why the " second room " he never learned.

" So," he said, as he mused in his misery, " so this place has been holy ground, consecrated.   Heavens! was ever a place of prayer turned to such vile use since the Temple became a den of thieves ? "

As thus he pondered he heard the doors outside clanging, and a moment afterwards, the unbarring of the chapel door and the harsh grating of the key in the lock, a sound which was followed by the entrance of the turnkey, Bluet—who appeared now more drunk than before—and another man, also a turnkey.

"Ha!" said the former with a hiccough, "now to arrange the boudoir. Georges, disgorge thy burden and be gone. I have alone to do with Monsieur le Capitaine," and, as he spoke, he reeled across the room with a small folding table he had brought with him and placed it under the barred and latticed window, where the light streamed on it. Meanwhile, the other turnkey, Georges, had thrown down a huge bundle of what was evidently bedding, and departed, to return again a few moments later, with a tray, on which were several dishes.

"*Voilà!*" Bluet muttered as he arranged the table, "behold your first meal as guest of Madame la Bastille. A soup—of lentils—*bon! bon!* some cockscombs in vinegar—*pas mal ça!* some chip bread, beef full of gravy, with a garniture of parsley. Also the quarter septier of wine—and good, too, you see, of Bourgogne. Now for more furniture to accommodate our new guest." Whereon he reeled off to the passage and brought back a sound wooden chair, which he placed by the table, exclaiming, "*Voilà! monsieur est servir.*"

Seeing that the fellow, in spite of his drunkenness, was doing his best to treat him well, and reflecting also that much of any comfort he was likely to obtain might depend on him, Bertie resolved to make a friend of Bluet if possible; so, sitting down to the meal, he made a semblance of eating it; and as he did so he said:

"If I did not perceive that already you have been making free enough with the drink, I would ask you to join me. This great jar," touching the quarter septier, which contained half a gallon at least, "is more than I can consume in a week, yet you, I judge, could drink it all at a sitting."

"*Facilement.* I often do. And the wine is of the best. When St. Mars was governor here, he robbed the visitors, they say; took the King's money for the best and gave the worst. De Launey, now, is different."

"He is more generous, then ?"

"Nay, more timorous. For, observe, he fears the King should find out he is being hoodwinked. Yet, all do not drink nor eat alike here. Some get only a *chopine* of the thinnest, one *plat* to each meal, coarse bread, and no fruit. It depends on the degree of the personage, also the probability of the length of his visit. Because, you see, Monsieur le Capitaine, some seem never likely to depart—and there are many such, I assure you, who become forgotten ; there is no hope they will ever go forth ; they have no money to give away in fees—for if a visitor wishes to reward us for our little cares, he may make an order on De Launey to distribute some of the money he holds ; they become the guest who has outstayed his welcome. You understand, monsieur ?"

He spoke with an air of drunken gravity, and, although in drink, showed so much intelligence that Bertie guessed this was the man's normal condition. Also, the latter observed that the state he was in by no means prevented him from being able to fulfil any duty he had to perform. Indeed, during the time he had been enlightening Bertie as to the customs of the Bastille, he had been arranging in a corner of the room some furniture the other man had come back with, as well as that which he had originally brought. Thus he had fitted up a little truckle bedstead in one of the corners near the fireplace and under the statue of St. Matthew which stood in the wall above, a bedstead which had some curtains of dirty flowered stuff, with a bag of straw for a mattress, and also a blanket as dirty as the curtains, and full of holes, and a quilt of flock. Likewise he had brought in a great pitcher of water, a ewer and mug, all of which were of pewter.

"*Avec ça,*" he said, regarding these things with a look of satisfaction, "monsieur is well provided. Oh, well provided! Now for this you must pay six livres a month—none of which comes to me, alas!—and if you wish more it can be hired. Yet, faith! it is a chamber for a King. Shall I send for a fagot and make a fire to purge the air of the room?"

"Nay," said poor Bertie, "it is very well. Yet I would that the chamber was not so vast; it is large, and draughty, and dark. Can I not be removed into a better one—at least, a smaller one?"

"That will come if you remain with us. Lengthened sojourns are not made in this one. So you may content yourself with this, namely, while you are here —in this apartment—you may go out at any moment. Now, I have other guests to see to; I will return later with the dinner. Adieu, monsieur," and he went away, banging, and locking, and barring the heavy door behind him.

Through the glazed window above, which had two great shutters to it that were always closed, but had an iron gate or smaller window within them, while outside was a green wooden lattice, Bertie could see that the sun was shining; nay, a ray or so even forced its way through the iron gate and illuminated a foot's breadth all along the dungeon, or room. In one way it was, perhaps, not very welcome, for it showed plainly the filthy condition of the floor, all incrusted with dirt as it was, and with other refuse, such as small meat-bones, fish-bones, egg-shells, and pieces of bread-crust trodden into it. Yet, also, to his sad heart it brought some comfort; it spoke to him of the world without, of the gay streets and gardens of Paris; of her, his love. What was she doing now, he pondered; would she soon be wondering what had become of him, and why, as once before—so long, so long ago, as now it seemed—he had again disappeared from her and made no sign? Or would he be free before Thursday came again?

He thought, looking round the gloomy chapel, while he considered and mused on these things, that his head might reach that little iron gate, or *grille*, in the shutters if he placed upon the table the chair and then stood on that, and thus he would be able to obtain a sight of what was outside. So he set to work to place them in position, and then, on clambering up, found that he could obtain a view of the garden of the Bastille, and, owing to a low-roofed portion of the fortress almost immediately in front of him, of away beyond into the city.

In the garden he perceived a lady walking, accompanied by a dog that seemed from its action to be very old, for it moved slowly and feebly without any gambols; and he wondered who she was, and if she might be De Launey's wife, who was " young enough to be his daughter." The garden itself, he could also perceive, since the chapel was no higher than the first floor, formed the interior, or courtyard, of all the towers of the prison, and he saw that, by glancing upwards, the windows of other rooms, or cells, were visible to him. Indeed, not only were they visible, but so also was one of the inmates, who, as Bertie observed him, was leaning against his little window frame with his face at the bars as though to catch the air. He was a man somewhat over middle age, with scowling features and long, unkempt hair, and as Bertie regarded him he saw his lips moving as though either he was talking to some fellow-prisoner within the room or muttering to himself. This man fascinated Elphinston so that he could not remove his eyes from off him —for in those other eyes there seemed to be a hell of despair—and, as he thus looked, the man, shifting his gaze, glanced down and across, and so saw him at his lattice. For a moment he stared at Bertie and then made a motion to him with his finger—it seemed as though to bid him stay where he was—and then disappeared from the window to return a moment later with a little piece of light board in one hand to which he pointed with the other.

Made more curious than ever by this, Elphinston continued to regard him and his actions fixedly, which were as follows: First the man held up in his right hand—his left still grasping the board—something that appeared like a piece of burnt wood, and then, applying it to the board, drew on it the letter N. Pointing to it, he next drew the letters O, U, and V, then E, then A, then another U, until at last he had spelt out the whole of the word *Nouveau*. Next, after a glance across at Bertie, as though to ask if he understood, and seeing that he did, he again went on with four more letters, making the word *Venu*, and carefully finishing the sentence by drawing, last of all, a solitary note of interrogation, and looking over to Bertie as though awaiting his reply to the question. Receiving from him two or three emphatic nods of the head, he began again, and this time produced a longer sentence, which, by recollecting each word as it had been found, Bertie made out to be (in French, of course), "I have been here twenty-one years."

At this melancholy information he tried to throw into his features—for no action of his body could be at all apparent to the man—as much sympathy as was possible, whereon the other again pointed to his board and continued with his letters until he had formed the sentence, "Have you been before the Judges?" and receiving a negative shake from Bertie's head, again worked out, "*Nor I, yet,*" and waited as though to see what effect this stupendous piece of information might have on a newly-arrived prisoner.

If the unhappy man desired to see horror depicted on that newcomer's face—if such a sight could be gratifying to him who had lived forgotten there so long, without, perhaps, even knowing why he was so detained, he must indeed have been gratified. For as that terrible sentence came out letter by letter on the board, Bertie shrank back from the lattice, while his countenance must plainly have shown to the other the emotions of pity mixed with dread and dismay with which the communication had filled him. "Twenty-one years," he muttered to himself, forgetting even for the moment his new-found acquaintance opposite, "twenty-one years without knowing what he is charged with ; without hope. My God! what has his life been during that time ; waiting, waiting always ! And it may be so with me," he thought, shuddering as he did so, "it may be my case. I am twenty-six years old now ; at forty-seven I may still be in this prison, untried, uncondemned, yet unreleased—no nearer to my freedom than now." And again he shuddered.

He glanced over to the unhappy prisoner in the opposite tower as he finished these reflections, and saw that he was waiting for his attention to begin his letters again. And, once more fascinated by their terrible revelations, he watched eagerly as the next sentence was formed.

Slowly the words were composed, letter by letter; slowly they met his eyes, and seemed to numb his brain and strike a chill to his heart. "I am not the worst case," the prisoner spelt out. "Above you in the Tour de la Bertaudière is one who has been here for forty-two years. Untried still!" Then, with a wave of his hand, the man vanished from his window—perhaps because he heard the gaoler coming into his room—and Bertie saw him no more that day.

Yet that which he had gleaned from his opposite neighbour was enough to furnish him with sufficient food for miserable reflections all through the remainder of the day, and far into the night when he lay sleepless on his unclean bed. Bluet had visited him twice during that period, bringing him two more meals — each good enough in its way, and with different meats at each, but badly cooked; and on the second occasion, and when he could perceive through the lattice that night was coming on, the turnkey had offered to let him have some light if he wished it. High up above the latticed window there was an iron socket into which a candle could be fitted, or on to which a lamp might be swung, and Bluet had volunteered to bring in a ladder and place the light there if Elphinston desired it. But he replied, "No, he wanted nothing. He would try to sleep till daybreak, try to rest. The day had been long enough for him already."

"*Ma foi ! sans doute !*" the fellow replied, he seeming neither more nor less drunk than he had been at
nine o'clock in the morning. "*Sans doute*, monsieur is
fatigued, yet he must not lose heart. If the judges
do not release him ere long, he shall be moved to
another chamber where, perhaps, he will have some
society. There is plenty here. Of all sorts. Then
monsieur will be gay."

"Gay!" exclaimed Bertie. "Gay! In this
place ?"

"And why not? Oh, figure to yourself, there is
gaiety here and to suffice. Hark now to that! Hark,
I say!" and at the moment he spoke Bertie heard a
voice in his own tongue trolling forth a drinking song.

"Ha! ha! *Mon Dieu !*" exclaimed the turnkey, "it
is the gallant captain. Also a captain like monsieur,
but of the road. They say he stopped the Cardinal's
carriage at Fontainebleau not so long ago, yet this he
denies. And a spy, too, of England, they say. He
plays the big game. *Mon Dieu !* listen! he sings well,
though I understand no word of your somewhat severe
and sombre tongue."

Severe and sombre though it might be, it did not
sound so as the gallant captain shouted forth his
drinking song.

"He's gay," said Bluet ; "he has found a new companion—one, however, who will scarce join in his
mirth. A miserable creature sent in by the priests, a
murderer, they hint. *Mon Dieu !* either he will deso-
late the captain or the captain will drive him mad with
his carousings."

After which, and having wished Bertie "a good-night
and good repose," he took himself off, and, ere the latter slept, he could have sworn he heard Bluet's harsh

voice joining in a song with the captain, though this time in the French language.

"So," he thought to himself as, after having knelt by his wretched bed and prayed for mercy from his God, he flung himself upon it, "so 'tis to this pass I am brought—I, who have served the French King faithfully for years, who have committed no crime against him. And am I doomed to remain here forgotten? Perhaps be like that other one with whom I communicated to-day, or that still more unhappy man whose life has been spent in these awful walls. Forty-two years, he said of him—forty-two years!" And again he applied that second case to himself as he had done the first. "Forty-two years! I shall be then sixty-six. All, all will be dead and gone. My mother long since, Kate almost of a certainty; Douglas, too; even the scoundrel Fordingbridge! O God!" he cried, wrought up by these reflections, "release me from this place, I beseech Thee, release me; even though it be only by death. Let me not linger on here untried for a fault I know not of, uncondemned and forgotten. Take my life, but not my freedom while I live. What have I done? What have I done?" And with such a heart-broken prayer as this on his lips Bertie Elphinston fell asleep at last, if that can be termed sleep which was no more than a disturbed forgetfulness—a broken slumber from which he would wake with a start as some sound from other parts of the prison penetrated his chamber, or a rat would scamper across his bed and touch his hand with its foul, dank coat.

CHAPTER XXIII.

AT LAST.

THE days went on slowly and without anything to distinguish them from one another, until, at last, it seemed to Bertie in his dungeon that he would soon lose count of them, would forget how many had passed since first he entered the prison, and would become confused as to the days of the week. Every night he heard the roaring of the English "captain"—if such he was—and every day he communicated with the prisoner in the tower opposite to him, but these alone were the incidents of his life, for beyond the visits of Bluet with his meals, no one came near him. And he thought ever of what those outside would imagine had become of him. With that opposite prisoner, for whose appearance at his window he looked eagerly every morning, he had now established an almost perfect system of corresponding, so that, although their intercourse was naturally very slow, it was at least something with which to beguile many weary hours. He had been unable to discover any board which would answer to the one on which his strangely made friend wrote and rubbed out letter after letter and formed his words, but as he had found several large pieces of paper in a corner of the chapel, he had managed to shape a number of large letters—indeed, all of the alphabet—which, by holding each up successively, answered the purpose equally well. And thus they corresponded slowly and wearily, but still intelligibly, and in that way the monotony of their lives was relieved. Yet even this was not always practicable, and sometimes they had to desist from communicating with each other at all since, on certain days the sentries were set on the tower in which the man was, and would have discovered their correspondence had they not discontinued it. But at other times the men's duty took them to other parts of the prison roof—for the *corps de garde* was not strong, the walls, locks, and bars being alone considered sufficient to prevent any attempt at escape—and then they were uninterrupted.

"I am alone in my cell," the other had communicated to Bertie, "and my name is Falmy. I am of Geneva. Of the Reformed faith. I know of no other reason why I am here so long. Fleury sent me here the year before he was Cardinal."

Every morning, however, he prefaced any other message to Bertie by the question, "Have you been examined yet?" and as each day the other shook his head he seemed by his expression to show that he regretted such was the case.

"If you are not examined soon, your stay may be long. But take heart," he signalled, "the principal examiner is extremely irregular, yet he comes at last in most cases."

"He has not done so in yours, poor friend," returned Bertie, "nor in the case of him who has been here forty-two years! Who is he?"

"Le Marquis de Chevagny, of near Chartres. It was the Grand Monarque who sent him here. He is forgotten. In December he will have been here forty-three years."

"What was his fault?"

"He wrote a *pasquinade* on Madame La Vallière. She obtained the lettre de cachet from the King."

"And," signalled back Bertie, "for that he has suffered forty-three years!"

"He will suffer till he dies. Louis and La Vallière have been long dead, so have all of their time. He is forgotten. He will never go forth. Nor shall I. Those who are forgotten are lost."

With such recitals as these it was not surprising that Bertie's heart should sink ever lower; that as days followed days and grew at last into weeks, he began to feel sure that for him the gates of his prison would never open. He, too, would be forgotten by those who had sent him there; would he, he asked himself, be forgotten by those who loved him? No one knew that he was incarcerated in those dreadful walls, that fortress in which one was as much shut off from the world as in a tomb. No one would ever know!

He consulted Falmy one day as to whether there was no possibility of communicating with that outer world, no chance of letting some friend who could interest himself in his behalf know where he was, but in reply the other only shook his head moodily. Then, after staring out of his window for some moments, with always in his face that look of despair which Bertie had observed from the first and had been so fascinated by, Falmy made a sign to him to attend, and began his letters again.

"There is," he signalled, "one chance alone. To be confined with some prisoner whose release may come while you are together. Then to send a message to your friends. By word of mouth alone. No written

line can go forth.   All are searched for letters ere they
are let go."

Bertie thought a moment, then he asked:

"Can I get changed to another room?"

Again Falmy shook his head gloomily and pondered.   But another thought appeared to come to his
mind, and he signalled:

"You will be changed ere long if you are not released or examined.   None remain in the chapel who
are to stay in this devil's den.   I have made many
friends at your window, and lost them all.   Soon I
shall lose you," and as he finished the last word Bertie
saw Falmy's face working piteously and knew that he
wept.   And he, his heart torn with both their griefs,
wept too, and left his window suddenly to throw himself on his bed.

And still the days went on, and the weeks, and he
knew, by the notches he made on the wall as each
fresh dawn broke, as well as by the increased cold,
that the depth of winter had come.   On the roof of
the Tour de la Bertaudière he could see the snow
lying now, or heard it fall into the garden with a thud
when a slight thaw happened, while the cold became
so intense that neither he nor Falmy could stay long
at the window to communicate with each other.   He
had given various little orders to Bluet for payment
out of his stock of Louis d'ors during this time, so that
the man still looked after him well, and he had a few
fagots of wood allowed him, or rather found him, in
consequence, over which he would sit and shiver,
though the large bulging bars in front of the grate
prevented him from getting near enough to the sticks
to derive much warmth from them.   And often
he was driven to seek his pallet and lie huddled

up in the foul bedding to keep himself from perishing.

And still the weeks went on now, and he was there, though he had begged the turnkey to ask the Governor to remove him to a warmer and smaller room, and also to some place where he might have company. But Bluet had only shrugged his shoulders and said that such a request was useless, adding that De Launey was a brigand who would do nothing until it pleased him.

"Yet," replied Bertie, "he said he would do his best for me and make me comfortable. Comfortable! comfortable! My God!"

"Poof! poof?" exclaimed Bluet. "You must not believe in him. He is full of words to those who come in—*le sal Gascon !*—because he knows not how soon they may go out again, nor whether they may not have come in by mistake—as *mon Dieu!* many have —nor what trouble those who go out may plunge him into. But once he finds they are not going—that is to say, not going just at once—why, then he possesses the Bastille memory which, *ma foi!* means an agreeable forgetfulness. *Tenez !* have no hopes from that shivering *escargot !*"

"I am doomed, then, to die in this vault—to be killed by the cold and the draughts!"

"*Non, non,* be calm. You will go forth. None but princes and marshals stay long here. And there has been a clearing from above; many have departed; there is room for you now. Soon I shall remove monsieur."

"Who are gone? Any who have been here long?"

"No. Many new ones, and one who was here

eight years—by a mistake. He was a Hollander, a doctor, and—*mort de ma vie !*—they thought he was Schwab, the Alsatian poisoner. He now is gone, and the pig, De Launey, entertained him to breakfast ere he went, though he would allow him only *la petite bouteille* while he remained. And the captain of the road, the sweet singer of songs, he is gone too, only 'tis to the Place de Grève, for a certain purpose," and he motioned to his throat as he spoke and winked at the other, who shuddered. Vile and dissolute as the man's roarings and carousals had been, they had served to cheer him up in his loneliness and desolation, and he regretted his fate.

Another week passed, and Bertie, who had now contracted a terrible cold and cough that plagued him at nights, began to believe that he would never leave the chapel alive, when Bluet, coming with his breakfast one morning, told him that he was to be moved.

"Thank God!" exclaimed the poor prisoner, "thank God! it cannot be worse than this."

"No," said the turnkey, "because where you are going to you will find *la société.* Though, *par hasard,* I know not if it will enchant you much. There is the oldest pensioner of Madame La Bastille, the Marquis de Chevagny—a sad man, taking little enjoyment of his life—though he should be used to it by now! and another, a fool, a madman, they say a murderer. But I know not. However, he is a compatriot of Monsieur le Capitaine, an Englishman."

"What is his name?" asked Bertie.

"Monsieur, to many there are no names in the Bastille. Only numbers, with few exceptions, such as that of De Chevagny, of whom we are justly proud. He is a credit to us and to our care. Still, I doubt not you will soon find out the idiot's name. He has his sane moments, though they are few. But his principal remark is that he trusts the wheel is not too painful. "Tis to that he is bound to go."

"An idiot! And sent to the wheel, even though a murderer! Will they do that?"

"Faith, they will. For, *tenez*, monsieur "—and he laid a dirty finger along his nose and looked slyly at Bertie—"he is a prisoner of the Church, of the priests. He has outraged them. Do you think he will escape their claws if he were forty thousand times as mad?"

"When shall I join this company?" asked Bertie. "I shall be glad to go. At least, the Marquis de Chevagny should be an interesting companion."

"At once. I will go fetch Pierre to assist in carrying up your baggage and furniture, and then the King's Lieutenant will escort you to the *calotte*. And, cheer up, 'tis high, but pleasant; you can see *tout Paris*, and the top windows of the Rue St. Antoine. *Ma foi!* a gay view, a fine retreat."

While the man was gone, Bertie placed the table and chair against the wall and sprang on top of them, and since it was Falmy's usual time for being at the window, was happy in finding him there. "Adieu," he signalled as rapidly as he possibly could, "I go to one of the *calottes*. I pray we may be able to correspond as before." Then in an instant he knew by the light in Falmy's face that such was the case, for he nodded and himself began to signal back: "If not the one above me, we can. I——" but at this moment Bertie heard Bluet coming back to the door, and, hurriedly jumping down, replaced the chair and table in their accustomed position. He had never been able to judge whether the turnkey would have remonstrated at this correspondence with another prisoner, and perhaps have caused it to be stopped. He did not, indeed, think he would do so, but he had always taken precautions to prevent him knowing what they did, and he took them now on this the last occasion.

Bluet was attended by the other turnkey, Pierre, and accompanied by the King's Lieutenant, who was second in command in the prison ; and while the two former busied themselves in getting together his bed and linen, as well as his furniture, the latter addressed him with that French etiquette and politeness which so often does duty for kind-heartedness.

"Monsieur has, I trust, found himself as comfortable as circumstances will permit," he said, "and has wanted for nothing. The food served in this chapel is always of the first order."

"I have nothing to complain of," replied Elphinston; "since I am here, I must take what comes. Yet, I wish you would answer me a question or so, monsieur. You are, or have been, a soldier, like myself. May not that ancient comradeship of arms make you gracious enough to do so ? "

"It is not the graciousness I lack," replied the officer, "it is the power. For, Monsieur Elphinston, you must surely know we are vowed to silence and secrecy within these walls. It is more than our posts, nay, our heads, are worth to answer questions or divulge secrets."·

"If I could know," said Bertie, "when I shall be interrogated it would be much."

"No mortal man in the Bastille can tell you that," the King's Lieutenant interrupted, "not even De Launey himself. The examiner, or judge, comes at fitful times and without warning. He came a week ago; he may come again next week; he may not come again for a year, or for two years."

"Is it because he did not concern himself with my case a week ago that I am now moved?" Bertie asked wistfully; "is it because I am passed over and may have to wait a long time now that this change takes place?"

The officer shrugged his shoulders and turned his face away. He was a soldier and had a heart within him, in spite of being the Lieutenant of the Bastille, and he could not reply that Bertie had guessed accurately, that it was because he had been passed over, and might, in consequence, be passed over for years, that he was now removed from the chapel.

"I see. I understand," Bertie said. "I understand very well. I may linger on here till I am old; I may become, if I live long enough, the oldest prisoner!" Then, once more addressing the Lieutenant, he said, though without any hope of receiving an answer:

"If I could only know to whom or what I owe this incarceration it might ease my mind; might, perhaps, enable me to confute the charge that in years to come may be brought against me. Can you not help me!—me, a brother soldier?"

Bluet and Pierre had left the chapel with the furniture and bedding, so that they were alone now, and the Lieutenant, glancing round the place, said softly:

"Have you no suspicion? Can you not guess? Does not your memory point to one whom you have injured?"

"My memory," replied Bertie, "points to one who has injured me and those I love so deeply that, if he had the power, he would have caused me to be sent here. But even his devilish malignity could not procure him that. He cannot have the power."

He had thought of Fordingbridge over and over again as the man whose hand might have inflicted this last deadly blow, yet he could never convince himself that it could indeed be he. He would be almost as much an outcast now, if in the city, as he would have been in London with a price upon his head. How, he had asked himself, could it be Fordingbridge?"

And the Lieutenant's next words, uttered in almost a whisper, in spite of their being still alone, seemed to confirm his doubts.

"Think again," he said; "reflect on some other than this one you mention; on one whom you injured, whose ambition you thwarted in its dearest design; on one who is powerful, has the ear of the King, who could send you here, and did so. Reflect!"

Bertie drew back in amazement and stared at the Lieutenant, unable to believe his own ears. Then he repeated:

"Whose ambition I thwarted! One who is powerful—the friend of the King! Oh, 'tis impossible, impossible! Some awful mistake has been made. I know no one such as that. No one."

Then, clasping his hands together, while his voice rang out clear and distinct in that vaulted chapel, he exclaimed, "For God's sake, help me in this! For God's sake, tell me to whom you refer!"

"Hush!" said the other. "Hush! They are coming back. And as for the name, it must never pass my lips. If the recollection of your own actions cannot help you now, I can do no more;" and, seeing the turnkeys at the door, he said in his usual tones, "Monsieur, follow me to your new apartment."

Dazed with what he had heard, Elphinston obeyed him, and slowly they went through the gloomy passages and up more stairs through iron-plated doors, until they stood at the one which opened into the *calotte* of the tower above the chapel—so called because, being the topmost chamber in the roof, it resembled a *calotte*, or fool's cap, or extinguisher.

"Messieurs,' said the Lieutenant to the inmates of the room when the door had been unlocked and unbarred, "allow me to present to you a comrade. Let me trust you will be agreeable to each other. Monsieur de Chevagny, you are the father of the house; I commit him to you." Then, glancing over to a bed in the corner, on which a dark-haired man lay sleeping with his face turned to the wall, the Lieutenant shrugged his shoulders and said, "*Mon Dieu! le fou* sleeps heavily. Well, we need not disturb him. No presentations are necessary with him."

The man addressed as Chevagny—whom Bertie could not but regard with interest, despite the whirl in which his brain was at the strange, inexplicable revelations of the Lieutenant—rose with courtesy from a chair as his name was mentioned, and, coming towards Bertie, held out a thin hand. His hair was snow-white and of great length, while his face, partly from age and partly, perhaps, from long confinement, was shrivelled and wan. What his clothes might have originally been it was impossible to guess; now they were a mass of rags and tatters, patched in some places, in others hanging in shreds. Round his neck he wore for a cravat the sleeve of an old shirt; while the soles of his shoes, which were full of holes, were joined to the upper parts by pieces of pack thread. All over his face there grew a great beard as white as the hair on his head, and this may have helped to keep him warm, especially as over his breast it was tucked inside a shirt that was almost black from long wear. Yet, with all this ragged misery, those features of his face which his hair and beard allowed to be seen were refined and elegant, were the features of a well-born man.

"Sir," he said to Bertie as he held out his hand, "what there is here I welcome you to, and I can only pray that it may not be your lot to grow as familiar with this place as I have become. For now—now—" and Bertie could see his old lips tremble as he spoke, "this place has grown through my unhappiness to be the only spot on earth that I know of—my only home."

"Monsieur le Marquis," said Bertie, "for your greeting, sad as it is and sad as is the spot where we meet, I thank you. So long as I am here—so long!— I shall respect and pity you."

He had taken no heed of the figure on the bed while he was speaking, having, indeed, his back turned to it, but now it forced him to observe it.

For, as he spoke for the first time, that figure—its wild eyes staring as though about to start from its head, and its hands opening and shutting convulsively —was kneeling on the bed, muttering, whining, gasping behind him.

And, turning round suddenly and seeing its contortions and its awful maniacal fear, Bertie reeled back across the *calotte*, exclaiming:

"My God! Fordingbridge! Face to face at last!"

CHAPTER XXIV.

BROKEN HEARTS.

YET in that very moment he knew that once more
Fordingbridge had escaped his vengeance. He recognised in the creature which had flung itself at his feet
and was moving, grimacing, and chattering there, that
he was mad—that he could no longer right his wrongs
by choking the life out of it. Those wild, misty eyes,
extended to their utmost with fear and maniacal frenzy,
told only too plainly that the brain behind them was
gone for ever, that henceforward he had to do with a
thing that lived, it was true, but had no sense nor reason. Yet the maniac recognised him, he observed,
was striving in his way to sue for mercy—could he be
so mad as to be safe from his revenge?

"You know him?" asked the marquis, in his sad,
weak voice, he having witnessed the scene with astonishment. "You know him?"

"To my bitter cost. Until to-day I thought—so
much has he wronged me—that to him also I owed my
detention here. Yet that, it seems now, can hardly be.
Monsieur, how long has he been your companion?"

De Chevagny paused a moment as though endeavouring to count the time since first his companion
had been there—his blue eyes gazing out wistfully to
the Rue St. Antoine, the roofs of which could plainly
be seen from this room—then he shrugged his shoul-

ders and said, "I cannot tell. I do not know. I have lost the power of keeping count. Yet—yet—it must be many weeks. We had no fire when first he came, and—and—the swallows were—— No," he broke off, "I cannot remember."

That told Bertie much; told him that it could scarcely have been Fordingbridge who had been the cause, even though indirect, of his being seized and sent here. They must have come in almost at the same time. Who, then, was the strange, mysterious man of power—the friend of the King, of whom the Lieutenant had spoken, the man whose deadly vengeance he had incurred?

"Begone!" he said to his old enemy, still grovelling at his feet; "away from me, I say. Heavens!" he exclaimed, "must this companionship be added to my other sufferings? Is the Bastille so small, or are its chambers so crowded, that this wretch and I could not be kept apart? Oh, what an irony of Fate that I who have sought him so long must meet him thus!"

"Monsieur," said De Chevagny, while still Fordingbridge knelt at Bertie's feet, wringing his hands and muttering, "monsieur, if his wrongs to you, his evil doings, are not beyond all forgiveness, you may pardon him now, almost pity him. He is doomed to death, I hear; nothing, not even his madness, can save him."

"Pity him!" exclaimed Bertie, "pity him! He has ruined, broken my life for ever; how can I pity him? And, even though he be not the cause of my presence here, I curse the hour that he was born, the day that threw him across my path!"

"They say," repeated the wretched maniac, his eyes glinting about the room in his frenzy, "they say nothing can save me. The priests will have my blood, will have me broken upon the wheel, will even refuse me absolution at the last. Yet I confessed to one of them—I confessed—I should be spared."

"What fresh crime have you committed that brings you here?" asked Elphinston sternly of him. "What deed of treachery—or worse?"

"I slew him," said Fordingbridge, still shaking all over, "because I hated him, because he wrought my downfall. I came behind him on—on—the *place*. I had the knife up my sleeve thus," and he bent his hand as though to illustrate the holding of a concealed dagger's hilt in it, "and when he turned from me I drove it home. He was dead a moment afterwards. Dead! Dead at my feet!" and he leered hideously as he spoke.

"Who was it you assassinated thus, in a manner so well becoming all your actions? Some poor, feeble creature unable to protect himself; some old man or stripling, perhaps, and unarmed?"

Was it well that Bertie did not suspect? If he had known, if he could but have known or guessed that, so far from being such as he imagined, the victim had been his own stalwart friend and comrade who had fallen beneath the foul assassin's knife, could he have restrained himself enough not to have dashed his brains out against the prison walls?

"Ha! ha!" laughed Fordingbridge, while at the same time there came into his eyes the awful look of cunning so peculiar to maniacs—"ha! ha! I know. But the secret's mine—mine—and the priests'. Yet, though I confided in them—confessed to them—they still denounced me, will now slay me. They say," he went on, putting out a long, shaking finger and endeavouring to touch the arm of the poor old marquis, who shrank back from him as from some foul creature, "they say that not even my English peerage can save me, since the priests are determined to have vengeance. Do you think that is so? Will they kill an English peer?"

"There is," said De Chavagny coldly—for now he knew that the creature he had pitied when first he came to this room was a cold-blooded assassin who had probably gone mad from terror afterwards—"there is no reason why they should not. The priests have slain many French peers who were not murderers—Son Eminence Grise more than a hundred, they say. Why should they not slay an English peer who is such as you are?"

"But not by the wheel," Fordingbridge moaned, "not by the wheel. Oh, to think of it!" and again he mowed and mouthed as he spoke. "I have seen men killed thus—there was one at—at—I forget the place—my memory is gone—but I saw him. They broke his bones with iron bars, and finished by beating in his chest-bone, and——" breaking off inconsequently, "I want my dinner; I am hungry."

In disgust the others turned away from him, while he threw himself on his bed in the corner and moaned again that he was hungry.

"I have had many strange companions in this cell in my time," said Chevagny, in his quiet, sad tones, "but never one like this. It is an insult to put such as he is in with us."

"Will they execute him as he fears?" asked Bertie. "I had always thought that the Bastille detained its prisoners or sent them forth free. I knew not that condemned men went from it to meet their death."

"Many have so gone forth," the other replied, "though generally only traitors. Yet this man stands in evil case, too; he has murdered, I judge from what he has now said, a priest—a Jesuit; if so, he must die, for the Jesuits are powerful in the Bastille—Gerville, the chaplain, is himself one. And, if he is a murderer, he should die."

"In truth he should," replied Bertie, "nor would I lift a finger to save him. For he is a murderer in more senses than one: he has slain two lives already—my own and another. I had sworn to myself to kill him if we ever met; we have done so, and lo! I cannot slay him. No matter, let the Place de Grève do its work!"

That he should feel no pity for the wretch lying there on his bed was not strange; he had wrought far too much bitter woe to Elphinston for such a sentiment to rise into his heart. Indeed, instead of pity, there had come into his mind now a great desire to discover, if possible, who the victim could be whom Fordingbridge had slain. He had not actually said it was a priest, though the Marquis de Chevagny had suggested that it was one, and as Bertie pondered on all this a terrible idea flashed into his mind—was the victim Archibald Sholto? He knew that Fording-bridge hated him, he knew that Archibald possessed many secrets of his; could it be that he had come upon him unawares and slain him? If so, if such was the case, then it was not strange that the Jesuits had determined upon his execution. And as he reflected on all this he determined that, if Fordingbridge were not taken away to his doom at once, he would find out who it was that had fallen victim to his treachery.

Bluet came in as he made these resolutions, and

began busying himself with preparing their midday meal, laying three covers at the table in the middle of the room. As, usual the fellow was in his accustomed semi-drunken condition, which Bertie had long since discovered was owing to his habit of abstracting some or all of the prisoners' wine ere he brought it to them—a pleasing custom none complained of, since he was, otherwise, an obliging rascal; and, as usual, he began to chatter in his familiar manner to those in the *calotte*.

"*Ma foi!*" he exclaimed, "if things go on as they now are, we shall soon have no guests at all. The examiners come again to-night; we are informed they will dine with *le vieux singe* De Launey; there will be some clearances to-morrow morning."

It was natural that at these words hope should spring into the breast of Elphinston; that he should be excited with the thought that now his case might be considered. Also, perhaps, it was natural that to De Chevagny they caused not the slightest emotion.

" Is—is there any possibility, any chance of knowing who will be called before them ?" asked the former. "Can you, Bluet, give any guess ?"

"*Mon Dieu! non*," replied the other, "not the least. When D'Argenson, who is the presiding Examiner, has supped—and, Heavens! he will punish old De Launey's *vin de Brequiny*, which is a wine to make the goats dance—then he will call for the list of our visitors, and will go over it from the first here to the last; and from that list he will select the names of some, but who they will be D'Argenson and his friend, the devil, alone can tell."

"There will be one," said the marquis softly, "whose name at least he will not select—one who is forgotten by all outside these walls. Yet, how well he was known and loved once by many—by many!"

"Ah, Monsieur le Marquis," said the good-natured vagabond, trying to cheer him, "what should we within the walls do if he did not forget you? *Mon Dieu!* I would disband myself, would go forth also if you, the father of our company, our Bastille flower, left us. *Non, non*, marquis, we cannot part with you. You are our father, our pride."

"I was here," said the poor old prisoner, shaking his head—and as he did so he shook a drop from each of his eyes on to his long beard—"when Bernaville was Governor. He put me first in the Tour de la Comte, where Lauzun had been, and where, when he tried to escape, they hanged his servant outside his door as a warning; him they dared not hang; and then I thought always that the Examiner—it was D'Argenson's father in those far-off days—might send for me. But he never did, he never did. And none have sent for me yet, and never will. You will go," he said, looking at Elphinston, "as the others have gone, and he," looking at the maniac on the bed, "will go to his doom, but I shall remain until I go, too—unto my grave. Ah, my grave, my grave! And then—I may see again the young wife they took me from—'tis almost forty-three years ago—and the little babe I left slumbering on her breast; the little child that we were going to make so brave a feast over and christen Brigide because it was my mother's name, because it had blue eyes like hers."

Bertie had turned his face away from the old man to hide his tears, and now he took him by the hand and wrung it softly, while Bluet, who, for a turnkey of the Bastille, seemed also much affected, exclaimed boisterously :

"Courage, courage, monsieur! We may lose you yet to our desolation. And Madame la Marquise may welcome you still—without doubt she lives for you—and *la petite mademoiselle*, now surely a great lady, as a De Chevagny must be. Heart of grace, monsieur, heart of grace, and see the fine dinner I have brought you! *Regardez moi ça.* Here is a fish—*ombre chevalier*, of the best—and two pigeons, some beef with the gravy in it, and a salad, some rennets and biscuits, and, for the wine, two little bottles. Because, you see, monsieur," turning to Bertie with a husky whisper, "here in the *calottes* the visitors drink not with such·abundance as in the chapel rooms. 'Tis not my fault."

"Why," exclaimed the marquis, in a stern voice very different from that in which he had just spoken, and regarding the table fiercely, "have you placed three covers? Who are the three?"

"*Mon Dieu!* you are three, monsieur. *Le fou*—the English lord—must eat too, is it not so? The portion is for three, and a good one at that."

"He is a villain!" exclaimed the old marquis, his eyes flashing. "He shall not sit at the table. I thought his drivellings of murder were not true, until this gentleman came, and that he was a harmless idiot. Now, I know he is a villain. And—and—I am a gentleman—a peer of France—he shall not sit at meat with me."

"Faith! then he must eat on his bed. Here, fool," Bluet exclaimed, going up to Fordingbridge, who seemed more dazed than ever, though he had been regarding the food eagerly; "the marquis will not have you at the table; eat there!" and he flung a platter down before him, on which there was some of the beef and salad, and an apple, or rennet, all mixed together.

The miserable wretch sprang at the portion like a wild beast that was famished, and devoured it in a few moments, and then threw himself on the bed again and either slept or pretended to do so, while the marquis and Bertie, taking no notice of him, discussed their meal, which, in spite of Bluet's eulogies, was not a very solid one. And during its progress they took the opportunity of telling each other a good deal of their various affairs and history, though, since the poor marquis had been immured so many years, his did not take long in the recital. Yet it was pitiful to hear.

"I had been married but a year," he said. "I was young—but twenty-five—well to do; nay, rich and happy. Then I wrote a little *ballade*, a harmless one, upon La Vallière; it was sung about the streets, it reached Marly and Versailles, and—and—that was all! A week later I was here—and it is forty-three years ago. O Jeanne, my wife! O Brigide, my little child, my babe! where are you both now? Forty-three years! Forty-three years! Forty-three years! If they should see me they would not know me. Jeanne could not recognize in me the young husband who was torn from her side; my little girl never knew me, will never know me now."

That Bertie's expressions of pity and sympathy with the poor old prisoner eased his grief he could not flatter himself, nothing could bring comfort, he knew, to that broken heart and wasted life. Moreover, he was himself too appalled, too overshadowed, by the dread of what might be his own fate to give much consolation to the other. He was young, almost as young as the marquis had been when he was brought here; he might be here, in this very *calotte*, forty-three years hence. Could there be any horror greater than this to look forward to? Anything more dreadful than such as this, to freeze the very life out of him!

Yet, he hoped that it was not possible; he even hoped that to-night, when the judges came, might see his liberty announced. For he knew now that he must be the victim of some awful error; there was no man in France whom he had injured, no man whom he knew who held the rank and power which the King's Lieutenant said his enemy held. How, then, could he have come here except by a mistake?

Bluet brought their supper at eight o'clock and announced to them that D'Argenson had arrived with two other examiners, or judges, as they were termed indifferently; that they were supping with De Launey, and that, when this was finished, they would proceed to the great hall, where those who were to be examined would be summoned one by one before them.

"And when—when," asked Bertie, "shall I know if—if—I am passed over?" while it seemed to him as he spoke as though his tongue cleaved to the roof of his mouth so that he was scarcely intelligible.

Bluet shrugged his shoulders ere he answered, then he said:

"'Tis scarce possible to say. *Mon Dieu!* in this place day and night scarce know distinction. They may sit till daybreak—I have known them do it when making a great clearance, and we have had to rouse our guests from their beds to go before them. Yet, 'tis not always so; ordinarily, by midnight, the affair is finished."

"So that," said Bertie, "I can know nothing for certain until the morrow."

Again Bluet shrugged his shoulders, again he answered dubiously that, "*en vérité*, that might be so;" and then, saying that "Monsieur le Capitaine must hope for the best," he took himself off.

So, in this hapless frame of mind, Bertie sat down to pass the first night in his new lodging. That he should sleep was impossible, and therefore bidding the marquis, who had already got into his bed, "Good-night," he dragged a chair in front of the barred fire-place and sat there brooding through the hours. Of Fordingbridge, who was lying outside his bed, neither of the others had taken any heed, and even when he muttered incoherently Bertie regarded him not.

As he sat there watching the fire die, he heard the great clock over the gateway strike eleven; as he still sat on, listening for any sound which might announce the coming of those who would be sent to fetch him, he heard it strike twelve. Yet still no one came. By this time the candle in the socket high up out of reach was flickering and flaring at its last ebb and throwing great shadows on the walls; and once, as he looked round the room, disturbed by some movement of Fordingbridge's, he saw that the latter was sitting up on his bed peering at him with his great hollow vacant eyes, in which the glare of madness was almost intensified by the unsteady waverings of the candle's flame. Then, as the great clock tolled one, the light went out, and he heard Fordingbridge throw himself back on his bed.

Still the time went on—once Fordingbridge laughed in the dark, an imbecile, vacant laugh; once, he could have sworn, he heard him mutter "Sholto!" and once

he moved uneasily on his pallet and groaned—and
then the clock struck two. But still he sat on in the
darkness before the dead fire, waiting, waiting. And,
at last, he heard a sound of a door opening in a distant
corridor, then another, and then footsteps approaching. And a moment later Bluet's voice was speaking
outside.

"Monsieur," he heard him say, "*Je regrette beau-
coup*, but the judges have departed; monsieur's chance
is not yet arrived."

And with a heart-broken groan Bertie groped his
way to where his bed had been placed and flung himself upon it, while, as he did so, he heard his maniacal
foe at the other end of the *calotte* muttering to himself
and laughing once more.

CHAPTER XXV.

AFTER that night Bertie ceased to believe that he would ever go forth from the Bastille; a lethargy, which was partly despair and partly a fierce, bitter repining at the inexplicable, unmerited cruelty which had consigned him to such a place, took possession of his spirits, and he came to regard himself as one who was dead to the world for ever.

Yet from the other—to whose long sufferings his own could at present form no comparison—he received consolation in many forms; from De Chevagny, continual exhortations were made that he should never lose heart, while even Bluet would tell him, in his own familiar, good-natured manner, that he was far too young a visitor to consider himself a permanency as yet.

" There have been men here," said the marquis, repeating the same stories over and over again to him for his comfort, "who have not given up hope for years, who have then done so and become despairing, and have then, after still more years, gone out free." After which he would tell of the Dutch doctor who had been mistaken for the Alsatian poisoner; of others who had been there ten, fifteen, twenty years, and had at last got away; indeed, to solace poor Bertie, the marquis more than once said that even he himself, after forty-three years, had not lost all courage, and hoped to spend some few of those remaining to him in freedom. Yet, as the other looked in his face and heard his sad, trembling tones, he knew that it was but pity that inspired the words; that, in his heart, De Chevagny knew he would never be released.

From Falmy—by use of their letters which, in spite of the change in lodging, they could still make visible to one another—he received also many sentences of encouragement and counsel, while one day there came from that unhappy man a piece of information which once more set his heart beating with hope, and raised great expectations.

"I have been joined by another prisoner," he signalled across to the window of the *calotte*. "He is, however, about to obtain his liberty—awaits only his signed acquittal from D'Argenson. If you have messages to send, he will deliver them if possible."

In an instant Bertie had snatched from an old trunk that had been brought by De Chevagny the letters which he used, and a few moments later he had begun to signal a message to his mother, which he intended to augment by another to Kate. His heart beat high as he did so; he knew that, if this prisoner who was to be released was only faithful, in a few days at most the two women who loved him so would know of his whereabouts, though they were powerless to obtain his freedom. Yet, could even that be possible? Who could say? His mother might represent to the King his long and faithful services in the regiment; Kate might have powerful friends at court who could do something.

With trembling hands he formed the words, letter by letter. "Tell him my name is Elphinston. Bid

him seek out my mother. She lives at the Rue——"
Alas! as he finished the last letter of the word "Rue,"
upon the *calotte* about the tower in which Falmy was
there appeared the cone-shaped shako, or cap, worn
by the *corps de garde* of the Bastille, followed by the
body of a sentry, and, hastily leaving the window, he
desisted from his work. He was foiled for the day at
least; the sentry he knew, was set on that particular
tower, and either he or those who relieved him would
be there for twenty-four hours. And as he reflected
that in those twenty-four hours the *acquit* from D'Argenson might come for the prisoner who was about to
be released, he felt as if he would go mad.

Falmy appeared at his window often during the
day, looking wistfully up to the *calotte*, though Bertie,
who could still observe him when standing back from
the window, dared make no sign. It would matter
nothing for the soldiers to see him at the opening—
the prisoners were allowed the privilege of looking
out if the windows were low enough to permit of their
doing so—but the slightest communication that should
be observed to pass between them would be visited
with the most severe punishment, even to confinement
in the dungeons beneath the ditch. He perceived,
therefore, all the signs of distress on Falmy's face; he
even observed him turn round, and saw his lips move
as he gesticulated to his new companion within the
room; he could guess, as plainly as though he had
heard him, what the Genevese was saying. He felt
sure that he was explaining that there must be a sentry above them, and that therefore Elphinston dared
not signal across.

"Oh!" exclaimed poor Bertie, "oh, if I had but
acquainted them with my mother's address at once be-

fore the guard was set! that would have been enough. Fool! fool that I am to lose so fair a chance! The very visit of a man set free from this place to my mother's house would have alarmed her suspicions, would have told her all. And now, now, he knows not where to go. God help me! it was my only hope, and I have lost it."

All day he watched the roof of the opposite tower, hoping against hope, for he *knew* the guard would only be changed, and not removed. He watched still as the shadows of the winter evening deepened into night, and still also he watched until the night itself had come and both tower and sentry were obscured in darkness. And as he kept his dreary vigil all through the day, he saw Falmy's face at his own window, staring at him with sad and melancholy glances, but without any sign being made by him, so that he knew that a guard had been placed above the roof of his tower as well.

"On any other day it would have mattered nothing," he moaned to himself. Oh, why to-day of all days should these towers have been selected!"

It was so absolute a chance, such a coincidence, that the guard should happen to have been placed at this part of the Bastille on this particular occasion that his misery and mental anxiety were not strange. Of all the days he had been in the *calotte*, there was scarce one that could have been worse for him and his prospects.

The restless night passed, the dawn broke, cold, grey, and miserable, and springing from his bed he rushed to the window—only to see above the opposite tower a sentry still there. The twenty-four hours' guard was not yet finished, would not be until the great clock over the gate should clang out nine. And it was not yet eight o'clock on this dreary February morning! But at last the hour arrived. The sentry presented arms to the King's Lieutenant who came to dismiss him from his post. As the clock struck, the roof was deserted, and a few minutes later Falmy's face appeared at the window. But he shook his head mournfully, and then, with his board and piece of charcoal, he communicated the melancholy words, " The prisoner went forth at eight o'clock."

And now, indeed, Bertie gave himself up to despair—black despair that grew deeper and deeper as the weeks crept by one after the other; as slowly the cruel, griping Paris winter passed, and gradually they knew that spring was coming. Yet to him who had once welcomed the birth of new summers with such eagerness, the one now on its way to gladden the earth brought no comfort. The swallows came back and circled round and round the towers of the prison, and began, with countless chirps and squeaks, to build their nests below the gloomy eaves, yet he only found himself wondering vaguely why, when they were free, they should choose so foul a place. Also, over in the garret windows of the Rue St. Antoine he saw daily a girl tending some flowers in a box, even saw the tint of the flowers themselves as they burst into bloom, and wondered, too, if she, who had her liberty, ever cast one thought to the poor prisoners confined so near to her.

As for his companions, De Chevagny and Fording-bridge, they seemed, from opposite reasons, to be in-different to any changes that the season might bring, though sometimes the former would stand at the window and hold out his hands and let the warm May sun—for May had come—stream down upon them and his face, and whisper sadly that for those who could be out in the woods and fields it was good, very good. Then, when he was tired of standing or sitting thus, he would cast himself on his bed and sigh, and so sleep away the hours.

With Fordingbridge, both he and Elphinston had ceased to hold any converse at all; nor, indeed, had they been willing to talk with him, was it possible that he could either have understood or replied to them. His madness seemed to grow upon him daily, and, while he became more taciturn, also he became more imbecile. Once he woke Bertie in the early morning by crawling to his bedside, and, holding out a piece of string which he had found imbedded in the filth of the floor, asked him to hang him ere they could lead him to the wheel; and one night he raved and moaned so through the dark hours—and on this occasion the other heard him beyond all doubt mutter the name of Archibald—that the prison doctor was sent for the next day.

This official, who was addressed diversely by Bluet as *Monsieur le Docteur* Herment and *Monsieur l'Abbé* Herment when he brought him in, seemed to be in about the same state of semi-drunkenness as the turn-key generally was, and to be also an inordinately vain creature. He had on his head a golden-haired wig which, while he was examining the unhappy wretch Fordingbridge, he was engaged in telling Bertie had been made from the hair of one of his *chères amies* who loved him truly; and he also remarked that some silver buckles on his shoes had been given him by a *grande dame* who had recently been released from the Bastille.

"What of the patient?" asked the latter sternly, such observations being unwelcome to him. "Will his lunacy increase, think you?"

"*Ma foi!*" exclaimed the *abbé*, or doctor, "so much so that it is my duty to warn the Society of Jesuits to be expeditious with what they have to do. Otherwise they will miss their victim, and our good Parisians will lose a spectacle. The wheel furnishes many a *fête* in the Place de Grève."

"Will they do that?" asked Bertie. "Will they execute so miserable a wretch as this?"

"*Bien sûr*, they will. Was there ever a Jesuit who forgave?"

"What has he done? They say he has slain a priest."

But the other was not to be entrapped like this, so, with a wink, he replied: "Monsieur, you should know by now that Madame La Bastille keeps her secrets well. But this I will tell you," and he pointed as he spoke to Fordingbridge, who was writhing on his bed, though none in the room could guess whether he understood what was being said or not, "he is doomed. And since he appears likely to escape the examiners if there is much more delay, his time will not be long now. Not long. Not very long! Oh, no! *Bon jour*, *messieurs*, I have my report to make to the Governor. Yet, since we must not lose our friend, I will send him a draught."

Whether the creature really made his report as he said he should, and thereby hastened Fordingbridge's end, Bertie Elphinston never knew, but at any rate it came soon afterwards.

It was on one night, one 14th of May, when the weather had taken an extraordinary change, and all the warmth of the coming summer seemed to have disappeared and winter to have returned, and when from their window they could see slight flakes of snow mingled with the falling rain, that Bluet, bringing in the supper, appeared to be especially solicitous that Fordingbridge should make a good meal.

"*Mangez, mon ami*," he said, as the other crouched on his bed, staring round the room with the hunted expression that was always now in his eyes—"*mangez bien*. Make a good supper. *Mon Dieu!* you eat nothing of late," and he came over to the table where the others sat and asked their permission to tempt the idiot with some meat and biscuits. Then, as he bent over to take them from the dish, he whispered significantly:

"He goes to-morrow. Before daybreak."

If Bertie had known that the doomed man had, to his other crimes, added that of cowardly slaying his bosom friend Douglas, could it have been possible that into his heart there could have come the feeling —was it pity—that now arose? At last, then, Fordingbridge's end had come; he was to pay for all! And—and—for of such complex emotions are we formed—as Bertie heard that his doom was sealed, he forgot the wrongs he had suffered at this man's hands; he forgot the wreck of his and of Kate's life; if he did not forgive him, he compassionated him. Rising from his chair he went over to the bed where Fordingbridge was seated, and on which he shrank from him as he approached, and, pointing to the biscuit he held in his trembling hands, he said, very gently, "Eat, Fordingbridge, eat. It will do you good. And, see, you have nothing to drink," and going back to the table he poured out a cup of wine and brought it to him.

With still trembling hands the madman took it from him, glinting at him over the cup as though afraid, and watching him as though fearful that at any moment a blow might be dealt; and then, when he had drained the last drop, he began slowly to munch the biscuit, which he kept shut in the palm of his hand, as though someone was about to take it from him.

"Do you ever," asked Bertie, speaking slowly and distinctly, as if he might thereby make him understand what he was saying, "do you ever think of those who —who were once dear to you? If—if—it should please God in His infinite mercy that, some day, perhaps in some far-off, remote day, I may depart from here, and you—may not—not accompany me, is there any word, any message, you would wish to send?"

Still Fordingbridge shrank from him, creeping, edging farther away from where he had sat down by his side, but he uttered no word. Only, still his eyes roamed restlessly over Bertie's form, and still his mouth worked convulsively as ever, and his hands twitched.

"Think. Reflect, I beseech you," the man whom he had wronged so much continued, "you are not well—you may—at any moment—be worse. And I, forgetful of the past, would, if it ever comes into my power, very willingly do this for you. Fording-bridge, you may trust me. As I sit by you to-night, I cast away for ever from my memory the evil you have wrought me; I desire only that, if I can, I may serve you. Can I do nothing?"

And still the other shrank from him, understanding, perhaps, not one word that he said. Once more, however, Bertie continued:

"If you can comprehend me, I pray you do so.

Think, remember. You had a wife once; before God I believe she is your wife now, and always has been; I do not believe that you deceived her. Have you no word for her, no plea for pardon, no request that, as time goes on, she may come to think of you without bitterness? Also there are others—Archibald Sholto and Douglas——"

A cry from the maniacal lips interrupted him—a hoarse cry such as an animal in pain, an animal that had been struck suddenly and unawares, might utter.

"Douglas! Douglas! Douglas!" he shrieked. "Douglas! Douglas!" and so continued muttering that name again and again. Then, with another sound, half wail, half sigh, he flung himself back on his bed, and thus spent his last night on earth. Yet, even on that night, through the whole of which he chattered unintelligible words to himself, he laughed once or twice convulsively, and as though suffocating with suppressed mirth.

.   .   .   .   .   .

As the shadows of the night departed and the morning gave signs of breaking, with still the snow-flakes mingling with the rain that beat against the windows of the towers, they came for him—the King's Lieutenant, accompanied by four of the *corps de garde*.

"Put on your cloak, if you have one," that officer said to the miserable creature shrinking back to the wall, while he shivered all over and uttered his broken cries—"put on your cloak, and come."

"In pity leave him!" exclaimed Bertie; "in the name of Christianity, of humanity, refrain from taking so miserable a life as this! Vile as he has been, see, see what he is now! It is as though you took the life of a helpless child, of a dumb brute.   As you hope for mercy, show some."

"I am but an instrument," said the Lieutenant; "I have my orders; willingly or unwillingly I must obey them.   And if I would spare him, nay, if my master the King would spare him, the Church would not.   He is in their grip; it will be unfastened an hour hence, when he is dead."   Then, turning to the soldiers, he said, "Bring him away."

They took the shaking wretch—no longer a man but only a living thing—by the arms and led him moaning to the door; yet, when he had arrived there, he had the strength to wrench one of them free; and looking round at Bertie for the last time in the world, and with his starting, scintillating eyes fixed on him, he raised that arm, the hand clenched as though grasping a weapon, and—once—twice—struck downward fiercely with it.

Then he was gone for ever.

CHAPTER XXVI.

KATE LEARNS SHE IS FREE.

A GREAT masked ball was over at the opera house; the candles were burning down into their sockets in the girandoles and lustres; the May morning, which under ordinary circumstances should have broken so soft and bright, had dawned foul, rainy, and snowy; and carriages, hackney coaches, and sedan chairs were pushing their way up to the doors of the theatre and carrying off their employers to their houses and beds.

But all were not yet departed; some still sat drinking or chatting at the supper tables; some danced in groups without any music to accompany them except the airs which they hummed or whistled themselves, for the orchestra had put up its instruments and gone also to its bed; and some, principally men, struggled and pushed in the *vestiaires* to obtain cloaks, roque-laures, hats and riding hoods, and swords—which latter could not by law be worn in the ball-room. Mock harlequins jostled imitation Henrys of Navarre; mock monks swore at supposed Crusaders; minotaurs and cavaliers and priests all contended against one another for their and their female companions' wraps, and at the same time laughed and jested and pro-posed breakfasts at neighbouring taverns, or a visit to the gambling hells, which on such nights as these kept their doors perpetually open.

Amidst all this confusion there ran through the whole place a rumour—a whisper, which reached first those in the *vestiaires*, and next the people at the supper tables—that those who so chose might yet finish their night's enjoyment with another spectacle—a grim and dismal but still enjoyable one—which was far better than any tavern breakfast or punting at the gaming table.

"*Figurez-vous!*" screamed one reveller, a deformed creature by nature, who had, with true Parisian appreciation of ludicrousness, arrayed himself consequently as Venus—"*figurez-vous, mes enfants*, there are two for execution, although, *malheureusement*, but only one is to be broken. The other, they say—because, *peste!* he is a *sal Anglais* and also of high rank—escapes the wheel and is only to be decapitated. A curse upon the law, say I, that treats an Englishman better than us!"

"*Ma petite Vénus de poche*," remarked another to him, clad as an arquebusier, "have a care how you curse the law; otherwise you may get broken yourself. There are plenty of police here in disguise, and if they hear you, that goodly hump of yours will stand a fine chance of being smashed by the executioner's bar. *Ma foi!* the *coup de grâce* is generally administered to the chest bone; with you, I presume, it will be administered on the *bosse*."

"I spoke only in jest," exclaimed the deformed one, glancing round apprehensively; "I meant no harm. A good subject, I, of the King of France and all his ministers. But come, let us away. Who's for the Grève? *Mon Dieu!* we must not miss the show!"

"I am for it, for one!" screamed a girl not over twenty, whose golden hair hung down over her back, and whose tones and glances proclaimed her to be already far sunken in dissipation. "I have never yet seen a man done to death; and as for the wheel, why, I have prayed often for a chance of seeing it. They say the *coup de grâce* is magnificent if the—the patient —is still sensible. Now, in our old village, before the young lord brought me to town, we never saw anything but a beggar in the stocks. And, *dame! les ceps* cease to be interesting after one has pelted the occupiers for half an hour."

"Pretty things," said the arquebusier, looking down sardonically on her, "have a care, *ma chère*, that you never come to worse than *les ceps* yourself. I have known many country girls brought to town by their young lords, and—hem!—who got worse shift than the stocks when they were discarded."

"*Ah! voyons!*" exclaimed the girl, "*avec ça!* Look you, my figure of fun, you are insolent. Get you home to your wife and family, and earn bread for them. We of the fashion desire none of your *banalités*."

Yet, as she spoke, she was being inducted into her long cloak by some of her would-be admirers, and also many others were getting ready. For Paris had not had an execution for some two months now, and the "half-tiger, half-monkey nature" which Voltaire attributed to his countrymen was thirsty for its favourite form of entertainment.

In the ball-room itself there sat, however, a group very different from those in the vestibule, who, since the masquerades were open to all who could pay for admission, had attended the ball. This group consisted of Sir Charles and Lady Ames—once Lady Belrose—and Kate, who, in spite of her melancholy and her ill-health, had been persuaded to accompany them.

Heaven knows such diversions were little enough in her way now! yet Lady Ames had been kind to her when she needed kindness, and, at the express desire of Sir Charles and his wife, she had consented to go with them.

In one way she was not unhappy: she knew, she felt certain, that this second disappearance of Bertie Elphinston from the knowledge of the world was not of his own accord. That something terrible had happened she could not doubt; yet she knew also that, whatever that something might be, it was not due to any desire to hide himself from her—that was, if he was still alive. But was he?"

Douglas's awful death by an unknown hand might also have been Elphinston's lot: who could tell? And then her own husband's disappearance! Did not that point to some catastrophe? Over and over again she had meditated on all these things, lying awake for nights together, pondering over them, wondering, wondering always. For even now she was in total ignorance of who the murderer of Douglas had been, of what Archibald had discovered. He had written to her at intervals, it was true, but he had either avoided all reference to the tragedy, or had said that, if the murderer was ever brought to justice, she would doubtless know all. Her husband he never mentioned.

Yet, those who are aware of what she could not guess can understand how difficult a task it would have been for the Jesuit to tell her that he had discovered the assassin, and that Fordingbridge, her husband, was the man. It may be that, after he had handed him over to the proper authorities, he hoped, nay, endeavoured so to arrange that she should never discover that her husband was the criminal. Better that he should disappear from her knowledge for ever, go to his doom without her dreaming that he had paid for the crime with his life, than that she should know to what a foul thing she had been united.

The candles guttered lower in their sockets, the attendants were putting out even the few lights that still burned; it was time to go. The opera house was emptying fast of all who had danced the night away there; amidst shrieks and whoops and yells the lower class of visitors were departing in coaches and chairs or on foot—some to their homes, but many to the Place de Grève. The spectacle of one man being broken to death and another decapitated was not to be missed.

"They say," exclaimed Sir Charles, as he returned with the cloaks and hoods of the two ladies, "that an execution takes place this morning on the Place de Grève. Hark! you may hear the creatures chattering over it as they go forth. Well, our coachman need not go through .the *Place*, though it is on our road. Surely he can skirt round it. At least, I will bid him do so," and he escorted his wife and Kate to their carriage.

Outside, the crowd that was making its way to the place of execution was stamping down the now fast-falling snow as it fell, and hurrying forward for fear it should be too late for the show. With renewed shrieks and yells it went onward, singing songs and choruses, roaring out ballads that perhaps it deemed suitable to the occasion, beating on *tambours-de-basque* and little tabours which formed the accompaniments of many of the masquers' costumes, and hammering on doors that were as yet unopened, with their shepherds' crooks and wooden swords (which were allowed to form part of their dress) and canes, and howling at the inhabitants to arise and come forth to *le spectacle*. They halted very little on their short way, sometimes only to shake the falling snow off their clothes, sometimes to wipe the paint and raddle from their faces which the wet snow had turned into sticky filth, and sometimes to kick over the braziers of the early morning chestnut-sellers, or to run into an early-opened wine-shop, hastily gulp down a drink, and then go on again.

"Heavens!" exclaimed Sir Charles, as the slow-progressing coach kept pace with the creatures that passed along the miserable three-foot sideways or crunched along the road—"heavens! what a crowd is a Parisian one! Their laughter is as ferocious in its way as the roughness of our English rabble—nay, I believe, far more deadly. How they revel in what they are going to see!"

"I tell you, my friends," screamed one painted harridan from the sedan chair she was being carried in, to a number of her friends who walked beside it, "that it is a great, a magnificent spectacle. I have seen it, *voyez-vous*, at Lyons, on the Place Bellecour, often—once, twice, thrice. *Ma foi!* the shriek at the first blow as the man lies back, his body tied to the wheel, is *pénétrant écrasant!* And so on, the cries becoming lower, till they are no better than sobs or groans, until the *coup de grâce*. Then, sometimes, but alas! not always, there will be one more wild shriek, and *voilà! c'est fini*. After that it is always time for breakfast."

One or two girls in the crowd making its way onward glanced at the ogress in the sedan chair and turned white; and Kate, who had heard all her words, grasped Lady Belrose's hand; while a man, walking steadily along through the snow, answered the woman, saying:

"*Peste!* 'tis not always as good as that. I waited once all through a summer night at Caen to see a man broken—I remember we played cards, I and the others, in the moonlight, and I lost four gold pistoles —and, *dame!* the fellow was a favoured one. Favoured, you understand. A vile aristocrat. So, as we thought, they strangled him as they bound him, and, *malediction!* he suffered not at all. Never screamed once—not once. 'Twas a cruel wrong to the spectators."

"'Tis an aristocrat who suffers to-day, they say," another man exclaimed.

"Nay," screamed still another, "not so. The aristocrat will suffer not; they will but slice his head off with the axe. There is no suffering in that; 'tis done and over in a moment. Yet I would see him die, too. He is an English aristocrat, and I hate all English; one beat me the other day for regarding his flaxen-haired wife too admiringly! I have never seen an Englishman die. They are brutes, yet they have the courage of devils."

"An English aristocrat!" said Sir Charles to his companions. "I do not understand this. There have been no Englishmen arrested in Paris for a long time; otherwise I must have heard of it among our friends here. What does he mean?"

"My dear Charles," replied his wife, "you do not know the Parisians very well. An English aristocrat to them is any Englishman who is outside his own country for pleasure and with his pocket well lined with guineas. Doubtless, however, this is some needy ragamuffin or copper captain, who has come to the scaffold for his sins, and they suppose him an aristocrat."

Whatever Sir Charles may have replied was drowned now by an increase of the howls and yells of the crowd, by fiercer beatings on the *tambours-de-basque* and tabours, by snatches of wild, frenzied songs, and by bursts of hysterical laughter.

The Place de Grève was in sight.

"Turn off!" said Sir Charles, putting his head out of the window and addressing the coachman—"turn off, I say! I told you to leave the route to that infernal *Place* and avoid it. Why have you disobeyed me?"

The man shrugged his shoulders as he looked round from his seat—doubtless, in spite of the orders he had received, he meant to see *le spectacle* himself if possible—then he said:

"Monsieur, it is impossible to turn off, or scarcely now to proceed. The crowd encompasses us. Yet the *Place* is not so full but we may pass through it. *Mon Dieu!* if it had been a fine May morning, a fly could not have passed."

"Is—is there anything—dreadful—taking place yet? If so, we will not proceed."

The driver stood up on his box and gazed forward; then he shook his head and said:

"*Non,* monsieur, there is nothing. Only the erection itself, and the soldiers and people; not many of the latter, either. *Nous autres,*" pointing to the howling crowd from the Bal Masqué seething around them, "will double the sightseers." But he muttered to himself, "Ere we get into the middle of the *Place* we shall see something, or I'm a stupid *escargot.*"

"Go on, then," said Sir Charles, "as quickly as you can, since you cannot now turn round. Lose no time." And he spoke to his companions, saying, "Best put on your masks. This is no place for ladies to be seen in. But we shall be through it all in five minutes."

Lady Belrose and Kate did as he bade them, and then the coach went on, slowly following all those in the road before them. Unfortunately, it had no curtains to the windows, which shut from within as was the custom of the day, otherwise the baronet would have closed out the whole of their surroundings. But this was impossible.

And still the crowd accompanying them shrieked and howled more and more—fighting and struggling to pass each other; thrusting those in front of them away; elbowing and pushing—the man who had waited all night at Caen playing at cards, throwing another almost under the wheels of Sir Charles's coach, while a girl was borne down in the crush and dragged aside fainting—stamping with glee and excitement, almost dancing in frenzy.

For the bell of the neighbouring church was tolling now, and, through the flakes of snow as they fell, the wheel and the block for the two condemned men were visible on the scaffold.

That scaffold itself was a platform some seven feet high, around which stood a company of the grenadiers, with, on either side of it, a guard of the musketeers. On the left of it was the wheel itself, fixed horizontally between stout wooden supports let into the platform, it being a large cannon-wheel. On the right side was a headsman's block, with, beneath it, a basket filled with sawdust, now half covered by snow. By the wheel and leaning against it was a huge club, iron-bound at the head, and at this sight the crowd became still more excited, if possible, pointing it out to each other and saying, "Behold, *la massue*. She will dò her work well. *Ça pese bien*," and laughing and screaming once more, and rubbing their hands.

Next came a roar, with shrieks from women and more faintings among them, while, by some impulse unrecognised perhaps by themselves, all of the latter produced their masks and put them on. It may be that something feminine, some feeling of womanly shame, prompted them to hide their features, to disguise their presence there. As for the men, the excitability of their natures affected them in a different way, for at what was happening now some of them, even strangers to each other, shook hands effusively, and some clapped others on the back.

For the condemned ones were in sight.

They came forth together from a small door in the wall of the *Hôtel de Ville*, side by side, these two who were to suffer ; one—he who was to perish on the wheel—being nearly naked, and having on him nothing but a short pair of breeches reaching to his knees and a sleeveless singlet. He was a great, bull-chested man, with massive limbs that would have become a gladiator, and, as he strode along attended by a confessor with a crucifix in his hand, he seemed to the mob to appear like one who would suffer severely. Therefore they roared and shrieked at him, and some waved handkerchiefs and clapped and cried, while he regarded them almost with contempt. Yet there was a glance in his eyes as if he could not comprehend why all these people, whom he saw through the falling flakes, should be thus fantastically dressed and should also be masked.

In truth it was a weird scene in the Place de Grève that morning, with the condemned men approaching the scaffold through the snow, and with, for the greater part of the spectators, these women, through the holes of whose masks their eyes glittered, and whose grotesque costumes were but little suited either to the occasion or the wintry morning.

Yet still there was the other doomed one. He, however, approached the platform very differently from the manner in which the man whose portion was the wheel came forward. He, too, had by his side a confessor with a crucifix—after each there walked the executioners, and also the officials—and it seemed as if he would shelter himself behind the robes of the priest. Yet sometimes, too, he smiled and gibbered at the crowd as though it was composed of his friends, and only when he saw the masked faces of the women and all the quaint garbs of the onlookers did he seem astonished.

At his appearance the crowd appeared startled, the shouts died down; instead of them a whisper ran through their ranks. "He is mad! *Il est fou!*" they cried, and again some women fainted.

"Great God!" muttered Sir Charles Ames hoarsely, catching sight of him. Then, suddenly, he said: "Kate—Lady Fordingbridge—do not look out; for pity's sake do not!" And to his wife he made signs that she should prevent her friend from glancing at the scaffold.

But he was too late! Already she had done so; already she, peering from the window of the coach, her own face masked, had seen the face of the trembling, grinning wretch ; and, since gradually the coach-man had edged the carriage through the crowd until it was not now ten paces from the platform, he, too, saw her—the woman with her face disguised—glaring at him.

She herself was nearly fainting at this time, yet she could see the headsman grasp his axe and motion to the victim to kneel down and place his head upon the block, and in her agony she raised her hand to her brow. In doing so it struck and loosened the mask, so that it fell off, leaving her face exposed.

And then the crowd's enjoyment culminated!

For he saw the mask fall away from her—he saw her face.

And with a wild scream—a scream that penetrated to the hearts of all in the Place de Grève—he shrieked :

" Kate! Kate! I have seen him! He forgives! He is a prisoner in——" and fell back, dying, into the executioner's arms.

The frenzied brain had failed at last.

CHAPTER XXVII.

KATE had been, as already stated, far from well of late; the horrible revelation of that snowy morning brought her near to death's door; and, after she had been taken back to the Prince's house in a prostrate condition and put at once to bed, her life was for some weeks despaired of.

Meanwhile she was carefully ministered to by all the Scotch ladies who formed a part of the establishment, and also by Lady Ames, who refused under any circumstances to quit Paris; though, indeed, her indulgent husband did not press her to do so.

"The King," she said, "may call me a Jacobite, may even prosecute me for one when I return to London, yet I shall not leave Lady Fordingbridge now— no, not even if I have to become an inmate of Charles Edward's house. Oh, the horror of seeing one's husband brought out to such a doom, villain though he was; the horror of it! How shall she ever recover from such a catastrophe?"

"How, indeed?" replied Sir Charles, who, worldling though he was, had been as terribly shocked as she at the end of Fordingbridge's career. "Yet it might have been worse. It was a merciful providence that saw fit to end his life at the moment it did. Think, only think, if, added to all else, she had seen his head fall, as she would have done had he not died at the instant!"

Lady Ames nodded her head reflectively as she agreed with him; then a few moments later she said, speaking from the deep *fauteuil* in which she was sitting in their lodgings, which they had now taken on the Quai des Théatins so as to be near her:

"You heard his last words?—'I have seen him. He forgives. He is a prisoner in——' and then died before he could conclude. What, Charles, do you think they pointed to?"

Sir Charles shrugged his shoulders; then he asked significantly, "What does *she* think they pointed to?"

"Alas!" his wife replied, "she does not refer to them; seems scarcely to have heard them uttered, or, if she did, not to have understood them. Remember, she is but a woman, and, although it is impossible she should regret his death, the horror, the shame of it, has broken her down completely. She longed—any woman would long—to be free of a man who had deceived her from the first as he had done, yet no woman could desire her freedom should come in such an awful form. They say," she continued, sinking her voice to an awestruck whisper, "that he died of fright upon that scaffold."

"Possibly," replied Sir Charles, "possibly. He was a cowardly fellow, as it seemed to me, when Sholto and I had that interview with him in your morning-room. I should not be surprised; other men have died on the scaffold, at the foot of the gallows, before now. Why not he? But," he said, changing the subject, "since we can do nothing, we must be what assistance we can to her. Now, I propose to set about discovering what he was led out to execution for;

what his crime was. It must have been something
horribly grave to lead to a man of his position being
executed in France ; for, although no treaty of peace
has as yet been signed between them and us, we are
no longer at open strife. And if," he added, " France
would but send this Stuart packing, and harbour him
no longer, a lasting peace might be secured." *

"What could it have been, think you ?" his wife
asked. "Something terrible, to lead to such a conclusion."

"Yes," he replied, "yes. Something terrible."

Then he devoted himself to the task of discovering
what that something terrible could have been.

Meanwhile, Kate, after being utterly broken down
and lying between life and death for something short
of a month, began to mend at last, her naturally fine
though delicate constitution enabling her to triumph
over the blow she had received. Then she, too, told
Lady Ames that she must discover for her own future
ease, if not peace of mind, the reason why her wretched
husband, after having disappeared for so many months,
had met his end in such a way. Also she undeceived
her friend in the belief that she had not heard that
wretched husband's last words.

"For," she said, "I heard them all, clearly and
distinctly. Heard them ! I hear them now—at night ;
all day ; as I lie here. ' I have seen him. He forgives.
He is a prisoner in——.' And," she continued, laying
a white, wan hand on that of the other who sat by
her bedside, "I know well enough to whom he referred.
It was to Bertie, to Mr. Elphinston."

"Great heavens !" exclaimed Lady Ames, who,

---

* As happened the next year, by the Treaty of Aix-la-Chapelle.

in the excitement of all that had happened since that terrible morning, had absolutely forgotten that this other one was also as mysteriously missing as Lord Fordingbridge had been—"great heavens! to Mr. Elphinston. Yes, it must be. Each word would apply to him. O Kate! what does it all mean?"

"God knows what it means; what it points to none can doubt—to the fact that in the prison from which they brought him the other one is incarcerated; though on what charge I cannot dream. Oh, my dear," she exclaimed to her friend, "beg Sir Charles to find out that—those two things, above all: the prison, and the reason why he is detained. Then, when that is discovered, we may do something to obtain his release, since I am known to so many who have influence."

"Yes," Lady Ames acquiesced, "yes; Charles must do that. Yet there are many prisons in Paris where men are kept unknown to the outer world—La Force, Bicêtre, Vincennes, the Bastille. And what can he have done to be sent to any one of them?"

"Heaven alone knows. Yet, in France, men are sent on the most trivial charges, on suspicion alone, sometimes. Oh, I beseech you, ask your husband to discover first where he is, and then we may learn of what he is accused, and do our best to free him."

Sir Charles, with now a clue as to whom the miserable man had referred, prosecuted his researches with great ardour, keeping ever two points before him for elucidation: the first being the reason for which Fordingbridge had been brought to execution, and the second the prison from which he had been conducted to the Hôtel de Ville; for, when he had discovered the latter, he would know almost of a surety where Elphinston was. Yet almost as well might he have demanded information of the stones in the streets and have expected to receive an answer, as from those whom, with infinite trouble, he sought out.

Commencing with the English ambassador—who professed himself profoundly ignorant of the execution of Lord Fordingbridge, as well as extremely shocked that such an outrage should have been committed upon a nobleman of our country, no matter what his fault was—he next managed to procure an interview with the Mayor of Paris and with the Prefect of Police, the former a more important functionary then than now. Yet all was useless; he got no further. After many visits to the ambassador, the latter told him plainly that Lord Fordingbridge's death would lead to very little discussion between the two countries; moreover, any discussion was just now to be avoided. France and England were by this time sick of warfare and wanted peace, and the only thing that stood in the way of that peace was the espousal of the Stuart cause by France.

"And," remarked the ambassador quietly to Sir Charles, in a private interview they had together, "the peace will come, and, if I am not deceived, the Stuarts will go. The Chevalier de St. George at Rome knows such to be the case; so does the Prince here; only they do not run away from the storm. Time enough for that when it breaks; anyhow, it won't be particularly hurtful—will only, indeed, lead to a residence in Paris being exchanged for the capital of some other country. Yes, everything points to peace— has begun, indeed, to do so for some time back. Now," and his Excellency leaned forward and spoke very gravely, "this Fordingbridge episode must not disturb that impending peace."

"No one wishes that it should do so," Sir Charles exclaimed; "we only desire a little information. He had a wife, and, although he had behaved as a thorough scoundrel to her, is it not natural that she should wish to know what his crime was, and what prison he was confined in before the morning when he was taken to what was intended for his execution?"

"Perfectly natural," replied the ambassador, with easy grace, "perfectly natural on her part. Only, how is the information to be obtained? I tell you frankly I cannot procure it for you. Lord Fordingbridge was, in London, what they term here 'a suspect'; he was under Government surveillance there; known to be a late Jacobite avowing Hanoverian principles—yet known also, of late, to have been one of the prime movers, if not *the* prime mover, in the attempted assassination of his Majesty before the invasion. Also he was known—I assure you," the ambassador interjected still more gravely, as he bent forward, "everything was known about him—to be the friend of Charles Edward's followers, yet to be, also, their denouncer. He disappeared from England, no one knew why, closed up his house, wrote to his attorney to say he should probably not return for many years, and also that the lady who had passed as the viscountess was not so in actual fact."

"It was a lie!" exclaimed Sir Charles.

"Without doubt," the diplomatist continued suavely. "I only mention all these things to show you that we need not trouble our soon-to-be-beloved French neighbours about the Viscount Fordingbridge, especially as, after all, it was a higher power than they who slew him. Remember, he plotted to kill the King; he was Hanoverian or Jacobite as it suited him;

in fact, Sir Charles, he was contemptible. Let us forget him."

"Everyone is perfectly willing to do so, I assure your Excellency," the baronet replied, in quite as easy a manner as the other was capable of assuming; "he is quite done with on all sides. Only someone else has to be remembered who is supposed to be in the prison he was led out from—someone whose freedom many of us desire to procure."

"An Englishman, of course ?"

"Yes. Not precisely so, though. .A Scotchman, and——"

"A Jacobite, perhaps ?" the ambassador asked with a sweet smile.

"There have been tendencies——"

"Precisely. Good-morning. You can hardly—— I protest, Sir Charles,. you can hardly expect King George's representative to interest himself in that quarter. *Good*-morning."

As regards the mayor and the *préfet*, he arrived no nearer. The former, a rabid hater of all things British, told him that, although he had no knowledge of what persons might be in the various prisons of Paris, he was quite sure that, if any Englishmen were incarcerated, they deserved to be. The *préfet*, more politely but with equal firmness, said he also was not aware of what English people might be detained in the prisons, but that, even if he possessed the knowledge, he should not consider it his duty to give any information on the subject.

Then Kate, by this time recovered somewhat from the shock of her husband's death, and, although she knew it not, rapidly mending in health through the knowledge of the freedom that was now hers undoubtedly, determined that she would lose no opportunity of herself discovering where Bertie Elphinston was incarcerated ; for that Fordingbridge had spoken the truth in his last moments, half mad though he seemed, she never had the faintest shadow of a doubt.

First she wrote, as was natural, to Archibald Sholto, telling him everything exactly as it occurred from the ending of the ball at the opera house to Fordingbridge's last words. Also she asked him to discover, if possible, for what crime her husband had been condemned to death. Above all, she begged him to find out from what prison he had been led to the Hôtel de Ville on the morning of his execution. "Because," she wrote, "in that prison Bertie Elphinston, your friend, your murdered brother's friend, will be found."

Her letter reached Father Sholto at St. Omer, to which he had removed from Amiens, and for some weeks he did not answer it ; while, when he did so, he simply wrote to say that he would endeavour to find out the reason why Bertie should be incarcerated in the prison from which Fordingbridge had been brought forth.

"'Tis a cold answer at best," he muttered to himself one evening, as he paced along the marshy swamps around St. Omer, unobservant of the ripening fruit in the rich orchards all about, and even of the glorious sunset behind him—"a cold answer, yet what else to make ? I cannot tell her that it must be the Bastille in which Bertie is confined. Merciful Father in heaven !" he broke off, "what can he have done to be there ? Because it was to the Bastille that I, determined never to loose my hold on Douglas's murderer, procured he should be sent. Also I dread to tell her what Fordingbridge's crime was, who the avenger of that crime is. I dread! I dread! It is more than I have strength to dare."

Still pacing the marshes, he turned over and over again in his mind all that he had pondered on for so long, with—now added to all that—the fresh knowledge derived through Kate that Elphinston was in the Bastille.

"In the Bastille! the Bastille! So that is where he disappeared to without leaving a trace, a sign behind him. To the Bastille! It seems incredible. What could he have done? A good officer, a favourite with all. It is indeed incredible."

Still musing, he approached the town, to be aroused from his meditations, in spite of himself, by the clash of arms from the guard being relieved at the gates, and by the blare of some trumpets from the walls. They seemed to chide him, he thought, for being so inactive; they seemed to reproach him for meditating so much and for doing so little.

"Only," he murmured as he almost wrung his hands, "what—what shall I do? He is in the Bastille, and, though I could send that other one to the same fortress, I have no power to obtain this one's release. Who can help me? To whom shall I apply?"

At last, tossing on his bed as he had so often wearily tossed before, he thought of Tencin. The cardinal, he knew, was no longer in the greatest favour, and had been sent back to his archbishopric as a punishment; yet he could not be the Primate of France and still be without some influence. If he could do nothing else, he could at least find out on what charge Elphinston, an officer of the King's army, had thus been thrown into prison. So he sat down and wrote to monseigneur.

Of course more weeks passed thus—long ones to the poor prisoner in the *calotte*, and almost as long to the woman outside who loved him so, and to the man at St. Omer who was doing his best for him; then, at last, the archbishop wrote, but could tell nothing. He was, he said, astonished that such a thing could be. The Scotch officers had served the King faithfully without exception; it was incredible that one could be thus incarcerated. The only thing his Eminence could suppose was that Elphinston must have mortally wounded or angered someone of high position at court—someone much in favour with the King himself, and able to procure a lettre de cachet from him without any questions whatever being asked. He could imagine nothing else but that. Then, having given vent to his surmise, he proceeded to suggest to Sholto the very best steps he could take.

"Of all men," his Eminence wrote, "there is none for your purpose like D'Argenson. As you know, all the family are of the same trade—lieutenants of police, Presidents of Parliament, judges; and the present one, like his father before him, is not only one of his Majesty's chief judges, but also the chief Examiner of the *internes* of the Bastille. The family is high in the world now, but some generations back were low—forget not that. Yet, neither will your remembrance of it have weight with D'Argenson. He has a heart of marble if he has any heart at all, but with it a sense of justice that it is impossible to excel. If Captain Elphinston is falsely detained, or detained in error, D'Argenson will set the matter right, though he may take months to do it."

"Though he may take months to do it." Alas! it soon seemed to Archibald Sholto that he was more like to take years. He had got into communication with this important personage through the influence of the cardinal, but once in communication had advanced, or seemed to advance, no further. The judge wrote in his tablets, it is true, the name of Elphinston, and said that if he were in any prison in France he would take care that his case was inquired into sooner or later. Beyond that he refused to say another word.

And with this Sholto had to be content, and to try and persuade himself that it was at least something toward the desired end. Also he wrote to Kate, saying that it was from the Bastille that Fordingbridge had been brought to execution, and that therefore doubtless it was the Bastille in which Bertie was. And he bade her be of good heart and hope for the best, since one of the principal examiners of prisoners detained in the prisons had promised that his case should be inquired into.

"Though he may take months to do it!" the cardinal had said. Verily it seemed as if he had indeed known the man of whom he wrote.

For the months passed away outside the Bastille as they were passing away inside, and to those without there came no news of him within; so that, at last, Kate was led almost to believe that, as her husband had lied to her from the very beginning, so he had lied to her at the end. For it seemed to her that if Bertie had ever been in the gloomy fortress, by which she now so often walked and to which she went and stood before and gazed upon, he must have been released ere this, or in some way have found an opportunity of communicating with her.

CHAPTER XXVIII.

IT was in the early part of May, 1747, that Fordingbridge had been led out to his doom, and month after month had passed, another May had come and gone, and, at last, another December—the December of 1748—had come round. Then even the hopeless state into which Bertie had been so long plunged was quickened back to life by the behaviour of two people with whom he held some intercourse.

Although Falmy and he had almost ceased now, from very weariness during the passage of time—perhaps from heartbrokenness—to communicate much, they did occasionally do so when either considered that he had anything to tell the other that might cause him some faint stir of interest; and one morning the former, appearing at his window, made signs to Bertie that he was about to signal. Then when the other nodded to show that he was attending to him, the Genevese traced on his board the sentence, " Have you heard anything unusual?" To this Bertie, with a bound of his heart—for, in spite of his long incarceration and his growing hopelessness, he still had, although he knew it not, a ray of courage, of presentiment, left in him—shook his head, and by eager facial signs asked Falmy to explain his meaning. But he, whether it might be that he was afraid of communi-

cating too swiftly anything he had gathered, only
signalled back, "Say nothing to De Chevagny as yet.
It is rumoured that they have remembered him."

"Remembered him," thought Bertie, "at last!"
and as he so reflected he looked round upon the poor
old man sitting with his white head bent over his
knees, and wondered if, should this be true, it would
be for his good to go forth."

"'Tis now forty-five years," he said to himself,
"since he came here. A lifetime! Of what use for
him to regain his liberty? He said once to me, when
first I was brought to this room, that this awful place
was his only home. Heaven grant, if they release him,
that he may not find it to be so!"

He watched Bluet's manner when he removed the
remains of their next meal—which meals had gradually, as month followed month, become more sparse
and meagre, possibly because De Launey had now
come to suppose that neither of them would ever be
able to publish to anyone outside those gloomy walls
the story of his neglect and parsimony, to call it by
no other name—and as he did so he noticed that this
good-natured fellow seemed even kinder to the old
man than ever.

"*Mon Dieu!*" he began now, with his usual exclamation, varied only occasionally with his *ma foi*—
"*mon Dieu*, 'tis cold, Monsieur le Marquis. Yet, I'll
warrant me, there are blazing fires in many a happy
home in France. *Par exemple*, now, in the Château de
Chevagny I will dare to say they keep good fires for
monsieur."

The old man looked up at him with a startled, hurt
look; then he said softly:

"Bluet, you have always been good and kind to

me. In the ten years you have been here I have come to look on you as a friend. Yet, when you recall needlessly to me my—my long-vanished home— that I shall never see more—you hurt, you wound me."

"Ah! *avec ça!*" said Bluet, "I'll wager you see that home again yet. Or, perhaps—*mon Dieu!* why not?—the Hôtel de Chevagny in Paris itself. Monsieur le Marquis is not to suppose we shall entertain him for ever; no, no! Neither is he to imagine that because he has dwelt with us so long—it is a little long, I concede—he shall never leave us."

The old man regarded him fixedly for a moment, then he sighed and gave a true French shrug to his shoulders. "If," he exclaimed, in his gentle, well-bred voice, the aristocratic tones of which he had never lost—"if it pleases you to wound me, Bluet, you must do so. Yet I know not why. We have always been such good friends."

"Cease," said Bertie to the turnkey in a whisper. "Why play with an old man thus?"

"It is no play," Bluet replied in the same whisper, only that his was a husky, vinous one. "He is remembered. D'Argenson comes to-morrow night. He will go before him. It may be that on the next day he will be free. Break it to him if you can."

"You are certain of this?" Bertie asked, intensely startled and interested now. "Certain? I thought you told me long ago that no one knew who the judges would call before them."

"*Ordinairement*," replied Bluet, while he glanced at the marquis, who was again warming himself at the fire, "no one does. But this is different. The minister sent a day or so ago asking if there was one incarcerated here of his name. They say the primate, Tencin, stirred him to it. Then—then—*voyez-vous*—D'Argenson's secretary came and—poof!—we hear many things, we jailors! D'Argenson will come himself to-morrow night, and, *mort de ma vie!* we shall lose the prison flower! Where—where will he go to? May the good God protect him!"

The name of Tencin roused many bitter reflections in Bertie's heart, many recollections of how it was this cardinal and archbishop who had been the mainspring, the prime mover, in the Scots' invasion of—of—was it a year ago, or two years ago? He had to pause and count over to himself the time ere he could recollect, for he seemed to have lost all power now of reckoning the period that he had been in the Bastille. Then, when he had arrived at the remembrance that he had absolutely been here for two winters and was in the third December of his detention, his mind went back to the name of Tencin again. Tencin, he repeated—Tencin, the minister who brought about the invasion of England, who was the friend, almost, indeed, the patron, of his own master, Charles Edward. Yet he, a devoted follower and adherent of that Prince, a man who had followed him until the last, had had to suffer so cruel an imprisonment as this which he had undergone! Tencin! Would he allow that if he knew of it? Would he let one who had served the Prince so well be incarcerated there? It might be not, if he but knew that such was the case. Only, how could the fact be brought to the powerful cardinal's knowledge? That was the question.

He glanced at the marquis, who was still sitting gazing into the embers, and he remembered that Bluet had said again, before he left the *calotte* with the re-

mains of the supper, "Break it to him if you can."
Well, he would try and break it to him; only, he
prayed Heaven that in the breaking he might not kill
the old man with the shock. And, if that did not happen, then—why, then, perhaps, through him the cardinal might be apprised of how a faithful adherent of
the cause he had championed was wrongfully immured
in the Bastille—immured, neglected, and forgotten.

"Monsieur de Chevagny," he said, drawing up
another chair by the side of the old man, "are you
fatigued to-night? You seem so—seem more weary
than usual. You are not ill?" In truth, the old marquis had been presenting signs of late that his strength
was failing rapidly, and that he was fast nearing the
only escape from the Bastille that had for forty-five
years seemed likely to come to him; and to-night he
appeared even more feeble, as well as more absent-
minded and lethargic, than ever; also he was more
dazed than was his wont. But he replied:

"No, no, not ill—or only so from having lived for
seventy years; and also from having passed forty-five
of those years in prison. A long while! A long while!
A lifetime! My father's whole life was not so long."

"Yet," said Bertie soothingly, "it may still be pro-
longed; it may——"

"Would you desire for me that it should be pro-
longed?" the other asked, lifting his eyes to Bertie's.
"Is that to be wished, think you?"

For a moment the younger man hesitated, then he
said, speaking very gently:

"Yes, if—if you could find happiness thereby.
For suppose—only suppose—that some great chance
should come to you; some undreamed of, unsuspected
chance, by which you might be enabled to see once

21

more the wife you so tenderly loved, the little child you left sleeping on her bosom——"

"Stop! For God's sake, stop!" De Chevagny exclaimed. "You torture me; you wring my heart worse, far worse, than ever Bluet did. You conjure up hopes that my senses tell me can never be realized; you bring before me thoughts and ideas that I have been trying to bury and put away for many, many years now."

And, as he spoke, Bertie saw his old eyes fill with tears; again saw those tears drop from his eyelids to his snowy beard.

"Oh, my friend, my fellow-prisoner," he said, "believe me, I would not torture you unnecessarily. Think you that I, before whom this living tomb yawns as it yawned before you years ago—that I, who, Great Powers! may be here, in this very room, forty years hence—would say one word to distress you? No, no. Never, never! But, listen to me, I beseech you; and, above all, listen to me calmly. I have something to tell you, something that I pray earnestly may make you very, very happy."

As he spoke he dropped on one knee by the old man's side, while, taking one of his hands in his, he passed his arm round the other's waist, and, drawing him to him, supported his now trembling form as a son might have done. And as he did so he felt how worn and thin his poor old body was.

"What is it?" whispered the marquis. "What is it? You—you frighten me! I—I cannot bear a shock."

"Pray, pray," continued Bertie, "do not be frightened nor alarmed. Indeed, you have no cause. But, oh, my dear and honoured friend and companion, there has come strange news into this place, strange news for you—nay, start not! Strange news! It is said—strive to be calm, I beseech you—that, that—be brave! as you have been so long—your release is at hand. It may come soon, at any moment now."

He felt the old man's feeble frame quiver in his grasp; he felt him draw a long breath, and saw him close his eyes. Then for a long while he was silent, sitting enfolded in the other's arms as though he were asleep or dead. But at last he spoke:

"If it should be so, if this is true, what will become of me? Can I hope to find my wife alive? And for my little child that was—she is almost old now, if she still lives. She will not know me; will not, perhaps, believe I am her father."

"Oh, how can she doubt it? And for your wife— she need not be dead; how many women live far beyond your own age—why, my mother is near it. Look hopefully forward, therefore, I beg of you, to your release; think of what happiness may be yours still."

But, although Bertie used every argument to prove to De Chevagny that there must be still some period of such happiness before him, however short that period might be, he could not bring him to so regard his forthcoming release. Above all, he could not make him believe for one instant that he would ever meet his wife or child upon earth; and he reiterated again and again that, if he could not have them with him, he would almost prefer to remain a prisoner.

"I have grown used to the filth and squalor of this place," he said, "to my wretched rags. My hotel across the river, even if it has not been long since confiscated, would be no fit abode for me. Better remain here without hope, better forget that I was ever a free man, loving others and beloved myself, than go forth into the world where I am unknown. And," he said tenderly, "I have at least one friend here—I have you."

On the next day, however, when Bluet had told him that beyond all doubt he was to be taken before D'Argenson that night, he began to show a little more interest in what was occurring, and, at last, to look forward eagerly to the hour when the Examiner should arrive.

"For," he said, "I shall have a piteous tale to tell him; perhaps when he hears it he may be disposed to look into the cases of some others who are here. There is that poor man Falmy, over the way; he, too, should be released."

At six o'clock the King's Lieutenant paid a visit to the *calotte*—De Launey had never been known to visit a "guest" from the time he was first received by him —and asked the marquis whether he would choose to have a change of linen and some fresher clothes in which to appear before the judges; but this offer he firmly refused.

"As I am," he said, "as I have been for so many years," and he held up his arm, from which his sleeve hung in a hundred tatters; "so I will go before him, and, if he releases me, so I will go forth into the world again."

"That," said the King's Lieutenant, politely and with a slight smile, "Monsieur le Marquis must know will not be permitted. No guest leaves us who does not sign a paper in which he undertakes most solemnly to divulge nothing of what has occurred within. He would scarcely, therefore, be allowed to depart in such a garb as that in which Monsieur le Marquis is now unhappily clad. Besides, the illustrious family of De Chevagny is rich; the head of the house will scarcely adorn himself with such raiment when he goes back to his proper position."

"Rich!" the old man echoed with bitter scorn—"rich! What have I to do with riches now? If I find not my wife or child, I shall not live a week in my unaccustomed lot. A garret such as this will do well enough for me."

The Lieutenant departed after this, saying that the marquis—as he was scrupulous now to call him on every occasion—might expect to be sent for early in the evening; and those two, who had grown to be such friends, sat down to pass what, with the exception of the night, would probably be their last hours together. All was arranged between them as to what was to be done on Elphinston's behalf when once De Chevagny was free—he was first to seek out his mother and Kate, being careful to say nothing to the latter about her husband and his end until he discovered what she knew about him, and in any circumstances to be very discreet in what he revealed. Then he was to strive in every way to bring Elphinston's case before Tencin, so that something might be done as soon as possible.

"For," said Bertie, "never will I believe that when once his Eminence knows that I have been thrust in here under what must be, cannot help but be, a false charge, a mistake, he will allow me to remain. Oh, my friend, my friend, lose no time, I beseech you, in releasing me from this death in life!"

"Have no fear," replied De Chevagny, "I shall remember. First your mother, Madame Elphinston, at Passy; then to her who was that creature's wife; then—then to the King or to—what is his name?—Tencin! Tencin! I shall not forget. Yet, oh, my friend, how shall I leave you here—alone! And you so young—so young! Not yet in your prime."

"Fear not for me," replied Elphinston, assuming a hopefulness he by no means felt; for he doubted if, even with the Marquis de Chevagny at liberty and free to plead his cause, his release was likely to be obtained. If there was, indeed, as the King's Lieutenant had hinted, some terrible and powerful enemy in the background whom he had injured without knowing it, it was possible that even Tencin's exertions and influence might be of no avail. Yet still he sought to cheer the other.

"Fear not for me. Once you are free to bring my case before the King I have no fear myself"—then he started, for he heard the clanging of the doors. "Hark!" he said, "hark! They are coming for you. Oh, I pray God that when you return from your examination you may do so with your liberty assured—as it must be! As it must be! Otherwise they would not send for you at all," and he kissed the old man's hand as he spoke, and whispered to him to be calm.

"God bless you!" the marquis replied—"God bless you! I will be brave."

As he did so the door was unlocked, and once more the King's Lieutenant came in, accompanied by four turnkeys, one of whom was Bluet, who behind the officer's back kept gesticulating and nodding his head and winking at Bertie—who stood a little behind De Chevagny—in an extraordinary manner.

"The fellow had indeed a good heart," he thought to himself, "which even the miseries he is witness of in this living hell are unable to suppress. One would think that De Chevagny was his dearest friend, so overjoyed is he." And still, as he reflected thus, Bluet's grimaces and becks and nods continued.

"Réné Xavier Ru de Chevagny, Marquis de Chevagny," read out the King's Lieutenant from a paper in his hand, "the Viscomte d'Argenson, Judge and Examiner of his Majesty's fortresses, desires your presence."

"I—I have waited the summons long," the marquis said, with quiet dignity; "I am ready to obey it."

And he turned round to touch Bertie's hand in a temporary farewell, when again the voice of the King's Lieutenant was heard reading from the paper:

"Elphinston—baptismal name uncertain—captain of the Regiment of Picardy, formerly of the Regiment of Scots Dutch——"

"What!" exclaimed Elphinston, dazed by being summoned at last so unexpectedly, and also at the last description—"what!"

—"the Vicomte d'Argenson, Judge and Examiner of his Majesty's fortresses, desires your presence."

"I, too, am ready," he replied in a low voice.

"*Avancez!*" said the Lieutenant, and at the word the party left the *calotte* and descended the massive stairs, the officer with two turnkeys leading the way, while Bluet and another followed.

And as they went to the Hall of Judgment, Bertie whispered to the marquis:

"I begin to understand. I know now why I have been here so long. It was another Elphinston, not I, who served in the Scots Dutch—the Elphinston who eloped with the daughter of the Duc de Baufremont!"

CHAPTER XXIX.

FREE.

WHEN the stairs had been descended, at the foot
of which were several soldiers who, as ever, removed
their hats and placed them before their faces so as not
to observe the prisoners, they passed through a little
door into a great court and, traversing this, entered
what was known and served as the arsenal or armoury.
There Bertie observed a number of gorgeously dressed
footmen and coachmen seated about, whom he supposed to belong to the judges, as well as a number
of exempts and several messengers of the Bastille,
known to all Paris by the badge they wore—a brass
plate, having on it an engraved club full of points and
spikes, with round it the motto "*Monstrorum Terror*"
—most of whom, perhaps from long habit, regarded
the party very indifferently. Leaving this place behind, they traversed another court, and then, after the
King's Lieutenant had struck three times on an iron-
studded door, they were admitted to a large, stately
hall well warmed and lighted. It was the hall known
as the *Salle de Justice.*

At one end of the hall, seated in great padded chairs
let into niches, were four judges clad in scarlet robes,
with huge wigs upon their heads, while one, who was
undoubtedly D'Argenson, wore above his wig a richly
laced three-cornered hat, as a symbol that he repre-

sented the sovereign. At his feet sat his registrar, or secretary, with a long table before him covered with a great crimson cloth that hung down to the ground, and also with innumerable papers, while at either end of the table stood sergeants-at-arms with maces. In the midst of the court, or hall, near to these, was a railed-in space, within it two small wooden stools, and to these the sergeants motioned that both De Chevagny and Bertie should approach, while, as they did so, the registrar handed up to each of the judges papers which were copies of the interrogatories about to be administered. At another table, with some papers also before him, sat De Launey, shivering and shaking and smiling in exactly the same way that Bertie had seen him do more than two years ago. Poor wretch! smiles and shivers were alike to be soon over for him now; in another few months the worst form of paralysis was to end his life.

As De Chevagny and Bertie took their seats upon the stools in the inclosure, the judges half rose and bowed to them (a ceremony always observed, except when the worst class of *détenus* were brought before them), and, on their salutation being returned, D'Argenson, glancing down his paper of interrogatories, prepared to address De Chevagny, the first on his list. This judge, who sat as president, and was reported to work harder than any other twenty men in the French King's service, sitting, indeed, in the law courts during the whole of each day, and being able, consequently, to only make his examinations of the prisons at night, was a strange man to observe. His complexion was as swarthy as a mulatto's, his eyes enormously large and black, his eyebrows each as big as an ordinary man's moustache, while his reputation for austerity had spread through the whole kingdom. Yet he possessed also, in contradistinction to his appearance, a voice as soft and sweet as a girl's, or De Launey's own, and hands—one of which, covered with brilliants, generally lay extended on the desk before him—as white as marble.

"Monsieur the Marquis de Chevagny," he began now—while as he did so the old man rose from the stool and faced him as he leaned upon the rail—"Monsieur de Chevagny, you have been a resident in this fortress for a long period. I perceive you came here on the 30th of January, 1704," and the silvery tones ceased for a moment as though awaiting an answer.

"It is true," De Chevagny replied, "true." And he bent his head.

"The charge against you was the writing of a contumelious lampoon upon the then Marquise de la Vallière and holding her up to contempt and derision. For that the lettre de cachet concerning you was signed by —by a then illustrious personage. That letter was an open one, unlimited as to the continuance of its effect——"

"The charge was true," murmured the marquis, "the punishment cruel beyond all thought."

"Monsieur le Marquis," interposed the judge, while his voice sounded even sweeter, more silvery than before, "I must remind you of what doubtless in the passage of years you have forgotten: There must be no criticism here, no discussion of those who are, or once were, all-powerful. Monsieur, I represent the King's Majesty; let me beg of you to offend—unintentionally, no doubt—no more."

He paused a moment, and it seemed as if some

bird had ceased to warble its innocent notes; then he continued:

"The family of La Vallière is now practically extinct. The King, in his sublime goodness, is therefore pleased to ordain that you shall no longer be asked to remain here. Monsieur le Marquis de Chevagny, permit me to congratulate you. You may depart at any time most convenient to you."

The old man raised his hand to his long white beard and stroked it thoughtfully for a moment; then he, in his clear aristocratic tones, replied:

"You congratulate me, monsieur, on what? On a wasted, ruined life, perhaps; a prison for forty-five years; an existence given me by God and taken away by man; a home desolated; a broken heart—nay, two, if not three, broken hearts; and all for what? A youthful folly, a joke made in the exuberance of a young man's spirit. Oh, monsieur, spare me your congratulations! If you were even born when I first came here, think, think of the passage of those years, think of what lives you have known, think of the use they have been put to, and then reflect on mine. Surely your congratulations are the last bitter drop."

"Monsieur de Chevagny," replied the judge, "I must not argue with you. Yet one word I will say: I had no part in sending you here; my share is only to tell you that you are free." And he took up in his jewelled hand a fresh batch of papers, and, stooping forward, whispered something to the registrar.

As the old man tottered back to the stool he had risen from, that functionary said:

"Elphinston, captain of the Regiment of Picardy, formerly of the Regiment of Scots Dutch, answer to your name."

"My name," said Bertie, advancing to the rail and standing as the marquis had previously stood, "is Elphinston, and I am of the Regiment of Picardy. I never served in the Scots Dutch Regiment."

With an almost imperceptible start D'Argenson bent his dark, luminous eyes on him, as did all the other judges, who had sat like dead men in their seats, while De Launey, with the King's Lieutenant and the registrar, also cast surprised looks on him.

"You say that you were never in the regiment of Scots Dutch, monsieur?" asked D'Argenson, still holding the papers in his hand and glancing at them; "what, then, is your *nom de baptême?*"

"Bertie."

The judge glanced again at the papers, then he conferred for a moment with the other judges, and then spoke again:

"Pardon us our ignorance of your Scotch name, monsieur; but this name 'Bertie' we do not know it. Albert we know, but not Bertie. Is that the whole name, or a part of one—an abbreviation?"

"My name is Bertie, *tout court.*"

The white hand of the judge rubbed his chin softly, and he said:

"You were never in the Scots Dutch Regiment? And, *par exemple*, you will perhaps also tell us if you are the husband of Mademoiselle de Baufremont, daughter of the duke of that name."

"I am not. I am the husband of no woman."

A visible stir went through the others in the *Salle de Justice* at these words, while D'Argenson shrugged his shoulders. Then, sweetly as ever, he continued:

"There are many noble Scotch gentlemen serving his Majesty. Would it be known to you if there were any others of your name—your family name—in the army?"

"I know of one other," Bertie replied. "*He* was in the Scots Dutch."

"Ha!" exclaimed D'Argenson. "And his first name, what is that?"

"Basil."

D'Argenson threw down his papers and for several minutes conferred again with the other judges; and during the time he did so Bertie could not but muse on how the Bastille and its accursed uses had been lent to one more crime, one more mistake that was in itself a crime. For that he had suffered for the man who was his namesake there could now be no doubt; the only wonder in his mind was that it had never occurred to him before, never dawned upon him that such was the case. And now he only prayed that the judges might never have it come to their knowledge that, innocently enough, he had rendered assistance to that other Elphinston.

"God knows," he mused, "that I have suffered sufficiently already by doing so; 'twas through that assistance that I lost my love; surely I shall not also have to suffer further; surely the Duke de Baufremont's vengeance will not be permitted to still fall heavily on me." And once more he prayed that his share in the transaction might not be known.

Then D'Argenson spoke again:

"*Monsieur le Capitaine*," he said, " your answers to my interrogatories appear to show that, by grave misfortune, you have been confused with another man. Such errors are always to be regretted; nay, more, when they have been made, it is always the custom of his Majesty—a most gracious sovereign!—to make atonement for them and to nobly recompense those who have been injured. I shall to-morrow take steps to ratify your statement: if I find it accurate, you may expect to go away from here in a very short time. His Majesty will sign your acquittance at once. You will be free."

"Sir," replied Bertie, "I might have been free two years and a half ago, might never have suffered this long misery—while much other misery might have also been spared to those whom I love and who love me —had this examination taken place when I was first brought here."

"Doubtless," D'Argenson replied coldly. "But the laws of France have their mode of procedure and cannot be altered for any case in particular. *Monsieur le Capitaine*, your examination is concluded," and turning to his brother judges, he said, as he rose:

"*Mes frères, la séance est terminée.*"

Of what use was it, Bertie asked himself as he and De Chevagny were conducted back to the *calotte*, to rage or fret against this legal wall of adamant? As well hurl one's self against a rock and hope to make an impression on it. For a fault not his own, he had been forced to endure two years and more of miserable imprisonment, and now, by chance alone, he was likely to be set free.

Yet the very word "free" sent his blood dancing and tingling in his veins once more; it brought to him the happy hope of seeing his mother, his beloved Kate again. And when he saw her, there would be no further barrier between them; she, too, was free—free to become his wife. Then, at last, their long vexations would be over—at last—at last !

"Make yourselves as comfortable as you can, *mes*

enfants," said Bluet to them when once more they were back in the *calotte*, "it will not be for long now. Meanwhile, to-morrow, I will see if I cannot snatch from that villainous cellarer a bottle of the best *vin de Brecquiny* wherewith to celebrate your sortie. And I —though I am but a poor drinker at best—will drink to your happy restoration to your friends and families."

As the turnkey had said, so it happened. From the next morning their meals were improved; the best wine was served to them; everything gave promise that their imprisonment was at an end. One morning —which was the third day from their examination by D'Argenson—Bluet, accompanied by another turnkey, came in, bearing a large basket, in which was a quantity of new linen, with some ruffles and lace for both of them. Then, next, the tailor was brought in to prepare a plain but serviceable suit for the marquis, and also to repair Bertie's clothes, his suit being, though much used, still wearable. And, to complete all, Bluet arrived on another morning with the necessary implements for cutting and trimming their hair and beards, which, with the exception of the attentions they had been able to render each other with a rusty pair of scissors they had discovered imbedded in the filth of the floor, had not been done at all since the younger prisoner had been there.

"*Avec ça!*" exclaimed their cheerful janitor, "messieurs will go forth into the world again as though to a *fête* or a wedding. *Ma foi!* Monsieur le Marquis, you look not fifty years of age. You will both do very well. Ah, but the brave day is at hand!"

And at last it came. One evening, a week now after the judge had pronounced that the Marquis de

Chevagny might go back to life, and had said that the Captain Elphinston might cherish hopes of doing so, the King's Lieutenant again made his appearance in the *calotte*, unaccompanied this time by anyone but Bluet, for the purpose of unbarring the doors.

"Messieurs," he said, "have the goodness to accompany me to the *Salle de Justice.* The commissary attends you to hand to you your *permission de sortie.* You will depart to-morrow, if it so pleases you."

Rising, they followed him through all the passages and courts as before, and arrived at the great hall. Here they observed that the judges were not again present, but in their place, and seated at the scarlet-draped table of the judges' registrar was the commissary, a little, old, wizened man, who bowed to them as they entered.

"Be seated, I beg," he said, motioning them to two chairs placed in front of him—two *fauteuils* very different in appearance and comfort from the stools that had previously been accorded them; and when they had done so, he instantly read from two papers before him:

"Réné Xavier Ru de Chevagny, Marquis de Chevagny," he began; "his Majesty, King Louis XV, graciously accords you this his permission to depart out of this fortress, the Bastille, from this present moment. This permission I now hand to you as a certificate of his Majesty's gracious goodness." Here he held the paper out over the table to the old man, who took it from him without uttering one word. Then the commissary continued: "And in consideration of your having been unable to attend to your own interests, properties, and estates of late, his Majesty ordains that you may draw upon the captain of this his fortress, Monsieur Jourdan de Launey, for a sum not exceeding fifty *Louis d'ors*, for your present expenses, to be by you recouped later on."

"I—I want nothing," De Chevagny began, when, as he did so, his eye fell upon Bluet standing near and behind the King's Lieutenant, and remembering all the fellow's kindness to him—kindness which he had never been under any obligation to show—he ceased what he was saying; while the commissary continued:

"From this moment you are at liberty to depart. Monsieur le Marquis you will consult your own pleasure as to when you do so."

Then turning to Bertie and addressing him, he again read out the rigmarole about "his Majesty's gracious goodness," and handed to him his certificate of freedom. And also he informed him that he, too, could draw on De Launey for fifty *Louis d'ors*, to be recorded later on.

"If, monsieur," Bertie exclaimed, however, at this, "I draw them, I know not how they are ever to be refunded. I was an officer in the French King's army when I was brought here. I can scarcely suppose I am one now. When I quit this prison I am as like as not to be a beggar in the streets. This incarceration has stolen my life from me for two years; now I am free, its effect will be to deprive me of the means whereby to live in the future."

"*Monsieur le Capitaine*, I think not. I am authorized to tell you that a commission in his Majesty's service will still be provided for you, in consequence of your residence here being due to a slight mistake."

"So be it," said Bertie; "I rejoice to hear that so

much justice will be done to me." Yet, as he spoke, he took a vow that never more would he serve the French King, never more draw sword for a country in which such errors could happen as that which had imprisoned him for those two years.

"Now," said the commissary, "you must please to sign these papers, and to swear upon your honours that you will neither reveal, when outside this fortress, any of the situations of the various chambers, apartments, towers, halls, or courts of which you have obtained any knowledge, nor the names of any other persons here with which you have become acquainted in any way. Also you must, upon your honours, state that you carry no messages from anyone within this fortress to anyone whatsoever outside of it, either written or verbal. And when you do go forth at the time it shall please you, you will also sign another paper stating that you have been deprived of nothing, neither money, clothes, jewellery, nor trinkets of which you were in possession when you arrived."

De Chevagny shrugged his shoulders as he answered :

"I may sign with safety. I have no recollection of anything I had about me when I came here in the year 1704. I know not what I had. And what matters it ? What matters it ?"

"As for me," said Elphinston, "I had but a few gold pieces in my purse when I came here, and they have been exhausted long ago in payment for my bed. There can be nothing left; and if there is, I want it not."

That night, however, both he and De Chevagny decided to draw each upon De Launey for ten *Louis d'ors*, with which to reward the faithful Bluet, and also

—for such was the custom even in this hateful place—
to give a treat to the turnkeys. So, ere they slept for
the last time in their miserable chamber, these men
were called in, and, bringing with them various sorts
of wine, chocolate, pasties, and ratafias, were rewarded
also with pieces of money, while they drank to the
health of those whom they termed the "parting
guests."

One other had, however, to be taken a sad farewell
of—one whom there was no likelihood of their ever
meeting again in this world—the unhappy Genevese,
Falmy. At daybreak Bertie was at the window looking for him, and a few moments later he appeared at
his; and the tears streamed down the former's eyes
so as almost to blind him as for the last time he sent
his message across to the opposite tower. "Farewell!
I leave with De Chevagny," he signalled. "God ever
bless you, and may He at last release you! Is there
no message for anyone outside?" For, in spite of
the promise he had given to take none from any
prisoner, he felt absolved from it when he thought of
the bitter agony of those incarcerated still. Indeed,
such was the feeling of all who went forth from that
living death.

But Falmy shook his head sadly; then, listlessly, as
though hopeless and heartbroken, he signalled back,
"None; I have no friends. If I ever had any, they are
dead or have forgotten me. Farewell!" and, with a
look upon his face that Bertie never forgot, he left the
window.

Down through the corridors and passages they
passed, away through the *corps de garde*, with, for the
last time, their laced hats held before their faces, until
they reached the wicket and so to the great gates

which opened to admit their exit. And a moment
later, as the great clock struck nine above their
heads, they stood outside the prison walls.*   They
were free !

---

* The Bastille.

CHAPTER XXX.

THE MARQUIS GOES HOME.

THE turnkey had provided a *fiacre* for them, and into this they stepped from the outside of the great gate, while Bluet; looking as sad as though he were parting for ever from his dearest friends, asked where the man should be instructed to drive them to? Strange to say, neither had given any thought to this matter, though, had Bertie been alone, no consideration would have been necessary on the subject. His mother's house would have been his destination; for, although often and often in his misery he had mused on whether she was still alive, and on whether she would ever fold him in her arms again, nothing would have kept him from going straight to Passy and at once resolving his doubts.

But now, with De Chevagny by his side—a poor old man cast back into an unknown world after nearly half a century's exclusion from it—he could not leave him; he must be his first consideration.

"Dear friend," he said, while still Bluet stood by the coach door, "have you thought of where we shall proceed to? Will you go to your own home first, or come to mine—if—if—God! if I have any left there. At least we will not part—or not now, not now."

The poor old marquis wrapped the dark blue cloak they had provided him with around him as the other spoke, for the December morning, although bright and sunny, was cold and crisp, then he said, " Home! to my home?   What home have I ? "

"*Mon Dieu !*" exclaimed Bluet, consoling to the last, "*sans doute*, a beautiful home.   Monsieur must well remember—even I, a prison watch-dog, have heard of it—the Hôtel de Chevagny.   Monsieur will doubtless go there.   And, *parbleu !* when I have a day's release from my labours, I shall make a little visit to the marquis.   He will be glad to see his old friend and servant, Bluet *N'est ce pas ?* "

" Yes," the marquis whispered, dazed, as it seemed to the others, by his freedom—" yes, I shall always be glad to see you, Bluet.   Let us go—let us go," and he held out his hand to the turnkey, as did Bertie.

" Hôtel de Chevagny," said Bluet to the driver ; " you know it without doubt.   Away with you to the house of the noble marquis ! "

" De Chevagny ! " said the man from his box—" De Chevagny ! No, I know it not. What is the quarter ? "

" St. Germain, naturally. Monsieur," looking in again at the window, " the name of the street—of the street, monsieur ? " he repeated, seeing that the marquis appeared to scarcely understand him.   But a moment later he muttered :

" The Rue Charles Martel.   That is it."

" *Bon !* " said the coachman, he having caught the words—" *bon !* Rue Charles Martel," and as once more Bluet exchanged farewells with them, he lashed his horse and drove off, while De Chevagny cast one last look on the Bastille and shuddered.

" Forty-five years," he murmured, " forty-five years. A young man when I entered there, an old man now— worn out and near his end."

"Nay, nay," said Bertie, "do not think so. Remember, you may find many alive who are still dear to you. Let us pray so at least."

But the marquis, burying his head in the collar of his cloak, spoke no more, though Bertie, regarding him from time to time, saw that he was gazing out and observing the places they passed by; and as they traversed the Pont Neuf, he observed a brighter look in his face than he had hitherto seen. "This, at least, has not changed," he muttered. "It is the same as when I was young—as when I passed over it to go to the Bastille. Forty-five years ago!—forty-five years ago!"

Presently—for it was no great distance from the Quartier St. Antoine to that of St. Germain—the hackney coach arrived at the end of the Rue Charles Martel; a long, sad-looking street, having high walls all along it into which were set great wooden gates, and behind which were large courtyards belonging to the various mansions or hotels of the nobility. Yet, as they entered this street and observed a large, modern, and very gaunt-looking house, De Chevagny seemed more bewildered than ever, and raised his finger to his forehead as though confused.

"I—I—do not understand," he said. "Has the man mistaken the way? Bellancourt's house stood here—years ago—when I was a lad. I have played in the gardens often—oh, so often, with his children! It was an old, old house, built in the days of Henri of Navarre. Where is it? That is not it."

"This is a new building," replied Bertie; "is it not possible the present owner may have removed the old one to make way for this?"

"Yes, yes," De Chevagny whispered—"yes, it is

forty-five years ago.　I should have remembered. Forty-five years ago.　And sixty since I played under the cedars in the garden.　My God!"

The hackney carriage rolled along slowly, for in this old-fashioned street the road, like so many in Paris in those days, was far from good, and a slight thaw had now set in which rendered it particularly heavy.　Then, looking out, the marquis pointed to an antique mansion the roofs of which could be seen behind the walls.

"See," he said excitedly, "see, it is the house of De Montpouillan, the man whom the King delighted to honour!　I was at a ball there three nights before I was taken, and he—Louis, the Grand Monarque—was there too.　He danced in the ballet * with the daughter of St. Hillaire, a blonde whose hair shone like the gold of a new *Louis d'or*.　*Mon Dieu!* observe—there is a hatchment over the house.　Someone is dead."

Again Bertie tried to soothe him by reminding him that, whomsoever it might be, he could scarcely have known them after his long and terrible absence; yet this consolation, unhappy as it was, only served to remind him of his own sad fate and to set him once more murmuring, "Forty-five years!"

But a moment afterwards he gave a gasp—a cry, indeed—and exclaimed :

"My house! my house!　See, see, it is there!" and called feebly to the driver to stop.

Above the walls Bertie could perceive the red tiles

---

* The ballets in which the French kings, and Louis XIV in particular, frequently danced, were more in the style of a minuet than anything else.　There is a picture in the Luxembourg of one being performed, with Louis taking part in it and representing *Le Printemps.*

of a long, low hotel; could observe also that in many places some of those tiles had fallen away and left great gaps yawning; and also that the whole gave signs of being in a ruinous condition. The huge, double wooden gates hung loosely on their hinges, while one or two beams in them bulged inward from rottenness and the lock, once large and handsome and a triumph of the smith's art, was rusted and almost fallen from its wooden socket.

"Alas! alas!" thought Elphinston to himself, "it is not here that he will find his wife or child. He must look farther for them—perhaps in heaven!— who knows? Poor De Chevagny—poor, unhappy man!"

There hung a great iron bell-handle on the side of the vast door, and the marquis, grasping it, rang a peal that could be heard echoing in the house itself across the courtyard—a peal that met with no response. Then they waited for a minute or two, the marquis leaning on Bertie's arm and gazing up wistfully into his face, as though seeking to read therein what his thoughts might be, and the driver staring over the wall at the unshuttered and uncurtained windows.

"*Mon Dieu!*" the man muttered to himself. so that they could not hear him, "after having dwelt in the *palais des grenouilles* * so long, it is not strange if the master is no more expected," and he cracked his whip vigorously as though hoping, perhaps, to thereby attract some attention from within.

Still the old man looked up sadly at his companion's face, and muttered, "My home, my home!"

---

* A derisive name sometimes applied to the Bastille, especially by the lower classes in Paris.

so ruefully that the other had to turn away from him so that he should not see his eyes; and then Bertie, seizing the bell handle, rang a strong, lusty peal upon it.

"If there is anyone here," he said, "that should arouse them. The bell has a tongue that might wake the dead!"

He could have bitten his own tongue out a moment later, for at his words, especially the last one, De Chevagny started, and then muttered, "The dead—the dead. Ah! it is the dead who never come back to us. They are gone. All are gone! When shall we meet again? Never, never, never!"

As though in answer to that question which his own weary heart had answered for itself, a door was heard to open in the front of the house—it creaked wofully on its hinges—and then steps were also heard upon the stones of the courtyard, the steps of some-one in sabots, and next the key was turned in the rusty lock and one half of the great gate pulled back; following upon which, a woman of about forty years of age appeared at the doorway, and, after regarding the *fiacre* and the young man with the old one now leaning so heavily on his arm, asked them what they desired.

"To come into my own house," said the latter, looking at her, though he could see at once that she had been born since he last stood upon that spot. "I am the Marquis de Chevagny."

She was not an uncomely-looking woman, neither did she appear hard nor severe; still she answered, with a look of suspicion in her face:

"There is no Marquis de Chevagny. The title exists no longer."

"Yet," said the old man feebly, "I am he. This is my house. Woman, I have but left the Bastille an hour ago. I have been a prisoner there for forty-five years."

She took a step backward, as though to regard him more particularly, while her brow wrinkled a little and her colour came and went, as she exclaimed, "My God, it is not possible!"

"It is true," he said. "I pray you let me enter. I am very old and feeble—older than even I should be by my years—and—and this *is* my house. Do not refuse me!"

"Enter," the woman said, pulling wider open the door. "And this—monsieur," glancing at Bertie, "who is he?"

"I also have been a prisoner in the Bastille, though for only a short space of time in comparison with his. I beseech you," he said, sinking his voice to a whisper, "answer him very gently—especially when he asks you of—of his family."

"I understand," the woman said in return as she walked by their side across the courtyard, in which one or two fowls were strutting about—"I understand. Is he truly the marquis?"

"He is, indeed."

"God help him!" and as she spoke, they reached the door of the house.

They entered a great hall with a tiled floor and, above it at the back, a window of stained glass, some panes of which were broken—a hall in which there was no furniture except a plain oaken bench, that looked as though it had been used to chop wood upon; and on to this the Marquis de Chevagny sank, exhausted already, while Bertie, saddened at such a home-coming as this, stood by to cheer and comfort him if possible.

"This is not as I left it," the old man said as his glance roved round the spacious but empty hall. "Has there been no one to guard it?" Then, as though such trifles were unworthy of consideration, he asked eagerly, while a strange light shone from his eyes: "I had a wife, a child, when they took me from here. Are they—they—still alive?"

"Is it possible monsieur does not know?"

"Know! What should I know? Woman, I tell you I have been dead to the world for forty-five years —buried alive in a place to which no news ever comes. Where," he continued, "where are my wife and child?"

"Alas! monsieur," she said, seeming while she spoke as though endeavouring to avoid answering him, "I have heard of you from my father; he was *garde chasse* at the Château de Chevagny many years ago."

"Lenoir! Was he your father?"

"Yes, monsieur, but he has been dead these twenty years; and then——"

"My wife and child!" he interrupted—"my wife and child! Are they dead, too?"

"Alas! monsieur, I never saw Madame la Marquise. She—she—died the year I was born."

De Chevagny straightened himself upon the bench —as he did so there came to Bertie's recollection how his own father had so straightened himself as he died in his arms a few years before, and he wondered why he recalled that incident at this moment—then the marquis said:

"The year you were born? How old are you?"

"Forty-one, monsieur."

"Forty-one!" he whispered, "forty-one! So! she lived four years. Four years. And I—I—have been hoping, praying—O God! how I have prayed!—to see her again—to see her again, while for forty-one years she has been lying in her grave—in her grave!"

He paused awhile, perhaps because he heard the sobs of Bertie and the woman mingling with his own; then he said:

"And the little child—my dear, dear little babe! Is—is she dead, too?"

"*Non*, monsieur—at least I think not. She——"

"Thank God!"

"She married, very young, the Vicomte de Brunet," the woman answered through her tears, "and went with him to Guadeloupe; and sometimes, at intervals, she writes to her friends in Paris, and they send me news of her. Also, she has once written to me."

"And she is well? Has she children of her own, perhaps?"

"No, monsieur. Her marriage has not been so blessed by the *bon Dieu!*"

He sat thinking awhile, meditating deeply ere he spoke again; then he said:

"But this house and the château—they were good properties; we have drawn large sums from them for generations. Who takes the rents, the produce, now—to whom do they belong?"

"To the state, I have heard, monsieur; to the King; though, it is said, in trust only. Yet, I know not. I cannot say. But I suppose so. Twice annually a monsieur comes from the minister of the King to visit us, and twice, also, I hear, one visits the château. If all has been saved for you, monsieur, during your long absence, you should be very rich."

"Rich," he repeated—"rich! very rich! Yes, yes, very rich." Then, turning on the woman suddenly, almost fiercely for him, he asked:

"Where—where, do you know—did my wife die? Where did my little child live until she married? If the state, the King, took possession of my property, they would not let them stay here nor at the château."

"Madame la Marquise went back to stay with her father after monsieur had gone away. Mademoiselle de Chevagny lived with him also until she married." Then, observing that the old man looked even more feeble and drawn than she had at first noticed, she said: "But, monsieur, do not stay here in this cold hall. Come into the saloon, I beg of you. There is no fire, but I can soon make one. Come, monsieur, come."

Slowly leaning on Bertie's arm, he rose at her behest—and now the latter perceived that he weighed more heavily on him than before—and, all together, they went into a fair-sized *salon*, or morning-room, to the left of the corridor; while the woman, preceding them, made haste to open the window shutters and to let a flood of light from the wintry sun pour into the room.

It seemed to have been left much as it must have been in those long-past years, when so dreadful a doom had fallen upon that unhappy family—perhaps had scarcely undergone any alteration since those days. Upon the walls there hung several pictures: one, of a man in half armour, bearing a strong resemblance to him who now tottered on Bertie's arm; another, of an elderly woman, of a long anterior date; a third, of a young man in all the bravery of the rich apparel of Louis XIV's date, a young man with bright blue eyes and a joyous smile—De Chevagny himself. Also, there were many chairs, none very comfortable, since, fifty years before this time, comfortable chairs were almost unknown articles; a table or so and a tabouret; also a woman's worktable in a corner by the fireplace, with, above it, a painting of a fair young girl with a soft, gentle expression, done in what was, at the period in which it was painted, quite a new style—the style of Antoine Watteau—and much embellished with a rural landscape behind the portrait.

With a gasp, a cry of recognition, De Chevagny regarded this portrait in the light of the thin December sun, and then, leaning now so heavily on Bertie's arm as to be almost entirely held up and supported by him, he exclaimed:

"See! see! She has come back to me; we have met again! Again, Jeanne, my love, my wife, my dear! O Jeanne, Jeanne, we shall be so happy now!"

The woman and Bertie regarded each other significantly, though neither could speak from emotion, while De Chevagny addressed the latter, saying:

"See! there is the table where nightly she sits and works, making little things for the child that is to come —the babe that shall make us so happy. Here," and he put his finger on a gilt nail by the chimney-piece, "where she hangs her workbasket at night; here," and he pointed to a low stool, "where I sit by her side and tell her all I have done at the court."

He broke off, and appeared to be listening.

"Hark!" he said, "hark! It is striking eleven—we are going to bed—the great *cloche* is ringing; there is a noise in the courtyard. God!" he screamed, "it is full of torches; the exempts are there; they have come to seize me—to drag me to the Bastille—to part us! Hide! oh, hide me!"

"Courage, courage, dear friend," said Bertie, soothingly, as he held him in his arms, and noticed once again how heavy and inert his poor form was—"courage, courage! They will never come for you again. You are free forever now. Dispel these illusions. Be brave."

"Free," he repeated, "free!" and his wandering blue eyes sought Bertie's once more, while in them there was again that wistful look which so wrung his heart. "Free! yes, I am free!" and as he spoke he released himself from Elphinston's grasp and flung himself upon his knees before his wife's picture.

"My darling," he murmured, gazing up at it, "*ma mignonne*, we shall never part more. I am free! free! free! And so happy! oh, so happy!" and he clasped his hands together and bent over the low chair before the picture. And once again he looked up and murmured, "So—so happy now!"

When at last they ventured to speak to him, and, getting no answer, to raise his head, they saw upon his face so sweet and placid a smile that, remembering all, Bertie would not have wished to call him back to the world in which he had suffered so much.

CHAPTER XXXI.

IT was the night of Monday, the 10th of December, 1748, and once again all Paris lay under the snow—snow that hung in great masses over the eaves of the houses, threatening, when the next thaw should come, to fall and envelop the passers-by; that was caked and hardened on the *chaussées* of all the streets by the recent hard frost; that, out on the quays, was of the consistency of iron almost from the same cause; while, so severe had that frost been, that on the river the snow had been frozen into huge solid blocks, which swirled round and round in vast masses as, under the stars, they floated slowly down towards the open country and the sea.

There were but few abroad on this cold night, certainly few pedestrians; yet, as the clocks from Notre Dame and all the other churches round struck eleven, there was one who, swiftly making his way along the Quai des Théatins, directly opposite the Louvre, seemed neither to heed the cold nor the snow beneath his feet. Wrapped in a long cloak, or roquelaure, held up sufficiently, however, not to impede his limbs in their stride, and with his three-cornered hat pressed down closely over his head, this man, without turning round to regard even the few casual passers-by, went onward until, as he neared the edge of the quay, on which stood a large, imposing hotel, from the windows of which issued a blaze of lights, he suddenly stopped in amazement! for outside this great mansion there was what he least would have expected to see—a large concourse of people assembled together, indiscriminately mixed with whom were exempts, other officers of police, and a considerable body of soldiers, as well as several sergeants of the grenadiers clad in their cuirasses and skullcaps. Also he saw a number of musketeers (or horse guards) standing by their horses ready to mount them, as well as several of the *guets*, or street watchmen, near them; while, to make this concourse more astonishing to those who did not know what might be its object, in the road were half a dozen scaling ladders, with, by them, several of the *guets*, with axes and hammers in their hands.

But that which was more astonishing for him to behold than aught else was that between the ordinary people or onlookers in the streets and the officials, civil and military, who stood in front of the mansion, was stretched as a barrier a thick, handsome, crimson silk cord fringed with gold. This cord, attached to gilt poles or staves about four feet high, served with the hotel itself to form an exact square, the house making the fourth side ; and inside that square itself it was that the musketeers, sergeants of the grenadiers, and superior officers of the police were standing, as well as several other officers of high rank, as testified by their gorgeous uniforms and trappings.

" It is the Prince's house," Bertie whispered to himself, for he was the man who had been making his way swiftly along the Quai des Théatins but a few moments ago—" the Prince's house! What can be intended towards him? He should be safe here in

Paris, if anywhere. And Kate is within—a lady of his suite—ill, and, my mother said, sick almost to death. Heaven! I may not be able to see her even now, after so long! What a fate is mine! On the first night that I am able to approach her after so long and cruel a separation, to find the way barred thus!"

He was about to ask a man in the crowd which he had now joined what the strange scene meant, when a murmur arose amongst those collected there, and at the same moment the order was given to the musketeers to mount their horses and the sergeants of grenadiers to form their men into double line. And at that instant the tramp of other animals' hoofs was heard and the roll of wheels. Then, a moment later, a handsome and much-gilded coach drawn by four horses came swiftly along the quay until it reached the crowd, and the astonished coachman, seeing the gilt-embroidered crimson cord with the military behind it, pulled his animals up sharply.

From the interior of the coach a voice, clear, crisp, and distinct, was heard exclaiming in French:

"What is the meaning of this assembly? Why am I prevented from entering my house?" and directly afterwards a gloved hand was put out from the open window, while a tall young man of about thirty years of age stepped from the coach.

He was clad, perhaps because of the wintry weather, in a thick rose-coloured velvet suit embroidered with silver and lined with peach-coloured satin and silver tissue, and his waistcoat was a rich gold brocade with a spangled fringe set on in scallops; his silk stockings were also peach-coloured; in his lace cravat there sparkled a magnificent diamond solitaire.

Over his shoulders he wore the insignia of the Garter of England and the order of St. Andrew, and on his breast there hung a gold medal by a blue satin ribbon, on which, if it could have been inspected, would have been seen the words, "Carolus, Walliæ Princeps, Amor et Spes Britanniæ." As to his appearance, his face was oval and of a good complexion, though now he seemed somewhat pallid in the torchlight, and his eyes, which were very prominent and full, were blue.

"God bless your Royal Highness!" cried Bertie loudly, in which he was imitated by many, while all the officers and soldiers saluted him, and the richly clad civilians in the inclosure uncovered their hats.

The Prince glanced at the spot where Elphinston's voice came from, and gave a look of recognition at his tall, stalwart form; then, turning to two of the gentlemen who surrounded him, he said, while he threw over his shoulders a small fleecy cape of ermine he had brought in his hand from the carriage: "Monseigneur le Duc de Biron, and you, Monsieur de Vaudreville, you are friends of mine—friends ever, as I have thought—explain to me, therefore, I beg you, why my way is barred to my abode, and why I see you amongst those who so bar it? And, Monsieur le Duc and gentlemen, the night is more than cold; be covered, I beseech you," and he put on his own hat, in the lace of which there sparkled another superb diamond as an aigrette, while the white cockade was visible.

But the others remained uncovered, while the Duc de Biron said:

"May it please you, monseigneur——"

"Monseigneur!" interrupted Charles Edward. "I am the Prince of Wales! Either that, or nothing!

Now, if you please, the reason of this *guet-apens*. Do I owe it to my cousin Louis?"

The duke shrugged his shoulders, as though deprecating the Prince's wrath, then he said:

"His Majesty regrets that your Highness would not conform to his desire that you should leave France, according to the terms of the recent peace made at Aix-la-Chapelle, as conveyed to you by the Duc de Gesvres——"

"Neither my royal father nor I had part in that peace," again interrupted the Prince.

"Therefore," went on the Duc de Biron, "his Majesty has thought it well that you shall be conducted, with all respect and reverence, to the frontier. Yet some forms must be observed, which I pray your Highness to pardon." Then, turning to Monsieur de Vaudreville, he said:

"Your duty."

"Monseigneur," said De Vaudreville, "I arrest you in the name of the King, my master."

"Then," exclaimed Bertie, as with a bound he rushed under the crimson cord, "arrest me also! This is the Prince of Wales, my master; we fought near to one another in the Scotch campaign; where he goes I go too!"

"Captain Elphinston," said Charles Edward, who had recognised him when first he spoke, "I am, indeed, rejoiced to see you by my side again. There could be no truer friend. Yet it must not be. Your services have already been too many; I can never requite them. Henceforth live for yourself and those who love you." And turning to the duke and De Vaudreville, who with the soldiers and the crowd had been astounded—indeed, touched—with this proof of devotion to the unfortunate Prince, he said: "I shall not dispute his Majesty's orders. Yet, I think the manner is a little too violent."

"I hope not, monseigneur," De Biron said. "I should be *au desespoir* if such were the case. But since there are other formalities to be gone through and your Highness does not contest his Majesty's decree, will you please to enter your house, and to permit of our accompanying you ?"

"As you please," replied the Prince. "But," he said, pointing to Bertie, "here is a gallant gentleman of the family of my Lord Balmerino, who was done to death on Tower Hill in my cause. He is a devoted adherent of our house, though I have lost sight of him for some time. Gentlemen, I am alone, save for my grooms. I beg of you to allow him to enter also."

The Duc de Biron and De Vaudreville bowed at his words, and bowed again to Elphinston, after which the order was given for the soldiers to stand out of the way while his Highness entered the house. Then, with another bow, the duke begged the Prince to precede them, motioning also to Bertie to accompany them.

"I am glad to see you, Captain Elphinston," Charles Edward said as they approached the hall. "I have thought often of you and of your poor friend, and mine, Mr. Sholto. And—you will find in my house one to whom your coming may be a new life. You understand ?"

"I understand, your Royal Highness. I should have been here long before, but that I have been a prisoner in the Bastille."

"In the Bastille! You! So that is where you have been hidden from all human knowledge. But stay—

we cannot talk now. What do they intend to me? Do you know? I do not, though I have long known that my presence in Paris is unwelcome."

Bertie shook his head mournfully, and then they entered the hall of the mansion which the Prince had hired from a French nobleman. A huge fire burned in the grate at one end of it, and to this Charles Edward advanced, and, holding out his hands to the blaze, warmed them.

"Your Highness," said the Duc de Biron, who by no means appeared to relish the task before him, "again I beg you to believe that in what we have now to do no disrespect is intended. Yet, it must be done. I have to ask you for your sword and any other weapons you may have about you."

The Prince started and coloured at these words, then, with a calmness which he never lost until the end of his life—when despair and, alas! drink had done their, worst with him—he said:

"I shall never deliver my sword to you, nor any man. But, since I am helpless—— No, Captain Elphinston," seeing a movement on the latter's part, "do not interfere, I beg you. Since I am helpless, you may take them, and what else I have of arms."

At a sign from the duke, De Vaudreville undid the sash of his dress sword—he had been that night to a gala performance at the opera in the Palais Royal— and took the weapon from him, and then, seeing a melancholy smile upon his face, the other, with many profusions of apology and regret, gently felt in his pockets and removed from them two small ivory-handled and silver-inlaid pistols and a little knife with two blades.

"Do not be surprised," the Prince said, "at seeing

the pistols. Since I was hunted like a wild beast in Scotland—ay, hunted even by dogs—I, a king's son —I have carried them ever. And here in Paris also my life has been sought."

"I have to ask your Highness to give a promise that you will make no attempt on your own life nor that of any other person," De Vaudreville said.

The Prince shrugged his shoulders and glanced at the pistols and knife in the other's hands; then he said, "I promise. What more?"

"Your Highness," said the duke, "will be conducted to Vincennes to-night. De Chatelet has received orders to prepare a room for you. To-morrow you will set out upon your journey. But, for the present, again I ask your Highness to pardon me," and he faltered as he continued, "it is necessary for the greater security that you should be bound."

"Bound!" the Prince exclaimed, and now he turned white as death. "Bound! I! The Prince of Wales!"

"Alas! sire," said the duke, "it is the King's orders. Yet, I pledge you my word as a peer of France, such orders are issued solely out of regard to your Highness's person, and to prevent you making any attempt on that person."

"I shall make no attempt," Charles Edward replied. "But I am unused to such proceedings as these. And I do not even say whether they are justifiable or not; the disgrace does not affect me, but your master alone."

While he was speaking, De Vaudreville continued to bind him, using crimson cord of a similar nature to that which formed the barrier outside, and at last both his legs and arms were securely tied, when the unhappy Prince lost his calmness, and, looking down on De Vaudreville with a glance that has been described as "menacing and terrible," exclaimed:

"Have you not enough now?"

"Not yet," replied the other, "though it is nearly ended."

It was, indeed, nearly ended, since the Prince's body was now so swathed with the cords that it would have been impossible for more to be placed round it or his limbs, and, looking at the duke with still his sad smile upon his face, he said:

"I hope, monsieur, no other Englishman will ever be treated thus. They are not made for such a purpose;" after which he asked what was to be done next.

"To Vincennes next," replied De Biron, with a low bow.

"My horses are fatigued," the Prince said; "they cannot travel so far and back to-night."

"Have no fear," the duke answered. "A coach has been secured."

And now they prepared to lift the unhappy descendant of a family of kings, the last descendant who ever made a bid or struck a blow for all that his ancestors had lost—since his brother the cardinal, Henry, Duke of York, was a mere shadow of a Stuart— and to carry him to the hired coach that waited without.

But Bertie, who had been a furious witness of this insult to him whom, rightly or wrongly, he deemed— in agreement with three fourths of his country people and perhaps one half of the English—to be the rightful heir to the English throne, could not part thus from him. As he saw him tied and bound, there arose before him once more the memory of the bright young chieftain with whom he had embarked at Port St. Lazare, with whom he had landed in Lochaber, and before whom the old Marquis of Tullibardine had unfurled at Glenfinnan his white, blue, and red silk standard, with, on it, the proud and happy motto, "*Tandem Triumphans.*"

Also before his eyes there rose the progress through Scotland, the joyous welcome at Edinburgh, the victory at Prestonpans, the surrender at Carlisle, the glorious march to and arrival at Derby, with the news which succeeded that arrival, to the effect that the German King was trembling for fear at St. James's, and all London mad with terror. And then Culloden! —that bitter day, when, as Cumberland's butchers hacked and shot the wounded and the dying, Charles urged on the living to avenge their comrades, and was at last forced off the field against his will, his face bespattered with the dirt thrown up by the cannon balls that fell around him.

And now to see him thus!

"Oh, sir," he cried, flinging himself at the Prince's feet, "let me go with you wherever the King of France may see fit to send you. Give me but leave to see her I love, to tell her that once more I have returned to her, and then let me follow you, as is my duty and desire, wherever you go!"

It was not only Charles Edward who was affected by this manly speech; even De Biron, who understood English well, and De Vaudreville, who did not, but evidently guessed accurately what he had said, were touched by it.

"No, Elphinston, no," the Prince replied. "As I said but now, the day is past for services to be rendered to me or my cause. That cause is lost; this is the last blow. When France joins hands with England, how can a Stuart hope? Farewell, Captain Elphinston; she whom you love—I know all!—will recover yet, ill as she is, I hope. I pray to God that He may bless you both. Farewell! we shall never meet again—never again! Yet, remember, I beseech you, when you hear my name mentioned, that we fought side by side once—that we were comrades—and—and—so, try to think well of me."

They bore him away after this, scarce giving Bertie time to kiss his hand, and from that night they never did meet again. To the Prince there were still to be forty years of life accorded; what that life became, with every hope shattered and every desire unaccomplished, the world well knows.

Between them the grenadiers and De Vaudreville carried him to the hired coach—for owing to his silken fetters he was unable to walk—and put him into it at the spot where it waited, behind the kitchens. And Bertie, following like a faithful dog who perceives its master departing, thus saw the last of him and received his last look. De Vaudreville, he observed, sat by him; two captains of the musketeers entered the coach and sat opposite to him; two other officers rode on each side of the vehicle, with a hand upon the door; six grenadiers with fixed bayonets mounted behind like footmen, and the rest of the soldiers accompanied them on foot.*

Thus the last but one of the Stuarts left Paris; thus the last hospitality and favour of France were withdrawn from the representative of the unhappy family whose cause France had so long espoused.

---

* Note E. Arrest of Charles Edward.

"And now," said Bertie to himself, as with a final courteous bow the Duc de Biron entered his own gorgeous carriage and departed to give an account of the proceedings to Louis—"and now for her whom I have pined for so long! God grant that the report of her ill-health may be exaggerated! If I lose her, I have nothing more to live for!"

CHAPTER XXXII.

"LOVE STRONG AS DEATH!"

NEITHER the Duc de Biron nor De Vaudreville had thought it necessary to place any of their soldiery or police within the mansion—perhaps because the person they required was himself outside it—and, consequently, there was nothing to prevent Bertie from making his way from the hall to the upper regions where he naturally supposed Kate would be—nothing, that is to say, beyond a few terrified-looking men-servants, who, on perceiving him mount the stairs, retreated before him, probably imagining that he had been left in possession of the place by those who had taken away their master. They were quickly, however, undeceived by the stranger calling to them to ask who was now in charge of the establishment, and to whom he should address himself with a view to finding Lady Fordingbridge.

"Lady Fordingbridge," one of the footmen replied, answering him in French, as he had spoken, though his accent showed plainly enough that he was a Scotchman—"Lady Fordingbridge! She sees no one; she is very ill. She is, indeed——"

"What!" interrupted Bertie, in so sad a voice that even the man refrained from concluding his speech, which he had intended to do with the words, "dying, they say."

But here a lady who had been descending the stairs from above, and now reached the corridor on the first floor at the same time that Elphinston did, came forward and said, as she motioned the servants back:

"It is indeed Captain Elphinston! Oh, why not have come sooner, and why, of all nights, be so unhappy as to select this one? Captain Elphinston, your disappearance has very nearly brought Lady Fordingbridge to her grave—that, and the tragic death of her husband."

"She knows that, then?" he asked, as he recognised the lady who spoke to him, she being the wife of Lord Ogilvie, whose title at that time was forfeited in England, though afterward restored—"she knows that, then?"

"Yes, she knows it," Lady Ogilvie replied.

"Does she also know the reason of it—of why he was led forth to execution on the Place de Grève?" Bertie next demanded. He himself knew it now; his mother, whom he found still alive and well, though terribly prostrated by the two years and more of anxiety which she had endured since his disappearance, having told him all.

"No," her ladyship replied, "that she does not know. We have never told her. Rather we have let her suppose that he was about to be executed for some political crime. We could not tell her how base he was. Yet," she went on, "it seems that you and he met in prison—that you forgave him. Did you forgive him *that?*"

"Nay," replied Bertie, "I knew not what he had done, and only saw that his mind was gone. And, not knowing, I forgave. Now, Lady Ogilvie, I beseech you let me go to her!"

"First," she replied, "I must warn her that you are here. She is very ill; she cannot bear a shock."

"Is she as ill as that?"

"She is very weak and feeble. Perhaps now you have appeared again, come back almost from the very jaws of death, she may recover. Let us pray she will!"

Then she left him alone, saying she would soon return.

Agonizing as had been the long hours, weeks, months that he had spent alone in the chapel-room of the Bastille, and nearly as much alone in the *calotte* with De Chevagny, when, both heartbroken, they had sometimes scarcely exchanged a word for days, none had seemed more bitter, more unendurable, than the few minutes during which Lady Ogilvie was absent. For everything that he had gathered as to the state of Kate's health, since he had emerged into the world once more, pointed only too plainly to the fact that he had but found her again to again lose her, and to lose her this time beyond all hopes of recovery.

"Come," said Lady Ogilvie, returning to him— "come; she is now expecting you. I have prepared her. Come."

He followed her up the great stairs to the second floor, and there his companion opened the door and ushered him into a large, well-warmed and lighted room, and then left them.

Seated before the great fire, yet with her face turned eagerly towards the door as though watching for him, he saw her once again—saw the woman he had loved so long, the woman whom Fate had parted him from. She was thin, now, almost to attenuation—

she, whose supple, graceful figure had once been one of her greatest charms—so thin that she looked more like a child that was unwell than a grown woman, and on her face there were no roses now.

"Kate," he exclaimed, advancing swiftly to her as she held out her thin worn arms to him, and falling on his knee beside her—"Kate, my darling, I have come back at last; am free once more! Kate, nothing can part us now."

For answer she let her head droop to his shoulder and lie there. It seemed to her that at last perfect peace had come, that all the black and dreadful past was gone and done with for ever; then she whispered: "Nothing part us! Oh, my dear, my love, there is one parting more only to be made; then—then—we shall meet to never part again. Bertie, you have come in time, yet too late—too late for this world."

"No, no," he said, "it shall not be! Kate, do not leave me now. Think, think, my darling, of how long we have waited, of all that has separated us so long, and that now there is no longer any barrier between us. Think of the dreary months in prison, months that I counted day by day, hoping, praying ever to get free and come back to you; think how brave you have been, always waiting for me. O Kate, my sweet, do not go and leave me now alone!" and as he spoke he wept, and buried his head upon her lap.

"Nay," she said, stroking his head and noticing how grey and grizzled it was now, though he was still so young a man—"nay, do not weep, Bertie. You are too strong to shed tears, too strong and brave. It was your strength and manhood I loved so much, was so proud of. Do not weep now; for it is best, Bertie, best so."

"Best!" he answered almost fiercely, and raising his head as he did so, while she with one wan hand put back softly from his forehead the brown locks flecked with grey. "Best! How can it be best; how, how? O Kate, think, think of all our hopes formed so long ago, the hopes of happy years to come to be passed together!—the hopes that we should grow old together, and then, together at the end, share one calm and peaceful grave. My darling, those years are still before us; I cannot lose you now. Stay, stay with me! Remember all our plans formed in the days of the Rue Trousse Vache, the days when we wandered forth hand in hand together. Oh, stay with me, my darling, stay!"

It appeared as if the rose-blush came back into her cheeks at his whispered prayer, as if a new life was dawning for her again. Then she murmured:

"Oh, my dear, it seems as though I must not leave you now. Bertie, I will stay with you, if I may—if God will let me!"

24

APPENDIX.

Note A.

The Reward offered by Charles Edward.

"Whereas we have seen a certain scandalous and malicious paper, published in the stile and form of a proclamation, bearing date the 1st instant, wherein, under pretence of bringing us to justice, like our royal ancestor King Charles I of blessed memory, there is a reward of thirty thousand pounds sterling, promised to those who shall deliver us into the hands of our enemies, we could not but be moved with a just indignation at so insolent an attempt. And though from our nature and principles we abhor and detest a practice so unusual among Christian princes, we cannot but out of a just regard to the dignity of our person, promise the like reward of thirty thousand pounds sterling, to him or those who shall seize and secure, till our further orders, the person of the Elector of Hanover, whether landed, or attempting to land, in any part of his Majesty's dominions. Should any fatal accident happen from hence, let the blame lie entirely at the door of those who first set the infamous example. CHARLES, P. R.

"Given in our camp at Kinlocheill, August the 22nd, 1745.

"By His Highness's command. JO MURRAY."

Headed.—Charles, Prince of Wales, etc., Regent of the Kingdom of Scotland, England, France, and Ireland, and the dominions thereunto belonging.

Note B.

Jesuit Priests in England.

A long proclamation was issued, headed "George R.," and dated December 6, 1745, which, after threatening all kinds of penalties against those who knew of Jesuit priests being in England, or those who harboured them, continued :

"We, for the better discovering and apprehending of such Jesuit and Popish priests, do by this our royal proclamation, by and with the advice of our Privy Council, strictly charge and command all our judges, justices of the peace, magistrates, officers, and other our loyal subjects, that they do use their utmost care and endeavour to discover, apprehend, and bring to trial, all Jesuit and Popish priests, except such Popish priests, not being our natural born subjects, as, by the law of this our realm, are permitted to attend foreign ministers." A reward of one hundred pounds for every such priest was offered.

Note C.

The Duke of Cumberland's Vengeance after Culloden.

Extract from a letter written by an officer in the King's army:

"The moor was covered with blood, and our men, what with killing the enemy, dabbling their feet in the blood, and splashing it about one another, looked like so many butchers."

A gentleman named George Charles, who wrote an accurate history of the rebellion, also says: "Vast numbers of the common people's houses or huts were likewise laid in ashes; all the cattle, sheep, and goats were carried off; and several poor people, especially women and children, were found dead on the hills, supposed to be starved. Even places of worship were not exempt from the ravages of the unprincipled soldiery; several mass-houses about Strathbogie were pulled down by them; some non-jurant Episcopal meeting-houses were likewise burnt and destroyed, and they were generally shut up all over the kingdom. The commander-in-chief was at this time amusing himself and his staff with foot and horse races."

Note D.

The Bastille.

In presenting the Bastille to the readers of these pages exactly as it was according to every authority on the subject—although in considerable opposition to the usually accepted and melodramatic and transpontine ideas on the fortress—I do not feel that I have robbed Romance of any of her charms. The true Bastille offers the fictionist quite as much opportunity for his powers as the fusty, tawdry thing which, under its name, has heretofore done duty in its place.

The Bastille was never the place of indescribable horrors which
fictionists and dramatists have contrived—"out of their own heads,"
as the children say—to represent it ; indeed, I may truthfully assert
that I have never read a description yet of the place in fiction, nor
seen a representation of the place in drama, which could by any possibility have approached very near accuracy. And this is the more
extraordinary, because there are something like forty authorities
who may be referred to on the subject, including among them such
men as the Duc de Richelieu and Voltaire, both of whom had in
their time been prisoners in it.

In truth, the Bastille was more a house of detention than anything else, and in many cases was regarded as a shelter or harbour
of refuge from outside storms. Instances are frequent of men peti-
tioning to be sent there to escape their enemies, and of others re-
fusing to come out and be forced to meet their enemies. Moreover, if a young man of fashion contracted debts or low amours, or
gambled, or was too intimate with undesirable women—as was the
case with the Duc d'Estrées, the Duc de Mortemart, the Comte
d'Harcourt, and others—nothing was more common than for his
father to pack him off to the Bastille, accompanied by his tutor and
his valet. Also, the Bastille was often regarded by the Parisians as
a suitable object for poking fun at. Voltaire, after having been incarcerated there for objecting to being thrashed by the Chevalier de
Rohan for being a poet, told Louis XV, when he promised to provide
for him, that "he trusted his Majesty's provision would not again
include board and lodging." Another poet, referring to the moat
round the fortress, delivered himself of the lines :

> Que vois-je dans ce marécage
>   Digne de curiosité,
>   Se tenir sur sa gravité
> En citadel de village ?
> A quoi sert ce vieux mur dans l'eau ?
> Est-ce un aqueduc, un caveau ?
> Est-ce un réservoir de grenouilles ?

And Langlet du Frosnoy (an abbé and a most prolific writer, who
passed half his life in various prisons, and died at eighty by tum-
bling into the fire while reading a book) used to take his papers, his
snuff, and his nightgown off to the Bastille when rearrested, and
calmly go on with his work there on being once more locked up.
As regards the surrender of the Bastille (for, as Marmontel truth-

fully says, it was only threatened with siege and never really besieged) in 1789, and the release of the "unhappy prisoners," it may be mentioned that there were but seven of them there, and that one was an imbecile Englishman named Whyte, whose friends had had him shut up to keep him out of harm's way. Four of the others were common forgers awaiting trial; the sixth was the Comte de Solages, detained at the request of his family and on their paying his expenses; and the seventh was Tavernier, a man who had conspired against the late King. No record of torture being practised in the Bastille—after the middle ages—can be found; while, as for food, the Kings allowed so fair a sum to each prisoner—generally one hundred sols, or five francs, a day—that often the latter petitioned that, instead of so many meals, they might be allowed some of the money for other things. In the case of a prince of the blood, fifty livres a day were allowed; for the Cardinal de Rohan one hundred and twenty were granted. Discipline had, however, to be maintained, and where the "guests" were too obstreperous they were sometimes confined alone in dark, solitary cells, instead of being in rooms with others for companions. Latude, who has been regarded as a martyr, was frequently punished for swearing, roaring so that people outside could hear him, and "playing the devil," to use the words of the officials; yet he was allowed tobacco, seeds for the birds he was permitted to keep, new clothes when he asked for them, fur gloves to keep his hands warm, and almost whatever food he desired. Allègre, who escaped from the Bastille with him and was retaken, was also a troublesome man; he broke all the windows, china, and pottery in his room daily, and tore up his mattresses and shirts, "which cost the King twenty francs each," and his pocket-handkerchiefs. He died mad at last at Charenton, did not know Latude, who went to see him, and told everyone that he was God.

The instrument of torture found in the Bastille on its fall turned out, when regarded by intelligent people, to be a small printing press left behind by one François Lenormand, who had been permitted to have it in his room for occupation; also a billiard table was discovered which was provided, the year before the Bastille surrendered, for the amusement of the "prisoners"! The "awful cells," which have furnished so much matter for powerful writing, were "the ice houses" in which wine, meat, and fish were stored. In truth, the "King's furnished apartments" seem to have been a far from unpleasant abode to many, as the Abbé de Mehégan acknowledged when his mother implored the King to keep him there as long as possible, because he was so dissolute and extravagant and such a terror to all the girls in his parish.

Of course, in the days of Louis XIV and Louis XV some prisoners were detained for long periods, and one there was who was detained the same length of time—forty-four years—as I have accorded to De Chevagny. Falmy's case was also possible in Louis XV's reign. But in Louis XVI's first year the Bastille was cleared of all but Tavernier and some others whose trial was close at hand, and even the revolutionists acknowledged that no "court" victim had been incarcerated during that unhappy King's reign. The last man to enter the Bastille was one Reveillon, a furniture dealer, and he did so at his own request, and with a demand for the rights of "sanctuary," as his fellow-workmen were destroying his house in the Faubourg St. Antoine because he had used defamatory language against *them !* and he was afraid for his life.

Terrible, therefore, as the Bastille was, as a place in which one might be detained for an indefinite period, it was not what it has hitherto been represented ; yet, as I have said, it formed a sufficiently gloomy abode in which to secrete such characters as Bertie Elphinston and Fordingbridge when such secretion was rendered necessary in the interests of my narrative.

The descriptions of the Bastille have been gathered by me from the accounts of the spy, Constantin de Renneville, who was a prisoner for eleven years, and who, when released, went to London, and was there assassinated by an unknown hand ; of the adventurer, Jean Louis Carra, who, after writing odes of praise upon the fall of the Bastille, perished at the hands of the republicans ; of the Duc de Richelieu, who, when a very old man of ninety, could not resist visiting the place where he had been three times confined when a very young one ; and of Voltaire, who had had considerable experience of its hospitality, having been sent there twice ; and of many other authors of the past and present.

Note E.

Arrest of Charles Edward.

The arrest of Charles Edward took place under precisely similar circumstances to those which I have described, with one exception, namely, that it was carried out on his quitting the opera house in

the Palais Royal instead of outside his own house on the Quai des
Théatins, and it was from behind the *kitchen* of the Palais Royal
that he was taken away in a hired cab.   I have transposed the arrest
to the latter spot to suit the requirements of the story.   The Duc de
Biron took part in it, against his will, in the capacity of colonel-in-
chief of the guards.   He was the least celebrated of the many Ducs
de Biron, of whom a French writer said "all were celebrated and
some notorious."

THE END.

www.ingramcontent.com/pod-product-compliance
Lightning Source LLC
Chambersburg PA
CBHW021714110726
47902CB00005B/1182